SHANGHAI REDEMPTION

QIU XIAOLONG

First published in the United States in 2015 by St. Martin's Press

This paperback edition first published in Great Britain in 2015 by Mulholland Books
An imprint of Hodder & Stoughton
An Hachette UK company

1

All characters in this publication are fictitious and any resemblance to real persons, living or dead is purely coincidental.

A CIP catalogue record for this title is available from the British Library

Paperback ISBN 978 1 473 61682 0
eBook ISBN 978 1 473 61681 3

Printed and bound by Clays Ltd, St Ives plc

Hodder & Stoughton policy is to use papers that are natural, renewable and recyclable products and made from wood grown in sustainable forests. The logging and manufacturing processes are expected to conform to the environmental regulations of the country of origin.

Hodder & Stoughton Ltd
Carmelite House
50 Victoria Embankment
London EC4Y 0DZ

www.hodder.co.uk

ACKNOWLEDGMENTS

DURING THE WRITING OF the book, a lot of people have helped, in one way or another, and I want to mention here Quynh-Thu Le, Harlan A. Pinto, and Anna Fu in a list too long for me to go through. I am so grateful to all of them for their help, which makes the writing possible. I also want to thank my editing team, Keith Kahla, Margit Longbrake, and Hannah Braaten, for their extraordinary work.

While I have been inspired by real events in writing this novel, everything that happens in the book, and all of the characters, are a product of my imagination.

DURING THE WRITING OF the book, a lot of people have helped in one way or another and I want to mention here Quynh-Thy Le, Hahan A. Hinc, and Anna Fu in a list too long for me to go through. I am so grateful to all of them for their help, which makes the writing possible. I also want to thank my editing team, Keith Kahla, Margit Longbrake, and Hannah Braaten, for their extraordinary work.

While I have been inspired by real events in writing this novel, everything that happens in the book, and all of the characters, are a product of my imagination.

Because I do not hope to turn again.

—GUIDO CAVALCANTI

SHANGHAI REDEMPTION

ONE

APRIL IS A CRUEL month, if not the cruelest.

For Chinese, April 5 ushers in the Qingming Festival, a date in the lunar calendar considered appropriate for *qingming*—grave-visiting or -sweeping. During Qingming, people visit the graves of their family, present an offering, and express their feelings. It's an important and time-honored tradition. In the seventh century, Tang dynasty poet Du Mu wrote a quatrain about the scene.

Around Qingming Occasion, it drizzles / on the heartbroken travelers treading the roads, / "Oh where can we find a tavern, please?" / A shepherd boy points to the Apricot Blossom Village.

Confucius said, "If you present an offering at the graves of the dead, the dead will appear in front of you, as if still living."

In ancient times, Qingming wasn't an easy obligation. For graves that were far away, people had to travel—boat-taking, donkey-riding—carrying offerings, and were often left worn-out and miserable on a rainy day.

In the twenty-first century, there were special Qingming buses.

On one such, traveling to the Suzhou cemeteries, Chen Cao, ex–chief inspector and ex–Deputy Party Secretary of the Shanghai Police Bureau, was sitting stiff-backed among a group of grave-visitors as the bus crawled along the congested highway. He thought about Du Mu's lines as he looked out the window, then at his own reflection in the grimy glass. A flurry of raindrops fell from the roadside willows, glistening as if in grateful tears.

More and more, Qingming was becoming a national holiday, and that fact was giving rise to new problems, particularly for the people of Shanghai. With the price of land in Shanghai soaring, people seeking a place to bury loved ones had to look to cemeteries outside the expensive metropolis. The feng shui and the manageable distance had made nearby cities like Suzhou popular alternatives. During Qingming, train tickets sold out days in advance, and the highways and roads were all crammed with vehicles. It could take four or five hours, instead of the usual two, to travel from Shanghai to Suzhou.

Chen decided to make the trip several days after the official Qingming Festival. Still, he balked at the idea of standing in the long lines circling the Shanghai railway station. And those lines, were he to travel by train would be only the beginning. At the Suzhou station, he'd have to stand in another long line, either for a local bus or for a taxi to the cemetery itself.

So for this Qingming trip, he had decided to travel by bus instead. There was a seasonally dispatched one between the two cities that departed from the People's Square in the morning, went directly to the cemeteries in Suzhou, and then headed back to Shanghai in the early afternoon. Convenient and inexpensive, it was sometimes derisively called the "cemetery bus." In this new materialistic century, traveling by bus was too shabby for the status of the "already rich." Instead, they went grave-sweeping in their own luxury cars, sometimes driven by chauffeurs. The passengers on the bus, however, unable to afford their own cars or the expensive high-speed train tickets, were clearly not so well-to-do.

It was not much of a bus. Old, worn-out, and dust-covered, there was nothing fancy or even comfortable about it. From where he perched himself, the plastic seat was hard, the floor dirty, the windows cracked. At his feet, a couple of late-arriving passengers were sitting on the floor.

Chen hadn't done any grave-sweeping for several years. He had been too busy working one case after another with the Shanghai Police Bureau's Special Case Squad. But a change in his position had handed him an unexpected break, and he decided to seize the opportunity. He took out a pack of rumpled cigarettes, then stuffed it back into his pants pocket. The air in the bus was horrible enough, his eyes squinting against a gray shroud of smoke. Waving his hand in front of his eyes, he recalled a similar bus trip several years ago. At the time, it hadn't struck him as all that uncomfortable. But since then, he'd been spoiled by all the privileges of his position as a Party cadre.

Another drawback to taking the cemetery bus: there was no immediate return. On a day trip to Suzhou, most people liked to do more than simply grave-sweeping. After kowtowing at the cemetery in the morning, they might go to the Xuanmiao Temple Market for tea and snacks, walking around shopping and garden-visiting before returning on the afternoon bus, or perhaps enjoying a Suzhou-flavor dinner before finally taking the evening train back to Shanghai.

Chen was in no mood for tourist activities.

There was no deceiving himself—he was in trouble.

It had been announced the day before, without any warning, that Chen was being removed from his deputy Party secretary and chief inspector positions in the Shanghai Police Bureau and would now serve as the director of the Shanghai Legal Reform Committee.

The decision was presented as a simple exchange of positions. To the outside observer, it might even look like something of a promotion. As a type of cold comfort, the new position even had the same Party cadre rank—and didn't even have a "deputy" before the title.

But this was a familiar trick in China's politics, a demotion in the guise of promotion. The committee position was one without real power. The committee was decorative at best, mainly responsible for making reports or suggestions to higher authorities. Because the interests of the Party outweighed those of the legal system, the legal system was anything but independent, and thus a position on a committee focused on "legal reform" didn't compare to one in the police bureau.

The new appointment was merely a reassuring gesture to Chen and to the public, at a time when "stability maintenance" was a top political priority. Chen was known as a capable and honest police officer, and his sudden removal could have led to unwanted speculation.

But why? It gave him a headache to even think about it.

At the police bureau meeting where the change was announced, Party Secretary Li had said with a catch in his voice, "The higher authorities have decided that Comrade Chen Cao is to shoulder heavier responsibilities for the Party. His extraordinary work all these years is greatly appreciated. A legendary police officer, Chief Inspector Chen has always been our pride. So I'd like to suggest that the chief inspector maintain his office here. There is no rush for him to clear out and move his things. This is his old home, and we hope he comes back to visit us often."

Teng Shenguo, the chief of staff for Shanghai Party Secretary Lai Xi, also called Chen personally, emphasizing the significance of Chen's new job. "Congratulations! It's an arduous yet important task to build a legal society in China. The position requires a lot of research and experience. Comrade Lai agrees that you alone are qualified to take on this responsibility, Director Chen."

Given the possible candidates in the Shanghai Police Department, that statement was probably true. But it sounded like an echo from the *People's Daily*: hollow words, totally unconvincing. Whatever else it was, the new position was not something that called for congratulations.

So Chen found himself on the shabby, packed bus to Suzhou, deprived of the "chief inspector" before his name, a title which, to him, was almost like a shell to a snail.

This wasn't the moment to get lost in self-pity, he told himself. Yet he couldn't shake off the sense of foreboding, the feeling that this was not the end of his troubles.

As an "emerging Party cadre," he was not without connections—some of them within the Forbidden City, near the very top. But his "promotion" had come out of the blue, which in itself suggested the seriousness of the situation. None of his connections had tried to help or to warn him. Even Comrade Zhao, the retired secretary of the Central Party Discipline Committee, with whom Chen had worked closely on politically sensitive cases, had chosen to remain silent.

Two lines by Li Bai came back to Chen unexpectedly:

The cloud drifting, obscuring the sun, / it worries me that there's no visibility of Chang'an.

Chang'an was the capital during the Tang dynasty. Li Bai, though a brilliant poet, got himself into political trouble during the An Shi rebellion, which marked the beginning of the downward turn for the once-powerful Tang empire.

In the present-day world, however, Chen couldn't come up with a specific reason for his own troubles. As a chief inspector, he had ruffled enough high feathers, unwittingly or not, that any number of actions could have come back to haunt him. Any number of powerful people could have been waiting for the right moment to retaliate, now tackling him from the dark and putting a stop to his career. He was known to be "liberal," and in recent years, increasingly disillusioned with the contemporary politics of China, he'd made a point of shirking his duty to the Party. But he didn't think he posed a direct threat to those above him.

Still, Chen sensed there was an unusual urgency to the move to sideline him. With the national Party conference scheduled for the end of the year, there might be something brewing that conflicted with the Party's undisclosed political agenda. Perhaps a certain case being investigated by the chief inspector spelled serious trouble to someone high up. But as far as he could see, there was nothing special among the investigations waiting for his attention in his Special Case Squad.

The cemetery bus was not the best place for Chen to mull over possibilities. Abruptly, the pungent smell of salty fish surged up, derailing his thoughts. He glanced around, noticing a covered bamboo basket at the foot of an old woman across the aisle. Probably in her late sixties or early seventies, she had a sallow, deeply lined face and a prominent mole on her shrunken chin.

"My late husband likes salted fish," she said with an apologetic grin, aware of Chen's gaze. "I bought it at Three Sun. His favorite store. It's so expensive, but it doesn't taste like it used to."

Salted fish was supposed to be a special Qingming offering. It was traditional for people to bring the once-favorite foods to the dead. Chen hadn't brought anything with him this trip, a realization that hit him hard.

"Tastes different? Little wonder," a elderly man sitting behind her cut in. "You know how they preserve the fish? By spraying it with DDT. With my own eyes, I saw a fly land on a salt-covered belt fish. It twitched and died in two or three seconds. Poisoned instantly. No exaggeration."

"What rotten luck!" The woman started crying. "I can't even serve a bowl of untoxic salted fish to my poor old man."

"Don't cry your heart out here, old woman," another man said. "In an hour, you can weep and wail as loudly as you like at his tombstone."

Chen didn't know what he could say to comfort her, so he turned away, rolled down the window, and took out the pack of cigarettes again. A noise broke out behind him.

"No one in this bus is a Big Buck. Don't put on any damned airs. If you're a Big Buck, why are you huddled up in a stuffy, smelling bus?"

"We're all poor. But so what? You may have an iron and steel fence that lasts for thousands of years, but you'll still end up in a mound of earth."

"Come on, it's a mound in the Eight Treasure Hills in Beijing. What feng shui! No wonder their sons and daughters are inheriting powerful positions today."

It sounded like the onset of a squabble. People could so easily become querulous. And not without reason, including the ever-increasing gap between the rich and poor. The passengers on the bus had found themselves at the bottom of society. The myth of Maoist egalitarianism, promoted by the Party authorities for so many years, was fading into a lost dream.

His cell phone rang. It was Skinny Wang, the veteran chauffer of the police bureau.

"Where are you, Chief? It's so noisy in the background."

"I'm on a cemetery bus to Suzhou. Qingming."

"How can you leave without telling me?"

"What do you mean?"

"I'm your driver. Why are you taking the bus?"

"I no longer work for the bureau."

Chief Inspector or not, Chen could still have arranged a bureau car and a chauffer for the trip. He hadn't cleaned out his office yet. But it wasn't a good idea to arrange a bureau car for a personal trip.

"You're the one and only police officer that makes me feel proud about my job, Chief."

"Come on. You don't have to say such things."

"Let me tell you a true story. I went to a class reunion last month. At such events, people like talking about their jobs and about the money they make. Those of my generation, with ten years wasted by the Cultural Revolution, consider themselves lucky to have a steady job, though a job as a driver is nothing to brag about, let alone as a driver for the police department. But I got to declare, 'I drive for Chief Inspector Chen.' Several people stood up and came over to shake my hand. Why? Because of you. They'd heard and read about you. That you are a capable and conscientious cop—an almost endangered species nowadays.

"And then Xiahou, a multimillionaire businessman, toasted me. 'To your extraordinary job.' Seeing that I was flabbergasted, Xiahou explained, 'You mentioned Chief Inspector Chen. Now, you must have heard about "singing the red," the movement to make people sing patriotic songs. I could have been thrown in jail for refusing to have my company sing these songs like rituals. It was Chen that spoke out for me. Mind you, he didn't even know about me, he was just speaking out as a honest cop. He's a qingguan—like Judge Bao or Judge Dee.'"

"Qingguan," Chen murmured. In ancient China, *qingguan* meant incorruptible officials, those rare, practically nonexistent officials who were not the product of the system, rather an aberration of it. Consequently, they frequently got into trouble. That was probably why Skinny Wang brought this up just now. But Chen didn't remember any businessman named Xiahou.

"Anyway, you're my Chief Inspector," Skinny Wang went on. "I don't see anything improper in asking me to drive for you."

"But grave-sweeping is something personal. I don't think I should use the car for personal matters, even if I keep my office in the bureau."

"If you say so. Next time, I'll drive you in my own car, but you have to let me know."

"I will. Thank you so much, Skinny Wang."

Closing the phone, he turned back to look out the window at the passing landscape. Suddenly the bus erupted in noise again. A loudspeaker started broadcasting a red song called "No Communist Party, No New China."

Oh the Communist Party, it works so hard for the nation, / It wholeheartedly tries to save the country, / It points out the way of liberation for the people, / It leads China to a bright future . . .

It was one of those old revolutionary songs that sang the praises of the Party, though this version had a suggestion of jazz in its modified rhythm. It was surprisingly familiar yet strange. The message, however, was unmistakable. Only the Party can rule China, and whatever it does is justified and right.

For Chen, such a song brought back the memories of the Cultural Revolution, and of that morning, seeing his father standing, broken under the weight of a blackboard hung around the neck, pleading guilty repeatedly like a damaged gramophone. All the while, the Red Guards were shouting slogans and singing that song around a book-burning bonfire. . . . This red song, along with a number of similar ones, had disappeared after the Cultural Revolution. But now they were staging a fierce comeback.

"Turn the damned machine off!" a passenger shouted out to the driver. "Mao's dead and rotting in his grave. Go and play those red songs in the cemetery."

"Don't drag Mao into this, you pathetic loser," another passenger snapped back, glaring over his shoulder. "Don't forget the movie *Hibiscus Village*!"

"What about it?"

"The Cultural Revolution will come again."

"Come on. Those were nothing but the ravings of a lunatic at the end of that movie. You must have lost your mind too."

"Let's not fight. It's Secretary Lai's order that we play these red songs on the bus," the driver declared.

Was another Cultural Revolution on the horizon? Chen contemplated that idea. The revival of the old revolutionary red songs was a campaign that originated under Lai, the First Secretary of the Shanghai Party Committee. A relative newcomer to the city, Lai had lost no time leaving his mark through a series of political moves, made possible by his background as a princeling—a child of a high Party member—and the fast-changing political weather. He was regarded by many as a leading figure of the left in China. It was increasingly said that Shanghai was just a stepping stone for Lai in his inevitable rise to the very top of the Party power structure.

What Lai did appealed to some of the people frustrated with the problems of modern China, because it harkened back to the days of Mao. But Chen didn't think it could work. China was still changing dramatically, despite these old red songs.

A gray-haired passenger was nodding in front, as if lost in the familiar tune. He had perhaps heard the song many times in his youth, and what the words meant hardly mattered any more.

Of course, the man in front might be napping instead, his head merely bobbing along with the bumpy ride. Still, several others in the bus seemed to be humming along, one of them even tapping his foot on the floor. At least they didn't appear to be bothered by the song.

Another argument was just beginning to rise up as the bus jerked to an unexpected stop.

"What a lousy ride!" An old man cursed. "The bag of my old bones is being shaken loose."

"If you want to enjoy a comfortable, luxurious ride," the driver shouted back, "take the high-speed train."

"It's easy for you to talk. How can a retiree possibly afford the train?" the old man wailed. "Alas, why do poor people like us have to suffer like this? If he were alive today, Chairman Mao would never let it happen."

"Your brain must be totally addled, old fool. Mao had a special train just for himself, with pretty waitresses dancing attendance on him, and, from what I hear, dancing under him, too. Use your imagination! I saw a documentary that said that one of the train girls became his personal secretary, and later became a powerful politburo member."

"Let Mao lie in peace," another passenger said, from across the aisle.

"Under Chairman Mao, you wouldn't have been allowed to sweep graves during Qingming. It was forbidden as a superstitious practice."

Chen nodded along to the arguments flying back and forth, but he didn't get in the middle of it. It was then that his phone rang again. It was Detective Yu Guangming, his longtime partner at the bureau. At the same time Chen's departure had been announced, Yu had been named the head of the Special Case Squad. Chen trusted Yu, so it was a relief that Yu had succeeded him, but he tried not to put too much stock in the choice. Yu's promotion might just be another part of the reassuring show.

"Chief—"

"I'm sitting on a cemetery bus. You can hear the background noise—and the red song—can't you? It's no place to talk." He added, "And I'm not 'Chief.' Not anymore."

"But I need to discuss the cases we took over just before yesterday's announcement."

"No, you're the squad leader now, Yu. You don't need to discuss anything with me."

"Some of the cases are ones you'd already started reviewing, and your opinion may be invaluable to the squad."

He thought he knew why Yu had called him. A demonstration of solidarity. But that was the very reason he didn't want Yu to go on. The phone call might be tapped.

"I'll be back from Suzhou soon, Yu," he said. "I'll call you."

Detective Yu had a point, though. His sudden change in job duties could have something to do with one of the cases recently assigned to the Special Case Squad. The squad's cases were deemed "special" mostly because there were politically sensitive. What Chen was supposed to do with those cases was provide damage control for the Party. The problem was that he took the cases, and his role as chief inspector, too seriously. Now, he was in trouble.

But he failed to see how his current trouble was in any way related to the squad's current caseload, particularly the case he'd been handed the day before. It was about a dead tiger—a publicly disgraced official or businessman who wouldn't be able to fight back—and it was assigned to Chen's squad as a formality, because of its high-profile nature. Chen hadn't done anything with it and wasn't planning to. He left the case file unread on the bureau's computer.

He did have some other files stored on his laptop. Without going back into the bureau, he could review them again. For the time being, however, he wasn't going to contact Detective Yu.

The bus ground to another abrupt stop. The driver caught sight of several people walking along the road with their cemetery offerings. He pulled over, let them on, and charged them ten yuan each. It was his own bus, and it made sense for him to make money any way possible.

The bus started up again and then swerved onto a newly built highway. Chen didn't remember having ever seen that highway before, but the high-rises along both sides looked strangely similar. They were all almost identical, like gray concrete matchboxes precariously piled up.

The bus took another turn, rolling down narrow roads with old, ramshackle farmhouses lining both sides. Occasionally, though, there were newly constructed villas, just like those in the suburbs of Shanghai.

"Gaofeng Cemetery!" came an announcement on the bus's loudspeaker.

The cemetery bus pulled slowly into the parking lot.

TWO

"THE BUS BACK TO Shanghai will arrive around 12:30," the driver announced. "After that, there may be another one, but it's difficult to say when it will arrive. So please don't miss the one at 12:30."

Chen looked at his watch. It was about nine thirty. Three hours. No need for him to hurry.

Following the crowd, he headed toward the cemetery entrance. Even though it was after Qingming, the number of visitors was considerable.

Chen hadn't been to the cemetery in several years, and it, like everywhere else in Suzhou, had changed. The sign at the entrance appeared to have been recently repainted, and a new arch stood over the entrance, redolent with the grandeur of a gate to an ancient palace. It added a majestic touch to the scene, standing against the verdant hills stretching to the horizon. To the left, he saw a pair of imitation bronze burners inside a red pavilion, with a sign in large characters instructing people to burn their netherworld money in the designated burners. That was surely another "improvement with time"—a political catchphrase in the *People's Daily*. In the past, visitors would burn "money" in front of the graves, which had the potential risk of setting off wildfires.

Chen carried no offering with him. At the sight of others headed toward the burners, clasping enormous red envelopes or brown paper bags, he felt another twinge of guilt.

Several guards stood by the gate, serious and motionless as ancient statues. It was possible they were there to prevent people from sneaking netherworld money into the grave sites. But Chen doubted it. More likely they were there merely to add to the pompous appearance of the cemetery in this materialistic age.

To the right of the entrance, there was a booth with tiny cans of red and black paints and worn-out brush pens for rent. He picked up a cardboard box containing two cans and an almost brush-bare pen.

Next to the booth, a silver-haired woman sat hunched over a small table, which displayed bundles and bundles of netherworld money—in denominations of millions and billions. There was more wealth there than was held by most of the world's bankers, and all in "cash" too. She sat there counting, and recounting, in dead earnest, wearing a pair of polka-dotted oversleeves for the job. A crow flapped overhead, cawing. She looked up, gazing ahead at things unseeable to others, her elbows ceaselessly rubbing against the table edge, still counting. Behind her, shadows and memories appeared to be lurking.

He decided not to buy a bunch from her. For one thing, he didn't think his late father, a neo-Confucianist scholar, would have liked it, despite the filial piety it symbolized.

Checking the cemetery map in his hand, he wound his way uphill, making several turns. Before him were tombs heaped upon tombs, looking almost like overgrown shrubs and stretching all the way to the peak. It was a different sort of population explosion.

It took him more than ten minutes to locate his father's grave. With the tombstone dust-covered and half buried in wild weeds, the paint peeling off, the grave looked lonely. Apparently, not very much maintenance had been done. He squatted down and, out of his backpack, he pulled a tiny broom and a mop. He started grave-sweeping, dusting the stone and pulling at the weeds that had grown around the stone. He felt as if he was engaged in a belated effort to redeem something, and he soon became sweaty, his knees inexplicably weak.

He pulled some incense out from his backpack, lit a bunch, and stuck it into a weed-filled crevice. He bowed three times. With the incense spiraling up, he dipped the brush pen into the can of red paint and traced the characters of his father's name on the tombstone. He did the same with his mother's name, but in black paint, which indicated that she was still alive. The logic of the colors and what they represented in the netherworld confounded him.

When he stood up and looked around him, he noticed a striking difference between the older tombs and some of the newer ones. The newer tombs were impressive—larger stones carved from better material and placed on bigger plots. They also seem to have been better maintained, with the weeds recently cut and the shrubs freshly trimmed.

Were China's materialistic, money-oriented values now taking hold even among the dead?

His father's tomb had been constructed shortly after the Cultural Revolution. At the time, it might have looked as good as anyone else's. But not now.

The incense burned down, leaving a tiny pool of ash. Chen wondered whether he should light another bunch in the hope that the father might protect the son in trouble.

He took out his camera, having promised his mother pictures. Looking around, he hesitated. Then he decided that he didn't have to include those luxurious graves in the background. Instead he took a few close-up shots of the old tombstone with the newly repainted characters.

He lit a cigarette and stood there for a long while, the pine trees rustling in a fitful breeze. He remembered something he'd thought about during his last visit here—about the politics of being red or black in Chinese political discourse. Those terms, *red* and *black*, were like balls in a magician's hand. Now the red songs, popular during the Cultural Revolution, were becoming popular again. Lost in his reverie, Chen started to mentally assemble the pieces he knew of his father's life. . . .

His father, the neo-Confucianist scholar, had suffered horribly toward the end of his life. During the Cultural Revolution, his beliefs made him a target. Now, all these years later, the Party had started talking about Confucius again. So they were portraying him as a great sage of Chinese civilization, a sort of cultural basis for the present-day "harmonious society." There was even a new movie about Confucius, which included a lurid scene of a beauty seducing the sage. Ironically, in a TV lecture, a young political scholar managed to portray Confucian ideals as aligning with the "socialist realities with Chinese characteristics," quoting long paragraphs from Chen's father's work out of context. And not long ago, a statue of Confucius made an unexpected appearance in Tiananmen Square—close to the Mao portrait that hangs high on the Tiananmen Gate.

An entire cultural value system, however, was not something that could be quickly raised up or quickly removed like a statue. The return of Confucius into the public sphere got on the nerves of the Maoists. After only one week, the statue disappeared from the square, as quickly and unexpectedly as it had appeared. Chen shuddered at the thought of the power struggle at the very top that was evident in these signs.

All politics aside, Chen had let his father down terribly. That realization struck home as he stood there at his father's grave, surrounded by the eerie quietness of the cemetery. Chen had tried to justify his career choice to the spirit of his father, who had envisioned for him an academic path. In Chen's defense, it was a time-honored tradition, thus arguably proper and right, for an intellectual to secure an official position. It was through those positions that the intellectual served his country. However, those positions required an unquestioned loyalty to the emperor, himself empowered with a mandate from heaven. According to the Confucian doctrine, the ruler can ask anything of the subject, even his life, and the subject cannot say no. For years, Chen avoided thinking about these things, justifying his compromises with the belief that he was doing something good for his country. It had not been easy.

Chen no longer knew what the right thing to do was—certainly not that morning.

To be able to accomplish anything in today's society, he'd had to maintain his position as chief inspector. Chen had spent his career maneuvering carefully, constantly aware that in China's one-party system, the Party's interests were paramount. Anything good he could accomplish had to be in line with the interests of the country's authorities. Ultimately, that was how he'd survived so far.

With his position at the bureau lost, his survival in the system was in question. The water of China's politics was too deep for him. This trip to Suzhou was partly the result of his sudden sense of impotence, and partly a temporary vacation from his troubles.

Out of nowhere, a black bird flew by, seemingly about to alight on the tombstone. Instead, it circled in the air, then flew away. Chen shuddered again, reminded of Cao Cao's poem:

The moon bright, the stars sparse, / the black bird flies to the south, / circling the tree three times / without finding a branch to perch itself . . .

It was his father who had first recited this poem to him and told him about Cao Cao, the ambitious prime minister during the Three Kingdoms period. Ironically, Cao Cao, who had intended to be a scholar, ended up being a politician. At least he had been a successful politician.

So what could his father say to him now?

In his confusion, a number of Confucianist quotes mixed with fatherly advice floated to the top of his mind. *"Living in a poor lane, Yan Hui is still happy, though others may feel miserable. . . . At forty, one may no longer be that easily confused. . . . Heaven revolves vigorously, a man should unremittingly improve himself and things around him. . . ."* And then, in his father's voice, "At the very least, you have to take care of yourself. . . ."

There was no point in this sort of speculation. He might as well focus on doing something concrete.

For instance, something about his father's grave.

He should try to see that the grave was better taken care of. It looked too shabby. Perhaps, like some other families had done, he could arrange to have a picture of his father embedded in the tombstone.

Finally, he was ready to leave. He picked up the paint cans and the brush pen, then glanced at his watch. There was still some time before the bus was due to arrive, so he decided to visit the cemetery office. He was fairly sure he'd already paid the maintenance fee for the next several years, but he might as well double-check. So he made his way to the office at the foot of the hill.

He walked down the hill to the office and pushed open the door. Inside he saw several small windows where people were paying their fees, and along the opposite wall, a row of chairs where other customers sat waiting. Next to the row of chairs were two or three sofas marked with a sign reading VIP AREA. That section was probably for the people responsible for the luxurious new graves on the hillside. At the end of the room, there was an area partially cordoned off with screens in which an elderly man in a spick-and-span Mao suit sat at the desk, ramrod straight, smiling and leafing through a register book.

Chen walked over to the man at the desk, thinking that there were two items he needed to discuss.

One was that he needed to double-check on the yearly maintenance fee. Inflation had affected everything, even cemetery fees. He might as well make sure that he was up to date on the current fees. Secondly, he needed to talk about the maintenance of the grave.

The old man rose, gestured Chen to a chair, and introduced himself as Manager Hong. He lost no time showing Chen a list of fees.

"Wow. It costs more than a thousand yuan a year now," Chen said, studying the chart of fees in disbelief.

"Have you heard the popular saying, 'You can't afford to live, nor to die?' " Hong said. "The price keeps going up, like a kite with its string broken. In the current property market, it costs about fifty thousand yuan per square meter for only seventy years. Now, how much do you make a year? Less than fifty thousand, right? So your annual income would only cover a square meter or less. That's for a living space—a real-life estate—above the ground. The same logic applies to this kind of real estate—an afterlife estate—under the ground. One possible solution would be to pay the eternal fee—the forever rate."

"I'm confused, Manager Hong. What do you mean by the eternal fee or the forever rate?"

"Well, it means paying one lump sum now, and that's it. There are no more annual fees, and you don't have to worry about inflation."

Hong turned to the page marked "eternal service" before he went on. "Let me tell you something. Do you know why real estate is only sold—leased, really—for a period of seventy years? It's because the Party officials may have made enough from selling that land for themselves, and for their children, but they're concerned about their grandchildren. This way, their grandchild can sell the land again, once seventy years has passed."

"But how can they guarantee that their grandchildren will also be Party officials?"

"Well, look at the princelings, the children of the Party officials today." Hong added, "You're from Shanghai. For instance, Shanghai Party Secretary Lai. His father was one of the eight most powerful leaders in the Forbidden City, and now Secretary Lai's own son, Xixi, who has been studying abroad, has come back to China to attend some important meetings—like an official."

"Who can possibly guess how things will be in China in seventy years?"

"Exactly. If you had paid the eternal fee twenty years ago," Hong said, "it would have cost you only about two thousand yuan."

"The current fee is a lot more than two thousand yuan. It's quite a sizable sum," Chen said, pointing at the page, though it wasn't unaffordable for him. "But there's something else I want to discuss with you. My father's grave has not been well taken care of, Manager Hong."

"Well, that's another long story." Manager Hong unfolded a white paper fan, waving it about dramatically like a Suzhou opera singer. "That grave was constructed many years ago, and the service fee set at the time is unbelievably low compared to today's standard rates. The tombs constructed in recent years—do you know how much they pay?"

"Do you mean how much the Big Bucks pay for their service under the ground?"

"If that's the way you want to put it, what can I say? But the local farmers contracted at the old, pre-inflation rates are aware of what other people are making. So for the amount of money they get, what can you really expect from them?"

"That's true," Chen said. "So, let me ask you a question. If I chose to have a renovation project done on my father's tomb—not like those fancy ones, but something fairly decent, perhaps even with a picture embedded in the stone—and include the so-called eternal maintenance fee, then what kind of a quote can you give me?"

"What a filial son!"

"Don't say that, Manager Hong. It's just that I don't have the time to come here often."

"For the renovation of the tomb, first you'll have to settle on a specific design." Hong produced a larger book, which showed a variety of designs marked with prices and details. "The price depends on the style and material of your choice. There are lot of options too."

Going through the book, Chen did quick calculations, focusing on those decent yet not too expensive designs. He pointed his finger at a page tentatively.

"If that's the design of your choice, for a rough estimate—how about sixty thousand yuan? That's about a fifty percent discount."

"It's still too expensive for me," Chen said, though he didn't like bargaining. "My father was a Confucian scholar. I could pay to have all his work published for that amount."

"You will spare no expense for your father, I know." Hong worked on the calculator again, put some numbers on a piece of paper, and then added them up to a lower figure. "How about that?"

Chen was becoming uncomfortable, bargaining over his father's tomb as if they were in a fish market. There were several higher-priced cemeteries nearby. This one here had been developed years earlier, so the price was not unreasonable. Still, there was no telling whether they would do a good, conscientious job with the renovation.

So he whisked out a business card with his new official title printed in gold: *Director of Shanghai Legal Reform Committee*. The cards had been delivered to him last night, and he played it now like a trump card, hoping to further bring down the price. Chen being a filial son or not would make no difference to the manager, but his being an official might. However, Chen immediately felt a touch of superstitious uneasiness. It was possibly an ominous sign that he passed out the brand-new business card for the first time in a cemetery office.

"A most filial son, I have to say," the manager repeated in a loud voice, holding the card in his hand. Several others in the office turned in their direction. "I'm speechless. Trust me. I've seen many a man here over the years, but you're different. A filial son like you will be blessed by Buddha."

"You don't have to say that, Manager Hong. But what if I pay everything up front? Any additional discount?"

"If you pay everything at once, then I can offer you an additional ten percent discount," Hong said in earnest. "Both on the maintenance and on the renovation of the tomb. Your satisfaction is guaranteed."

Chen nodded. He wasn't that well-to-do, but doing this could put his mother's mind at ease—at least on this matter. After all, he didn't know how long he would be able to hold on to the position printed on the new business card and be able to keep paying the annual fees like before.

"Great. Then if you are able to take off another ten percent," Chen said, "may I have copies of the designs to take with me? Back in Shanghai, I'd like to show them to my mother."

"Of course. When would you want to start the project?"

"I happen to have a week off. So please start as soon as possible."

"That's fine. We can get started on it tomorrow or day after tomorrow. Now, about the payment—"

Chen took out his credit card. But there was a credit limit on it, so he could only pay half the amount now.

"Can you charge half the amount to my card now, and I'll pay the remaining half in a day or two?"

"No problem. For a client like you, no problem at all!" Hong exclaimed, apparently impressed.

Chen signed the credit slip, and after pocketing the receipt, he got up to leave.

Outside, there was no one left at the bus stop. He'd stayed too long at the cemetery office and missed the return bus.

There was no sign of a taxi. The cemetery was too far out of the way. The bus driver had mentioned another bus later in the afternoon, but how long he'd have to wait, he didn't know. But there was no reason he couldn't wait, there was nothing pressing back in Shanghai.

And he ought to start economizing, having just paid a large sum. He didn't have to pay anything more for the return trip to Shanghai on the cemetery bus.

He waited for another half hour without a bus showing up.

"There are no more buses today!" a passing local farmer shouted out to him.

"Are there any other bus stops nearby?"

"Follow this road, turn left at the small creek, and then turn right. In about ten minutes, you might be able to see a bus."

"Thanks!"

He decided to follow the farmer's suggestion, though he knew there was no telling how long he'd have to wait at that stop, either.

THREE

CHEN SET OFF ALONG the trail in the direction the farmer suggested. In the countryside, a passing bus would sometimes stop for a possible passenger waving it down, just like the cemetery bus had on the way from Shanghai.

But the weather was beginning to change. A drizzle blew over from beyond the hills. He quickened his step, but in only three or four minutes the trail became slippery and treacherous. Chen was trudging along with increasing difficulty, splashing muddy water around. Unlike the road in the Tang dynasty poem, there was no Apricot Blossom Village in sight. He was probably lost, seeing nothing like the creek the local farmer mentioned.

His clothes were soaked by the sharper and larger raindrops, and he felt like a chicken dropped into an enormous pot of boiling water.

There was still no sign of any vehicles cutting through the rain curtain. At another bend in the trail, he saw something that looked like a shelter. He hurried over in that direction, but as he got close to it, he came to a dead stop. It was actually a large straw-covered chicken shed, abandoned.

Then a white car came speeding down the road past him. Up ahead, it made an abrupt U-turn, its tires screeching on the gravel, and rolled to a stop beside him. It was new Lexus.

Was it possible that he'd been followed all the way here to Suzhou?

The driver rolled down the window, sticking her head out.

"Where are you going?"

An attractive woman in her midtwenties, the driver had an oval face with delicate features. She was wearing a custom-tailored mandarin dress.

"It's raining cats and dogs." She spoke with an unmistakable Suzhou dialect.

"I'm looking for a bus stop," he said, "or a taxi. I've missed the cemetery bus."

"You can never tell when the bus will come. You're from Shanghai?"

"Yes."

"Let me give you a ride," she said, her slender hand lifting the door lock.

"Oh, it's so kind of you, but—"

It was a luxurious car with a shining beige leather interior. He hesitated, afraid of making a mess with his wet clothes. She leaned over, pushing the door open for him.

"Don't worry about it. It's raining hard."

It was a surprising offer, one he couldn't afford to turn down. He got in and slumped into the seat beside her.

Her generous offer to a stranger had come out of the blue, but she lost no time demystifying it. "I saw you at the cemetery office. What a filial son! Paying the eternal maintenance fee, all of it, there and then."

"A filial son?" He then recognized her as one of the VIP customers seated on the sofa in the office.

"Well, I happened to overhear part of your conversation with the manager."

"I haven't paid a visit to my father's grave in years. It was the least I could do for him, and for my mother, too. This way, whatever happens, she won't have to worry about that."

That was the truth, which he blurted out at the spur of the moment, though its full meaning was beyond her.

"I see," she said. "So you're going to the railway station?"

"Yes. If you could just take me to the stop for any bus that goes to the station?"

"Oh, don't worry about the bus. Let me just take you to the train station."

"That would be extremely nice of you, but it's too much trouble."

"No trouble at all—not for a filial Big Buck," she said, not trying to conceal her curiosity. "Particularly one who doesn't have his own car. My name is Qian, by the way."

"And mine is Cao. However, I'm neither filial, nor rich. I've just completed a well-paid job, so I decided to pay the maintenance fee now, while I still have the money."

"It must have been quite a well-paid job!"

He wasn't in the mood for conversation, but since she'd rescued him from a long walk in the rain, he didn't think he had a choice. He took a pink napkin she held out to him and wiped his wet face and dripping hair.

"In a month or two, all that money may be gone. In fact, after today's payment, I might have to start cutting back."

"What kind of job was it?"

That was a difficult question. There was no point in telling her that he was a government official, which was neither a popular profession nor one that matched the "well-paid job" he'd just invented. And he saw no need to reveal his real identity.

"Well, I'm—sort of a cop—for hire."

He'd been a cop for so long, it was the first thing that came to mind.

"Oh—a private investigator?"

That was ironic. Old Hunter, Detective Yu's father, was helping out at a private investigator's office in Shanghai. For Chen, though, "private investigator" meant something else—an investigator who was independent of the Party's legal system.

"Well, you could say that."

"That's really interesting," she said., "You're based in Shanghai, aren't you?"

"Yes."

"Now we meet, though not known to each other before."

"Oh, it sounds like a line from 'Pipa Song.'"

"I like pipa. And 'Pipa Song' too."

Pipa, a zitherlike musical instrument, had been popular in ancient China and was still commonly used in Suzhou opera. Bai Juyi, a Tang dynasty poet, wrote a celebrated long poem about a forsaken artisan playing pipa, entitled "Pipa Song." It wasn't surprising that Qian, a native of Suzhou, liked the instrument. But the line she cited from the poem was a curious choice. The original couplet read:

Two pathetic souls adrift to the ends of world, / now we meet, though not known to each other before.

She was apparently well-to-do, and she had taken him for some sort of Big Buck as well. So why did she choose those two lines?

He began to feel a bit uneasy about her and felt pressured to say something merely for the sake of saying it. He decided to change the topic. "Why were you at the cemetery office today?"

"I was there to pay the annual fee for my grandparents' grave." She quickly changed the topic back: "Please tell me more about your business. I've only read about private investigators in foreign mystery novels."

He shouldn't have said anything about his work. One fib, however well meant, inevitably led to another.

"Like the PIs you read about in those translated novels, I work for my clients. Unlike them, however, the profession isn't legally licensed in China. It's still a sort of gray area."

"So you work like a cop—" she said, with a sudden glint in her eyes, "but for the client, not for the government."

"That's a good way to put it. There's another difference. A Chinese PI has to stay away from anything involving high-ranking officials and politics. It's just as hopeless as pitting eggs against rocks."

"That's so true. And so sad."

The car swerved and pulled onto the main road. Almost instantly, the traffic became heavier, and the car was caught in a traffic jam. They slowed down to a dead stop. Chen looked out the windshield. A long line of unmoving vehicles stretched as far as he could see.

"I can't even see the end of the line," she said apologetically. "I'm so, so sorry. You wouldn't even be on this road if it weren't for me."

"No, it's like this everywhere right now. It's just after lunchtime, and, particularly around Qingming, there are a lot of people like you, who are hurrying back to the railway station."

"Yes, the traditional lunch in Suzhou. A lot of Shanghainese like to do that after finishing their duty at the cemetery. Well, I'm in no rush. There are a number of trains to Shanghai leaving in the late afternoon and evening. I can take any one of them."

"Then how about having lunch here?" she said, casting a glance at a side road. "I know a couple of good local restaurants, not too far away. The traffic might be better when we're done."

It was another surprising invitation from this young woman, but this one made sense. It was no fun being trapped in unmoving traffic. And there was nothing urgent waiting for him back in Shanghai.

Chen again looked out the window. It was still raining, though not as heavily as earlier. Off to the side of the road, he saw a black dog loitering under a pear tree, uninterested in the line of vehicles standing stock-still. It was reaching out a paw in tentative exploration of a pool of rain water, where white petals fell in occasional flurries.

"Good idea. But I insist that it be my treat. You are giving me a lift in the rain, and now you're taking me to a Suzhou restaurant. That's two favors, and the least I can do is to pay for lunch."

"You're such a gentleman. I agree to your terms. Do you have a favorite place in mind?"

"It's your city, but in Shanghai, the best-known Suzhou-style noodle place is called Changlang Pavilion. It would be fantastic to eat at the original here."

"The original Changlang Pavilion? I've been to that restaurant in Shanghai, but curiously enough, I don't know of one here in Suzhou. But there's a Changlang Pavilion garden in Suzhou, so perhaps there's someplace nearby named after the garden. Let's go there and ask the locals. Someone there will be able to help us."

"Only if it doesn't take up too much of your time."

"I don't have any other plans—not at the moment, anyway. If we can't find the restaurant we're looking for, I'll take you to another one. It's not as well known, but it's quite good."

She maneuvered onto the side road, then onto another even narrower side road. An experienced driver, familiar with the back roads of Suzhou, she cut through a maze of secluded streets lined with old, dilapidated houses. They encountered very little traffic along the way, and it was less than ten minutes before they were in sight of the Changlang Pavilion garden.

They asked several locals about restaurants in the vicinity, but all shook their heads. They circled the area one more time, searching for a noodle restaurant, but without any success.

"Okay, let's just go to another one," Chen said. "Any one you recommend."

They drove over to a quaint street lined with ancient-looking boutiques and eateries. Qian pulled up in front of a tiny restaurant decorated in the unmistakable Suzhou style.

They picked a table with a view of a pleasant lotus leaf–covered pond.

"An ancient pond," she said gazing at it with a wistful smile, "as old as the city of Suzhou, still reflecting the Song dynasty cloud and the Tang dynasty moon."

"What?" Chen asked. He was surprised at her comment, even though he himself was inclined to speak in quotations.

"Oh, that was just something from Suzhou opera."

Her wistful smile reminded him of the plum blossom folding into a paper fan as tall weeds swayed, as if to an inaudible tune. It was a fleeting memory, a touch of déjà vu. He shook himself out of the strange reverie and began to study the menu.

"In Suzhou," she said, "you really can't go far wrong with noodles."

Chen settled on the special of the day—crispy fried green onions and shredded pork. Qian ordered plain noodles with peeled shrimp fried with Dragon Well tea leaves, in across-the-bridge style.

"The local live shrimp are very fresh—caught just this morning," the waiter recommended. "Every one of them is still jumping in the kitchen."

They decided to split a special platter of river shrimp in saltwater, along with a couple of cold side dishes and a pot of fresh jasmine tea.

"I know a good restaurant near the Southern Garden Hotel," she said, pouring a cup of tea for him. "On Ten Perfections Street."

"Southern Garden?" The hotel name sounded familiar. He wondered whether he'd stayed there.

"The restaurant is also near a club that I've been to quite a few times. The owner is an eccentric man. A native of Suzhou, he made a fortune in real estate, and then he quit to run the restaurant. Loyal to his childhood memory of Suzhou noodles, he tries to maintain the standards of those old days. It's open only for breakfast and lunch, so it's closed now. You should try it next time you're here."

"It sounds wonderful. Thank you for telling me about it."

Their noodles came along with the extra dish of shrimp, which was placed on the table between them. Chen's choice proved to be not disappointing. The crisped fried green onion and shredded pork on top of the noodles was delicious, though perhaps not as exquisite as it had been in his childhood memories.

"So you're living in Shanghai," she said, once the meal was under way. "I have a proposal for you."

"A proposal?"

"You said that you're a cop for hire. I'd like to hire you for something."

"Oh, thank you so much," he said, in a rush. "But I've only recently started doing this kind of work. You can easily find a more experienced private investigator."

"Well, since you're such a filial son, I'm sure you'll be a conscientious private investigator."

She was sharp and practical. It was even possible that she had picked him up with this conversation in mind.

"On your last assignment, you mentioned that the pay wasn't bad," she went on. "How about ten thousand as a guarantee? For the job, I'd be willing to pay you eighty yuan an hour plus any necessary expenses. If, after a couple of days, your progress is satisfactory to both of us, then we can discuss the hourly rate again."

It probably wasn't a bad offer for a PI—which Chen wasn't. If he took the job, and the Party found out that he was "moonlighting," it could mean even more trouble for him.

"But I'm in Shanghai—"

"Actually, you're going to investigate in Shanghai, not in Suzhou."

"But I might have to travel here frequently over the next two weeks—you know, for the renovation of my father's tomb."

"Why do you keep coming up with one excuse after another to say no? The job I have for you is not one that is to be done in a hurry. And if you need to make frequent trips to Suzhou, well, that may even help. We can discuss your progress while you're here in Suzhou, and, of course, we can talk about your rate as well."

"The rate is not the important thing," he said, feeling trapped. "As a rule, I don't take a case without having at least some background information."

"Yes, you are special," she said. She paused, leaned back, and looked Chen over carefully, as if reappraising him.

"You don't have to tell me everything right now. Still, some basics will be necessary."

"I want you to check up on someone in Shanghai—and not just her, but the people she meets with as well. In particular, a man she's seeing."

"What's her name and address?"

"Jin Jiani, and she lives in Gubei. This is her address." She scribbled the address on a pink paper napkin.

He could guess what this was all about. She wanted him to catch a cheating husband. Once she had evidence of his infidelity, she could make her move.

But Qian's here in Suzhou, he reflected. "So the man goes to Shanghai to meet her?"

"No, he lives in Shanghai. You'll find out more about him."

That's strange, Chen thought, but he refrained from commenting.

"He's *somebody*, I can tell you that much. But for the moment, you don't have to do anything regarding him. For that matter, you don't even have to know his name. Focus on the woman instead. When you find out more about her, you'll decide whether you want to move forward or not."

She was reasonable and persuasive, carefully taking into consideration his earlier statement about professional taboos. He found it difficult to respond with an outright no.

"Alas, it's most difficult not to return a favor to a beauty," he quoted in spite of himself.

"What a flattering line!"

"It's not mine, but I forget the poet's name. Fine, I'll take a look for you. Don't worry about the hourly rate or paying me a retainer, since I might not take the case. Give me your phone number, and I'll call you if I think I can be of any real help."

Such a vague promise wasn't really a commitment at all, he told himself.

Soon, they finished the noodles, and she had the remaining shrimp boxed. Chen paid the bill and picked up one of the restaurant's business cards on their way out.

When they reached the street, the rain had stopped. To Chen's surprise, right next to the restaurant, there was a bus stop for a route going directly to the train station.

"Oh look, there's a bus stop right here. I can just take the bus, and you won't have to go any farther out of your way," he said. "I'll contact you once I know if I want to take the case."

A silence ensued. She gave him a wan smile. He heard a faint sound behind him, like something had burst. It was a bubble of mosquitos. He looked over his shoulder, and saw the air bubbles burst on the surface of the green water pond.

FOUR

THE NEXT MORNING, BACK in his apartment in Shanghai, Chen woke up quite late.

A glance at the clock on the nightstand showed that it was past nine thirty. Stretching in the morning light, he felt refreshed and reenergized.

He hadn't been able to enjoy a good night's sleep for a long time. Perhaps it was due to satisfaction of doing something for his father and to exhaustion as well. Yesterday, all the trains to Shanghai had been sold out except for the last one of the night. Chen had to wait hours at the station, so he spent some time with a cup of coffee in a station café, stirring up the details of the Special Case Squad's latest cases. Detective Yu had a point—there might be something in one of these cases that would explain the reason for Chen's sudden transfer. Chen jotted down a lot of notes, most of which would probably turn out to be irrelevant. He kept going over those cases in his mind during the trip back to Shanghai, and then again as he waited in the long line for a taxi at the train station. He didn't get home until after midnight, where, exhausted, he fell asleep almost immediately.

Now well rested, he got up and went to check his e-mail. It was no great surprise when he found more than thirty messages waiting in his in-box.

A number of them were enthusiastic congratulations on his new position. Was it possible that so many people had no clue what this new assignment really meant? Some of them were probably sent as a formality, but at least it seemed that people weren't trying to avoid him. Perhaps they were thinking that since power struggles within the Party were unpredictable, there was no telling if, or when, Chen would stage a comeback. Whatever interpretation one placed upon recent events, Chen was still a Party cadre with the rank of a bureau head.

There were already several e-mails marked "urgent" from his new office, along with a number of attached documents. He didn't open any of them immediately.

On his answering machine, Chen found a number of phone messages waiting for him, including several from senior Party officials in the Shanghai city government. The messages all sounded more or less the same, perfunctory expressions of congratulations. Chen knew better than to take any of them seriously.

There were no calls or e-mails from Beijing, though.

He made himself a pot of coffee, took a sip, then sat back down at his computer and began surfing the Internet. He was looking for articles about legal reform. In China, the first sign of change would have appeared in cyberspace. There was still a week before he was to start his new job, but Chen might as well get a head start and do some research.

After an hour or so, he gave up in resignation. He hadn't found anything interesting, except some old news about Zhongtian. Zhongtian was an "independent scholar" who had posted articles on his blog about the idea of separation of powers between the legislative, executive, and judicial branches of government. The *People's Daily* had responded with an editorial declaring that this idea would never work in China. Zhongtian had argued that under the one-party system, where it was taken for granted that the Party's interest was above the law, any talk of legal reform was just a show, full of politically correct language, yet empty of anything real. As a result, Zhongtian had been invited by Internal Security to meet them for "a cup of tea," which meant a serious warning delivered in person. When Zhongtian continued posting, he got into some "tax trouble"—at least, that was the word on the Internet.

That incident spoke to the possible role of the Legal Reform Committee, Chen thought, with a frown. *Reform* was just another umbrella word in the politics of China, capable of referring to anything, or nothing. At bottom, the legal system was part and parcel of the Party system.

Annoyed at the whole concept, he began replying to the e-mails from his new office, using similar, equally empty language. He didn't bother to download, much less read, any of the attachments.

It soon wore him out. He got up and put a bowl of instant noodles in the microwave. While waiting, he sent his pictures from Suzhou electronically to a nearby convenience store to have prints made for his mother. He selected same-day service, so he could pick them up later that afternoon.

He called his mother to tell her about his visit to Suzhou. He made a detailed report about the planned renovation of his father's tomb and promised to bring the pictures over soon, possibly that evening. She sounded pleased.

Afterward, as he was throwing the paper bowl of the noodles into the trash bin, he started going through the pile of junk mail he'd let collect on his kitchen counter. Among the piles, he found an invitation from White Cloud for the grand opening of her high-end hair salon on West Huaihai Road. The envelope contained a VIP voucher in the amount of five thousand yuan. He'd already missed the event.

He'd met White Cloud on a case several years ago. At that time he was an "emerging cadre"—a man on the rise—and she was a "college/karaoke girl" working in a KTV salon. Afterward, she briefly worked as a "little secretary" for him while he was doing a translation project. They'd kept in touch ever since. On several occasions, she'd been helpful, and he was sure it wasn't because of his position. She had no need to curry favor with him. This invitation was yet another of her generous gestures.

It really wasn't easy for a provincial girl, with no connections or background, to become a successful entrepreneur in Shanghai. Now she had her own salon, and on West Huaihai Road at that. The very location spoke volumes. On impulse, he ordered a large bouquet of flowers to be delivered to her salon.

And with that, he was ready to set out.

Half an hour later, Chen arrived at the Shanghai Foreign Liaison Office on Shanxi Road.

The visit was related to a recent incident assigned to the Special Case Squad, the so-called dead pig case. The trouble had all started when a British visitor came down with food poisoning from some sausage made with bad pork. Then everything got out of control: pictures of thousands of dead pigs floating down the Huangpu River turned up online, creating an embarrassing international scandal for the Shanghai government. Interpretations and speculations flew around the Internet. People panicked, and there were rumors that there was a plague going around. The government and local farmers denied the rumors repeatedly, but the question remained unanswered: why were there so many dead pigs if there was no plague?

Finally, the matter was sent to the squad as a "special case." Assuming it was a damage control assignment, Chen had barely looked at it. Still, as Detective Yu had pointed out, it was one of the newest cases. So this morning, Chen was going to make a few inquiries—not in his former role as chief inspector, but in his new one as the director of the Legal Reform Committee. He thought he could come up with a plausible enough pretext to get away with it.

The director of the Shanghai Foreign Liaison Office was a man named Sima, known as a capable, hardworking cadre who started out as an ordinary clerk. He was also rumored to be connected to Internal Security, which would be no surprise given his job. He still managed to keep good working relations with everyone, including Chen, who, as a member of the Shanghai Writers' Association, sometimes met with Western writers.

In the early days of China's economic reform, the main function of Sima's office was to make arrangements for people either coming into or leaving the country. It wasn't easy in those days for regular Shanghainese to get a passport approved. Applicants had to pass a rigorous political screening. State-arranged junkets abroad, in contrast, were very important to the officials making those government-funded trips, and required swift processing. In recent years, however, making those travel arrangements was no longer an important role of the Foreign Liaison Office. Nowadays people had little trouble getting a passport and international travel approved, and as more and more Western expatriates moved to Shanghai, the work of the office had shifted. Foreigners had to apply for a Shanghai residency permit—something like the United States' green card—in order to move here. In addition, the office also had some say regarding which foreign enterprises were allowed to set up offices or factories in Shanghai. Rumor had it that director of the Foreign Liaison Office was a lucrative position, but Chen knew better than to be too nosy about such things.

In a spacious office basking in the morning light, Sima stood up with an affable smile and reached out his hand to Chen as he arrived for his unannounced visit.

"Congratulations, Director Chen."

"For what?"

"Your new position."

"Come on. Surely you know better, Director Sima."

"Well, I've just read an article from the Associated Press saying that Beijing is determined to give China's legal system a thorough overhaul. The article said that it's possible that new judges at the highest level will be appointed. So your transfer to this new position may be another step toward that reform."

"Really! I've not heard anything about that."

"But it's possible, right?" Sima said. "What favorable wind brings you here today?"

"Oh, I'm here to familiarize myself with some aspects of my new responsibilities."

"Great! What can I do for you, Director Chen?"

"To start with something specific, are there any regulations involved in the matter of the dead pigs?" He added in a hurry, "I'm just curious."

"You mean the dead pig scandal? What a shame that was! I'm not an expert in that sort of thing, but when the scandal broke out, I did look into it. Because there were Westerners involved in the background, as you know. What I found out is that the regulations are vague. Theoretically, the farmers should see to the proper disposal of any livestock that dies, in this case the dead pigs, but that means extra labor and money. It was simply more cost-effective to throw carcasses into the river."

"Is there any legal recourse? A law requiring proper disposal or a penalty for dumping them in the river like that?"

"None that I know of," Sima said, shaking his head. He shifted the topic easily. "There are so many foreigners in the city these days that I really have my work cut out for me. It's not even possible to effectively control all the hotels."

"The pig scandal started with a British tourist, right?"

"Oh yes. He actually posted a picture of his hotel meal online, just an hour before he was taken to hospital. From there it just spread like a virus. The Internet can really create trouble. Pictures and blog posts were forwarded and reposted God knows how many times. Someone even posted the patient's diagnosis from his hospital records. And then, after all that, the pictures of the pig carcasses floating down the river showed up. The city government lost a lot of face, and they had to conduct some sort of internal investigation."

"Tell me more about that investigation."

"The dead pigs were traced back to Jiaxing. In the past, farmers there raised only a few pigs, perhaps five or six per family. Pig farming is now a matter of mass production. There are thousands of them, maybe even more, crammed together. They are now raised on chemical feed and whatnot. So naturally there are more sick or dead pigs in the picture. Some 'entrepreneurs' saw an opportunity there. They bought the pig carcasses from the farmers for practically nothing, and with their special connections, they sold the pigs to food companies at a slightly lower price. After all, once it was made into sausage, who could tell the difference?"

"Then why were all the dead pigs suddenly floating down the river?"

"The National Party Congress is scheduled for the end of the year. After the British tourist's bad sausage situation became so public, the city government tried to do something to address food safety issues. They arrested a couple of the businessmen who were selling the dead pigs. Those arrests scared the others, so they simply dumped the remaining pig carcasses into the river."

"But what about all of the others?" Chen said. "I mean, it's a long chain of corruption, starting with the farmers and then moving on to the middlemen, the food companies, and the supermarkets. How can all of them be so unethical and irresponsible?"

"People don't believe in anything these days except the money in their own hands. As the proverb says, everyone is just sweeping the snow in front of their own door. Secretary Lai is right. There's something wrong with the introduction of Western capitalistic ideas and values into our society. The result has been a spiritual vacuum. We have to reintroduce revolutionary ideas to the people."

There was something to Sima's analysis. But whatever it was that had caused this general "spiritual vacuum," singing the old red songs wouldn't be the solution. Sima was just using the official language and speaking the Party line. Chen saw no point in discussing it with him any longer and quickly made his farewells.

Emerging from Sima's office, Chen decided to walk for a while and try to sort out what he'd learned from Sima. The story of the dead pigs was absurd, conceivably another blow to the prestige of the local Party government, but he couldn't see how it could possibly be related to him. He was still wondering what the invisible connection was, when he got a phone call from Wuting, the acting head of the Shanghai Translation Publishing House.

"I've got great news, Chen. The new T. S. Eliot translation is coming out. We are going to have a book launch party tonight. As one of the main translators, you have to come to the party and speak about it."

Chen had started translating Eliot in the mid-eighties. His collection of translations had turned into an accidental bestseller at the moment China was becoming interested in the concept of modernism. The surprise success was attributable to a misleading statement by an old scholar: "Without modernism, without modernization." The latter referred to the Party's call for four modernizations—in industry, agriculture, national defense, and science—which was the principle political slogan at the time. But it befuddled censorship officials, who approved the translation as a result. Afterward, however, the translation disappeared from the bookstores for more than a decade because of copyright issues. Now, the publishing house had finally cleared the rights to the poems, and a new edition was coming out. It included most of Chen's earlier translations, along with some by other translators.

"It was a compromise born out of necessity," Wuting said, going on at the other end of the call. "We had to include some work from other translators so we could present it as a collective effort, but yours are definitely the best, so we put your name on the cover."

"That's great. A variety of translation styles collected in a single volume," Chen said, though he didn't really believe it. But it was by no means easy to get a collection of poetry in translation published these days, so Chen felt obliged to at least attend the party. "I'll come, of course, but you can't expect me to give a talk on such short notice. I haven't even seen a copy of the book."

"We can't afford to let the opportunity slip by, Chen. Guess who is sponsoring the party tonight?"

"Who?"

"Rong Pan, a Big Buck fan of T. S. Eliot—and to be exact, of your translations of Eliot. He's going all out for the launch party tonight, sparing no expense. Do you know where he wants to hold it?"

"Where?

"The Heavenly World."

"You're kidding, Wuting. I've heard about that place. It's a notorious nightclub, rumored to be exotic and obscenely expensive."

"Obscenely expensive, indeed! You're right about that. And quite exotic as well."

"Then why drag T. S. Eliot to such a place?"

"In today's age of conspicuous consumption, an invitation to this nightclub is worth a lot of face. Just to be invited is a recognition of one's elite status. Those who are invited will definitely come. What's more important, they are financially able to buy books—a lot of books. Rong promised to buy five hundred copies himself as an encouragement to others. Now, if the party were held somewhere appropriate, like a library, then some people might still come, but how many copies do you think they'd buy?"

It was an invitation to which Chen couldn't say no, not when it involved five hundred presold copies of the book. The party was essential to book sales. Poetry couldn't make anything happen in this age, but money always could.

Personal reasons were also contributing to Chen's feeling that he couldn't decline the invitation. It was his translation of Eliot that had first made him known among then-young readers, and it was under Eliot's influence that Chen himself started writing.

"You owe it to Eliot to give a talk at this party," Wuting concluded. "You don't have to speak for very long. Ten to fifteen minutes will be more than enough."

"When you put it that way, I don't have any choice."

Chen flapped the phone closed. Whatever reasons he might have for not going to the party were outweighed by his desire for the collection to succeed.

So he hurried back home to prepare for the talk he'd have to give at tonight's party.

The more he worked on it, however, the more unsure he was about tonight's event. At a bookstore, he'd have no problem holding the interest of the audience. Not so at the Heavenly World. What would the Big Bucks who showed up there want to know, particularly about a modernist poet like T. S. Eliot?

Also, he didn't know how to dress for the occasion. Looking at his disheveled reflection in the mirror, he thought he'd better at least get his hair cut.

He picked up the phone and dialed.

"Oh, thank you so much, Chief Inspector Chen," White Cloud said, recognizing his number. "I've just received your flowers."

"Thank you for the invitation to your opening, White Cloud. My hearty congratulations, and my apologies too. Sorry to miss it—I wasn't in Shanghai."

"Don't worry about it. You're always busy, traveling here and there. But it's been such a long time. You may have forgotten what I look like."

"How can that possibly be?"

"Then come see me at my salon."

There seemed to be a subtle complaining note to her words. Did she think he'd been avoiding her? Perhaps, he admitted to himself, he had been, for a number of reasons. It wouldn't do a high-ranking police officer any good even to be seen in the company of White Cloud, given her background as a karaoke girl, let alone get entangled in a close relationship.

But now that he was no longer a cop, was he still going to worry about what people might think?

He put the question aside: right now, he had a more immediate agenda. White Cloud, in addition to helping with his hair, might also be able to tell him something more about the nightclub, since she moved in those circles.

"Drop by any time you like," she repeated. "I'll be here every day—and at your service."

"I will. You've come a long way, White Cloud. The first time we met was at a salon, as I recall, and now you have your own salon."

"You still remember, Chief Inspector Chen."

"I'm no longer a chief inspector, as you might have heard."

"Mr. Gu has mentioned that, but so what? You're still a Party cadre. If anything, you might have more time for yourself, and you'll be able to do what you really want."

"I hope so. In fact, there's something I have to do this evening. A new volume including my translations of T. S. Eliot is coming out, and the publisher wants me to attend a book launch party at the Heavenly World."

"A party for T. S. Eliot at the Heavenly World? That's mind-boggling."

"It really is, isn't it? So let me ask you a question. What can you tell me about the nightclub?"

"Well, a lot of Big Bucks go there. There are a lot of high-ranking Party officials there too, but they usually keep a low profile. The officials, that is, not the Big Bucks. There are a lot of stories about the place, so many that it's hard to know which, if any, are true.

"The owner is a middle-aged man named Shen, and he allegedly is connected to people both at the top of the Party and to people in the black way. He's untouchable, and his customers don't have to worry about police raids or anything like that. That's why the elite are willing to pay so much for an evening at the Heavenly World. I'm told that there's even a secret passage connecting the garage and the club's most 'private suite.' So for those that really want privacy, they can get in without being seen. I can find more about it you if you like—"

"No, don't worry about it. I don't need any secret passage. I'm just going there for the poetry. But what's the dress code?"

"The dress code is either formal or fashionable, but it doesn't really matter to the upstarts who hang out there. They're just like monkeys, wearing and doing the same thing as all the others. Though I will say that there's no such thing as 'too expensive' for that crowd."

"Thank you. That helps. You know what? I thought about coming by to get a haircut at your place, but then I realized I wouldn't have enough time. I have to prepare a talk about Eliot for tonight's party."

"Come by any time you like. We have a number of well-trained hairdressers. Or, if you prefer, I'll take care of you myself."

He thanked White Cloud again for her help and they said their good-byes.

While there wasn't time for a cut today after all, it might not be a bad idea to pay her a visit someday, he thought, as he put down the phone. Certainly before he officially started his new job and put in an appearance at the new office.

He picked up the phone and called the convenience store again, this time asking them to deliver the printed photos to his mother. It was already five thirty, and he wouldn't have the time to take them to her himself.

Chen stared out the window and watched a lone bat flipping by, flying erratically. The light outside was getting dim.

FIVE

SHORTLY AFTER SIX, CHEN was sitting in the backseat of a taxi crawling along Wuning Road. Neon lights began appearing against the city's night sky like stamps on a huge somber-colored envelope. He couldn't shake off an uneasy feeling about the party at the Heavenly World.

"You're going to Wuning Road near the Inner Ring?" the taxi driver said, looking over his shoulder.

"Yes, I'm going to a nightclub there."

"Wow, the Heavenly World."

Chen didn't respond immediately. The notoriety of the club was a given, and he didn't have to justify going there to the cabdriver. Chen looked out the window instead. The streets seemed to be continuously rediscovered in the ever-changing fantasies of neon lights.

"The cover charge alone is more than what I make in a month. You're a rich man, sir."

Shanghai taxi drivers could be either garrulous or grumpy. This one obviously belonged to the former group.

"I have no idea. I've never been there before."

"*Spring warm, flowers blossom*. It's a different world, that Heavenly World," the driver went on. "You'll enjoy yourself to the fullest."

"Oh, I'm going there for business," Chen said.

"Business, you say. And you're no ordinary businessman, I say."

Perhaps it was sarcasm on the part of the taxi driver. But the ex-chief inspector wondered if his long immersion in the system had left something recognizable in his look or his manner.

"I'm going to a book launch party there this evening. I'm a translator."

"A book launch party there?" The driver sounded incredulous. "What will the girls do tonight—demonstrate all the positions in the *Inner Canon of the Yellow Emperor*?"

"You've read some books," Chen said, surprised. The *Inner Canon of the Yellow Emperor* was sometimes compared to *Kama Sutra*, though to do so was to take the work grossly out of context.

"Whatever kind of a party it is, the place is untouchable. It's connected with both the police bureau and the city government."

Chen thought back on what he'd learned from White Cloud. Under Chinese law, organized according to what the government called "Socialism with Chinese characteristics," prostitution was still forbidden. But customers at the Heavenly World didn't have be wary of police raids.

"Money-intoxicated, gold-dazzled," Chen said, thinking of two Tang lines: "*Those Shang girls know nothing about the doom of the country, / still singing about the flower blossoming in the backyard.*"

"The flower blossoming in the backyard—that's so vivid, so true to life."

"So true to life?"

"Come on. Don't play dumb with me." The driver chuckled with great gusto. "They will do anything for you, from the front, to the back—"

"Oh that—"

"The club is expensive for a variety of reasons. Not just because of the service in the front or back. Some of the girls there are said to be highly qualified: college educated, fluent in English or French, able to cry out in whatever language you fancy when they come."

The taxi driver brought his monologue to a reluctant stop at the sight of a tall building topped with an elaborate neon sign that read, "The Heavenly World," which was just beginning to flash nocturnal conspiracies against the corner of the sky.

Chen got out and noted one thing immediately: the hustle and bustle of the valet parking. The attendants in red uniforms seemed to know their customers well, nodding and greeting each one by name. All the cars that pulled up were luxury models, and Chen alone arrived in a taxi.

Wuting was waiting near the front entrance, with another middle-aged man dressed in a black suit and a red bow. He was beaming at Chen.

The red-bowed man reached out his hand. "Director Chen, I'm Rong Pan, your loyal fan. It's a great honor for us to have you here."

"Thank you for your generous support of literature, Rong. Wuting told me all about it."

"Wuting may not have told you one thing, Director Chen. I began reading your translations as early as the mid-eighties. Oh, those were truly the good, golden years for literature."

Rong was apparently aware of Chen's new position, though that didn't seem to have damped his enthusiasm.

"Let's move inside," Wuting said with a smile.

The book launch party was being held in a large hall with a banner stretched across overhead, bearing the name and portrait of T. S. Eliot. Chen wondered about the original function of the room, noting a colored poster near a closed door to the left.

In the middle of the hall stood rows of leather chairs. In front of the first row, there were some marble coffee tables, and further up, a cordoned-off area with a dais in the middle. To the right of the dais was a long table with piles of books stacked on it.

It turned out that Rong did know something about Eliot. Not only were copies of the new volume displayed around the room, but there were also several girls dressed up like cats scampering around, just like in the musical.

The party started off with a fairly long introductory speech from Rong, one full of Eliotic lines. He did bring up one interesting detail about how the English poet was the catalyst for a crucial change in Rong's life.

"In those years, I would bring a copy of Director Chen's translation of Eliot to bed with me every night. I dreamed of becoming a poet myself, but it didn't take long for me to realize that, as a young college graduate, I had neither the time nor the money for poetry. One night, I happened to reread a paragraph in Director Chen's preface. It talked about Eliot's early career as a banker. Eliot became a banker because there is no money in poetry, but making enough money as a banker made it possible for him to write. This hit me like a bolt of lightening across a black sky. If Eliot could do that, then so could I. I took a job in a state bank and worked my way up, until eventually I left to start a private bank of my own. That part is a boring business story, which I don't need to tell here. But it all came about because of T. S. Eliot. And because of Director Chen too."

Applause broke out across the room. People put down their drinks and their cigarettes so they could clap.

"Time flies. This all happened so many years ago," Rong said. "Unfortunately, I couldn't make my way back to poetry, but through Director Chen's masterful translation, I might be able to relive my old dream tonight."

Rong's likening his career path to Eliot's seemed far-fetched. Eliot never earned much at the bank, and he never quit writing. Nonetheless, it probably made sense from Rong's point of view. People interpret their own past however they want, seeing and believing their personal history through the perspective they've chosen.

It was now Chen's turn to speak. The lights were dimmed, and after a brief silence, they were brought back up, as if Chen were onstage.

"Speaking as a translator of T. S. Eliot's work, thank you, Mr. Rong. Or may I say, on behalf of T. S. Eliot?" Chen started with an awkward attempt at a joke, wondering to himself whether Eliot would have been amused at the book party.

He fumbled, struggling to find his rhetorical footing in this talk. With the exception of Rong, who kept nodding and grinning, there was barely any real response from the audience. As he looked around the room, Chen couldn't help but think of some of the characters from Eliot's poems. There was a red-faced, middle-aged man in the front row with a girl nestling against him like a pussycat, purring as his finger caressed her shoulder-length hair. A gray-bearded, cigar-chomping man in the back spilled red wine on his silk Tang dynasty costume, and another young girl dressed as a cat hurried over to lick up the wine. Spiraling cigarette smoke from all corners of the party began to spread out like a shroud over the room. Distracted by the tableau in front of him, Chen continued to stumble, make more mistakes, ultimately deciding to rush through to the conclusion of his speech.

As Chen stepped down from the dais, a well-known actor stepped up and started to read "The Love Song of J. Alfred Prufrock" in a rich, self-possessed voice that was absurdly incongruous with the persona in the poem. In the dimming background, a mermaid floated out of nowhere, naked except for green gauze wrapped about her loins, and began dancing, moaning, singing, groaning . . .

"*For me . . . for me . . .*"

At the conclusion of the reading, Wuting stood up and announced, "Now it's time to sign some books."

To Chen's astonishment, once this announcement was made the

room was plunged into darkness. He could hear hurried movements about the room, like ragged claws scuttling across a sea floor.

When the lights came back on, the hall had been turned into a ballroom. Most of the chairs were folded up and leaning against the back wall; only the long table with stacks of the book on it remained unmoved. From the side of the ballroom came pouring in yet more attractive cat girls. Unlike in the musical itself, they were practically naked, covered mainly by body paint.

It was a bizarre scene. The girls were not singing, swirling, swaying in tight choreography as in the musical *Cats*. Instead, they were each dancing with various Big Bucks.

Once again, Rong stepped into the limelight and began addressing the crowd. "I still have a copy of Director Chen's earlier translation. Someone on Confucius.com offered to purchase that cherished copy for one thousand yuan and, mind you, it's not even a signed copy. Of course, I didn't sell it. Here it is—the same life-changing poetry collection. I brought it with me tonight so I could ask Director Chen sign it for me. With his signature on this collectable item, it'll be worth at least five times as much as before." In one hand, he raised his copy of the older edition high. Then, with a flourish, he waved a check in his other hand. "And this is for five hundred copies of the new edition, all of which I'll get signed. What a great investment!"

Wuting, all smiles, walked over next to Chen and whispered in his ear, "Confucius.com is an online site for rare and old books."

"You don't have to sign all of those copies tonight," Rong said. "But if you could, please sign my personal copy now, Director Chen. Wuting, please send all the other copies to his home so he can sign them at his leisure."

Chen heaved a sigh of relief. It would break his wrist if he were to sign five hundred copies at one sitting. And that wasn't to mention the rest of the copies that others wanted signed. Chen walked over to the table where a line was quickly forming.

He took up a position in the middle of the table, and two of the girls in cat costumes came to squat beside him, one on each side. The one on the right, Red Coral, opened each book to the signature page, while the other, Green Jade, wrote down the buyer's name on a piece of paper. Sandwiched between the two, Chen scribbled his name on one book after another, brushed on the cheek by Red Coral's long hair, and tickled by the tail dangling from the bare buttocks of Green Jade.

"The party's a huge success," Wuting said, wandering over to Chen's side again to comment. "People are snatching up copies like potato chips. We'll sell almost as many copies as a memoir of a celebrated movie star."

The assistance of the two cat girls helped keep the signing line moving. Several customers bought a bundle of copies, "giving face" to Rong, and some of them didn't even bother asking Chen to sign their copies. The cat girls carried their books out for them.

In the room the girls come and go, / talking about anything but Michelangelo.

After another tall pile of copies was gone, Chen looked up to see Rong sidle up to Wuting and whisper something before heading out of the room.

"Rong had to leave for an urgent business meeting," Wuting said, coming over to speak to Chen. "He asked me to pass on his regrets."

Chen nodded. It made sense that a busy banker would have to leave early, having delivered what he'd promised.

People began to leave. They'd come as a favor to Rong, and with the host gone, there was no reason for them to stay. Some of them might continue to enjoy themselves at the club, but they were done with the book launch party. A couple of them even left with a cat girl on their arm.

There weren't many copies of book left, and Wuting looked pleased.

Then Wuting got a phone call and stepped aside to take it in relative privacy. It was a fairly long call, and by the time he finished, the last Big Buck was limping out, leaning heavily on the bare shoulder of a slim cat girl.

"Sorry, I can't stay," Wuting said, closing the phone with an embarrassed smile. "I have an emergency conference call with the City Propaganda Ministry. I have to hurry back to the office. But please stay. Rong will be back around ten for a celebratory banquet. Some other Big Bucks will be coming as well, and if the conference call doesn't last too long, I'll be back here for it. Everything has been arranged. So please, for the sake of Eliot, stay. It's essential for the success of the book."

Once again, Chen felt he had no choice but to comply.

After Wuting left, Chen was the only one remaining—except for the two cat girls who had helped him with the signing.

The lights was starting to dim again, suspiciously.

"Mr. Rong thought you might want to take a break in the inner room before the banquet," Red Coral said.

"It's much more comfortable there," Green Jade said.

They dragged him through a side door into the inner room, which turned out to be a bedroom furnished with a large bed, a leather sofa, and an antique dresser with a large mirror on top. As soon as they entered the inner room, the two girls started shedding their remaining clothes.

"Now you can enjoy a break in privacy," Green Jade said.

"Why don't you relax on the bed?" Red Coral added.

Chen retreated to the sofa.

"Let's sit and talk," he said in a hurry,

Red Coral moved in beside him, kneeling on the couch. "You must be tired, sir. Let me give you a massage."

For other customers at the nightclub, this might be a natural part of any party, like a cold appetizer before the banquet.

"A special oil massage," Red Coral pushed.

"But your hands—"

"Don't worry about it," she said, noticing the greenish paint on her hands. "I'll take a quick shower. Green Jade will keep you company."

He had no idea that the room had a shower as well, but considering the stories he'd heard about the Heavenly World, it was no surprise.

"Mr. Rong has engaged us for the night," Green Jade said, edging up more closely. "He's paid for the full service, whatever you like. And there will be a nice tip for us from him if you're satisfied."

"I don't know what to say. I don't know anything about the arrangements he's made. I just came for the book party."

"I can promise you an unimaginable night."

"A night like never before," Red Coral said, calling out from the door of the bathroom. She was giggling, her naked body glowingly pink like a skinned cat. "Flying in pair, with both of us serving you at the same time if you prefer."

Green Jade was reaching for his belt, and he hastened to stop her. His hand deflected hers and brushed up against something throbbing in his pants pocket. It was his cell phone, he realized. It had started vibrating as if on cue. He sat straight up.

"Hold on," he said, pulling out his phone. He looked at the number—it was his mother. She probably had questions about the restoration of his father's tomb. "It's urgent business."

Pushing the girl aside, Chen stood up and headed to the door. It was the perfect excuse to disengage, and he didn't want his mother to hear the background noise.

The moment Chen stepped out into the corridor, the door of the next private room over flew open. A girl, her robe unbelted and largely fallen off her shoulder, ran out of the room. She was bare-legged and barefoot, swaying her hips exaggeratedly, like a seductive robot. A sturdy foreigner rushed out after her. All of a sudden, the dimly lit corridor felt stifling.

Chen hurried to the elevator at the end of the corridor, holding on to the phone. A girl in a yellow dress with a sweet smile like a flowering apricot blossom held the elevator door open for him.

The lobby on the first floor turned out to be no less noisy, crowded with girls and customers milling around. An elegantly dressed lady was barging in through the revolving door, followed by a couple of fierce-looking men who looked like bodyguards. She was definitely not a "girl." Confused, Chen wondered whether female customers came to the club as well, but quickly dismissed the question. It was none of his business.

He slipped outside the club, then looked around. His phone was no longer vibrating. He saw a convenience store on the corner and headed over to buy a pack of cigarettes. Before lighting one, he took a deep breath of the fresh night air to clear his head. There was no need to go back inside, he decided. At least, not until it was time for the banquet.

Not far away, he could see the Wuning Bridge stretching across Suzhou Creek, unfolding like a splendid dream, with golden statues glistening atop the magnificently lit arch. Shanghai had changed dramatically, but in spite of all the complaints, some of those changes were welcome.

He pulled out his phone again, ready to call his mother back, but he stopped abruptly. He caught a glimpse of a black-clad man moving stealthily toward the nightclub. He was not alone: there were several others in similar clothing following him.

Chen recognized the first one as a cop named Tang Guohua. He was in the Sex Crimes Squad of the Shanghai Police Bureau. Whatever Tang's appearance here signified, Chen knew better than to step back into the club.

Instead, he moved a few steps farther to stand under the awning of a small café, the phone in his hand undialed. He sat down at an outside table on the street corner side and watched as the black-clad team entered the nightclub. There were seven or eight of them in all.

For the next twenty minutes or so, Chen remained at the table, finishing a cup of espresso and three cigarettes. Strangely, there seemed to be no commotion inside the nightclub. Fashionably clad men and women kept coming and going, visibly undisturbed.

The Sex Crime Squad was a relatively new one in the bureau, and it was directly responsible to the city government. It was even more "special," so to speak, than Chen's Special Case Squad. The hair salons, nightclubs, karaoke rooms, and other such places where sex business was conducted in the back rooms were usually run by people with connections. Deciding which establishment to target was often the most complicated matter of police politics. It was no secret—not even to the taxi driver who had brought him here—that the squad worked in accordance with specific orders from above. Some of the raids were conducted as part of some political campaign, but the targets were often tipped off ahead of time.

So a raid against the Heavenly World could be politically motivated, part of another campaign to "Sweep Away Pornography." But as far as he knew, there was no such campaign going on at the moment.

He shuddered at another possibility.

The target of the raid might not be the club, but somebody in it.

Grinding out his cigarette, Chen rose to leave, his questions unanswered. He glanced over at the nightclub one more time. The neon sign of the Heavenly World was still dancing fervently.

There was no point in lingering there anymore.

As he turned down another shaded street, he felt vulnerable, superstitious, as if weighed down by a sudden oppressiveness of the black night sky. If not for the phone call from his mother . . .

He didn't want to think about it.

SIX

THE NEXT MORNING, CHEN woke up with a splitting headache. He hadn't slept much last night, tossing and turning for most of it.

It portended another rotten day with an unshakable headache. But it wasn't a morning that he could stay in bed, groaning in self-pity.

He rolled out of bed with an effort and brewed a pot of black coffee. When the coffee was ready, he poured himself a cup and swallowed a couple of aspirin.

It was time to get started. The first thing on his agenda was to find out more about what went on last night.

He turned on his computer to see what he could find on the Internet. It was about all he could do to move the mouse around, while gulping down the bitter, strong coffee and rubbing his eyes against the morning light reflecting off the screen.

Chen tried several different searches, but he couldn't find any news whatsoever about the raid at the Heavenly World. He stood up, shaking his head in confusion. So much for the new media; maybe he could find something in the old media. Chen walked downstairs and, at the street corner newsstand, picked up several different newspapers. Looking through them on the way back, he didn't see anything about the raid.

Back in his room, he went through the newspapers one more time, looking through them page by page for any reference at all. With another cup of coffee in hand, he finally found something. On the fourth page of *Wenhui Daily*, there was a tiny piece tucked in a corner.

"A new collection of T. S. Eliot's poetry is finally being published, which has been much anticipated by poetry-loving readers. A grand book launch party was held by Shanghai Publishing House last night, and a large number of people came to the celebration."

It didn't mention where the party was held, who attended, or anything about Chen, the primary translator, giving a talk at the event.

It was possible that the journalist simply wrote the piece based on a press release, without so much as a fact-checking phone call about the details of the party. Or was it possible that no one there, including Wuting or Rong, was aware of the raid? It would certainly be understandable for the nightclub management to keep mum.

All of this, however, pointed to the scenario that occurred to him last night: that the raid was targeting not the Heavenly World, but rather someone who was there—a surprise attack by the police in collaboration with the nightclub management. Chen recalled the surprising overtures of the cat girls and realized that it was very possible that the person they were targeting was the former chief inspector Chen himself.

If so, if he was indeed the target, then he'd had a very lucky escape last night. But that kind of luck wouldn't last long.

That kind of political assassination was most thorough. Pan Ming, the former Shanghai Propaganda Minister, had been personally and professionally annihilated in a very similar way. During the eventful summer of 1989, Pan had chosen the "wrong side" and was removed from his position. But his political enemies worried that he might be able to stage a comeback. So one evening, he was caught in the company of a naked massage girl. It was obviously a setup, but there was evidence and witnesses, so Internal Security nailed Pan to "the pillory of humiliation." After he was released from prison several years later, it was rumored that Pan was a broken man, running a small eatery somewhere near Shanghai.

The sponsor of the book launch party, Rong Pan, undoubtedly had close ties to the local government, otherwise his non-state-run bank wouldn't exist in the first place. As for his fondness for and knowledge of T. S. Eliot, he could have been stuffed with it like a Peking duck, all for the purpose of staging that party.

Was Wuting involved? To what extent? It was a convenient fact that Wuting got an emergency phone call, causing him to leave the nightclub shortly before the raid. Chen had always thought of him as a capable publisher. But it wasn't easy to run a decent publishing house in this materialistic age, especially under the constraints of Party censorship. That Wuting's survival might have required some sort of collaboration between the publisher and the authorities wasn't unimaginable.

But for his mother's call, Chen—if he was indeed the target—could have ended up like Pan, caught by the police in the company of the two undressed cat girls. There would have been no use in his arguing or trying to explain. Being discovered in such a scenario would have finished him and put him beyond redemption.

Suffering another assault from his dull headache, Chen didn't want to speculate further.

He picked up the phone and called his mother.

"I'd planned to come over yesterday, Mother, but something unexpected came up. So I had the pictures delivered to you instead."

"Don't worry. I know you're busy. The pictures arrived," she said. "Last night, I placed them on the small table in front of the Guanyin image and burned incense and candles. Guess what? Sparks flew up from the candles like small flowers, and then the picture quivered a couple of times. It's a sign."

She was a devout Buddhist, capable of seeing signs in many things. Chen never tried to argue with her.

"What time, Mother?"

"It was almost ten, I think," she said. "I was thinking of your father. So the candle must have been his message to us. He's still around here, blessing and protecting us."

"Yes, I think so too." That was around the time the black-clad police were sneaking into the nightclub.

"About the grave renovation—you do whatever is necessary, but don't spend too much. And don't go out of your way. You already have a lot on your hands."

"I have a week's vacation time right now, so I'm going to go to Suzhou and supervise the renovation. But I'll come back from time to time."

"That's good."

He said his good-byes and put down the phone. He thought that the sparks from the candle were just another coincidence. As a cop, he didn't believe in coincidences for the most part, but neither did he see it as a sign.

He started pacing about the apartment. It was a two-bedroom apartment, assigned to him in accordance to his cadre rank. His new bureau head position would entitle him a larger one. In China's one-party system, to be a Party official meant access to all sorts of privileges, including better housing. In return, he was supposed to place the Party's interest above everything else.

The pacing didn't really help him think. The ex-inspector felt an attacking wave of nausea instead, and a cold sweat broke out all over his body.

During the trip to Suzhou, he had thought about lying low, but doing so hadn't made a difference. The day he came back to Shanghai, he had been lured straight into what might well have been a devilish trap. He wasn't going to just sit there worrying, with his arms crossed, waiting to be crushed.

But was he absolutely sure that he was the target of the police raid? Or was he being paranoid?

He had to find out.

It would be difficult for him to "investigate." He had no idea who might be plotting against him in the dark. For years, he had acted, unwittingly or not, against the interests of many people: random speculation was useless. So he decided to start by checking into the nightclub and the people associated with it. But he wasn't a cop anymore—he didn't have access to resources like he used to, and any move he made might be closely watched. He looked up the phone number of Tang, the cop who was at the nightclub last night, but before he called Tang, Chen hesitated again. A low-level cop in the Sex Crimes Squad, Tang might not have been told anything about the real target of the raid, particularly one conducted at well-connected place like the Heavenly World.

It wasn't a good idea, he concluded, for him to contact Tang—at least, not at this moment. There was no telling how Tang would react. Still, if Chen was in fact the target, information from Tang would be essential before Chen could make any definite move.

Had he still been a chief inspector, Chen would have been able to check into the background of the nightclub and its untouchable owner, Shen. As it was, all he could do was stir up the snake.

Approaching Rong could also backfire, given all his possible connections to the people in the city government. For the same reason, Chen thought he'd better not contact Wuting either.

At the same time, he knew that if he was being targeted, he needed to try and buy some time, however short, before the next strike against him.

Finally, Chen wandered back to his desk and settled down to compose a request for one more week's leave from the city government. In his e-mail, he maintained that he needed more time to prepare for the new position. As a chief inspector, he'd been too busy handling one case after another, and he hadn't had any time to study the legal system properly. He thought that such a request might not appear unreasonable to the higher authorities. The Legal Reform Committee was rumored to be one of the offices where Party cadres were sent as they prepared for retirement: a nondeputy position, with all the corresponding perks and benefits but not much responsibility. As such, a week off didn't really matter.

At the end of his e-mail, he added a personal touch, talking about his father's grave in Suzhou being in bad repair and claiming that his mother had requested that he personally oversee its renovation.

"She's old, in frail health, and her days may be limited. I'm not in a position to say no to her. The renovation of my father's grave will take just about a week. While there, I can also continue reading up for the new position. The moment the project is completed, I will start working with unlimited concentration for our Party, for years to come."

This note sounded like an echo from *Chenqing Biao* by Li Mi, a Jin dynasty scholar-official in the third century. Li Mi compared his grandmother to the evening sun declining against the western hills; "*The days I can serve my old grandmother are short, and the days I can serve your majesty are long, long indeed.*"

He wondered whether the superior cadre reading it would catch the reference. Still, it sound credible, for Chen was known to be a filial son, a pose in line with his bookish character. To some, it might also look like a feeble protest about his new position: Chen could easily be doing nothing more than dragging his feet, delaying the onset of his new role.

To do nothing, it says in the Taoist classic *Dao De Jing*, makes it possible for one to do everything. Chen wanted to make his enemy believe that he was doing nothing, thereby allowing him to do whatever was necessary while they weren't watching.

He stepped outside again, this time going over to a newsstand several blocks away. He was sure no one recognized him there. He asked for several SIM cards. Theoretically, in accordance with government regulations, he should have shown ID to buy SIM cards. Those SIM cards would then be registered under his name, but newsstands usually didn't bother to check ID. Sure enough, the young girl there sold them to him without any question.

He started to put a new SIM card into his cell phone, but he had second thoughts. He walked down another block and went into a phone store. There he chose a couple of inexpensive cell phones. He put the new SIM card into one of them—this would be his special phone, designated for confidential calls, to avoid any possibility of his calls being tapped or traced. It would also be easier. This way he wouldn't have to change the SIM card frequently.

As for the other phone and cards, he kept them to use on special occasions, or perhaps to give to others.

He used the special phone to dial Mr. Gu, a successful and well-connected businessman, who had proclaimed himself to be a staunch friend of Chen's ever since they had worked together back in the early days of Gu's New World project. Gu might be able to tell him something about Rong.

Gu picked up at the first ring and, on hearing Chen's voice, said, "Oh, you. I'll call you back in one minute."

Was Gu calling back on a special phone? The businessman was a cautious one and might have heard something about Chen. The phone rang almost immediately.

"You're calling from a new phone? I recognized your voice, if not the number," Gu said. He had indeed called back from another phone, one with a different number. "Oh, I got the invitation to the book party at the Heavenly World yesterday, but I had a business meeting. Sorry I couldn't make it."

"You don't have to feel sorry about missing it."

Chen told Gu what had happened at the Heavenly World, including the party sponsored by Rong and the raid on the nightclub. He didn't say anything about the possibility that he himself was the target of the raid.

"How could that be possible?" Gu exclaimed. "Shen is connected to someone at the very top. Everyone knows that."

The surprise in his voice sounded genuine.

"Then why?"

"Let me make a couple of phone calls and see what I can find out about Rong. I've met him before, but I don't know much." Gu then added deliberately, "I don't get involved in politics, Chen, but I've heard some whispered words."

"Really!"

"You know how businesspeople are always gossiping about one thing or another." Gu abruptly changed the subject: "I have a new vacation center in Kunshan near Suzhou. It's finished but not open for business yet. Why not go there and stay as my special guest? Enjoy a vacation. It's time for you to take a break from your work—a break in absolute privacy."

"Absolute privacy?"

"Well, some of the successful elite nowadays work hard to maintain a low profile. For them, staying at a five-star hotel is no longer a good idea, what with cell phone calls being monitored and surveillance cameras everywhere. So I had a vacation center built for my special guests. Each of them will have a whole floor to themselves, and from the garage, they can go directly to their designated floor. They won't have to worry about being seen by others, and they enjoy all the services of the vacation center in complete privacy. You can stay there as long as you like, and you can drive back to Shanghai in less than an hour."

Gu was making the offer in spite of the "whispered words." It was a practical suggestion, too, for Chen to lie low. Should he request additional leave? Out of sight, out of mind—and how things might change in two or three months, no one could tell. The emphasis on privacy and service, however, reminded Chen of the scene at the Heavenly World.

"I'll think about it, Gu. It's so thoughtful of you, I appreciate your offer," Chen said. "And your business has been expanding beyond Shanghai. Congratulations!"

"You don't have to say that to me. It's just that I've been drinking wine today, and I'm a little drunk. Who cares about the flood coming to drown the world when I'm no longer here."

That didn't sound like Gu. Chen waited for him to go on.

"Surely you remember Lu Xun's prediction. Today's society is like a sinking ship at night, with most of the passengers in a deep sleep. It's probably not a bad idea for them to sink into another deep sleep, so to speak. There's no point in trying to wake them up. It would only add to their suffering if they were to become aware of the inevitable end. At the same time, however, the few who have profited are awake and are jumping ship."

"Imagine you saying that to me, Mr. Gu! You, the chairman of the New World Group."

"Well, I'm reading a book about Jiang Cun, a Qing dynasty salt merchant, who at the peak of his success said, 'You may have mountains of silver or mountains of gold, but overnight the emperor can take it all away without even condescending to say "I owe you."' That was China then, and that is China today.

"So I'm thinking of emigrating. I'll have my wife and daughter go to the United States first. Then, if worse comes to worst, at least they'll be safe and secure somewhere else."

Chen didn't respond.

"You have a girlfriend in the United States," Gu went on thoughtfully. "And you once talked to me about furthering your studies there."

"Yes?"

"I'm planning to set up an office in New York. What about serving as the office head there? It's condescending of me to make such a suggestion, I know, but it's something for you to think about."

"I will think about it, Gu. I really appreciate your suggestion."

Afterward, Chen felt increasingly uneasy about what Gu had said.

The well-connected businessman hadn't tried to distance himself from the ex–chief inspector. But his suggesting instead a vacation—and then an overseas job—was a subtle warning about the terrible mess Chen had landed himself in.

Chen looked at his watch. It wasn't noon yet. He swallowed another two aspirin, still without eating anything. Then he set out again.

Around one thirty, Chen got to the intersection at new Western Huaihai and Wulumuqi Roads. White Cloud's new hair salon was there.

He looked over his shoulder, slipped in through the front door of a packed Starbucks, then out the side door, making sure he wasn't being followed before he turned onto a side street. Then he zigzagged along alleys and side streets, slowly making his way back to the original intersection. Chen took another look around the area near the hair salon before walking inside.

White Cloud was there, surrounded by several girls. She was standing bare-legged in a short white uniform dress, just like the others. Still, there was something that made her stand out as the proprietor. Possibly her ankle tassel sandals added a necessary distinguishing touch.

"Welcome," a hostess said.

White Cloud turned around. She was opening her mouth in recognition when he made a point of saying formally, like a new customer, "I'd like to have my hair cut, madam."

"I'll take him," White Cloud said to other girls. To him, she asked, "It's your first time here, right?"

"Yes, a friend of mine recommended your salon."

"You won't be disappointed with the service."

It reminded him of something the cat girls in the Heavenly World had said. If there was something dubious about this salon, he didn't know. And he didn't really care.

"Please follow me," she said, leading him to a sort of a private room in the back. It was a secluded hair-washing area, furnished with a sink, a reclining chair, a swivel stool, and a blue velvet-covered couch against the wall. She locked the door after her.

"I just heard something about your change in position. I called you at the police bureau, and the people who answered wanted me to leave my name and number. It sounded strange, so I hung up without telling them anything."

"You did the right thing," he said. "It's a complicated story. The long and short of it is, I'm in trouble. The position I've been assigned at Shanghai Legal Reform Committee is just a smokescreen."

"But you've been doing an excellent job, and the people of Shanghai all know that."

"It's not just that I've been moved out of the police department. Last night, I nearly fell into what I think may have been a trap set for me at the Heavenly World."

"The Heavenly World?" she exclaimed. "Yes, I remember something about a book launch party. But a trap?"

He proceeded to tell her what had happened last night, making no attempt to play down the seriousness of the situation.

"But for the call from my mother," he concluded, "I might have been finished there and then."

"Thank Buddha," she said, patting her chest involuntarily like a little girl. "It was a setup, no question about it. The water is so deep there."

"Too deep. I don't even know who's giving the orders behind the scenes."

"What can I do for you, Chief Inspector Chen?"

The directness of her question perplexed him. There was no hesitation whatsoever in her voice.

"Anything for you," she repeated emphatically.

"First, I need to learn more about the club. Last night's raid might have nothing to do with me. If it does, though, I have to find out who is behind the Heavenly World. But I know almost nothing about the nightclub—"

He stopped himself. His words carried unpleasant implications about her associations in that circle, past and the present. But there was no avoiding it: that insider knowledge was the reason he was here.

"I'll do my best to find out. I have my connections, and perhaps they can tell me something about what was going on last night." After a short pause, she added pensively, "But I'm worried about you."

Once again, he was surprised by her stealing the initiative, saying what was difficult for him to say.

"Thank you, White Cloud," he said. "But you have to be careful. Don't share a single word about our talk today. Not even to Mr. Gu."

"Have you talked to him?"

"Yes, but not like I've talked with you. For the sake of caution," he said, producing a cell phone for her, "keep this. If anything comes up, I'll call you at this phone. If you have to call me, better use a public phone."

"Got it."

"Let me know anything you find out," he added, "or anything people are talking about at the Heavenly World."

"Don't worry, Chen. Will you come back here again soon?"

"Not anytime soon, or I wouldn't be able to pass myself off as a customer, right?" He tried to work a humorous touch into his words. "I'm going to Suzhou for a few days. I'm too easy a target here. But I'll travel back and forth between the two cities."

"Too easy a target—you're scaring me, Chen," she said. She paused and then produced a business card from her purse.

The card was a simple, elegant one, black and white. It had only her name with a red seal chop hand-printed beside and a cell phone number beneath it. She scribbled several words on the back. "That's my home address. Drop by any time you like. You don't have to call ahead."

"Bingjiang—the one in Pudong? In Lujiazui?"

"Yes, that's the one."

He'd heard of the apartment complex. It was one of the most expensive in the city and a symbol of wealth and status. Not long ago, he'd seen people at a temple burning offerings that bore the name of the subdivision—an indication of affluence for the dead. She'd been doing well, and having an apartment there was yet another indication of just how well.

"It has a nice view of the river—and the Bund across it. You like the Bund, I know."

"Thanks. I'll come to see you."

He was about to get up, her business card in his hand, when she put a hand on his shoulder, smiling.

"I have to wash your hair first, Director Chen."

"What?"

"You just said that we have to be careful, didn't you? Now you've come to my salon and stayed for a long time. You can't leave without having anything done to your hair. What will the others think?"

She had a point. He had no choice but to lie down on the specially designed recliner, his head sticking out over the sink.

She leaned over him, lathering his hair luxuriously, her fingernails scratching his scalp, her bosom almost touching his face. He caught a glimpse of her cleavage through the opening of her low-cut uniform.

"Relax. You're a first-time customer here. I'm doing my best, so you will come back."

Subconsciously, he had been aware of her feelings for him, and that was the reason—at least, one of the reasons—that he had come here. He was banking on that.

He let his head be buried in lather. Bubbles of shame. Still, it was very comfortable with her fingers moving in his hair, and he closed his eyes as his highly strung nerves began to relax.

He almost fell asleep, with the water gurgling overhead, as if out of a gargoyle's mouth somewhere far away, like in a blurred dream.

SEVEN

OLD HUNTER WAS WORKING part-time for Zhang Zhang's Consulting and Investigating Agency more out of boredom than anything else. It was mostly a one-man operation—the owner, manager, chief investigator, consultant, and whatnot were all one man: Zhang Zhang. Zhang Zhang, however, had declared that he needed Old Hunter, a retired cop with a lot of experience and a lot of connections—not just his own connections, but his son's as well. Old Hunter's son was Detective Yu Guangming of the Shanghai Police Bureau, the longtime partner of Chief Inspector Chen.

Old Hunter was only supposed to come in a couple of days a week, and those days were flexible depending upon his availability. There wasn't much work to do, but during slow times he enjoyed talking to Zhang Zhang, spinning tales about various investigations from his long career with the police. True to his other nickname—Suzhou Opera Singer—he indulged in long, drawn-out narratives full of tantalizing details and digressions, to his audience of one.

Zhang Zhang was a capable entrepreneur, but he hadn't received any formal training in investigation, so whatever stories Old Hunter could share were not merely intriguing: they were educational. In return, having such genuine attention gave the old man a boost. So Old Hunter was often at the office more than was really necessary, content with office chores, taking the occasional phone call, sharpening a pencil or two, and, when Zhang Zhang wasn't there, listening to Suzhou opera on the radio.

For lunch, he usually went out to a cheap eatery nearby. For less than five yuan, he could get fried mini pork buns covered with white and black sesame and a bowl of beef soup strewn with chopped green onions. That was something he liked about the city of Shanghai.

That noon Old Hunter was at his usual place, seated on the wooden bench outside, picking up a set of bamboo chopsticks and wiping them off with a paper napkin, when a middle-aged man came over, eyeing the same bench.

"Oh—"

It was none other than Chief Inspector Chen, who discreetly raised a finger to his lips.

"I've heard a lot about this place," Chen said, smiling, like a customer commenting casually to another, "particularly about the fried buns."

"Yes, the fried buns here are inexpensive and considered the best in the city: crispy at the bottom, yet the pork stuffing is juicy," Old Hunter said, picking up on the cue. "After eating lunch here, then holding a cup of Dragon Well tea from the teahouse across the street, I don't have anything to complain about."

In reality, he had his tea back at the office. And not Dragon Well tea, either, which could be expensive—not to mention the fact that, more often than not, what was sold as Dragon Well tea was fake. He made a point to purchase his tea through folks at his old home village. It wasn't a well-known tea—and it wasn't much cheaper—but at least it was real tea.

Chen hadn't bumped into Old Hunter at random, that much the

old man could guess. They had better go off to a quieter place. Not here, nor back at Zhang Zhang's office.

So five minutes later, he led Chen across the street, to the back room of the teahouse, which had once been a neighborhood hot-water shop. The owner, Mai, was in his early seventies, and he kept his business running in the hopes that if the old neighborhood was razed like so many others, he might get a large payoff as compensation. The back room consisted of nothing but a folding canvas bed for Mai's napping needs, a table, and a couple of chairs. Old Hunter took over the back room by the simple expedient of pushing a ten-yuan bill into Mai's hand. With the door shut, and a sign reading "Closed for Business" hung up front, the two ex-cops had their privacy, and their tea, if nothing else.

"The tea is not that good," Old Hunter said with a self-depreciating chuckle, "but you can have all the hot water you want for free."

"How is the PI business?" Chen asked, after taking a sip.

"Not too bad, but it's nothing truly exciting. I'm doing it more to prove I'm still alive and kicking than anything else. I've read those mystery novels you translated. Those private investigators, Sherlock Holmes and Hercule Poirot, have real cases. But here, the profession itself exists only in the gray area—it's not legally permitted in this socialist society of ours. According to the *People's Daily*, if you have any problems, you're supposed to go to the 'people's police.' And they will take care of them for you. Unless your problems are something you can't let the government know about, and therefore can't go to the police for help with. Then you really have problems.

"In the final analysis, the cops work for the Party system, and private investigators work for their clients. That's why even the term 'PI' is still taboo in the official media.

"That's why it is necessary for our agency to operate under a different name. The sign at the office says, 'Consulting and Investigating.' Consulting covers a broad range of activities. We're not licensed private investigators, but we're not illegal either.

"In short, it's like the names of those sex-service operations. You may call it a hair salon, a karaoke club, a foot-washing place, or whatever you like, as long as it's not about what the place really does. Last year, I planned to attend a PI convention in Hangzhou, but at the last minute, the convention had to change its name and cancel most of the sessions. Internal Security was going to be there, so I changed my mind.

"Of course, I don't have to tell *you* about these regulations. They are government-imposed, and then, as a consequence, self-imposed as well. One guideline we have in the office, we try not to accept cases involving Party officials. No matter what evidence we come up with, the authorities will never accept it. And Internal Security might come knocking on our door the very next day. The old proverb put it well; 'All the ravens are equally black under the sun, and officials protect and shield one another.' "

"You're a walking encyclopedia of proverbs, Old Hunter, but that one sums it up well."

"We also can't do anything if there's an ongoing police investigation—or even if the official media just *says* there's an investigation."

"Well, Confucius says, there are things a man will do, and things a man will not do. There are things a PI can do—like change one or two words in the name to keep your agency open—and things a PI can't do. But my question is, how can your agency manage to operate when it's burdened with such a long 'can't-do' list?"

"Exactly, Chief. It can be really tough. But it's not my agency. I'm only a part-time helper, so I don't think I have to—" Old Hunter caught himself abruptly. Why the sudden interest in the agency? He paused, then decided there was nothing wrong with describing the work in general terms. "Well, most of this industry is kept afloat by one particular lucrative niche market: you might not have a customer for three months, but then one customer might make you enough to keep going for three years.

"What's that lucrative niche? Now, I don't want to tantalize you as though I were a Suzhou opera singer. Simply put, it's the old practice of cheater-catching. Particularly when the cheaters are Big Bucks. As another ancient proverb goes, 'When you're luxuriously fed and clad, you can't help but dream lustfully.' " Old Hunter took a long, deliberate sip at the tea before going on. "There's no need for a lecture about the national moral landslide—our premier used those words not long ago. Today's Socialism with Chinese characteristics has room for many rich and powerful cheaters. Their wives spare no expense to save their marriages—or, failing that, to extract the maximum alimony from them in their divorce. So suspicious spouses are willing to pay us quite a handsome fee to bring them the evidence they need."

"Tell me more about it, Old Hunter. You're so experienced. As they say, older ginger is spicier. Zhang Zhang must depend on your expertise for these operations."

"For that sort of business, the clients want you to go to these notorious sex-service places and watch, waiting with all the patience you can muster, and from time to time, pretend to enjoy foot-washing or hair-washing like an old idiot. It's a shame that a retired cop has to resort to such, but to catch those red rats wallowing in money—millions and billions—it's what you have to do. Naturally, just a picture of the cheater in the company of a girl—with both still dressed, if only barely—may not be enough proof. In those cases, you may have to install a hidden camera to get the photos that are required. We always do a careful risk assessment before taking a job. The fee may not be worth the trouble.

"Some wives know better than to bother if their husbands just have fun on the sly. As a proverb in *Dream of the Red Chamber* goes, 'What cats are not keen on stealing fish?' What those wives can't stomach, however, are ernai—secondary concubines. If the husband is keeping a mistress with her own upscale apartment, paying for her expenses and all the luxuries on the side, well, that is too much. For cases like this, we have to go out of the way—"

"For wives to fight ernai?"

"Sometimes. Though it's not just the out-of-favor wives who hire us: the ernai come to us for help, too. Unlike concubines in the pre-1949 era, Socialism with Chinese characteristics doesn't acknowledge the existence of ernai or grant them any status. Once their men find younger, prettier replacement ernai, they will lose everything. To survive, they have to fight back by any means possible, even threatening and blackmailing their former lovers. That can be very effective, since official propaganda invariably portrays Party cadres as Communist saints. If photos and details were posted online, proving that a cadre kept a spicy ernai, that official would be removed from office, even disavowed."

"I could work as a private investigator too!" Chen interjected.

"It's a lot like those old detective movies from the thirties. The one difference is that you don't have to carry around a bulky camera. You can take all the pictures you need with a light cell phone, all the while mumbling into it on and on, pretending to talk to someone. That way you don't attract attention from anyone. Still, sometimes you have to wait patiently for hours, even days. And you have to know where to wait."

"Where?"

"If the target is in one of the well-guarded apartment complexes, it's useless to wait outside. You're not going to be able to get inside, much less stand outside the bedroom door, waiting—"

"Hold on, Old Hunter. What if the cheating spouse is a Party official, but the fee is too good to decline?"

"Well, there might still be some room to maneuver."

"How so?"

"In my day, the newspapers used to portray the Party cadres as good and honest with only the rare exception of a few rotten eggs. People believed that then, as did I. But now? There's another saying in *Dream of the Red Chamber*: 'Except for a couple of stone lions crouching in front of the mansion, nobody is clean.'"

"Another old saying that goes right to the point."

"You know only too well all the propaganda regarding our Party officials and their role-model lives. But what are they really up to in their secret lives? Little secretaries, ernai, concubines, three-accompanying girls, and whatnot." Old Hunter paused, breathing into his mug, creating a series of expanding ripples on the surface of the tea, before he went on. "Some of the wronged wives or deserted ernai are so desperate for revenge, they don't care how much it will cost. So our agency may occasionally accept some of them as clients. After all, there are many roads leading to Beijing. In such a case, we obtain evidence for them only on the condition that they agree to strict confidentiality. They even have to sign documents agreeing never to name the source."

"But if the evidence goes public, wouldn't the source eventually be identified?"

"You've investigated cases involving crowd-sourced Internet searches. Once the basic evidence is online, others see it and jump in, adding more information and pictures, until the evidence becomes overwhelming. Ultimately, the government has no choice but to investigate officially. A shrewd wife, however, wouldn't necessarily put the evidence online immediately. She'd use it as a bargaining chip first. Her husband would know all too well that once it's on the Internet, his political career is finished.

"To protect our agency, we usually keep a backup copy of the agreement stored in a secure place. If something happens to one or both of us, then the signed agreement will appear online as well," Old Hunter said. He heaved a sigh, then changed the subject. "Now, you don't go to the Three-Treasure Temple without praying for something. What's on your mind, Chief Inspector? You don't have to mince words like a singer in Suzhou opera."

"Oh? Now I've become a Suzhou opera singer too?" Chen said good-naturedly.

Chen proceeded to tell Old Hunter about his being removed from the police department and about his "promotion," and then about the events at the nightclub. He finished up by saying that he wasn't entirely sure he was the intended target of the raid.

"I'm glad you came to me today," Old Hunter said. "Yu hadn't told me that this was going on at the bureau. But whatever new position they've moved you to, you're still a high-ranking Party cadre."

"But what will happen next? That's why I wanted to talk to you. Soon I might have to start working as a private investigator, just like you."

"I don't think you have to worry about that, but what went on at the nightclub does worry me, Chief Inspector. Sorry, I should call you Director."

"I wish I could tell you more about the raid, but that's all I know right now. There's another proverb you like to quote: 'A desperately sick man will seek help from any doctor.' Not that you aren't a really good one."

"You remember Pan Ming—" Old Hunter asked, looking up from his cup, "the former propaganda minister of the city?"

"Yes, he came to my mind as well. As I remember it, he got into political trouble in 1989 and was removed from his powerful position. He was then caught at a massage parlor and charged with an illegal sex act. That destroyed him publicly and ruined any possibility of his staging a comeback."

"Exactly. You know the story, so I don't have to say any more," Old Hunter said. "Now, in my current job, I'm no stranger to nightclubs. I will go there and find out the information you need. You couldn't find anyone more experienced for a job like that."

"No, I don't want you to go to the Heavenly World, Old Hunter. I thought about directly approaching Tang, the police officer I recognized in the raid, but that may alert the snakes."

"You're right to be cautious. But I can approach him for you. Tang is getting close to retirement age, and I know how to talk to him."

"All right, but remember—you can't be too careful."

"I don't think people will pay much attention to an old man like me. What could be suspicious about a retiree talking to a former colleague? But what's your own next step, Chief Inspector?"

"I'm going to go to Suzhou to oversee the renovation of my father's grave," Chen said, with a wry smile. "I may even visit a Suzhou opera house, if I can find one."

"It's a good idea for you to lie low for a while. You can always come back to Shanghai as need be."

"Yes, I can do that." Chen added, as if in afterthought, "I'm also going to double-check some of the latest cases assigned to the Special Case Squad, particularly the cases that were sent to me just before I was transferred to this new job."

"That's right. Someone might have been determined to keep you from checking into a particular case."

"The day my new position was announced, I happened to have with me electronic copies of the files on the dead pig case, and a case involving Shang's son. But the other few case files are still at the bureau. I'll go back to my old office in the police bureau in a day or two and pick them up."

"I've heard about the dead pig scandal. It made a laughingstock of the Shanghai government. Thousands and thousands of dead pigs came floating down the Huangpu River in a scene imaginable only in *Journey to the West*. Living people and dead pigs both enjoying the same river, and the city government subsequently declaring that the river's water quality is perfectly fine. What an absurd joke! But how did that come to be a case for your squad?"

"The city government wanted me, I think, to put up a convincing show of investigating that whole situation."

"Of course. You're known as a 'good cop,' so assigning you to investigate would show how serious the city government was. With so many scandals breaking out in our miraculous society, people will probably soon forget about that one. But what is this case about Shang's son? Why is it such a big deal?"

"You know who Shang is, don't you?"

"Of course. He was very popular in his day, back during the Cultural Revolution. He was known for singing the songs for a movie called *Little Red Star.* He must be quite old now, perhaps even my age, and probably long retired."

"You haven't been keeping up, Old Hunter. In fact, he's been making frequent appearances on TV of late."

"Really! Why?"

"You just mentioned that song from the movie. A red song. As the original singer, Shang is seen as embodying the revolutionary spirit. He's being used in the current political campaign that encourages 'singing red.' He may have been pushed back into the limelight by others, but he's definitely profited from it. Not too long ago, he was made a general—at least, in terms of cadre rank. And the other day, he claimed that when he sings that old red song, he becomes energetic. What a shameful lie."

"I'm sure he welcomes being used by the Party. As the proverb says, 'The one is anxious to slap, and the other is eager to be slapped.' But what is the case that involves him?"

"After the Cultural Revolution, Shang married a young singer—she was more than twenty years younger than he—and they had a cute son, Little Shang, just like the little revolutionary in *Little Red Star.* For a while, Little Shang appeared to be growing up to be the red revolutionary teenager they expected him to be. About a year ago, however, he got into a car accident, and then savagely beat up the other driver. When police arrived, he started shouting, 'My father is General Shang.' The police officers hesitated, afraid to do anything to the son of a high-ranking cadre, but a passerby recorded the scene with his cell phone. When he uploaded the video online, it became an instant scandal. Before even that scandal blew over, Little Shang got into more trouble. He and some of his buddies dragged a young, drunk girl out of a bar. Took her to a hotel and gang-raped her."

"That's outrageous. Why haven't I read anything about it?"

"It only happened a couple of weeks ago. But you'll never read anything about it in the newspapers. The only place it's being discussed is on the Internet. Someone even made a playlist of all the red songs Shang had sung, and paired them with pictures of him standing on various stages, accepting congratulations from Party leaders."

"Like a bad apple, society is really rotten to the core," Old Hunter said, shaking his head. "In those red songs, only the Communist Party can save China. No one can ever question it. Now, corruption has been exposed as being deep-rooted in the one-party system. People can't help but be disillusioned and cynical."

"Right before I was removed from my position at the police bureau, Shang's son's case was sent on to our squad. Quite possibly it was sent to us as a public example of the Party's propriety, or as just another damage-control job. Or both."

"I don't know what to say, Chief Inspector. Today's China is beyond my understanding," Old Hunter said, draining his tea. "Perhaps I'm meant to be just a private investigator. I'll get Tang talking and see what I can find out for you."

EIGHT

THE NEXT DAY, CHEN made his way back to Suzhou and the cemetery with his father's grave. This time, he brought with him a hardcover book.

It was a study of neo-Confucianism written by his father and published posthumously just last year. The publication quite possibly had something to do with Chen's then-position as chief inspector and rank as a Party cadre. Now it was his mother's request that, once the renovation of his father's grave was complete, the book be buried in the casket.

There had been almost a supernatural aspect to his first trip to Suzhou, Chen reflected. Because he went to visit his father's grave, because he decided that he needed to have his father's grave restored and renovated, and because he took pictures of the grave and sent them to his mother, he'd gotten a call from his mother while he was at the nightclub. All these things seemed to be connected through the inexplicable links of yin and yang, as if guided by an invisible hand.

Had he told his mother about what happened at the nightclub when he stepped out to return her call, she would have declared that he'd been protected by his late father. It seemed the least he could do to return the favor was to pay personal attention to the restoration. The trip might also serve as a signal to anyone who might be trying to ruin him that the ex–chief inspector had given up, and instead of trying to fight back he was simply keeping himself busy among the graves in Suzhou. Providing them with a sideshow wouldn't hurt, whether they believed it or not.

If no one else, his mother believed in Chen's trip to oversee the renovation of his father's grave. She wasn't materialistic, but the knowledge that the grave of her late husband would be properly tended to would help her sleep at night. Her request that Chen have his father's book buried with his remains originated in a dream of hers in which the late Confucian scholar was frantically searching for his copies of the classics stored in the attic room, worrying that they had been burned. During the Cultural Revolution, one of the crimes his father had been accused of was his condemnation of the first Qing emperor's burning books as a means to control people's minds. Mao happened to admire the first Qing emperor.

At the cemetery, on the hillside with his father's grave, Chen saw two farmers in their early fifties standing nearby. They were smoking and talking, but not working. These were the workers supposed to be doing the restoration job. Chen introduced himself and lit cigarettes for them. Then, as Chen stood watching, the workers picked up their tools with undisguised reluctance.

Chen decided to stay there for a while, take a look around, making a comment every now and then and pretending to supervise. At one point, Chen walked over to a moss-covered stone step, sat down, and opened the book he'd brought with him. But he couldn't concentrate on all that Confucius said. Soon he got up and started pacing about, making a renewed effort to visualize the details of the renovation.

Around eleven, the farmers declared they had to leave for lunch, tossing down their tools. It was still early, but Chen chose to say nothing.

With the workers gone, Chen, too, walked down the trail, casting a look around and wondering if he was being followed. So far, he hadn't noticed anything suspicious. It was more than possible, however, that somebody would check with the cemetery office. Chen might as well stop in and let the office confirm that Chen was in Suzhou.

Manager Hong welcomed Chen to the office with open arms, leading him to the same sofa as the last time.

"Let's talk about the project," Chen started, moving straight to the point.

"We're doing our best, Director Chen. You can be assured that progress is being made. And that the work is of good quality, too."

"I have a week before I must get back to work in Shanghai. So I plan to spend some of that time here in Suzhou." Chen showed Hong the book he was carrying. "This book was written by my father. It's my mother's request that I place this copy of the book in my father's casket myself."

"Let me say it again, Director Chen, a filial son like you will be blessed. But you don't have to worry about the restoration work on your father's tomb."

"For the work to be completed in time, however, the farmers might have to work overtime. I understand that this might cost extra, and I want to reassure you that that'll be fine. Just make sure to give me an itemized list of expenses."

"To be honest, Director Chen, some of the local farmers might not be pulling their own weight. But I will visit your father's grave site frequently and keep an eye on the workers for you. I give you my word on it. If you want to stay in Suzhou for a short vacation, there is a lot to see in the ancient city."

A lot to see in the ancient city—that's what his father had said when they were in Suzhou many years earlier.

"Thank you, Manager Hong," Chen said, his tongue suddenly dry.

"Time alone will be able to show my gratitude. The blue mountains always stand, the green water flows along the unchanging course."

Chen's response sounded like something from a martial arts novel, but his mind had suddenly gone blank, and that was all he could come up with.

He gave Hong his regular cell phone number, which Hong entered into his own cell. Hong then called a taxi for him.

"Where are you staying, Director Chen?"

"It's a hotel called—" He had not booked a hotel yet, thinking that he could find a cheap one close to the cemetery. But that wouldn't fit the persona of a high-ranking director. "Southern Garden, I think that's the name."

"That's a nice hotel, the Southern Garden. It's just about twenty minutes from here. That should be very workable for you."

Chen said his farewells and walked out of the office to see a taxi driver waiting, arms crossed, a cigarette dangling between his lips.

"Southern Garden Hotel," Chen said, after settling into the backseat.

"Oh, the Southern Garden, I know it well," the driver said, nodding. "Years ago, Mao and other top Party leaders used to stay there. It's a really nice hotel, in the old city section. Most tourists don't know anything about Suzhou, and they swarm to newly built five-star hotels in the new city section."

As a result of China's economic reform, Suzhou had grown into a much larger city. There was now an outer ring called the new city and an inner section called the old city. The hotels in the old city were generally less desirable, with their old buildings and gardens little changed from the old days. Most visitors preferred the recently built high-rise hotels in the new city.

Fifteen minutes later, the taxi pulled up in front of a hotel located on Ten Perfections Street. What "Ten Perfections" referred to, Chen had no idea. Chinese people often believed in the power of certain numbers, and ten happened to be a lucky number.

Chen walked into the hotel, taking stock of the antique-style lobby and the southern-style garden in a sweeping glance. Things seemed to be little changed. The hotel was said to have been built on the site of a Qing dynasty garden, and the original grotto had been kept intact. The room rate was somewhat higher than what Chen had been planning on, but for a couple of days, he could handle it.

In the Ming and Qing dynasties, it was fashionable for the southern literati, when successful, to be Confucianists and to be intent on worldly achievements. When not successful, however, they tended to be Taoists focused on self-cultivation. For the Taoists, the southern-style garden represented a metaphysical landscape as well as a physical one, with the grotto, stream, and bamboo grove all clustered together in imitation of nature.

At the front desk, Chen registered, got his room key, and, just before he turned to go, decided to pick up a train schedule as well. Flipping through it, he saw that there was a Shanghai-bound train leaving Suzhou roughly every twenty minutes. If need be, he could leave Suzhou in the morning and return in the evening.

His room was on the second floor of the main building. It was a cozy, comfortable one, furnished partially in the Qing style. On one wall, there was an impressive row of pictures showing visits of high-ranking Party leaders in the fifties and sixties, eloquently documenting the hotel's glorious past. The wall opposite displayed a long rice-colored silk scroll of a seventh-century Tang poem copied by a modern calligrapher.

Chen decided to take a short rest and slumped across the bed. The mattress came as a pleasant surprise—it had a foam cushion covering the old-style mattress. Of late, he'd slept badly, and he could use a nap. However, he lay on the bed and tossed restlessly.

There was a strange sound—not loud, but persistent—a tapping against the window. Chen got up and saw that it was a lone twig trembling in the wind, creaking until it finally snapped. It reminded him of a story he'd read long ago.

The work at the cemetery seemed to be off to a decent start. What worried the ex-cop was his inability to do anything in Suzhou that could make a difference in Shanghai.

He pulled out his laptop. The hotel provided free Internet service, so he connected and started surfing the Web. He came across an anecdote marked as the daily top pick. It was written by Jian Hao, a Web-based writer popular in Shanghai, about a lunch of meatball rice on the train.

I was traveling on the high speed train to Beijing. An attendant came by selling meatball rice lunches. "Come on," he said. "The meat is a joke, I don't need to tell you that. The balls are made of nothing but flour with a generous pinch of MSG." Such an unbelievable tone of irony. The attendant was trying to pitch his wares by insisting they were fake. With the story of the dead pigs still so fresh in everybody's mind, nobody had any appetite for meatballs. Could the attendant be telling the truth? The heart of the matter is that the list of "truths" in China can be too long. It's not just dead pigs, toxic milk powder, contaminated fish, DDT-sprayed ham, and formalin-whitened shrimp . . .

I recently heard a joke about the people of Shanghai being blessed . . . they enjoy pork rib soup every day for free. There are so many things that are beyond imagination in this miraculous country. At the end of a TV soap opera I was watching, a Ming dynasty imperial concubine said to her secret lover, "Why are your brows knitted so deeply? I would love to smooth the lines with an electric iron." Can you believe that? Still, let us pray that there will be such a miraculous iron to smooth out all of our frowns and worries over a portion of meatball rice.

It was no wonder, Chen thought, that Jian Hao had so many followers online. He really knew how to effectively poke at social realities. Chen stood up and began pacing about the room, liked a cricket jumping in a corked bamboo container. His cell phone rang: it was White Cloud.

She spoke very fast, as if anxious to finish the call. There was some traffic noise in the background.

"Following your instructions, I'm calling from a public phone," she said. "About what happened at the club, nobody seems to have noticed anything unusual that night. A little disturbance at the Heavenly World is not surprising. But it might be because the people I've talked to—who are just girls like me, not the top management—know only a limited amount. I'm still working on it, though, and you can count on me. As for any particular topics that the clubgoers are talking about, you might as well simply check out the hottest topics on the Internet. Some of them that don't appear at first to be related to the club actually do have a connection. For instance, the notorious Watch Boss Yao. He was said to have spent a night at the club right after the scandal broke, spending time with two top girls in a private room before he committed suicide the next day. Then there is Shang's wife, who was also seen coming to a party at the club. She was coming to sing, though not necessarily like one of those singing girls, you know—"

"Watch Boss Yao—hold on, I know who you are talking about, I think. He was the unlucky city traffic bureau chief who got into trouble because of a *Wenhui* picture of him at the scene of a traffic accident, smiling and wearing an expensive watch. Overnight that picture turned him into a target on the Internet."

"Yes, that's Yao. After that photo appeared, people started asking a simple question, 'How could he afford that gold Rolex watch if he's not corrupt?' That was even the caption for the picture when it was posted on some muckraking Web site. Soon after it was posted, other pictures of him showed up. Ultimately, photos turned up online showing him with a total of fifteen or sixteen other watches. Together they looked like window of a luxury watch shop, and it didn't leave him with even a shred of credibility—"

"Okay, so that was Yao. But who is Shang's wife?"

"She's Little Red Star's mother. You must have heard of Shang's son?"

"Oh yes, I have. Shang's son. I see. But how did she end up at the nightclub?"

"Before she married Shang, she used to sing professionally at a club."

"Used to?"

"That was years ago. I don't really know the details, but if you want, I can check. Nowadays, she might be just earning some money on the side. But it is strange that she was at the Heavenly World and performing at a private party for 'distinguished guests.' "

"That's strange indeed. I think I saw her singing on TV last year. She's not exactly—"

"She's not a beauty, I know. I wondered why she was hired for a private party as well, but I was told that the people throwing the party wanted to hear her singing red songs. That it was exciting for them."

"That's perverted."

"The fact that she is a PLA general's wife added to the kick. It was the juxtaposition of a red general's wife singing red songs in the middle of all the decadence and over-the-top luxury of the club."

"How absurd!" he said. "Can you find out more about her? Such as what was she paid for her appearance, and who paid her fee?"

"I'll try my best."

"Is there anything else?"

"Just more stories like that. All kinds of people come to the club, for all kinds of reasons. But there is one more big story going around—everyone is talking about the death of a client, an American client."

"He died at the club?"

"No, somewhere else. It was in a club or hotel in Sheshan. One of the girls told me he was very well connected and spent money like water. There are a lot of clubgoers like that at the Heavenly World, but there was something special about this one. People have been whispering about it. Perhaps it's because he was a regular at the club, and some of the girls knew him well.

"As for Rong, people there haven't heard of him before—at least, not in connection with the nightclub. It's possible that he knew somebody there and that that's why he chose to hold the book launch party there." She then added with a touch of hesitancy, "Finally, about Shen, the owner of the club. I don't know him well, but I know how to get to him, if need be. He might have something to say."

"I don't know how I can ever thank you enough, White Cloud."

"I wish I could do more." The noise in the background was getting louder, and she paused. "Sorry, someone outside the booth is knocking, waiting to use the phone. I might be able to call you later with another message. Bye."

After White Cloud hung up, Chen sat there for a few minutes staring at his cell phone. Her failure to find any real clues didn't surprise him. Nor did the fact that no one was aware of the attempted raid or any other disturbances that night. As for the hot topics of discussion at the club that she'd uncovered, none of them seemed to be worth following up on.

For instance, Watch Boss Yao's visit to the nightclub. A corrupt official, aware of his doom, Yao very likely wanted to have his last "heavenly fling" there before leaving the world. It was understandable that the visit was never mentioned in the official media. Chen hadn't paid much attention to the situation. The punishment of a Party cadre was the responsibility of the Party Discipline Committee, not the police.

Chen also didn't see anything relevant in the death of the American clubgoer. There were so many Westerners living and working in Shanghai these days that it was nothing shocking that some visited the club. That night he was at the Heavenly World, Chen himself had seen a foreigner chasing a half-naked girl down the corridor.

As for Shang's wife, she would have been even less relevant

except for the case of Shang's son having been assigned to his former squad just before Chen was promoted out of the police department. While he didn't see a connection, he couldn't help feeling curious. Who were the clients paying her to sing red songs in that environment? Red songs supposedly meant a lot to the down-and-out, the people who missed the days under Mao. But why would they interest the elite who rented that private room?

What White Cloud was able to learn couldn't help but be limited. The hair salon of hers was nothing compared to the high-end club. She had made her way up from the bottom, but she was still a long way from the top. Her current associates and contacts were mainly the girls who worked at places like the club. There was something vaguely disconcerting about the way she referred to her contacts as "girls like me."

Opening the window, he saw that it was a fine day outside. A chirping note, off and on, came from the peaceful garden. It was still too early in the year for crickets, he thought.

Chen decided to go walk around the garden. He left his room, bought a pack of cigarettes at a kiosk in the hotel lobby, and headed out into the hotel's garden.

Once he was in it, the garden somehow seemed smaller. Nonetheless, it was a pleasant scene. He cut across a white bamboo bridge, which spanned a pond with a shoal of leisurely golden fish, lit from below by lambent lights on the pebbled bottom. Chen stopped for a moment, leaning against the bamboo rail, and wondered whether the fish enjoyed the artificial effects.

Master Zhuangzi says, "You are not a fish, and how can you tell whether a fish enjoys itself or not?"

As he walked off the bridge, another hotel guest enjoying the garden nodded at him. Chen strolled farther, reaching the back of the garden, where he seated himself on a stone stool at a round stone table, partially obscured from the view of others by a bamboo grove. He took out a notebook and a pen and placed them on the table.

A *go* board was carved into the tabletop. Running his fingers over it, Chen found himself missing Detective Yu, his longtime partner. Yu was an enthusiastic *go* player, and his wife, Peiqin, was a great hostess and chef. Chen had spent many evenings at their home, playing *go* over tea and, sometimes, delicious appetizers. In Chinese, *go* was sometimes called "hand talk." Sitting in the garden, Chen was tempted to give Yu a call, but he decided against it. The present situation resembled a *go* game in some ways. He was in trouble, waiting for the coming attack, without knowing when or where.

In a *go* game, however, one knew who was attacking and why. Chen did not have this advantage.

Once again, he thought about the cases recently assigned to the Special Case Squad, wondering which, if any, might have posed a real threat to someone powerful, who then neutralized Chen by removing him from the police bureau.

When a *go* player didn't know how to respond, one option was to position a piece anyway. Though it was a questionable move, it added the element of confusion to the game, and an opportunity might arise from the opponent's surprised response. It was sometimes referred to as a response-seeking move.

As Chen was lost in thought, his pen in hand and notebook in front of him, a young hotel attendant came over. She was dressed in an indigo period uniform, possibly that of the May Fourth movement. She placed a teacup on the table near him and a bamboo-covered hot water bottle on the ground.

"Are you writing a poem, sir?" she asked, speaking in a soft voice, her long black queue swaying at her back.

It was almost a scene from a classical Chinese painting: a poet enjoying the tranquil landscape of a picturesque garden, musing on something while a young, smiling, pretty maid stood in service.

"Well, I'm thinking about it, but not a single word has come up yet. Somehow, the garden seems smaller?"

"The Lion Garden is just a five-minute walk away," she said, not responding to his question. "It's larger and fairly quiet too."

"Thanks. I might go there. But for the moment, let me sit here in peace for a while. If I need anything else, I'll let you know."

"I understand. Enjoy."

He watched her retreating figure, struck with a sense of déjà vu, recalling the lines by Yan Shu, a poet in the eleventh century.

A new poem over a cup of wine, / the last year's weather, the unchanged pavilion. / The sun is setting in the west— / how many times? / Helpless that flowers fall. / Swallows return, seemingly known. / I wander along the sweet-scented trail / in the small garden, alone.

Then his reverie was cut short by a wave of panic. Was he being watched even here—perhaps by this pretty young attendant, who was now looking back in his direction?

Since that night at the Heavenly World, he'd started to react to nearly every situation with paranoia. He took a deep breath and tried to reassure himself.

He gazed into the cup of the tea, the leaves rising to the surface, then sinking reluctantly, with an occasional ripple.

One thought returned yet again. His enemy wasn't going to stop after just one failed attempt to entrap him. His attempt at calming himself was shattered.

Then his cell phone buzzed. It was Old Hunter, who jumped right in.

"I've just been to see your favorite chef in her restaurant."

"Chef?" Chen didn't know what Old Hunter was talking about—the old man wouldn't have called him to talk about chefs.

"She talked to me about some new developments in the office," Old Hunter went on. "The computer was taken away overnight, and everything in the office was turned upside down. Her husband protested, but he almost got fired as a result."

Chen got it. The restaurant Old Hunter was talking about was a coded reference to Peiqin's cooking, and thus to information from Peiqin and Yu: the office was his own at the Shanghai Police Bureau, from which the computer apparently had been taken away, possibly as part of a thorough search. That was mean. When Chen had been told he was being promoted out of the police department, Party Secretary Li had assured him that there was no rush for him to start packing up his office. Chen had planned to go back there in a couple of days to start cleaning it out, though he hadn't left anything really important in the office or on the computer. What infuriated him, however, was learning that Detective Yu was at risk because of his relationship to the now ex–chief inspector. Chen thanked Old Hunter for his call and quickly hung up.

Chen then pulled out his regular cell phone and dialed Party Secretary Li. It wasn't a call he'd rehearsed, but it was one he'd thought about.

The call might be recorded, which was what he wanted.

"Director Chen," Li started cordially, "how are you getting along in that new position of yours?"

"I haven't started yet. I'm in Suzhou at the moment."

"In Suzhou again?"

Chen didn't remember telling Li anything about his first trip to Suzhou, but that wasn't something to worry about now.

"I'm currently having my father's grave renovated and restored. It looks terrible, practically in ruins. My mother has been complaining about it, and she's right, it's long overdue."

"As we all know, you are a filial son. Do whatever you need to do in Suzhou, and if your mother needs any help while you're away from Shanghai, I'll see what the bureau can do."

"Thank you, Party Secretary Li. This morning, as I was standing at his grave, I couldn't help thinking about what my father said to me long ago. As a Confucian scholar, he always wanted me to pursue an academic career. For years, though, I thought I'd been doing a good job, in my own way."

"You've been doing an excellent job. There's no question about it."

"No, I don't think so. Things are so complicated in China. What appears to be the right thing may turn out to be wrong. I've learned that lesson the hard way. So I can't help but doubt my ability to fulfill any official position, including this new one at the Legal Reform Committee. This might be an opportunity for me to think it over."

Li didn't respond immediately, so Chen plowed ahead.

"So that's what I am planning to do. While I'm supervising the restoration of my father's grave in Suzhou, I'll spend some time reading and studying before I'll decide if I'm qualified for this new assignment. If I decide that I'm not, I'll try doing something entirely different. In college, I dreamed of a career as a poet. Perhaps that's what I'm meant to be, instead of a chief inspector." Without waiting for a response, he then added, "In the meantime, I've been doing a lot of thinking about recent events. Particularly about what happened that night at the Heavenly World."

"What happened at the Heavenly World? I'm totally confused, Director Chen. I haven't heard a single word about it."

Chen couldn't see Li's expression, so it was impossible to tell whether he was lying or not. Li should have been briefed by the Sex Crimes Squad about the raid, but Chen gave him a brief account about that night nonetheless.

"In Suzhou, I've been listening to Suzhou opera," Chen said, seemingly shifting the topic. "There are so many wonderful proverbs in it. For one, 'You'd better not chase the desperate foe too hard.' And for another, 'The cornered dog can jump over the wall.' "

"You're really into the proverbs, Comrade Director Chen."

"Some of the investigations I've conducted involved people higher up, and I, being too bookish, might have made things difficult for them. So now it's payback time. I'm not complaining, far from it. The Party has always emphasized the importance of acting in the interest of things larger than oneself, but what good is it, if one drops dead because of it?"

"You should take a break, whether in Suzhou or back here in Shanghai. After all these years, when you've worked so hard—"

"Party Secretary Li, what this sudden promotion really means, both you and I know only too well. At one point, you were my mentor in politics. So I want to consult you about what I'm going to do now."

"No, don't say that, Director Chen. I've never been your mentor. By no means," Li said in haste. "We've worked together, but—"

Apparently Li was only too aware that their conversation might be taped and was anxious to separate himself from Chen.

"I mean it, Party Secretary Li," Chen insisted, taking a perverse delight in Li's embarrassment. "Thanks to your showing me the ropes at the bureau, I've been able to become first a chief inspector of the Shanghai Police Bureau, and now director of the Shanghai Legal Reform Committee."

"Now—I'm lost, Director Chen. The decision to move you to your new position was made by higher authorities. I knew nothing about it until it was announced that morning."

"But you know what?" Chen said, barreling ahead. "I haven't been a cop all these years for nothing. I've put something away, in case there was a need to protect myself."

"Whatever you may have put away—" Li said tentatively, before changing direction. "I knew so little about your work, about those special cases you worked on. Nobody else in the bureau knew anything about them either, except for your longtime partner, Detective Yu."

"That's another reason I'm calling you today. Whatever I've put away, it's not with Detective Yu. You can be assured of that. I've worked on too many special investigations to make such a mistake. And don't think I've kept anything on the office computer. I definitely didn't leave it in any of the obvious places that others could lay their hands on. If I fall, then what I've stored away will automatically come out on the Internet."

This time, there was no response from Li.

"For what I've done, I'll take responsibility. My late father used to say, 'There are things a man will do, and things a man will not do.' But if anything happens to Detective Yu because of me, then anything is possible. Then we'll all learn what it's possible for me to do."

"I don't know what you are talking about. Detective Yu is doing a great job as head of the Special Case Squad. How could anything happen to him?" Li managed with difficulty. "You must have overworked yourself. I'll have a word with the leading comrades about the stress of your job."

Li was playing dumb. But there was no point in pressing him too hard. Events must have been planned at a level way above him.

"Take care, Director Chen," Li said, in a hurry to get off the phone. "Bye."

With a dial tone suddenly sounding in his ear, Chen put down the phone. He wondered whether the call, made on the spur of the moment, would make any difference. Perhaps his enemies might have to slow down a bit and think about their next moves more carefully. Optimistically, it could make Chen's opponent narrow down his "enemy list." Pessimistically, well, it could hardly be any worse than it already was.

But it was a call he had to make, for Detective Yu's sake.

The young attendant was coming over to him, carrying two saucers on a stainless steel tray. One saucer contained fried watermelon seeds, and the other, white-sugar-covered yang mei berries.

"I saw you were on the phone," she said, "so I didn't want to interrupt."

It had been a long time since he'd had a sweet bayberry. When he was a child, his mother once bought him a tiny bag, which he finished, to her chagrin, in less than ten minutes. Now he picked up only one berry from the saucer, satisfied with both the taste and service.

"Your room number?" she asked.

So it would be charged to his room. But it had been naive of him to think otherwise. When she presented him with a slip, he signed his name without bothering to check the amount.

He got up, wrapped the remaining berries in a paper napkin, and walked back along the winding trail like any other tourist.

A black bat flitted around overhead, first circling, then uttering a strange sound that sounded just like Chinese character *shou*, and finally disappearing into the dusk. The heat was steady, enclosing him like a grasp. The eerie noise reminded him of another garden—the Qing Dynasty Summer Palace. The Empress Dowager Cixi had the palace in the north built lavishly, imitating the southern landscape, thereby spending all the money in the treasury that had been reserved for the navy. In the Summer Palace, the *shou* sound made by the bats, a character that could mean longevity in Chinese, was so pleasant to her that she kept a skyfull of them.

China changes, and China doesn't change. Apparitions of the emperors and empresses seemed to be presenting themselves again in the flickering light in the ancient garden. Dusk was spreading out against the sky, and the last pale cloud began to retreat.

He thought of the rapid emergence of the princelings, the children of the party elite assuming high positions of their own. That was something new and yet old in China's political landscape. And he thought of the newly resurgent red songs and their call for the Party to rule for thousands of years.

He left the garden and strolled out of the hotel. He turned right onto Ten Perfections Street, moving past small local stores and a bookstore tucked in behind the landing of a stone bridge that spanned a dark green canal. It was a scene he remembered from a literary festival several years earlier, one session of which had been held in the bookstore. There was a peach tree blossoming near the landing, just as there had been the last time he was there. Like before, the bookstore seemed more like a café, with a blond waitress flitting among the chairs and tables outside. He wondered whether the waitress was the same one as before. It might not a bad idea to come here for breakfast tomorrow morning, perhaps stir up possibilities in a cup of coffee.

One block farther on, the stores were interspersed with small workshops and factories, all unsightly in the dimming light. He turned and walked back the way he'd come.

Soon he found himself at the entrance of the hotel, but he walked past it in the other direction and was soon in sight of an impressive-looking Suzhou noodle restaurant with a black and gold sign: CAI'S NOODLES. It was closed for the day, which struck him as strange, as it was almost dinnertime. He took a look at their business hours. From six a.m. to one p.m.

He recalled something the young woman named Qian had said the other day. She mentioned a really good noodle restaurant close to that hotel. That was probably why he'd thought of that hotel back in the cemetery office. She also mentioned an interesting detail about the restaurant being open only for breakfast and lunch, but if she'd explained why, he'd forgotten.

He made his way back, absentmindedly, to the hotel again. A bright red convertible sped past him just as he walked in one of the side entrances of the hotel. To his surprise, Chen saw something that looked like a nightclub on his right. Why was there a nightclub in an ancient-style hotel garden? As fragments of music came wafting over, he saw a flashing neon sign saying Southern Heavenly World.

A uniformed doorman hastened toward him with an obsequious smile.

"Welcome, sir. I can see that you're a guest at the hotel. Now, let me tell you that we have the best girls in the city of Suzhou and an incredibly large number of them for you to choose from. Superior quality, affordable price. Satisfaction guaranteed."

Grinning from ear to ear, the doorman spoke like an experienced salesman.

"So the nightclub is part of the hotel?" Chen asked.

"Yes and no. The nightclub was built in the hotel complex, and the profits are split with the hotel."

"So the club was built on the grounds of the ancient garden?"

"There are too many old gardens in Suzhou, and no matter how ancient, a garden doesn't bring in much income."

"But don't people choose the hotel because of the garden?"

"Well, truth be told, more guests stay here because of the nightclub," the doorman said. He added in an exaggerated whisper, "It's so convenient. After a couple of hours at the club, you may take a girl back to your room at no extra charge, since you've already checked in. And no one will say anything—"

His enthusiastic introduction was interrupted by a skinny girl who emerged from the club's interior and scampered over to their side.

"So you're a guest at the hotel, sir. Welcome."

The doorman slipped inside, as if on cue.

"You've got nothing to do this evening, right?" she went on. "It's lonely for a traveler, I know. So you need someone to keep you company—"

But she broke off right there and abruptly turned her head to watch a Jaguar that was pulling up at the curb. A plump woman in her fifties, wearing a light Burberry trench coat and a large diamond ring, stepped out of the car and walked toward the club. The doorman rushed past Chen and hurried outside to get the car keys from her.

"I've a question for you," he said to the young girl after the older woman disappeared into the club.

"What's your question?"

"Are most of customers here staying at the hotel?"

"No, not necessarily, but it's easy for hotel guests to walk over to the nightclub. And it's also easy for them to make arrangements afterward."

"I see," he said, nodding. "I've another question, if you don't mind my curiosity. The lady who just went in was in her fifties . . ."

"Of course, we have female clients as well. She's a regular here. If you have money, you can buy anything—ducks too."

"Ducks?"

"Gigolos," she said. "You've got so many questions, sir. How about coming inside with me? In a cozy private room, you may fire away to your heart's content, and I'll try my best to respond to your satisfaction."

If it weren't for his experience at the Heavenly World in Shanghai, he might have agreed. Instead, he pulled out a hundred-yuan bill and gave it to her. "Just buy yourself a drink tonight. Next time we'll go inside. For now, I have just a couple of questions more."

"You mean—" she said, snatching the bill in surprise.

"For instance, the lady customer who just arrived," he said. "She must be someone important."

"Yes, she has a meat company that went public about half a year ago."

"So she's a well-known Big Buck here. Aren't people like her worried about police raids?"

"Are you from Mars?"

"What do you mean?"

"The club owner is connected all the way at the top, so customers don't have to worry about their security."

"So it's just like the Heavenly World in Shanghai?"

"Oh, you've been there? Then surely you know better. Our club is affiliated with the Heavenly World."

"Affiliated—how?"

"The owner of the Heavenly World owns shares in this club. When his Big Buck customers come to Suzhou, he refers them here. And his connections help too. But that's about all I know."

"That makes sense. The name of this club makes the association with the club in Shanghai clear," Chen said, nodding like a truly bookish customer. "But cell phones and surveillance cameras are everywhere, and all it would take is one picture of someone prominent going up on the Web for their presence here to cause damage. That would seem particularly true for Party officials."

"For those people, there are also private clubs."

"Private clubs?"

"Not open to the public like this one. They offer absolute security. Each floor has its own private garage that leads directly to a particular floor offering all the services imaginable."

"Really!" he said, thinking of the vacation Gu had suggested to him.

"Have you heard of the Obama Club?"

"What?"

"Some rich female clients fancy black studs . . ."

"Have you been to it?"

"A friend of mine worked at such a place in Sheshan. And she saw a number of untouchable elites there, including the one at the top."

"Sheshan in Shanghai—there are a lot of villas there," Chen said, thinking. He knew he had heard something about that area lately, but he couldn't remember what.

"Of course, not everybody is there to take advantage of the available services. They might just want to meet someone in private to discuss important business. No one knows." She added, "But you have nothing to worry about here. Our club is connected in both the white and the black ways."

It was then that Chen caught a glimpse of a black-clad man loitering near the hotel's side entrance. He was raising a cell phone to his mouth. Something about the man struck Chen as suspicious. Was it something real or just Chen's high-strung nerves?

"Thank you for all that you have told me, but I'm not ready to go into your club yet. I think I'll go and eat something first."

"We serve dinner at the club too."

"I like the street food in Suzhou."

It was a lame excuse, but it was nonetheless a true one.

When he looked over again, the black-attired man had already vanished.

"Here is my cell phone number," she said, handing him a card. She was probably tired of being a consultant, even if she was paid not too badly. "I'm usually here a little after one. Give me a call, and I could come to your room. For a good man like you, I won't charge you any extra."

"Thank you," he said, slipping the card into his pants pocket. "I'll think about it."

"Think about it indeed," she said, touching his cheek with the tip of her slender finger.

He stepped back and then fled.

Outside the hotel and across the street, he saw a hot pot eatery named Little Lamb and a Hunan cuisine restaurant with young waitresses clad in Xiang style standing on the sidewalk, soliciting customers. There was also an American steakhouse just a stone's throw away, sporting a large bilingual sign. The neon lights flashed and reflashed delicious temptations. Neither of them looked too bad, but to his surprise, he didn't see a single restaurant offering authentic Suzhou cuisine. It would have been fantastic if the noodle restaurant were open for business at this time of day.

Another luxury car pulled into the hotel, honking and rolling in through the side entrance.

A thought struck him. "The restaurant is also near a club that I've been to quite a few times," Qian had said. She'd been to this very club frequently, which wasn't surprising, given the job she'd offered him. He wondered if she'd be able to tell him something about this nightclub—or, more importantly, about its connection to the one in Shanghai.

It was a long shot, but it was better than nothing.

He pulled out his cell phone, but he changed his mind as a motorcycle rumbled past.

Instead, he headed over to a phone booth at the corner of a side street.

NINE

OLD HUNTER FELT LIKE a cop once again, in the middle of an investigation. He strode out of the subway in Pudong, holding a city map in his hand.

To an old man from Puxi, which was west of the Huangpu River, the area of Pudong, east of the river, was almost an unexplored world. The new subway system hardly helped. The underground hub was a maze, with confusing signs about line transferring and retransferring between Puxi and Pudong. It was supposed to be convenient, but to Old Hunter, it was not.

In the early eighties, he had had an opportunity to move to Pudong, but he chose not to go because of a then-popular saying: "A bed in Puxi is far preferable to a room in Pudong." At the time, Pudong was basically farmland. Since then, however, it had undergone an unbelievable transformation. Now, featuring some of the fanciest commercial and residential developments, Pudong was almost unrecognizable. The old saying about changes in the world came to mind, "as dramatic as from the azure sea to the mulberry field."

He plodded among the unfamiliar streets, rubbing his eyes, studying the signs and comparing them to the map in his hand, which proved to be of little use. It had been printed two or three years earlier and was already out of date.

But he knew how desperate the situation was. He understood why the ex–chief inspector had turned to him for help rather than to his son, Detective Yu. As a retired cop, he probably wouldn't be noticed. And the crisis was escalating. Soon Yu could be involved in it, too.

"You're a really experienced cop, but you can't be too cautious." That's what Chen had said at the end of their conversation in the teahouse.

Experienced or not, Old Hunter would have to come up with an excuse to approach Tang, the cop from the Sex Crimes Squad. He was pretty sure he'd have no problem. Before retirement, Old Hunter had rarely worked with Tang, but there was still a common bond between the two. Despite their good, hard work, somehow both of them remained at the bottom of the ladder.

After several wrong turns, Old Hunter succeeded in spotting Jufeng Road, and from there, the sign for Carrefour Supermarket told him that Tang's home was close. Old Hunter pulled out his phone.

"Hi, Tang, it's Old Hunter."

"Oh, such a surprise! What favorable wind has brought you over to Pudong today?"

"I'm on an errand here for my part-time job. I just walked out of the subway, got lost—guess what—and I'm now near the Carrefour. You once told me that your home was close to the supermarket, and fortunately, I have your number stored in my phone. What about joining me for a cup of tea?"

"You're still thinking of me, Old Hunter. I'm flattered. Stay in front of the supermarket and I'll come find you. There's a neighborhood recreation center just about a block away, and we can get tea there."

Tang appeared in less than five minutes. He was a gaunt man in his midfifties, with his hair streaked white and with a slight suggestion of shuffle in his steps. Tang was pleased by the unannounced visit.

Instead of the neighborhood center Tang had suggested, Old Hunter dragged him to a street eatery about a stone's throw from the supermarket.

"This is still a developing area," Tang said. "It's too far away from Lujiazui, the center of Pudong, and there aren't many decent restaurants here. Still, it's much better than when we first moved here."

"That was when the state housing assignment was still in effect, right?"

"That's right—so the apartments here can't compare to the new ones people are buying, but I still count myself lucky. We couldn't afford an apartment in today's market, and with the new subway, this area may see some improvement soon." Tang said. Then he added shamefacedly, "To tell the truth, my place is overcrowded, now that my daughter has just moved back in with her crying baby. That's why I didn't invite you home."

"You don't have to feel alone in that, Tang. I'm still living in one room at that old shikumen house, with my old wife bedridden. My two daughters and their children are all squeezed together in the same wing."

"But this street stand is run by provincial sisters and is nothing more than a coal stove with benches and tables. I don't think—"

"But it's inexpensive, and it's my treat."

On the recommendation of a "provincial sister" waitress, Old Hunter ordered a small tableful of food—red-pepper-oil-immersed catfish in an earthen pot, fried frog legs with tender green beans, steamed stinking tofu on top of wild mushrooms, grilled lamb cubes, and cold shepherd's purse blossoms mixed with dried shrimp and new sesame oil.

The waitress, who spoke with a strong Anhui accent, trotted back and forth from the wok, carrying steaming hot dishes stacked on her right arm and two bottles of Qingdao beer in her other hand.

"People have been talking about toxic food, polluted water, gutter oil, and whatnot. The country is really going to the dogs. But I'm in my seventies, already a man of longevity in Confucius's time," Old Hunter said, putting a piece of hot stinking tofu in the hot sauce for himself and tearing up a large piece of fish meat for Tang. "And you're almost in your sixties, too. So why worry?"

Old Hunter had assumed the role that had earned him his second nickname, Suzhou Opera Singer. Suzhou opera was known for frequent digressions, sometimes with false surprises or suspense at the end of an episode to lure the audience back for the next. There was a reason, however, that he had adopted that style. It helped with his police work. In interviews, people wouldn't easily guess what he was really pushing for, and, as a result, they frequently came out with what he needed.

"You have ordered too much food. It'll be a waste if we can't finish everything."

"If we don't finish it all, we can box the rest. Your home is just around the corner, isn't it? At the agency I'm working for, they have some quite lucrative cases. What I'm being paid for today's errand, more than covers our lunch."

"That's quite a lot."

"At my agency job, in two weeks—working only two days a week—I make more than my pension."

"Wow, tell me more about this line of work. I'm retiring next year, and with my son laid off, unable to take care of himself, and my daughter divorced and squeezed back with us, I need to find a job like yours."

"Believe it or not, I landed the job because of Chief Inspector Chen."

"How?" Tang asked with the cup suspended in the air.

"Chen is a good man. I was once made a special consultant to the traffic control office because of him, remember?" Old Hunter said. He was watching for a change in Tang's expression, but he didn't see any.

"Yes, Chen served as the acting director of that office for a short while," Tang responded, his tongue not beer-loosened yet.

"Zhang Zhang was working there as a clerk then. About two years ago, he left and started the PI agency. It really is a niche market—take today's job, for example. A rich woman wants us to find evidence against her cheating husband, and she offers to pay twenty thousand yuan—all in cash. What I need to do is to get pictures of her husband in a notorious foot-washing salon—in the company of a half-naked girl."

"That's not bad—I mean the pay," Tang said, helping himself to a spoonful of the green shepherd's purse blossoms mixed with dried shrimp.

"From time to time, we also have to go to one of those fancier nightclubs. There are so many Big Bucks and high officials there, as your squad knows only too well. Oh, I just heard a new Q and A joke. In today's China, who is the most formidable force in exposing corrupt officials? Their wives and ernai! It's so true. Of course, it's because they are desperate and capable of doing anything. That's why it's such a profitable market for us. Just the other day I went to a notorious nightclub on Wuning Road. You must know it. It's called . . . damn it, my old memory really sucks. What's the name of it?"

This story was not entirely fiction, improvised for Tang's benefit. Old Hunter, in his work as a PI, had visited some of those nightclubs, though not the one on Wuning Road.

"Those notorious nightclubs," Tang said, echoing Old Hunter's phrase, his face slightly flushed from the beer. "You're right about that. My job takes me to those places frequently. But there's one difference. At your agency, you don't have to worry about politics. Not so for us."

Tang didn't go on, staring instead into the empty cup before him. Old Hunter signaled the waitress to bring over two more Qingdao, and said, "Anything can be political in today's China. It's really too much for me. There are so many unheard of or unimaginable practices going on in those places. I feel so ancient."

"The government wants to give the appearance that we're fighting against corruption," Tang said, jumping back into the conversation with growing enthusiasm. "So the squad puts on the occasional show. But we have to move carefully. I've learned that lesson the hard way."

"Really?"

"I was almost kicked off the squad for asking about a possible connection between a nightclub and someone in the city government. Party Secretary Li flew into a rage. I would have been fired on the spot, had all the squad members not begged him for my sake. As a man getting close to retirement, do I have any choice?"

"No. No, you don't. Not when jackals and wolves run amuck in this country. That's one of the reason I'm so into Suzhou opera. It represents a different world—that of law, of justice, and of everything you can't find in the real world today." Old Hunter continued, draining his cup, "Oh, yes, I remember. That nightclub on Wuning Road is the Heavenly World. By the way, there was some disturbance there a couple of days ago. Have you heard of anything about it?"

"How did you know?"

"I went there that night, but long after everything had happened. I was there after eleven thirty, and people were talking about something like a police raid. But apparently no one was caught. No one seemed to have any idea about what really happened, so of course it was all anyone could talk about."

"An unexpected disturbance at a place like that should actually be expected." Tang's answer was curt.

A seasoned cop like Tang would not let his falcon loose without spotting a rabbit first. Old Hunter, sighing inaudibly, leaned over to pop another bottle of beer.

"I used to be so proud of my job. The People's police, the proletarian dictatorship, and all that. But now I'm too old to be befuddled by the editorials in the *People's Daily*. What's the point of us working our butts off for those fattened red rats? At the agency, at least I earn my money without getting involved in dirty politics."

"But I still work at the bureau. So does your son, Detective Yu," Tang said slowly. "He was the longtime partner of Chief Inspector Chen. Have you heard anything from him lately?"

That sounded like a probe. Old Hunter chewed on a frog leg with his remaining good teeth before responding, "Nothing. Chen knows better than to contact Yu with the way things are now. When I think about Chen's trouble, I can't help but feel even more justified in taking on the PI job. Let me make a suggestion, Tang."

"What's that?"

"Why don't you start working for the agency now? Just part-time. Over the weekend, let's say. A simple visit to a nightclub could fetch you a thousand yuan."

"That's really something."

"Start working on the side now, and by the time you're retired, you'll be an experienced PI. A number of agencies will be interested in you. I know a few people in this line of work, and I'll introduce you to them."

"That's fantastic. You would be doing me a huge favor, Old Hunter."

"If we old-timers don't help one another," Old Hunter said after a deliberate pause, "who will?"

"Exactly. For old-timers' sake," Tang said, raising the cup. "Now, what were we talking about before you opened this bottle? Oh yes, the disturbance at that nightclub. Believe it or not, I was there that night. We were on some sort of a special mission. It was one of the raids I don't know anything about, either before or after."

"It sounds just like a suspenseful Suzhou opera. Go ahead, Tang. Now I'm all ears."

"In our squad, it's no secret that these raids are often performed for political reasons. For example, when people start loudly complaining about the 'moral landslide,' or when there happens to be a political campaign to fight sex crime, then the number of raids our squad is set out on increases. It's more like a show than it is police work.

How could those salons and clubs have mushroomed up in the city otherwise? Here, in our undeveloped neighborhood, if you walk along Wulian Road for ten minutes, you'll see four or five Wenzhou Massage Palaces or Yangzhou Foot Paradises."

"In Socialism with Chinese characteristics, that's definitely one of the characteristics."

"Since these places can be very connected politically, it's not uncommon that we don't know anything about a raid beforehand. Ji, the head of our squad, frequently is the only one with any information, and even that may be no more than some vague clue about the target. It was like that this time. Without any notice, we were sent to a city government office, where a gray-haired man pulled Ji aside and whispered instructions in his ear. Outside, there was a black van waiting for us. The driver was a stranger, who drove in silence the whole way. It wasn't until the van pulled up on Wuning Road that I realized why everything was so secretive."

"Why, Tang?"

"It was the neon sign of the Heavenly World. It was the one place we never dreamed of touching. There are so many stories about the owner being connected to the very top. The government might occasionally slap at a fly, but not at a tiger like that. So I was excited that the city government was finally determined to crack it.

"But then we were told not to rush in but to maintain silence instead. A manager came out to discuss something with Ji, and then he led us to the elevator in the back. In silence, and taking care not to disturb any of the clubgoers, we were taken straight to a large luxurious suite on the second floor. So the Heavenly World is still untouchable except for—"

"Except for one man who was there. You've got it right, Tang. Sorry for the interruption. Please go on."

"When we got to where we were going, it was a large suite that was decorated for some event. It looked like a party had just finished. There were drinks and snacks still scattered around, a long table with books on it, and some chairs here and there, but there was no one in the room. Then a faint sound came from an attached room. We burst in on two girls sprawled on a large bed. One had greenish paint on her bare breasts, and something like whiskers painted on her face. The other was stark naked, with only a towel wrapped about her groin. They were shocked speechless at first, and then became hysterical and started screaming. The manager seemed to be no less astonished. It took him several minutes to sort things out with the sobbing, stuttering girls.

"Apparently, they'd been entertaining someone in that room, but then he got a call and stepped out. He left not five minutes before we got there. They didn't know anything about him, not even his name. But he was a very important client, obviously, because a Big Buck had booked them both for that man—those two in particular—and had paid for the full service. They were just waiting for him to come back when we broke in."

"So where was the mysterious client?"

"I haven't finished yet, Old Hunter. We were told to wait for him. We turned off most of the lights so the room was as before, and we stood there, holding our breath. Nobody came back. After about ten minutes, the manager got a phone call from the security. There's no telling what they really discussed, but from what I overheard, there was no sign of the man anywhere in the building.

"Then the manager called someone and reported their failure to find the man. He talked apologetically. Ji looked on with confusion written on his face, just like the rest of us. Whatever was going on, it was a raid carried out on specific instructions from someone higher up. A young cop in the squad suggested that we search the other rooms in the nightclub, but we were told not to bother.

"There was no point waiting there any longer—our target had obviously fled, so we left quietly. With a group of seven or eight cops in the club, none of us dressed like regular clients, not to mention the screams and shouts of the two girls when we burst into the inner room, it's no surprise that some 'disturbance' was noticed."

"What a story," Old Hunter exclaimed. "Did you hear anything more afterward?"

"We were told not to talk to others about it—and in particular, not a single word was to be spoken outside the department. Of course, you're not an outsider."

"Of course. I won't say a word to anyone," Old Hunter said, raising the cup again. "Have you talked to Ji?"

"Not about any of the specifics. To us, he simply said that it might be just as well."

"Why do you think he said that?"

"I think Ji might have guessed something. The target in question might have been someone important, possibly a high-ranking official. If a powerful person is caught, there can be consequences for the squad. Ji usually keeps to himself, you know. That's why he was made the head of the squad."

"A different question. Do you remember which room at the nightclub?"

"As I said, it was on the second floor. It was the one overlooking the street . . . let me think. Suite 230. Why do want to know?"

"I'm just curious. A Suzhou opera singer has to grasp all the details," Old Hunter said. "Who was the manager that met you outside the club?"

"I have no idea. He didn't introduce himself to us. Likely he was the boss there—or one of the bosses. The girls knew him. They were cringing, speaking of him in awe." Tang went on, after finishing the last spicy catfish nugget in the earthen pot. "Now that I think about it, there was something else weird. Usually, raids like this are reported in the newspapers the next day. This one wasn't."

"It must have been a setup. What tough luck for the person who arranged it all!" Old Hunter said, shifting the direction of the conversation. "Thanks, Tang. Things in those places can be so complicated."

What Tang had told him about that night confirmed the suspicions Chen had expressed to Old Hunter when the two had talked in the teahouse.

As Old Hunter sat there, thinking over the implications of Tang's narrative, the beer spilled from his trembling hand.

TEN

EARLY THE NEXT MORNING, Chen found himself at Cai's Noodles, sitting at a mahogany table in a slightly raised section on the second floor. His table was leaning against a quaint lattice window that overlooked the somber green canal. He was one of the first customers. He'd slept badly the night before, so he decided to come as soon as the restaurant opened at six.

The other customers appeared to be locals, mostly in their sixties or seventies and some of them even older. He wondered why they were clustering around the lower section near the staircase, instead of sitting on the second floor, close to the windows with their pleasant views.

A waitress placed saucers of local specialties along with a pot of green tea on the table. The dog-eared, oil-stained menu she handed him spoke for the popularity of the restaurant. He began flipping through its pages. The prices weren't too expensive, especially considering the location of the place. Perhaps Qian was right: the proprietor wasn't so concerned with making money with the restaurant, having made enough elsewhere.

Sipping at his tea, Chen remembered a vacation not too long ago, when he was still a chief inspector. He was waiting for an attractive woman in a tiny eatery, in another city not too far away. . . .

Now, he was no longer a cop. He was not on vacation. In no mood for romantic fantasies at all.

Last night, he'd gotten another phone call from Old Hunter. The information from Tang confirmed what Chen had suspected. He was the sole target of the raid. The room number, the statements from the two cat girls, the books piled in the room . . . all of this led to one unmistakable conclusion. The book party had been a setup orchestrated at a higher level and was designed to entrap him.

After the phone call, Chen couldn't fall asleep. He lay there, awake, trying to put the pieces together in his mind, but got nowhere. By morning he was worn out, and haunted by the ominous feeling that he was far from grasping the crucial piece of this puzzle.

The waitress came over to pour him another cup of tea.

"I'm still waiting to order," he said, holding up the menu.

Glancing at his watch, He began wondering whether Qian would appear. It was now seven ten. It didn't really matter, he thought. All he really wanted to do this morning was enjoy a bowl of Suzhou noodles, not dwell on his troubles.

As he was breathing deep into his second cup of the fragrant tea, he heard a flurry of footsteps coming up the stairs. Qian appeared on the landing in a ray of dazzling morning light, waving her hand.

She was wearing a light blue, short-sleeved mandarin dress, with a white cashmere shawl over her shoulders. It accentuated her slender figure, as if she was stepping light-footedly out of another poem by Du Mu.

Down and out, I wander around / crossing rivers and lakes / with a cup of wine, / and her waist willowy, / as if capable of dancing / on my lone palm.

Chen stood up to greet her and then poured her a cup of tea, rather than the wine featured in the Tang lines.

"It's such a nice place. Thank you for your recommendation, Qian."

"You have a good memory, Chen."

The waitress came over to take their order. Chen chose the double topping of smoked fish and slow-cooked pork belly and the noodles in red soup, while Qian settled on shredded pork fried with pickled cabbage in white soup.

"The deep-fried rice paddy eel is the chef's special. It's from Cai's personal farm, so it's guaranteed to be hormone-free."

So along with the noodles, they agreed to share a platter of the eels.

"I didn't think you'd call," she said, chopsticking up the noodles as the waitress withdrew with an empty tray.

"I'm a detective for hire. So why not? But I'm here in Suzhou to oversee the renovation of my father's grave. My mother insists that I personally attend to the details, and I happened to have a few days off."

"You're a filial son, aren't you?"

"Well, you may tell my mother that," Chen said, picking up an eel slice for himself.

"How did you happen to pick that hotel?"

"Because of what you said about this restaurant the last time we met. The hotel is a nice one; it's also close to here and to the club."

"So you have also been to the club?"

"No, not yet. But I'll go there."

"I didn't know you were a Suzhou opera fan."

"What does that have to do with Suzhou opera?"

"You just mentioned the club."

"Don't you mean Southern Heavenly World, the nightclub that's in the hotel?"

"Oh. No. I was talking about the Suzhou opera club. It's just two minutes' walk from here."

"A Suzhou opera club—" That was a disappointment. He'd invited her out for information of a different kind. "Of course I'll go there too."

"The Southern Heavenly World nightclub murders the landscape."

"I couldn't agree more. Because of my job, I have to visit such places. It reminds me of the Heavenly World in Shanghai, which has almost the same name."

"I've heard that the nightclub here is affiliated with the one in Shanghai. A former colleague of mine works in the Shanghai nightclub."

"I see," he said. This was the second time someone had mentioned the affiliation of the two clubs, and this time it was from a more reliable source. "This noodle restaurant is fantastic. There are a lot of customers this early in the morning. We're lucky to be able to get such a great table, with just the two of us sitting by the windows."

"This raised section by the windows is more expensive. They charge double for the view, and for the service. The other customers at this hour are mostly local retirees who are not well-to-do like you with your lucrative jobs."

"Ah, that explains it."

"And there's another reason they come so early. They want to get the noodles from the first pot of the morning."

"Why's that?"

"When the noodles are freshly made, and boiled in the first pot, the taste is particularly delicious. As the day goes on, the chef has to frequently add water to the pot. Let's say you come here around noon. At that stage, the water can be floury from all the noodle residue, and there's a huge difference in the taste."

"That's intriguing," he said. "Is that why it's open for only half a day?"

"It might be part of the reason, but there's another explanation for why it's only open for half a day. To make traditional Suzhou noodles, the soup has to be cooked in a pot—a different pot from the noodle pot—overnight, for five or six hours, with all the special ingredients. Because of the great demand here, the soup is usually gone by noon. To maintain the highest quality, the proprietor, Cai, can only serve from morning till one thirty in the afternoon."

"Cai sounds like an interesting character."

"He doesn't come in early. He's another fan of Suzhou opera," she said, reaching into her purse. "I've brought a CD with me." She showed a disc to Chen. "It is Tang and Song poems set to Suzhou opera. You won't find it in any stores. It was produced by the Suzhou Opera Club."

"Tang and Song poems set to Suzhou opera!"

"It was an experiment we did at our club. An old proverb says, if you memorize three hundred Tang poems, you might be able to write a little. It's easier for people to remember words when they're set to music. And at the same time, people interested only in the classic poetry might also learn to appreciate opera."

"That's great. You are promoting poetry as well as Suzhou opera."

She took a slow sip at the tea, the morning light lambent in her eyes, a tiny greenish leaf between her lips.

The tenderness of the green tea leaf between her lips. / Everything is possible, but not pardonable. . . .

Did he write those lines himself? Possibly. It wasn't a morning, however, to indulge in poetic reveries.

"We didn't talk much about the job on the phone," Chen said, steering the conversation back to the reason they were meeting. "Tell me more specifically what you want me to do. Last time, you indicated that it involves somebody in the city government, someone big."

"He's not that big, but he is in a sensitive position. That's about all you need to know. You should simply focus on the woman. You'll find more about him as you investigate her—it's inevitable, and really only a matter of time. Once you reach that point, it's possible you'll decide the job's too much trouble. Once you understand what's involved, you can decline the job and not tell me anything of what you've learned."

It was basically what she'd said when they first met. But it would be difficult for him to back out now, since he'd invited her here, with his own ulterior motive in mind.

"I see," he said, putting down the chopsticks. "I still have to ask you some questions first."

"Go ahead."

"The identity of the man aside, why do you want information on this woman?"

"Do you really have to know, Chen?"

"Yes, I have to know what is motivating a potential client before I take on any job."

Chen was betting that Qian would choose not to answer, and then he would be off the hook.

She cast a plaintive look at him.

The waitress came over again, ready to clear the table.

"We're in no hurry," Chen said. "We want to talk for a while. Bring us another pot of good tea."

"Yes sir," the waitress said.

"And here is twenty yuan for you," Chen said, handing her a bill. "Once you bring the tea, I'd appreciate it if you could leave us alone to talk in peace."

"I understand, sir," the waitress said with a knowing smile. "For fifty, I can make sure that no other customers are seated near you."

"That's reasonable," Chen agreed readily. "I'll pay you when we leave."

Qian looked on in amazement. She expected a private investigator to know the ways of the world, but the way he tipped was surprising.

The waitress brought over another pot of Dragon Well tea in no time, leaving them with an obliging smile.

"You really must have been paid well for your last job," Qian said.

"Not too bad. The customer thought I did a good job."

"I see. And to do a good job, you have to know why you're being hired. I understand," she said slowly. "It's a long story. I'd better start from the beginning.

"In Suzhou opera, an actor might sing a couple of lines before starting into the narration. I don't want to be that dramatic, but there's a poem on the back of the CD cover, which might set up my story."

Chen picked up the CD, on the back of which was the silhouette of a graceful woman dressed in ancient attire leaning against a pavilion. Beside that image was a ci poem set in a special font that looked like petals.

Thanks to the long willow shoot bending / itself for her, she succumbs / to the mistlike catkins caressing / her face, as if touched / by an old friend.

"Oh, it's by Li Yu, the poet-emperor of Southern Tang in the tenth century," he said. "He was a lousy emperor, but a brilliant poet. . . ."

A group of customers appeared, laughing, talking, cursing, heading straight to their section, possibly having just come from an overnight mahjong party or a party at the Southern Heavenly World. It seemed the waitress wasn't able to keep her word.

One of the new customers shouted out to the waitress, "Double toppings for each of us, a couple of the best cross-bridge dishes as well. And a pot of your best Before-Rain tea."

"Sorry about that," the waitress apologized to Chen and Qian.

Since it was no longer possible for them to talk privately there, they paid their bill and left.

It was just past eight in the morning, and neither the Lion Garden nor the bookstore had opened yet. Chen, instead, led Qian to the back garden of his hotel. Considering the time of year, it was surprisingly pleasant sitting on a bench out by the pond. Faint music came wafting over on a fitful breeze.

No one seemed to be paying any attention to them. By all appearances, they were merely a couple from the hotel, stepping out into the garden to watch the goldfish in the pond after enjoying an early breakfast.

"It's a fairly long story," she said quietly. "Like a Suzhou opera, I think it's better told in the third person."

"Perspective is what makes a story. Please go ahead."

She was born in Suzhou. Her parents, both of them opera fans, dreamed of her growing up to be a Suzhou opera singer. She began showing a passionate interest in it as early as her primary school years. After middle school, she entered the Suzhou Arts School, where she was a top student. Soon she was hired by the Suzhou Number One Opera Ensemble. In the heyday of the opera, that would have meant a secure future. But times had changed. The audience, once huge in number, was shrinking rapidly, and frenzied real estate development led to the demolition of the old Suzhou opera theaters, one after another. As audiences dwindled, revenue fell, and once the government dropped their subsidy, the ensemble could hardly make ends meet. The dire financial situation meant the company could no longer continue as before.

Eventually, the ensemble had to resort to the old ways: having its members perform at whatever venue available. One night they performed at a restaurant, the next night a private performance for a wealthy family, and the day after, at a birthday party. Ultimately the members had to go their separate ways, with some of them going on the road and touring beyond Suzhou. Suzhou opera was said to have a considerable fan base in Shanghai, so Qian went there on her own, though nominally still a member of the ensemble.

In Shanghai, she came to play in a restaurant called Plum Blossom Pavilion, which was known for its inexpensive breakfast and was popular with the not-so-well-to-do retirees. The restaurant proprietor, a middle-aged man named Kang, invited Suzhou opera singers to perform every Tuesday morning. It was a marketing gambit—a free treat for customers to enjoy over a bowl of noodles or dumplings—but it gave the restaurant a reputation as "a conscientious enterprise intent on preserving the traditional arts." The Foreign Liaison Office heard about the performances and started to bring foreign visitors to the restaurant. Then Kang made a suggestion to her.

"Continue to sing every Tuesday as before, but during the rest of the week, you can work as a hostess and get paid accordingly. You'll also get free food and board, and a bonus whenever you sing for customers by special request."

To Qian, Suzhou opera could not have sunk lower. But the rapidly rising rent in the city already took more than half of the money she earned. She had no choice but to move into the restaurant—eating leftovers in the kitchen and sleeping on the hard tables after the restaurant closed late at night.

About a week after starting her new role, she was told that there would be a group of distinguished Western tourists interested in Suzhou opera coming in that evening and that she had to do her best. That evening turned out to be a huge success. Articles covering it appeared in several newspapers, some with pictures, and among the tourists was a well-known American sinologist who spoke highly of the Shanghai government's efforts to support the local dialect opera. For Kang, publicity like that meant more profit.

For her, however, it was more about a man whom, for the moment, she would call S. He was the one who arranged for the Western tourist group to visit the restaurant, initially as a gesture of support for the traditional art. He was in a position to make decisions for the Shanghai Foreign Liaison Office, and he arranged for several groups to come in quick succession.

In S., she saw "someone who understands the music," an echo from the traditional romantic stories celebrated in Suzhou opera. And S. saw her as "the youthful, vivacious embodiment of the ancient art," as he told her one evening after her performance. In him, she thought she'd discovered hope for a revival of Suzhou opera. He had the power to make impossible things possible. Because of the groups of foreign tourists who came to the Suzhou opera at the restaurant, and the coverage of it in the media, the opera started to attract some younger people.

All of this happened during a vulnerable time for her. She'd been in Shanghai for nearly a year, with very little to show for it. Her grandma had passed away back in Suzhou, worrying on her deathbed about her granddaughter. Qian was starting to wonder if there was any point in struggling any longer.

That was when S. stepped into the restaurant, and then, into her life. He brought with him flowers, red envelopes, and promises to make her a star in the revival of Suzhou opera. He was generous, though he might not have had to worry about the money, since it was all done under the cover of government business. He told her that he and his wife were separated and that they had filed for divorce. It wasn't long before he arranged for her to move into a furnished apartment in Xujiahui. He even managed to secure her a "research subsidy for Suzhou opera," which would be conducted under aegis of the Shanghai Foreign Liaison office.

What happened between the two of them seemed to be one of those old, yet always new, stories.

He told her that she didn't have to perform anymore—she didn't need the money, but she still went to the restaurant once a week. He was a busy official, so when he wasn't around, she worked on recording the CD of Tang poems as part of her research into Suzhou opera.

But that phase of the relationship didn't last very long. While S. tolerated her continuing to perform, he no longer brought foreign groups to the restaurant. He said that some people were already starting to gossip, and it was getting difficult to see her as much as he would have liked.

So he proposed that she move back to Suzhou. There he would

visit her whenever possible, and they wouldn't have to worry about being recognized. He bought an apartment for her there, and instead of a research subsidy through his department, he gave her a monthly allowance. Suzhou had more important appeal for her: she still had her position in the opera ensemble, and she hoped she might be able to do something more for the opera there. Not to mention the fact that she would be closer to her parents.

She accepted the seemingly reasonable arrangement, but she soon realized that it was something else entirely. He cared for his career more than he cared about anything else, and he wasn't exactly separated from his wife, who was in the United States with their son while he attended private school. But what could an ex–Suzhou opera singer do? Still, Suzhou held something unexpected for her—a new Suzhou opera club, whose members were devoted fans, and to which she was a welcome addition.

Then she started to notice that S. had changed. He didn't seem to be that crazy about her anymore. One evening, he even joked that when she was singing in her mandarin dress in Shanghai, she was animated with an irresistible glow, but here in Suzhou, she looked like any ordinary Suzhounese.

Shortly afterward, she found out that he had a new conquest in Shanghai, who was apparently younger and prettier. Qian was devastated by the realization that he'd sent her back to Suzhou to get her out of the way. Yet he still continued to come see her, though less and less, and to provide for her just as handsomely as ever.

Another devastating blow came from her parents. Initially, they were confused by the fact that she'd come back to Suzhou without a job, yet with very comfortable means. When they found out about the ernai arrangement with S., they refused to step into her apartment again.

Then an opportunity presented itself. The American professor who'd been part of the first group led by S. offered her a spot in his university's Asian studies program. He even offered her a tuition waiver, so that all she'd need would be the money to support herself. He suggested she could support herself by giving performances, but she doubted there would be enough Suzhou opera fans in the local Chinese community.

So she approached S. He was going to get rid of her anyway, this could be a kind of severance pay, she supposed. To her surprise, S. was furious. He thought that once she was out of China, she would start talking and damage his career. He forbade her from pursuing the opportunity any further and, through his connections, had her travel permit rescinded.

"Things can't go on like this," she concluded, switching back to the first person. "I was considering starting over in another country when we met near the cemetery."

She spoke in an amiable, soft Suzhou dialect, as if this were some sort of a theater performance.

Whether she was a reliable narrator or not, he wasn't sure. There was probably some self-justification woven into her story. Still, her story was probably not that different from those of other ernai, with the exception of her passion for Suzhou opera. If for no other reason than that, she deserved help.

He saw a parallel with his own passion for poetry, except that he was far more realistic.

She went on with a catch in her voice, "*He only sees the new one laugh, / but hears not the old one weep.*" It sounded like another Tang couplet.

"He's not worth it," he said. "Start over, but start over here—and start over for yourself."

"It's not that I haven't tried. But since my only skill is singing, it's difficult to find a real job in Suzhou. Besides, people have already started telling stories about me. So the prospect of studying abroad is very tempting."

"It's tough," he said, nodding.

"If only things could be just like when we first met—" Qian resumed.

It could be quote from a poem by Nalan Xingde, with a subtle intertextual allusion to a Han dynasty imperial concubine who compared herself to a silk fan that, once used, was forgotten, the memories of her first meeting with her lord now dust-covered.

As compelling as her story was, however, it was disappointing. He'd hoped that she'd be able to help him find out more about the Heavenly World.

"So you want to divorce him—" He cut himself short. She wasn't even the man's wife, and he was disturbed by the possibilities of who the man might be.

"No, I just want him to let me go, with or without financial help. But he says that if I try to leave him, he'll have me crushed like a bug."

"What do you want me to do?"

"I need you to gather evidence that will derail his career. It's only with that kind of information that I can even hope to negotiate with him."

"I see."

"The new woman in Shanghai—"

"You have met her?"

"No, but she called him one night while he was with me in Suzhou. I checked his cell phone while he was sleeping, and I got her name and number."

"That's something to start with."

"Whatever evidence you get, try to make sure it's as graphic as possible."

"But what are you going to do with this so-called evidence? If he's a high-ranking official, none of the official media will publish it."

"Now that the Internet exists, there's no point in bothering with the *People's Daily*."

That was exactly what Old Hunter had told him. Her plan could work.

In a determined voice, she said, "Even in the worst-case scenario, where the fish dies and the net breaks, I'll still have my freedom."

"Because of his position at the Shanghai Foreign Liaison Office," Chen said, "he might have special agents working under him. I'll have to move carefully, but I'll definitely look into it for you."

"Great," she said, taking out her checkbook.

"No, I don't know how far I'll be able to proceed, so I can't take your money now." After a pause, he continued. "But I have a question for you. Do you know anything about the nightclub attached to my hotel?"

"Southern Heavenly World?" she said. "He took me there one evening. I don't know why men are so crazy about it."

"You mentioned that it's affiliated with the Heavenly World in Shanghai and that you have a former colleague who works at that one."

"Yes. Why are you so interested? You're working on a case for another client, aren't you?"

He nodded without responding. It was a reasonable guess—he was pretending to be a PI, after all.

"Yes, one of my colleagues ended up working there. I can make some calls for you."

"That would be great. I'd really appreciate it."

"But, back to my case. You should at least let me cover your expenses."

"Don't worry about it. You are doing me a favor, so it's only fair that I do one for you. Now, about the new woman in Shanghai; you gave me her basic info last time we met, but I'm afraid I don't have it with me."

She scribbled the woman's name, address, and phone number on a piece of paper.

"One last thing. I'll contact you whenever I need to speak with you. But don't try to contact me at the hotel," he said, writing down his new cell phone number. "If anything, call this number and this number alone. That's very important. And don't call me unless it's an emergency and you absolutely have to speak to me. Otherwise, I'll call you as soon as I have something."

"I'll be waiting for your call."

ELEVEN

DETECTIVE YU WAS HURRYING home. He'd gotten a phone call from Peiqin, who had received a phone call from Old Hunter.

The old man had gotten straight to the point with his daughter-in-law, quite unlike his usual Suzhou Opera Singer self. He complained to her about how difficult it was to get hold of Yu these days. In response, Peiqin invited him to come over for dinner that evening. Old Hunter accepted the invitation with an enigmatic comment.

"Good idea. Your three-cup chicken is delicious. The fried mini buns near the agency are not too bad, but you can't have them every day. By the way, an old friend of mine, who recently lost his job, speaks highly of your cooking skills too, and even quotes a poem about it."

What Old Hunter had said was unusual, particularly the part about the mysterious old friend, so Peiqin had dialed Yu immediately. Half an hour later, Yu arrived home, having almost run there, arriving even before Old Hunter.

"Old Hunter's no gourmet," Yu said, still short of breath. "A cup of strong tea is about all he needs. I think I know which old friend he was talking about."

"Yes, the friend who recently lost his job," Peiqin said. "Also, the old man was calling from a new number."

"You mean a new cell phone number?"

"That's right."

Yu lit a cigarette. For once, instead of saying anything about it, Peiqin walked over to the stove.

Pouring a small cup of sesame oil into the wok, she started on the three-cup chicken by frying the chopped chicken. As it fried, she set up a cup of yellow rice wine, a cup of soy sauce, and a pinch of fresh basil on the kitchen counter.

Yu tried to help, clumsily, without much success. His mind kept wandering back to the conversation he had with Party Secretary Li back at the bureau.

Just the day before, Li had snapped at him, even threatening to remove Yu from his position when the latter questioned him about Chen's being removed from the bureau without notice. But then this afternoon, Li talked to Yu like an amiable Party secretary again. After a bit of small talk about the recent work of the Special Case Squad, Li came around to the point, telling him that the decision to remove Chen and to promote Yu to the head of the Special Case Squad had come entirely from the higher authorities. As far as Li was concerned, the promotion was long overdue. Even Chen himself had suggested it several times.

"The decision was unknown to us until the morning it was announced," Li said emphatically. "I had no choice but to read it word by word. Some people might have different interpretations of what the higher authorities intended with this decision. Have you heard any, Detective Yu?"

"No. I've been overwhelmed with the squad's caseload, particularly with Chen gone, and Jia away on vacation, and . . ."

"Has Chen spoken to you lately?"

"Only once, when he was on a cemetery bus to Suzhou. I tried to discuss the open cases with him, but like a filial son, he talked about nothing but his guilt over not having visited his father's grave in years."

"How did he sound to you?"

"A bit low. But that's natural for one on a Qingming trip."

"Did he mention anything about what he's planning to do?"

"That would be too personal a topic."

"No, I mean what he plans to do once he starts his new position."

"Nothing that I recall."

"Nothing?" the Party secretary asked, with a suggestion of seriousness in his voice. "You have to take the correct attitude, Comrade Detective Yu. As a Party member and the head of the Special Case Squad, you must trust the Party authorities. In today's society, things can be complicated. Whatever Chen might have said to you or whatever information he might have given to you, you know what you should and shouldn't do."

"Of course, Party Secretary Li. I'll report to you if there's anything new. The position as head of the squad is difficult, with a lot of new responsibilities unknown and uncharted. I'll look to move forward under your guidance."

"You're an old hand in our bureau. With Chen gone, there's nobody but you to help yourself. You know what I mean, don't you?"

"Yes, Party Secretary Li. I'll keep every word of yours in mind."

It was a talk in which Yu had decided not to give anything anyway, speaking only in respectful yet empty phrases. Li should have known better than to try to get him to reveal anything about the ex–chief inspector.

To Detective Yu, Chen was not just a partner or a boss but also a friend. What was more, Chen represented what Yu believed a cop should be. For that reason in particular, Yu was deeply disturbed by Chen's removal.

It was puzzling that, at this juncture, Chen chose to keep himself busy with the renovation of his father's grave, alone in Suzhou. Though it wasn't the first time that the ex–chief inspector had behaved in such an enigmatic way.

Chen had made no attempt to discuss the dire situation with Yu. Instead, Chen had contacted Old Hunter. Chen's reasoning wasn't difficult to figure out: as a retired cop, Old Hunter wasn't under scrutiny.

"A penny for your thoughts," Peiqin said, slicing the thousand-year egg with a thread for a cold dish. Another cold dish—tofu mixed with sesame oil and green onion—would be prepared once the guest arrived. "Thinking about the trouble your boss is in?"

Yu was indeed thinking about just that, though he had no clue what kind of trouble Chen had landed in.

"He's my friend," he said.

"Our friend," Peiqin said echoing. "And Old Hunter's too. But your father said very little on the phone."

"He'll tell us more this evening."

"What will happen to Chen, no one knows. Still, it might not be bad for him to start all over. He's not happy. As a Party-member chief inspector, he's a product of the system. He tries to make a difference but is that even possible?"

When Old Hunter finally appeared, the table was set with dainty cold dishes and tiny porcelain cups. Yu poured a cup of tea for him. Peiqin hurried to the stove, lifting the wok lid, adding a handful of chopped green onion and then drops of sesame oil to the slightly browned chicken.

"The three-cup chicken smells irresistible," Old Hunter said as Peiqin opened a bottle of yellow rice wine.

Raising his cup, Yu lost no time asking questions of Old Hunter. For once, the retired cop answered in a straightforward way. Without dwelling on his meeting with Chen, he launched into a detailed account of his meeting with Tang.

"That's about all Tang could tell me," Old Hunter concluded, "but he may be able to find out more soon."

"Tang has no idea that you're making inquiries for Chen's sake?"

"No, I don't think so. He doesn't even know that the target at the club was Chen."

"But he knows that Yu is a friend of Chen?" Peiqin cut in, pouring more wine for Old Hunter.

There was no answer to that. Old Hunter stared at a slice of the thousand-year egg, which was shining darkly, like a mystery covered in minced golden ginger.

Their conversation shifted to Chen's stay in Suzhou.

Old Hunter unfolded a white rice-paper fan with a dramatic flourish, as if ready for a lengthy digression in a Suzhou opera.

"You know Chen's in trouble. But you don't know why he's in Suzhou, do you?" he said, folding and then unfolding the fan. "Indeed, there's a lot you can learn from Suzhou opera."

Yu and Peiqin merely nodded, lest they interrupt the old man's narrative flow. Old Hunter took a leisurely sip from his half-empty cup, without immediately continuing.

"Why do you say that?" Peiqin asked, refilling the cup.

"I've been listening to the *Romance of the Three Kingdoms* over the last several months. Now that all of the Suzhou opera houses have been torn down, the artists can only perform in restaurants, like in the old days, before there were performance halls. There is a restaurant I go to every Tuesday morning where I can watch Suzhou opera performed over a bowl of plain noodles."

Peiqin and Yu looked at each other again. Old Hunter was back to his old self, tantalizing them before coming to a crucial point.

"In *Romance of the Three Kingdoms*, General Liu Bei is with Prime Minister Cao Cao in the capital. Cao Cao, wary of Liu as a potential rival, is thinking of getting rid of him. So Liu makes a public show of being interested in growing vegetables in his garden like an ordinary man, and a timid one at that. At a sudden clap of thunder, he drops his wine cup to the ground in the presence of Cao Cao. As a result, Cao Cao no longer takes Liu seriously, who then manages to flee from the capital."

"You think Chen is trying to do the same thing," Peiqin chipped in. "He's making a public show of weakness by pretending that he cares about nothing but the project with his father's grave in Suzhou. But do you think it'll work and his enemies will let him go?"

Neither the father nor the son had an answer to that.

Peiqin walked back over to the stove to prepare the green onion cake while Old Hunter started to ask questions of Yu.

"So, are there any new special cases passed on to your squad?"

"Theoretically, only special cases are referred to our squad, but as far as I can see, none of them are special enough to have Chen removed."

"Well, tell me about those cases assigned to Chen just before he was removed from the bureau."

Apparently, Old Hunter was thinking along the same lines as the rest of them, Yu observed, helping himself to a spoonful of refreshingly cold tofu.

"By the way," Old Hunter went on before Yu said anything, "Chen mentioned that he has electronic copies of the case files for Shang's son and the dead pigs on the river."

That meant Chen himself would look into those two cases and Yu needed to focus on the remaining ones. He then briefed Old Hunter on the other cases, particularly on a missing person case concerning an official named Liang, which had been assigned to the squad just the day before Chen was removed. Yu wasn't sure Chen knew it was a missing person case—he didn't know if Chen had even opened the file.

"The yellow rice wine tastes quite mellow," Old Hunter said slowly, at the end of Yu's briefing. Peiqin came back, her hands still partially covered in flour. “But it’ll be better when warmed just a little. As the old saying goes, after three cups of wine—and the three-cup chicken, too—it’s the time to come to the point.”

“Sorry, I forgot,” Peiqin said, hurrying to put another bottle in a pot of warm water.

“I just got a phone call from Chen. Guess what he wanted me to do this time? He wanted me to check out an ernai here in Shanghai. Ironically, it’s the sort of job we’re quite familiar with at the agency.”

“Why did he want you to do that?”

“I have no clue. I know only that it was a request from a young woman he met in Suzhou. He emphasized that I don’t have to go out of my way. Perhaps it’s unrelated to his current troubles, but I doubt that.”

“If that’s the case, I’m even more worried. It sounds like a shot in the dark, which means he might be desperate,” Yu said. “Did he tell you anything specific about the ernai?”

“She’s a young woman named Jin, who runs a café—a so-called ernai café—in the Gubei area. I wonder if Jin is somehow connected to the nightclub. I don’t think Chen would have asked me to do a job for someone he’d just met at random in Suzhou.”

“Even if it’s for someone pretty . . . ?” Peiqin wondered aloud. “No, not at this particular moment, not even for that impossible romantic.”

“No more interruptions, Peiqin,” Old Hunter said, after clearing his throat. “Now, a tale has to be told from the beginning. It’s about ernai. The new term originated at the time of China’s reform, but it evolved out of the old concubine tradition. Confucius says, ‘If the name is not properly defined, the story won’t come out right.’

“For more than two thousand years, concubines were legal and their social status acknowledged. In the *Book of Songs*, the first poem is said to be about the queen urging her lord to take a concubine. After 1949, however, monogamy became the new standard under Mao, despite there being no secret about how many women Mao had for himself in the Forbidden City. They served him under different job titles—personal secretary, nurse, dancing partner, special train attendant, and whatnot—but everyone knew what they actually did.

"The title *ernai* means something like 'secondary concubine,' but not exactly. For instance, in *The Morning of Shanghai*, a 'second concubine' simply signifies the number two, the second one taken into the household. Wives and concubines can live in the same house, with their status mutually recognized. But that's not the case for ernai.

"When China's economic reform began to unfold, Taiwanese businessmen came swarming over to the mainland. Their factories and offices mushroomed up everywhere, particularly in Shanghai. They had to stay here most of the time, with their wives and families far away across the strait, so some of them found girls in the city. Since these relationships lasted for weeks, months, or even longer, a sort of long-term businesslike relationship evolved. The chosen girls are not concubines—they don't have a concubine's social or legal status. Nor are they really mistresses in a romantic sense, since money is always involved. Most of them are kept in luxurious apartments provided by the men, along with additional allowances. It's convenient for the man, who can end the relationship without any legal entanglements. As for the woman, it's an easier life that carries with it the hope that one day her status might be 'normalized,' should the man divorce his wife.

"The local government was well aware of these arrangements but, because of the need for foreign capital, chose to ignore them. In time, the local Big Bucks and Party officials joined in, and *ernai* became a commonly accepted term.

"Jin is running a café in Gubei, an area known for the large number of women like her. Gubei is one of the earliest high-end property developments in Shanghai. At the beginning of the housing reform, property was cheap, so Taiwanese men snapped up apartments for these women. The subdivision in question is even referred to as 'Ernai Village.'

"Chen told me very little of the background to this case, so I did my homework, made some plans, bought a mini recorder—"

"A mini recorder? That's an excellent idea," Peiqin exclaimed, jumping up. "Hold on, Old Hunter. Excuse me just for one minute . . ."

She hurried off to the bedroom. Old Hunter and Yu looked at each other. It was unlike her to interrupt repeatedly like that.

But she was already running back to the table with a small tape recorder in her hand, saying, "You thought that actually hearing some of the café conversation could be helpful to Chen, right, Old Hunter?"

"Yes. He didn't say why he wanted me there. I knew that, with almost no background knowledge on the case, I could sit there for hours without learning anything from the conversation. It would be different for Chen, or his client."

"Exactly. I think the same thing applies to our conversation here. A Suzhou opera singer can be so full of digressions that it's not easy for the audience to grasp all of the important details. When we record the opera, though, Yu and I can listen to it later and get even more out of the story. In the same way, some of our discussions might be helpful to Chen."

"Peiqin, ours is indeed a family of cops!" Old Hunter said with a chuckle of approval.

"But not Qinqin," she said in earnest, speaking of her and Yu's son. "He shall have a different life."

"Now, the café has an interesting name: Naika. The first character is the same as the second in *ernai*. Might it be a hint about the owner of the café? Of course, it can also mean milk coffee or white coffee."

"Or latte," Yu cut in this time.

"The café serves a very specific niche market. Ernai can easily get bored: their men have to spend time with their business and families, often leaving them limited time for them. A neighborhood café that close and convenient enables them to walk over in their pajamas.

If their men make an unannounced visit, they can hurry back to their apartments in no time. Also, all of the women there are of the same status, so there's no one looking down on them.

"Not long after it opened, word about the café spread. Since ernai are typically young and pretty, male customers liked going to the café and looking at the sexy young women walking around in pajamas and slippers. To use a Shanghai expression, they let their eyes enjoy the rich ice cream. Then some other women came too, those who were anxious to be noticed by some Big Buck looking for an ernai. Essentially, the café was a place of opportunity, which added to its popularity.

"So I walked in like one of the customers, or, as the proverb puts it, like an old idiot stumbling into youthful blossoms. Anyway, being old gave me a sort of thick-skulled excuse. It wasn't a large café, but rather one with an intimate atmosphere. There were maybe nine or ten people there, only two of whom were men, including me. I picked a table not far from the counter, where the women flock around.

"And shallow, empty-minded women they are, gossiping and talking all day, since they have nothing better to do. In this materialistic age, they brag about their men's wealth and success, as if they themselves have nothing worth talking about. What I heard there was mostly empty conversation like that.

"A. got an incredible bonus because her man's company went public, pocketing billions of yuan at one scoop; B. had a luxury car bought for her; C. purchased an apartment for her parents, and so on . . .

"But Jin hardly talked about her man, even though he clearly has spent lavishly on her. He bought her not only an apartment in that subdivision, but also the café, including all the equipment.

"Jin might have a real passion for coffee, but she could enjoy it at home by herself. Why would her man let her run such a café? It's beyond me."

"How often do you think he can visit her?" Yu commented. "Once a week, or even once a month. What would a young woman do with all that money and time on her hands?"

"That's a good point. Anyway, not once did she talk about her man in the café," Old Hunter said. "And none of the customers talked about him either. However, they seemed to know something about who he was, which means he might be a government official.

"At one point, Jin left the café, went over to a BMW parked nearby, and drove away in a hurry. I took a picture of her license plate, so I should be able to find out more from tracing that. It's like I heard someone say in a reality show: 'I would rather weep in a BMW than laugh on a bike.' I have no doubt that her man bought the car for her.

"After that, I got a bit worried. In a tea house, I may sit for hours with a cup of tea, with the waiter constantly adding hot water for free. But in a café, I couldn't sit for hours with one cup of coffee hardly touched. And it's so expensive, costing more than fifty yuan for a cup. For these ernai, money is no problem. But I couldn't have them take me for a poor, suspicious old idiot ogling them with nothing but a cup of coffee. So I had a bottle of French water with gas, called Perrier, for eighty yuan, and a wedge of pie as well. All together, it cost more than two hundred yuan. Chen's really bankrupting me!

"After sitting there for more than an hour, I didn't think her man was going to stop by anytime soon. It's like waiting by a tree for a rabbit to run into it and knock itself out against the trunk. So I decided to push the matter a little.

"When Jin came back and sat behind the counter, I approached her. For a veteran tea drinker like me, it's not difficult to introduce myself as a tea salesman. I made a point about a lot of high-end cafés serving tea as well as coffee, and I offered to provide her some free samples. After bringing out all my tea expertise for ten minutes or so, she trusted me, and she gave me her phone number and an e-mail address so we could discuss future business opportunities. More importantly, it gave me a pretext to go back and visit her café again."

"You really are an experienced cop," Peiqin said.

"That's what Chen said."

Old Hunter then pulled out a small cassette tape. "Peiqin is right. No one can remember everything that's said, and most of their conversations are probably irrelevant, but Chen might be able to pick out what we're missing."

"Give me the tape," Peiqin said. "And the one with your conversation with Tang, too. I'll duplicate them, and you can come to my restaurant tomorrow morning to pick up the copies. I'll also make a copy of the tape of our conversation tonight. And, of course, I'll give you a bowl of our best noodles."

"That sounds good."

"If you think you're going to meet with Chen in the next few days, you can give him the recordings. But if necessary, I can also give them directly to him."

"But how, Peiqin?"

"He likes noodles. If he calls you, recommend the noodles at Shanghai Number One. That's what he calls our new restaurant, since he likes the noodles mixed with green onion and oil so much. He'll know what you mean," she said, then added, "Of the three of us, I might be the least noticeable. A lot of people come to the restaurant. So if Chen comes in, no one will suspect anything."

TWELVE

WHEN OLD HUNTER FINALLY left, it was already past ten thirty.

"Go ahead and go to bed, Yu," Peiqin said. "I'll join you as soon as I've finished cleaning up."

Yu lay on their bed, smoking, thinking, and listening to her footsteps in the kitchen. It would take her a while to clean up, he supposed. Turning over, he pulled out the cassette player and put in the tape that Old Hunter had recorded in the ernai café. The tape didn't start from the beginning, but that was fine with him.

A: We really are pathetic, spending hours with a cup of coffee, stirring our lives with a little spoon, serving our men from head to foot. And as a result, we're called all sorts of bad names, as if we're the ones responsible for the problems of a corrupt society.

B: Oh be content, woman. What those provincial sisters earn by working hard all day isn't enough to even buy a cup of coffee here.

C: Not only is it a pathetic life, we don't know even how long it'll last. Youth slips away like a bird. It's just a matter of time before we'll be dumped in the trash like a worn-out mop.

B: Enjoy it while you can. Why worry so much?

A: There are always younger girls out there, pushing forward, wave upon wave, as in the grand Yellow River. We live in a state of constant apprehension, afraid that we're going to be replaced at any time.

C: Kang is sending his daughter to private school in the States. The tuition alone is forty thousand dollars. And he's spending twenty thousand more for a chaperone.

E: Kang's daughter is nothing. Have you heard about the First Son? He's getting an apartment to himself in the best neighborhood in New York City. And it was all paid for in cash.

B: Well, my man is not heartless. He's promised to pay for me to go abroad in five years . . .

Yu pressed the stop button, wondering how the conversations on the tape could possibly lead to anything. Then he pulled out a granite *go* board along with a box of black and white stones from under the bed.

It was a game he enjoyed playing with Chen. Both of them felt like they were talking through the white and black stones, as if they were comparing notes. Chen was brilliant but eccentric, inclined to putting his pieces in positions unimaginable to others. In contrast, Yu preferred a more conventional approach, building up pressure, step by step, until the game reached a climax. They had one thing in common, however. Neither of them gave up easily. Each of them, when faced with a board that seemed hopeless, would persist, making one stubborn move after another, hoping for a dramatic turnaround.

Yu found himself positioning one black piece on the board, and then a white one, as if his right hand were playing against the left. Pondering the possible moves in both sides of a game of *go* was a bit like weighing all the possible actions he could take as the new head of the Special Case Squad.

At present, he was pushing ahead with the Liang case, whether it was relevant to Chen's current troubles or not. It wasn't really a "special case." Liang was a crooked official, the head of the commerce department for the Huangpu District, and he ran a private company on the side. Unluckily for him, his corruption had been exposed on the Internet.

Yu wasn't nearly as Web-savvy as Peiqin, but he'd learned how to run a search on the Internet, combing through all the online posts on a particular topic, some of them barely relevant, and some, barely reliable. Liang's case, however, was a classic example of unbridled corruption. Liang, as an official, was involved in the emerging high-speed train industry being established by the central government. Liang's private company supplied furnishings for the trains, such as chairs, tables, sinks, and other low-technology items. A couple of weeks ago, a copy of the invoice that Liang's company was charging the government for those furnishings had been posted on the Internet. The invoice caused a huge storm on the Internet because of the prices Liang was charging the government. A chair, for instance, was being invoiced at 200,000 yuan. On the Internet, people were raising legitimate questions about pricing practices and possible corruption and were demanding that a broad search be launched for any other corruption surrounding Liang and his company. Liang, however, had disappeared before the government could take him into custody. So right now, it was a missing persons case, which had been turned over to Detective Yu's squad.

Liang couldn't have pulled off a complicated scheme like that on his own, Yu suspected. According to the *People's Daily*, the high-speed train project was both a political and an economic priority. It was a symbol of China's great progress and was therefore a high-profile project for the central government as well as every department that had a piece of it, including the state council in Beijing, the Railway Ministry, and the Shanghai city government.

According to the rules, any contract had to be awarded to the company with the lowest bid and the most experience. Liang's company, however, didn't have any experience manufacturing equipment for trains, and it was widely believed that Liang had used his political connections to land those unbelievably lucrative orders.

There were several popular theories on the Internet about Liang's disappearance. One was that Liang had gone into hiding somewhere nearby. But with new information and photos constantly being posted on the Internet, he would be spotted the moment he poked his nose out—he couldn't expect to stay hidden long. Still, it couldn't be ruled out entirely. Liang might have fled in panic, without giving too much thought about the future.

Another possibility was that Liang had fled China entirely. If this was true, he had to have started preparing for it long ago, had a passport and visa ready, and a substantial sum of money stashed abroad. But would he really have left his wife behind? Other "naked officials"—people whose corruption was exposed on the Internet—sent their families out of the country before they themselves fled. However, there might be something special about Liang's wife that kept Liang from sending her abroad. Yu thought he'd heard something about her having a dubious background, but he couldn't remember anything specific.

There was yet another possibility, Yu thought broodingly, but so far there was nothing to support it except for a slightly odd conversation he'd had with Party Secretary Li. Li had asked Yu about the progress of the investigation into Liang's disappearance, and when Yu filled him in, Li clearly implied that it wasn't necessary for the Special Case Squad to go all out to find Liang.

Yu didn't have Old Hunter's passion for old sayings, but Yu couldn't help thinking of one in particular: *Treating a dead horse as if it's still alive.* Yu couldn't help wondering how Chen would have handled Liang's case. Of course, Chen had connections, some quite powerful, that Detective Yu couldn't imagine having.

When Peiqin finally came into the room, the ashtray on the nightstand was half full. She cast a glance at it, frowning.

"Old Hunter finished all of the chicken tonight," she said. "I'll have to scramble two eggs with onion for your lunch. I have to leave early tomorrow to go to the new restaurant, so there won't be time to make anything else."

About half a year ago, Peiqin and a partner had started a small restaurant of their own. She had managed to hold on to her job as the accountant for a state-run restaurant by agreeing to do the work mostly online at half pay. This allowed her to invest the time necessary to launch her own restaurant.

"Don't worry about it. I can eat lunch at the canteen."

"I don't even want to think about the food in your canteen."

She slipped into a blue-and-white striped pajama top that barely reached her waist, and slid under the quilt beside him.

Absentmindedly, he put his hand on her shoulder. She sighed, nestling up against him.

"What are you thinking about?"

"Old Hunter mentioned that Chen had electronic copies of two case files on his laptop. So I'm going to go through the rest of them. I was just thinking about the Liang case."

"What's your reason for focusing on that one first?"

"The case file was handed over to Chen the day before he was removed from the bureau," Yu said. "He didn't have to accept the case. In fact, corruption cases involving Party officials like Liang are usually handled by the Party Discipline Committee, so Chen could easily have said no."

"Then why didn't he?"

"I don't know. The Liang scandal first broke on the Internet, and then it snowballed rapidly. Before the Discipline Committee could do anything, Liang disappeared. As a result, it wasn't a corruption case, like it should have been, but a missing person case."

"I might have read about Liang online, but with so many corruption scandals, I didn't follow it closely."

"It started with an invoice posted online for the accessories like chairs, tables, and sinks that Liang's private company was supplying for the new high-speed train. The prices listed on the invoice were outrageous, at least ten times more than normal. How could Liang have gotten away with charging so much? That wasn't hard to figure out, and a lot of information about Liang and his dealings, from a broad range of sources, was quickly posted on the Internet. No more than a couple days later, Liang disappeared."

Yu picked up the laptop, clicked a bookmarked page, and the screen filled with the invoice in question. Underneath it were hundreds and hundreds of angry comments and armchair analyses.

"You've learned fast," she said, with an approving smile. "Your Internet search skills have really improved."

"I've learned it all from you."

"What have you done so far to find Liang?"

"Well, I tried to get his bank account records, but I was refused by the higher-ups. I tried to get a copy of his phone records, but again, no. As I mentioned, anything concerning a Party official is turned over to the Party Discipline Committee to handle. Any files or records that might prove Liang had corrupt dealings have been denied to my squad. We've been given only the missing person part of the case to handle."

"Perhaps he's in shuanggui," Peiqin said with a sigh. "You know how a disgraced Party official is frequently placed in secret interrogation, so the dirty details won't become known to the public. It's all done for the Party's interest, which is above and beyond the regular legal system."

"I made a list of what Liang did right before his disappearance—as much as I could find out, anyway. Considering the Internet storm he was facing, there didn't seem to be anything unusual. According to his colleagues, the day he disappeared, he received a phone call right before leaving the office in a hurry. The call came in about eleven thirty that morning. After he left the office, he wasn't seen by anyone. However, even though his colleagues were certain that he got a call at work, there was no record of any such call—according to the official in charge of office phone records—coming in at that time.

"After interviewing his colleagues, I went to Liang's home and interviewed his wife."

"Hold on. She's still there?"

"I had the same question. She's much younger that Liang, an attractive woman in her late twenties or early thirties. Her name is Wei. She apparently had a role in Liang's private company, and she's well connected in her way. But other than being married to Liang, there was nothing really suspicious about her."

"Tell me about your interview."

Yu sat up, propped against a pillow, and launched into a detailed account of his interview of Liang's wife, Wei.

"Officials who flee the country commonly move their families out first. That's what the term 'naked official' is about, isn't it?" Peiqin said, after Yu finished his account. "Is she an ernai-made-into-wife?"

"No. She's Liang's first wife, and she works in his office. She's in charge of PR," Yu said. "Of course, she claims that she doesn't know anything about his disappearance, but I caught a suggestion of genuine fear in her voice. She does seems to really care for him."

"What gave you that impression?"

"It wasn't anything she said, but it was apparent that she's worried sick about him. At first, I thought she might be just making a show of it, but at one point, she said something surprising. 'People might have said all sorts of things about our marriage. But I'll tell you what. I'm nothing without Liang.' "

"Was there anything else that caught your attention?"

"Yes. In answer to my question about whether Liang had any unique or identifiable physical characteristics, she shivered and said something even more surprising. 'If you must know, there's one thing. He has a tattoo on his lower belly, just above the hairline. It's a tattoo of a blue dragon interwoven with my name.' "

"Oh, that's really strange," Peiqin said. "Perhaps it was his way of saying he wouldn't have another woman—"

Suddenly, the room was filled with a shrill sound almost like crickets. Both were reminded of their younger years in Yunnan, when the sounds of crickets filled the night. Tonight, however, it was Yu's cell phone. Yu must have accidentally touched a key on the phone, changing the ring tone.

Peiqin went over to get the phone, which was plugged into a charger in the corner. She still had a fit figure—her bare legs firm, her ankles shapely—but Yu noticed the pajama top she had on was worn, threadbare.

Peiqin handed the phone over to Yu. It was a text message. It was a list of properties registered under the name of Liang's wife, Wei, a list Yu had managed to obtain through connections. The properties consisted of a villa, a condo, and three high-end apartments.

"I'm so sorry, Peiqin," Yu said.

"Why?"

"After all these years, we still don't have a decent apartment. Only these one and a half rooms. Compared to Wei's properties, I don't know what to say to you."

"You don't have to feel bad. I'm more than content," she said in a soft voice. "I have you. Whatever she may have can be taken away tomorrow."

"I doubt it. Nothing has been done about Liang's private company yet. For them, it's still business as usual."

"So what are you going to do next?"

"A *Wenhui* journalist is going to interview me tomorrow. He might want to speak to me because of my partnership with Chief Inspector Chen. But I think I'll focus on the Liang case. The number of high-end properties Wei has in her own name might prove to be an irresistible revelation to the newspaper."

"By the way, how did Party Secretary Li behave toward you today?"

"Surprisingly nice. It was quite a turnaround. Beats me what's going on with him."

"Your friendship with Chen is no secret to Li. I don't think he'll ever trust you," she said. "The business at our restaurant is picking up. Perhaps it's time for you to think about leaving the bureau and joining me."

The suggestion came out of the blue; he hadn't anticipated it at all. He was momentarily tongue-tied.

"Qinqin is in college," she went on. "We don't need too much for ourselves. There were a lot of years wasted in the Cultural Revolution and other political campaigns; I hope we can spend the rest of our lives without worrying about such things. Perhaps you can start a new career for yourself."

"But what other job can I really do? Nowadays, many young people are trying hard to get jobs in the police bureau because of the job security and the benefits. The Party needs the police to maintain stability, so the pay isn't too shabby." Yu resumed after a pause, "Let's discuss this after Chen gets out of woods. Then maybe I could look into early retirement, maybe try to come and help you at the restaurant. But with so many restaurants opening and closing in Shanghai, almost every day, there's no guarantee your restaurant would be able to provide for both of us."

"There's nothing you can take for granted in today's China. Not even Inspector Chen, in spite of his connections and abilities. There's no certainty at all."

Perhaps Peiqin was right.

He got out of bed and walked over to the window to smoke a cigarette. She walked over to him, barefoot, leaning against his shoulder. Outside the window, they could hear another shikumen block being pulled down. It was not too far away, the noise rising and falling, like the turbid ebb and flow of ignorant armies clashing by night.

"Come back to bed, husband," she said. "I want you to hold me."

THIRTEEN

ON THE TRAIN BACK to Shanghai, Chen took out his regular cell phone and called Manager Hong at the office of the cemetery in Suzhou.

"I slept late this morning, Manager Hong. I'm going to have a bite at Cai's Noodles and then I'll come over in the afternoon."

"No problem. Enjoy yourself. You've heard about the old, ideal Suzhou way of life, haven't you? In the morning, warm noodle soup in your stomach, and then a bathtub filled with warm water as an aid for digestion and relaxation."

"The Suzhou way of life indeed."

"Don't worry about the renovation. I'll keep an eye on it for you, Director Chen."

Their phone conversation was tapped. No doubt about it. Let others believe that he was in Suzhou, enjoying himself like an incorrigible gourmet, and supervising the reconstruction of his father's grave like a filial son.

At the Shanghai Railway Station, Chen took out his special cell phone and dialed Old Hunter, who picked up at the first ring.

"Oh, where I am? I'm in Zhangjiang, Pudong, with an important client this morning. I'm quite a distance from you. Go ahead to the noodle restaurant by yourself. The place you call the Shanghai Number One, the one that serves the noodles mixed with scallion oil, peanut butter, and fried shrimp. It's so tasty. There will be another real surprise for you there, and after you're done, you can call me."

"Another real surprise there!"

Old Hunter was speaking guardedly, possibly in the presence of a client. But Chen understood. Shanghai Number One meant Peiqin's new restaurant. Peiqin made a point of using traditional recipes and ingredients, and the noodle dishes were popular among Shanghai's budget diners.

Chen was heading over to the long line at the taxi stand when he caught sight of a subway sign. The number 2 line. It had a stop at the intersection of Nanjing and He'nan Roads, and he could walk to the restaurant from there. Given the invariable traffic jam that was in Shanghai, the subway was a more reliable alternative.

Thirty minutes later, he stepped into the restaurant. Looking around without seeing a familiar face, he chose a table in the corner.

An elderly waiter shuffled over to the table, clutching a mop in his hand. "What do you want?"

"I'm a friend of Peiqin's. Can you tell her I'm here?"

It was common for customers to mention it if they knew someone who worked at the restaurant. Sometimes it was for the sake of saying hi, and sometimes in hopes of getting special treatment.

"Peiqin, you have a friend waiting for you," the waiter called up the stairs.

When Chen was last there, Peiqin hadn't introduced him to her colleagues—at least, she hadn't mentioned his official position. She didn't like to show off her connections.

Peiqin hurried down from her attic office. To his surprise, she extended her hand rather formally.

"Welcome to our restaurant."

He took her hand in a similar manner and felt something in his palm. Without speaking a word, he clasped it—a small square object.

"It's been a long time, Mr. Chen. I hope you enjoy your meal today." She smiled and then looked over her shoulder toward the kitchen. "Please enjoy double toppings for China's number one noodles. They are the best. And on the house."

"Thank you," Chen said, playing along.

"It's now the number one dish in the noodle category on the Mass Review Web site. That's very significant, because it reflects the genuine opinion of real customers. Our small restaurant couldn't afford to simply hire people to vote for it online."

"The dish absolutely deserves the honor. Congratulations!" he said. "By the way, I took the subway here this morning. It's very convenient, and it might be the same for you too."

"In fact, I always take the subway—the seven fifty-one train—and it arrives at this stop at eight fifteen. From the number 3 exit, it is only a ten-minute walk to the restaurant. The subway is very reliable."

To anyone who happened to overhear their conversation, it would have sounded like a chat between two old acquaintances who hadn't crossed paths in a while.

But Peiqin seemed to be trying to pass on a subtle tip. If he needed, he should be able to get catch her at that particular time and at that particular subway exit.

"Shanghai Number One has a truly authentic Shanghai flavor, which is so different from that of Suzhou. My mother likes it too. I brought a box of noodles to her place one time, and she finished all of them in less than ten minutes."

"Sorry, I have been too busy to visit your mother lately. She doesn't live very far from here. Do you want to bring a box to her today?"

"Well, I'm really supposed to be in Suzhou today."

"I see—"

"Peiqin, you have a phone call from the Apricot Blossom Group CEO," another waitress said in a loud voice.

"The Apricot Blossom Group is named after the restaurant on Fuzhou Road. I still have my state job there," she said, by way of explanation. "I have to take this call."

"Of course, you take the call. I, too, have to leave."

Ten minutes later, he headed out of the restaurant without seeing Peiqin again. It might be just as well. The couldn't really talk openly in the restaurant.

He pulled out the envelope she had passed him, which contained a mini cassette tape. Peiqin had taken great care to make sure no one saw her hand it over.

Around the corner, he saw an electronics store, where he bought a player and a headphone set. He then kept on walking, going several blocks before he saw a shabby café with a bohemian ambiance. There were old worn-out chairs and tables both inside and outside. A young girl in a white T-shirt and threadbare jeans sat at an outside table, seemingly totally absorbed in a music player, her eyes half closed, her bare foot beating on the sidewalk. Chen chose a corner table inside, ordered a tall cup of black coffee, pulled out the new tape player, and put on the headphones. Drumming his fingers on the table like the girl outside, he put in the tape Peiqin passed him and started listening to it.

It started off with the conversation between Old Hunter and Tang. Chen already knew the gist of it, but some of the details might be helpful. Chen listened carefully, gulping black coffee, and taking notes.

Then came another section: the discussion between Old Hunter, Yu, and Peiqin. It was quite long, as they jumped from one topic to another over dinner. Chen listened with uninterrupted concentration. Old Hunter's account of the ernai café was hilarious, and their speculations as to Chen's reasons for having Old Hunter check out the café were no less intriguing. Some of the details proved to be thought-provoking, perspectives he himself wouldn't have considered. Yu's brief account of the missing person case was helpful too. Chen hadn't had the time to look into it yet.

He finished his second cup of coffee before he finished listening to the speculations of "the family of cops."

A waiter walked over and looked at him. Chen took off his headphones and asked for the menu again.

"I'd like a wedge of lemon pie," he said to the waiter, taking out his laptop and the CD from Qian.

"So few enjoy Suzhou opera nowadays. What a pity! I have to write something that will help people appreciate it," Chen said to the waiter.

The waiter appeared indifferent to opera. But that didn't matter. Chen just wanted him to see Chen as a bookish opera fan, working on an article in defense of it.

Taking another sip of coffee, Chen thought he might as well take a short break and listen to the opera CD. Roughly speaking, Suzhou opera consisted of two parts: singing and narration. The singing part could be blank verse sung in the middle of the narrative, performed to musical instruments such as the sanxian and pipa, but it could also be a song performed by itself. If it was the latter, the song was usually short, four or five minutes long, and was sung as the audience arrived at the theater, a kind of prelude to the narrative episode.

The CD was composed of songs adapted from classical poems. Qian was the singer, and her passion came out in her clear voice, but the choice of the poems also spoke to her own emotions. The pieces he listened to were quiet, sentimental ones. The first was a poem written by Liu Fangping:

The sun setting against the gauze curtain, / the dusk drawing nearer,

/ she sheds tears, alone, / in her magnificent room. / The courtyard appears so deserted, / the spring on the decline,/ pear petals fallen, all over the ground— / too much for her / to push open the door.

The last image was subtle yet striking. She'd had no visitors—the courtyard not swept, the door not opened—for a long time.

The next one, by Li Bai, had a similar ring to it.

Waiting, she finds her silk stockings / soaked with dewdrops / glistening on the marble palace steps. / Finally, she is moving / to let the crystal-woven curtain fall / when she casts one more glance / at the glamorous autumn moon.

The deserted beauty was a popular subject in classical Chinese poems. The person complains about—but doesn't really speak out against—her lord. In traditional literary criticism, these poems were often interpreted as being politically symbolic, representing the intellectual complaining about being neglected by the ruler.

Was that the reason these poems appealed to him at this moment?

Qian could have fallen for S. because of their apparent shared love of Suzhou opera. In this materialistic age, in which money was paramount and culture was frequently ignored, nobody seemed to be able to make a real difference in the declining fortunes of traditional opera. S.'s earlier help in bringing attention and audiences to her performances turned out not to be motivated by his love of Suzhou opera but by his lust for her. Once his objective was achieved, he didn't have to make any more efforts on behalf of opera.

Only an idealist like her, who saw only what she wanted to see, would go forward on blind faith alone. Even her plan to go abroad seemed too unrealistic. With her experience, she might be able to get into a university and earn a degree in opera, but the idea that she could earn a living from it was just another fantasy.

Chen couldn't help feeling sympathetic.

He forked up a bite of the lemon pie. Before he could eat it, though, his cell phone buzzed, sliding across the table as if it had a life of its own.

In a surprising coincidence, it was Qian calling him from Suzhou.

"I've made a couple of calls for you, Cao. About the nightclub in Suzhou—its main connection to the Heavenly World in Shanghai seems to be the law firm that represents it. S. once mentioned that law firm, though in a different context. Some of the Western companies that the law firm represented made things difficult for his office. Needless to say, someone in the firm is very powerful. Perhaps someone high up in the Party or government who is some sort of special advisor to the law firm. Someone powerful enough that S. couldn't do anything but throw in the towel."

"A law firm that represents the nightclub—"

"What's so surprising about that? The club pays a large retainer to the law firm because of the firm's connection to the people at the top of the city government. That way, no one can touch it." She then added, "Also, I've talked to him."

"Him? Oh, you mean Sima," he blurted out. Chen had guessed who it was that morning at Cai's Noodles. Sima, the head of the Shanghai Foreign Liaison Office, was someone Chen had known for years and had visited just a few days earlier.

"You moved fast, Cao."

He sort of regretted blurting out Sima's name, but it was probably just as well. She had confirmed his assumption.

"What did you say to him?"

"Not a single word about you, of course. But things can't go on like this, so I put a little pressure on him, hinting at the consequences if he doesn't let me go. He got it, I think."

"Be patient, Qian," Chen said. "In a couple of days, I may be able give you a progress report along with some evidence, and then we can talk about the next step. It'll be more effective if you have something substantial in your hands."

"Fine, I will wait for your report."

"In the meantime, if you learn anything else about the nightclub, let me know." He added in a hurry, "Don't put any more pressure on Sima. I'll definitely call you tomorrow."

Afterward, he had a bad feeling about having said so much on the phone, even though it was the cell phone he'd recently purchased, its number known to only a few people.

The coffee had gone cold, he discovered, as he sipped it with distaste.

He turned off the laptop and turned his attention back to the tape.

Next came the section of the tape that had been recorded by Old Hunter at the ernai café. It was mainly small talk among the regular customers there, who kept stirring up ripples of their bored lives in their cups of coffee.

Chen started to make notes again. Gossip seemed to be the primary characteristic of the ernai's conversation. Someone was buying a villa in Xiaoshan even more expensive than the one they owned in Binjiang; a vice mayor's son drove his Porsche so recklessly that he wrecked it after one month; a laowai met his end suspiciously despite the official announcement proclaiming that he died of natural causes; and dead pigs were reappearing, this time on a different river to Shanghai.

All of this chatter didn't amount to much. If anything, it spoke to the increasingly widespread corruption in society. Several of the ernai's men were officials, so a recurring topic was "naked officials"—officials whose families had emigrated, taking huge bank accounts along with them, while the officials themselves remained behind, in that sense "naked." The rationale behind shipping one's family abroad was simple. The officials were worried. They didn't know what would happen to them in the near future. For today, they would just use their positions to embezzle and steal as much as possible. The ernai, however, complained that their men gave "so much" to their families, leaving only little crumbs for them. Some of them actually hoped that their men would take them abroad too.

According to the ernai, about ninety percent of the officials were "naked." Chen did a quick calculation. That was probably about right, despite those red songs extolling the virtues of the great and glorious Party. Some Party officials might not have sent their entire families abroad, but at least their children were there, studying or working.

Then Chen heard something, one sentence that had almost slipped his attention. He pressed the stop button and rewound the tape.

"Lai's son studies at an Ivy League college, with several luxury condos purchased in his name in Boston and New York."

It wasn't entirely news. In a meeting, Lai had declared that his son was studying abroad because he'd won a scholarship. But what about the condos? For the moment, Chen decided not to give too much credence to the gossip of the ernai.

Sima was just such a "naked official." With his son studying at a private school in the States, and his wife staying there to keep her son company, Sima was free to find one woman after another for himself. He was also quite cautious, placing Qian in Suzhou and keeping Jin busy with her café.

Chen smiled at the part of Old Hunter approaching Jin. It was so funny, he couldn't help listening to it again.

OLD HUNTER: I used to be tea drinker. My nephew wants me to drink coffee, saying it's good for preventing Alzheimer's. I don't know if that's true, but I don't want to disappoint him. Still, I know far more about tea. In some fancy cafés in Western countries, they also serve excellent tea. It speaks for the sophistication of the establishment.

JIN: Yes, that's interesting. I've heard about that.

OLD HUNTER: I can have my nephew e-mail some pictures to you. He travels a lot.

JIN: That would be great. Here is my card, and I'll put my e-mail address as well as my cell phone number on the back of it.

Chen wasn't sure whether there was a real nephew at all, one who might feel avuncular toward the ex-inspector.

He was having his third cup of coffee when his cell phone rang again. It was Peiqin.

"I went to visit your mother during my lunch break. She had a bad scare this morning, I'm sorry to say."

"What!"

"She left to do her routine shopping at the food market this morning—you know, buying fresh vegetables for the day. When she got back home, she found that her room had been broken into and was completely ransacked. She collapsed in fright. When I got there, she was still sitting on the floor. I went with her to East China Hospital. You know a doctor there, Yu had said. Dr. Hou examined her thoroughly, saying there was nothing wrong, but for a woman of her age, it would be advisable for her to stay overnight at the hospital."

"You should have called me earlier, Peiqin."

"She didn't want me to call at all. I've just managed to step outside for a moment."

"I'm sorry, Peiqin. I really should be thanking you for your help."

"The doctor said there's nothing to worry about. He promised me she'll have a nurse in her room overnight. And I'll keep you posted."

Fury gripped him. After saying farewell to Peiqin, he closed the phone forcefully. What could a burglar have tried to steal from an old woman like her? It was hard to imagine why anyone would break in during the morning, not to mention into an old shikumen house with all the neighbors moving about. Unless it had been done by professionals, and for something not related to her at all, but to her son.

If that was the case, then someone seemed to be desperate, for reasons not yet known to Chen.

Or it could have been meant as a warning to him.

For years, he'd been telling himself that, although he wasn't a good son, he could see to it that his mother enjoyed a comfortable old age. Ironically, the very thing that made the plan feasible—his position in the Party system—was now threatening it. He would never forgive himself if she was hurt because of his problems with the system.

He had to do something—anything—to make sure that it wouldn't happen again.

But what?

His cell phone rang again with the sound of a wounded bird, startling him. This time it was Old Hunter.

"How did you like the noodles?"

"They were really delicious. Oh, I got the tape, and I've been listening to it for the last several hours. Is there anything new?"

"Well, the identity of the car owner was established."

"Who?"

"Sima."

That wasn't news. Qian had already confirmed that Sima was the official in question.

"I have something else for you. But it'll be at least an hour before I can leave Zhangjiang. And then I'd face all the traffic coming back from Pudong. How about we meet tomorrow morning?"

"Tomorrow morning?"

"You're still in Shanghai, aren't you?"

"Yes—" Chen hesitated, thought about his plan to return to Suzhou, and then decided against it. It wouldn't be a good idea for him to go back to his apartment under the circumstances. Because of his earlier subterfuge about being in Suzhou, if his enemies learned that he was in Shanghai, it would only add to their suspicions.

"Yes, let's meet tomorrow morning. At the People's Park as soon as the gate opens. The bird corner."

"I'll see you then, at the bird corner."

FOURTEEN

AROUND SIX THIRTY THAT night, Chen stood in a crowded subway train to Pudong. With people pushing in and out at every stop, he had a hard time holding on to the overhead handrails.

After the call from Old Hunter, Chen had mulled over his decision to spend the night in Shanghai. It was possible to travel to Suzhou and back again, getting in to Shanghai tomorrow morning. But an unexpected delay would wreck the plan, and he couldn't afford to be late for tomorrow morning's meeting in the park. The retired cop might be dramatic, but he knew what was at stake.

If Old Hunter had something new, Chen would be able to show Qian that progress was being made. Perhaps in return, she would try to find out more for him.

But that wasn't the only reason for staying in Shanghai. He was concerned about his mother, and it was reassuring to be in the city, somewhat nearby, in case he was needed.

But it wasn't advisable to stay at his own apartment, and he couldn't stay at Yu's place, for the same reason. A hotel wasn't an option, given that all hotel registrations were monitored. So he was going to see Overseas Chinese Lu. An old schoolmate and friend, Lu owned a large luxury apartment near Century Park and had invited Chen over several times. Even showing up unannounced, Chen would be a welcome guest at the Lus, who would most likely urge him to spend the night. Also, since Lu knew nothing about Chen's troubles, there wouldn't be many questions for him to answer.

He was reminded of an old Chinese simile used to describe a hopeless situation in which one has nowhere to go—*like a homeless dog.* The Party system, on which he'd once thought he could fall back, now seemed more like an omnipresent, omnipotent surveillance camera, following his every move.

He was then beginning to have second thoughts about the visit to Lu, who could be an overenthusiastic host, which was not something he was looking forward to.

The subway station announcements came every two or three minutes. He glanced up at the blinking station map opposite him. The train was now passing through the tunnel under the river, and the next stop was Lujiazui.

There he found himself moving toward the door.

White Cloud had told him about her new apartment in Lujiazui. He wasn't going to ask her to put him up for the night, he reassured himself. He just wanted to drop in for a short visit. It was on the way to Lu's.

What Qian had told him about the Heavenly World's law firm was a potential lead, and White Cloud might be able to tell him something more about it. She might also know some other details that she hadn't shared in her earlier phone call. Walking out of the subway in Lujiazui, he thought of a phrase he'd read years earlier—*the way up is the way down.* Why did he think of that phrase now? He had no idea. Near the exit, he saw an old woman with thread-bound white jasmine sprays in a bamboo basket. Fragrant and yet only one yuan for a single bud. It was something he hadn't seen for a long while. Perhaps it was too cheap for this new age. Leaning down, he paid for a single white spray. In his childhood, his mother would occasionally pick up a spray of jasmine for ten cents, wear it through a buttonhole in her mandarin dress, and then, one or two days later, put it in a cup of green tea.

At this moment, she was alone in the hospital, frail, frightened. He felt wretched at the thought of it. Once again, he was tempted to turn around and go to the hospital. But what about his meeting with Old Hunter tomorrow morning? From the moment he left his mother's side, Chen would probably be shadowed, which would then lead his enemies to the retired cop. The "burglary" of his mother's room could have been arranged simply to smoke him out, as well as those trying to help him.

He looked up to see a lone black crow flying overhead. In a forest of surrounding high-rises, the tiny darksome bird seemed to come out of nowhere. Possibly, it was another omen.

White Cloud had told him that the apartment complex was close to the subway, but the streets were new to him, and tall buildings obstructed the view, so it took him a while to find the Bingjiang subdivision.

Chen walked through the gate to the building. At the entrance, there was a gray-attired doorman sitting in a cubicle. He poked his head out and asked sleepily, "Who are you visiting?"

"3012. Miss Bai."

"The elevator is just over there, but you have to call up first." The doorman asked no further questions but simply sat back, grinning, with a cigarette in his hand.

Chen was about to push the intercom when the elevator came down. A young mother stepped out, pushing a red stroller. He got in without bothering to call up.

He got out on the thirtieth floor, found apartment 3012, and pressed the doorbell two or three times. There was no response. But since he was already there, he took out his cell phone and called on the cell he'd given her.

"Who's there?" she said, having picked up the phone on the first ring.

"Me. You gave me the address in your salon the other day, remember?"

"Yes, please come up. The top floor."

"I'm already at your door."

"Oh, just one minute."

The door opened, and she was standing there in a white robe, drying her hair with a towel, her face glowing.

"Sorry, Chen. I was taking a shower. I didn't hear the doorbell. Luckily I had the cell phone with me in the bathroom," she said. "What favorable wind has brought you over today?"

"I was in the subway, and I heard 'the next stop is Lujiazui,' so I decided to get out and drop by for a visit."

"I'm so glad you did." She looked excited, as she finished towel-drying her hair.

"I should have called first, but what a nice apartment! It suits your status as a successful businesswoman."

"You don't have say that, Chen. Besides, the room is a mess."

It was a spacious living room, but it was something of a mess. There were rumpled clothes on the couch by the window and a yoga mat stretched out on the floor, with a pair of high heels beside it. It looked like she'd been doing her workout routine before taking a shower.

Following his glance, she blushed. She pulled up a chair for him and seated herself on the edge of the couch. Her hair still wet, she gave off a clean smell, probably of herbal shampoo. Barely settled on the couch, she stood up again.

"What would you like to drink?"

"Water is fine with me."

"I've a bottle of very rare Irish whiskey."

"Whatever you have."

She took a bottle from a glass cabinet, poured for him half a glass of the amber-colored liquid, straight, and for herself, just two or three drops over a lot of ice cubes.

"Oh, I've forgotten to give you the apartment tour," she said, combing the slightly wet hair with her fingers. "Finally, I have something like a home in the city of Shanghai."

"That's the Shanghai dream, isn't it?"

"In a couple of hours, when all the lights are on, there is a fantastic view of the Bund across the river. It's your favorite part of the city, and you can't miss it." She added softly, "You told me how, as a student, you spent so many mornings studying in Bund Park, dreaming about the future."

So she wanted him to stay for "a couple of hours." After all, it was his first visit here. She was probably aware that there was something more than the merely social behind his unannounced visit. But for the moment, she seemed to be pleased to have him there.

Had we but world enough, and time. . . . But they were not in Andrew Marvell's world, and there wasn't the time.

Her cell phone rang. She picked it up and looked at the screen without saying anything. It was probably a text message.

"Sorry, it's about business," she said, typing a response. "I have to reply."

"What a hard-working businesswoman."

"You don't have to laugh at me."

"I'm in no position to laugh at a successful entrepreneur."

"Let's go into the other room," she said with a touch of coyness. "It's too messy in here."

It was to the bedroom rather than the office that she led him, however. She gestured him to a corner sofa, and then perched herself on the edge of the bed. She was half facing an antique mahogany dressing table, which must have been made in the days when a Chinese lady didn't have the luxury of a separate bathroom. Now the table served more as a decoration than as furniture. Not far from them, the bathroom door was ajar.

"Sorry, my hair is still wet," she said, taking a look into the mahogany-framed mirror above the dressing table before she sat down again, half reclining against the headboard.

He'd come here on the spur of the moment, but now the situation unnerved him. She was surprisingly nice to him, lying there gazing at him.

He was in such deep trouble. Why drag her in? There was no way he could ever pay her back.

She seemed to be reading his mind, but she said nothing.

"I want to thank you again for your help that day at the salon," he started with difficulty.

"You were my first customer there—my first personal customer. Usually, one of these girls would wash a customer's hair. And guess what? That afternoon I thought of something from my childhood in the Anhui countryside. In those days, it took a lot of effort to wash one's hair. For my father, it was almost like a ritual, and he did it only once or twice a year. On New Year's Eve, my mother had to boil two kettles of hot water, and then dip his head in and out of a small plastic basin, constantly mixing hot and cold water. I was a little girl then, and I remember giggling at the sight of his hair covered in grayish bubbles."

Was she hinting at something?

In the west, the sun was wrapped in the gathering dusk, as if it were on the wing of a black bird, sinking into the darksome water.

"They're still in Anhui. I thought about moving them to Shanghai, but I don't know whether they'd be happy living here with me."

"How could they not?"

"They are very old-fashioned, and they don't know anything at all about my business. I'm not a filial daughter," she said, contemplatively. "Anything new about you?"

"Well, I didn't say much on the phone the other day."

"Yes, please tell me about it, Chen. It may help if I'm able to focus on something more specific."

The big clock on top of the Customs House began chiming, the sound faint from across the river, as if accentuating her words in some sort of mysterious correspondence.

He made up his mind to tell her what had happened over the last few days. It wouldn't be fair to ask for more help without giving her a true, hopefully objective picture of the situation. Only then could she decide whether she wanted to get further involved or not.

She listened quietly, without interruption. But when he mentioned what had happened to his mother earlier that day, she sat up, crossing her bare legs.

"In her old age, my mother still worries about me," he concluded with a sigh. "Do you know why she refuses to move in with me?"

"Why?"

"She wants me to have the privacy to bring a girl to my apartment, so I can settle down and have my own family."

"Then why don't you?" she asked.

"There's something I've never discussed with her. Even though it looks like I'm successful and well connected, I'm actually holding on to the back of a tiger. It's just matter of time before the tiger throws me to the ground and finishes me up. The system doesn't have room for a cop trying to seek justice when it's not in the Party's interest.

"It's nothing short of miracle that I have survived this long. If it wasn't for luck, and the help I've gotten from people like you, Peiqin, Yu, and others, I would have perished long ago. So I've kept telling myself: I can't think only of myself. As a cop, I accept both the job and the consequences. But it wouldn't be fair to drag anyone else into all the troubles."

"But what if that someone doesn't care about those troubles?"

"Still, I have a responsibility for others, both as an investigator and in my personal life."

"You're always a cop, before anything else," she said, sitting up, her bare toes digging into the lush carpet.

"Now I'm a fired cop."

A short silence fell over the room.

"What can I do for you, Chief Inspector Chen?"

It was the first time that evening she had used his former title, and in doing so, she'd made herself clear. Whatever the changes in his position or troubles in his career, she was ready to help.

"I'm glad you've come to me tonight," she went on, "in the midst of your troubles. It shows that you think of me as one you can trust."

"This afternoon, when I first learned about my mother, I felt so sick and helpless. Perhaps it's not too late for me to throw in the towel—to forget about all the politics, to live an ordinary life, to be a filial son, at least one who doesn't bring trouble to her."

"You're just tired, Chen. Tomorrow morning, you'll be the ambitious, energetic chief inspector again," she said, suddenly standing up to open up the blinds behind her. "Look at the river. I remember the lines in one of your poems. '*It's not the river, but the moment, / the river comes flowing into your eyes.*' "

He gazed into her eyes rippling in the lambent lamplight, and behind her, the skyscrapers lit with the neon lights and signs, and vessels moving across the water.

Unexpectedly, another poem came to his mind.

The aspiration of rolling clouds and roaring wind gone, / I am leaning against the dressing table, / waiting on the ripples in your eyes. / Lest "Master Liu" grow despondent, / combing your hair, you pull up / the curtain to the view of the grand Yellow River.

It was a poem written by Gong Zizhen, a celebrated Qing dynasty poet who dreamed of making a contribution to the country. For most of his life, Gong remained down and out, unable to achieve his aspirations. During a trip to the capital, he visited a young woman named Lingxiao in Huai'an near the Yellow River. Lingxiao served in the Qing dynasty equivalent of the Heavenly World. That night, despondent and disillusioned with all the setbacks he'd encountered, Gong was about to give up and spend his life in her company, composing decadent poems in a Baudelairean fashion. Aware of his frustrations, Lingxiao encouraged him to continue pursuing his ideals. The poem was a scene between the two lovers: the first half unfolded as a monologue of Gong's, and the second half consisted of Lingxiao's reaction. At the time, a girl wouldn't raise her curtains before she was finished making herself up, so Lingxiao, while preparing herself, encouraged him by directing his attention to the grand Yellow River. In classical Chinese poetry, the river was commonly seen as symbolic of the magnificent and sublime.

Nevertheless, Gong ended up a despondent poet, never achieving the political reform of which he dreamed. His personal life was also a disastrous failure.

"What're you thinking?" White Cloud said.

"Nothing, really. Just about the Heavenly World. It's difficult for me to find out anything more about it. I'm not a cop anymore, and it's possible that I'm being watched day and night. Still, I have to make my move before anything else happens."

"I'll try to find out more for you, but can you tell me specifically what you're trying to learn?"

"You mentioned that you know Shen, the owner of the club?"

"Not exactly," she said, sounding vague. "We've met a couple of times."

Another short silence ensued.

"The law firm that represents the nightclub very likely employs a special advisor who is connected to the city government. That might be important."

"Yes," she said, waiting for him to go on.

"You've already been able to find out for me what the people who go to the club are talking about. But why are they talking about it? And are they talking about anything new?"

"I'll get in touch with all my connections and see what they can tell me. I'll leave no stone unturned."

"I really appreciate it, White Cloud," he said, glancing at his watch. "It's late now, and I think I have to go."

"Where are you going? Oh, that's right, you mentioned you were headed to somewhere in Pudong."

"I'm off to see my old friend Overseas Chinese Lu, who has a new apartment near Century Park."

"But it's—" she started, casting a look at the clock on the wall. She didn't finish her sentence.

She's right, Chen thought. It's already past eight fifteen. It could be nine by the time he got to Lu's.

"I have something important to do in the city early tomorrow morning. It's too much trouble to go back to Suzhou tonight, and then return to Shanghai tomorrow . . ."

"Well, stay here, then. You can take the bed, or the couch."

"It's so kind of you to offer, but—"

"Before your arrival, I was thinking of going out. Naturally, I would love to play the host, but I think I'll go out as planned. What time I'll make it back, I honestly don't know. So you can stay here, and don't wait up for me."

He wondered why she had suddenly decided to leave. Because of something he'd said? Because she wanted him to stay there and not feel awkward about it?

"But it's late."

"It's not too late for me," she said with a mysterious smile. "I might even go to the salon afterward."

"If you leave, I'd better leave with you, White Cloud."

"How can you be so obstinate? It's too late for you to go to your friend's, and clearly it's not advisable for you to go back to your apartment or your mother's."

"I can make do with a public bathhouse for the night. They don't bother to check ID regularly, and for one hundred yuan, I can enjoy a good foot massage and then sleep in a bath-towel-covered folding chair overnight."

"Come on. That's not only uncomfortable, it's risky too. From time to time, the cops raid those places. You don't need me to tell you that," she said. "Don't try to be such a gentleman. Besides, I might learn something about the nightclub tonight."

He didn't respond immediately.

"Oh, come to the study with me," she said, taking his hand. "If you want to use the computer, both the laptop and desktop are yours. The desktop is hooked up to the printer. So make yourself at home."

"I don't know what to say."

"Here, let me enter the computer's password for you."

She leaned over him, typing in the password, her long hair brushing against his cheek. He moved the chair closer to the desk, catching a glimpse of her breasts through the opening of her robe.

"In case you need to reenter it later, it's CC123."

Was that a coincidence? "CC" could refer to the initial letters of his name in Pinyin.

But she had already turned away and was padding back to the bathroom in her bare feet.

There, with the door half open, she slid off her robe, her snowy white back flashing under the light.

He stood up and walked out to the balcony. Out there, he took a deep breath of the night air.

Across the river was the Bund that was so familiar to him. It also seemed strange, as he looked at it from this different perspective. The Bund seemed to change and change again with the pulsing of the city.

Years slip away like water . . .

"How do I look, Chen?"

He turned to see her stepping out onto the balcony in a red mandarin dress with high slits. It reminded him of something from another case, several years ago, when she'd also helped him. For a moment, he was gripped by a sense of déjà vu. Was she wearing the same dress tonight?

"Ravishing, as always."

"Make yourself at home," she repeated.

She turned and walked out, looking back over her shoulder to flash another smile at him before closing the apartment door behind her.

She was gone before he had the time to ask where she was going. But was he really going to ask?

He stepped back inside the apartment and paced about the study before he finally sat down at the desk. Instead of working on the computer, he pulled out the cassette tape and listened to it again, focusing on the paragraphs he'd marked. He spent more than an hour listening to the tape, but he didn't find anything really new.

Then he turned on the computer, typed in the password again, and started surfing the Internet. Immediately he read about a new twist in the dead pig case. A Shanghai meat company was trying to buy an American meat company, as a way of reassuring domestic consumers by implying that the company's quality control standards were the same as those in the United States. All over the Internet, the move was being ridiculed as an attempt by Chinese socialism to buy superior quality from American capitalism.

Chen continued to surf around the Web. It seemed that Liang was still missing, but the high-speed train industry was being unanimously praised as another great achievement under the Party's leadership. As for Shang's son, he seemed to have been largely forgotten. With so many fresh scandals breaking every day, old scandals usually didn't last long on the Internet.

He looked up from the screen, feeling worn out. The screen stared back at him, untiring.

Outside the windows, the view of Bund at night was truly breathtaking. The neon lights along the Bund projected beautiful abstractions onto the water and into the sky, while occasional ships slid down the river, casting shadows against the dreamlike horizon.

Once again he thought of some lines by Liu Yong, a decadent Song dynasty poet from the eleventh century.

All these beautiful scenes are unfolding, / but to no avail. / Alas, to whom can I speak / of this ineffably enchanting landscape?

He was dismayed by his own recurrent waves of self-pity. Was he really giving up, ready to become a decadent poet like Liu or Baudelaire?

It was just past midnight. There was no telling when she'd come back, and he had to get up early the next morning. So he went to the living room, and without undressing, he stretched himself out on the couch. It was fairly comfortable, and he dropped off to sleep quickly, in spite of himself.

He is standing in front of a door, hesitating. Finally, he raises his hand to knock, but there is no response. He pushes at the door, which opens into an empty room. There is nothing inside except an embroidered silk robe lying rumpled across the bed. He touches the pillow, which seems to be still warm and slightly wet. A red slipper anchors the silence of the room. Where is the other one? Outside the window, the footprints left by a night bird are being covered by freshly falling snow . . .

He was awakened by a phone ringing in the middle of his fast-fading dream. Disoriented in the grayness of the early morning, he rubbed his eyes. The ringing phone wasn't just part of his dream. It was her phone on the corner table. Chen looked at his watch. Four twenty-five. He was alone in the apartment—she hadn't come back yet.

Then the answering machine picked up and played the recorded message, "Sorry I'm not available. Please leave a message and I'll call you back."

From the other end, the caller spoke up. "It's me—White Cloud."

He crossed the room and picked up the phone in a hurry. White Cloud's voice came rippling over the line. "I'm glad you're awake."

There seemed to be a strange gurgling sound in the background, like water coming out of a showerhead.

"I went to see Shen tonight, the owner of the nightclub," she went on. "As I mentioned, I've met him at some parties before, and several times he's invited me to his place. So he was pleased to see me tonight, but apparently he had something on his mind. Still, I managed to engage him in small talk, going over some of the currently hot gossip.

"About Shang's wife, he said that the people who hired her to sing for them privately are perverted. They were after the sensation of a red general's wife singing red songs in the same way that others hire a slut to entertain them in a private room. It's not that she's still young or pretty, but that they liked the very idea of it, for which they paid quite a lot. Some of the guests that night were quite high up in terms of their positions. So perhaps she didn't do it solely for money. But Shen didn't say who the clients were.

"About the law firm that represents the two Heavenly World nightclubs—Kaitai LLC—he mentioned an advisor. At first I had no clue who he was referring to, but then I realized that the advisor was actually the founder. She officially resigned from the firm out of political considerations—"

"She resigned?"

"Yes. I'm not finished yet. Sorry, but I have to speak in a hurry."

She didn't say why she was in such a rush.

"The founder is Kai, none other than the First Lady of Shanghai." She didn't have to say that Kai was Party Secretary Lai's wife—everyone in Shanghai knew that. "Because of her husband's position, the law firm attracted too much attention. Her resignation was just a show, of course, and she's still in control. The Heavenly World retained her law firm as their legal counsel, and that's why no one dares touch it."

Chen had heard of Kaitai, the law firm. On at least one occasion, Lai had talked about Kai's resignation from her firm as a sacrifice she had made for the best interests of the Party, a noble move to avoid any possible conflict of interest due to his position.

"There was something strange. While talking about Kai, Shen made a comment on an unrelated topic. He mentioned an American businessman who recently died. He was somehow related to the club, possibly a regular customer, I suppose. But there are so many foreign customers there that his comment struck me as odd."

"What was the context of his comment?"

"After mentioning the law firm, he jumped right to the topic of the dead American. And then, all of a sudden he said, 'The First Lady is a real bitch.' That's what he said," she said breathlessly. "She seems to be putting pressure on him."

"A bitch?" He was more than surprised.

The "First Lady" could be more involved with Shen than simply working as his nightclub's legal representative. Could she have been behind the raid that night?

Chen had never met Kai before, and he couldn't remember any of his investigations having anything to do with the law firm.

Even if Chen's troubles were somehow related to Kai and her law firm, Kai, after the failed raid, shouldn't have had any reason to put pressure on Shen. Shen wasn't in any position to do more, because Chen would never set foot in the club again.

"I've got Shen's e-mail address," White Cloud said. "Do you have a pen?"

He grabbed a pen, wondering at this unexpected piece of information.

"This is his personal e-mail, not the office e-mail," she said, reading it out to him. "He's a cautious man. Sorry, I have to go now. There's some movement in the other room. Bye."

It wasn't difficult to imagine where she was calling from.

She was with Shen, which she didn't try to hide, and calling from the bathroom, with water running in the background, like a shower, to cover the sound of the call. She had to be cautious, knowing that the man in the other room could wake up at any time.

Shen had invited her to the club several times, Chen knew, but she hadn't gone there until tonight. In fact, she hadn't said anything about going out tonight until after he'd asked for help. She was doing this for his sake, to uncover information about the Heavenly World, which could be crucial to his survival. Feeling sick to his stomach, Chen willed himself not to imagine what was going on with White Cloud anymore.

As he sat there on White Cloud's couch, more fragments of his dream resurfaced, but what the dream meant continued to elude him. He found himself thinking about the first time he met White Cloud. Almost to his irritation, several lines by Yan Jidao, a poet in the eleventh century, came crashing back to him.

Holding the jade cup, / her bare arms reaching / out of the florid sleeves, drinking, / unaware of her cheeks flushing, / dancing with the moon sinking, / in the willows, singing / until too tired for her / to wave the fan that unfolds / peach trees blossoming . . .

Or was he still imagining the scene between White Cloud and another man tonight?

She had done that for him—despite the cost to herself.

Her passing Shen's e-mail address on to him also spoke to her thoroughness. Had he ever told her about the help he'd gotten from a hacker in another case? He wasn't sure, but her hint was unmistakable—she expected him to use Shen's e-mail address to find out more.

Across the river, most of the lights along the Bund were off. The skyline appeared barren and lusterless, like an aging woman with all her makeup removed. Wherever White Cloud was, she wasn't coming back anytime soon.

It hurt for him to sit alone—he couldn't do it any longer.

The People's Park probably opened at six, and he couldn't afford to miss Old Hunter.

He found a piece of paper and scribbled a quick note.

"Thanks."

That was all he could think of to say.

He took the white jasmine spray he'd put in his pocket and placed it on the note.

The tiny bouquet was badly rumpled, and several petals fell onto the desk.

FIFTEEN

CHEN ARRIVED AT PEOPLE'S Park about five minutes before six and waited with a group of old people who had started queuing up earlier. When the park opened, they all walked in together.

He had no idea when exactly Old Hunter was going to arrive. Retired Shanghainese tended to get out early to do their morning exercise. Perhaps that would be true for Old Hunter, since he had to go to his job at the agency afterward.

The park was at the corner of Nanjing and Xizang Roads, its northern gate facing the First Department Store across a busy intersection. The park was much smaller than he'd remembered. Just like the garden in Suzhou, the park's location was too commercially valuable not to be exploited. All around it high-rises were jostling, elbowing against one another, encroaching on the park. It was a relentless effort that eventually had reduced the park to about one third of its original size.

Despite the early hour, Chen saw people here and there in the park, starting to practice tai chi, to sing Beijing opera fragments, to dance to the melodies from a portable CD player. He approached a half dozing man leaning on a dragon-head-topped walking stick and asked for directions to the "bird corner."

"It's near the gate on Huangpi Road, facing the Flower and Bird Market across the street."

Chen had read about people training birds like parrots or orioles to repeat simple human words. There was a scene about it in a documentary about Shanghai. But that morning, there was only one old man sitting on a jutting rock in the corner, with a bamboo birdcage at his feet. He watched as a tiny sparrow skipped out of the open cage and then hopped about on the ground, flapping its wings. It was strange. The bird could fly away, but the old man was watching it, completely at ease, as if the bird were attached to him by an invisible string.

This was the bird corner, there was no mistaking it, but Old Hunter wasn't there yet. Chen lit a cigarette and continued watching. The old man grinned a toothless grin, his shriveled face like a worn-out walnut, nodding as a proud master of the bird.

Chen, seized by an inexplicable impulse, pulled out his notebook. This wasn't a morning for poetry, but the impulse could be gone in a minute. He wrote furiously.

The little sparrow hops in / and out the tiny door / of the dainty bamboo cage, / parading about in dust, / its wings rigorously disciplined, / capable nevermore of flying, / but only of flapping at the air. // A world of self-sufficient, self-containing, barred enclosure— / with rice, water, vegetables, / and light fresh air . . . enough / for its survival. What's the point / of its breaking out, alone, / into the unknown? // Cheerful, it peeks back / at its aged benevolent master / with his face shriveled / into a walnut of satisfied smile. / A flash of the sparrow's wing / in the light. History keeps / depositing into the forgotten corner / of the park. What is meaningful / means only here and now, / in the little bird's ecstatic jump / under his blurred gaze . . .

He wondered how this scene had galvanized him into these lines. Then came the realization. Possibly there was a subconscious parallel between himself and the tamed sparrow—with its clipped wings, hopping around in a pathetic illusion of the infinite azure sky. Had he been that kind of a cop for years?

At about a quarter past six, Old Hunter appeared, sauntering along a trail to the corner, a shiny birdcage in his hand.

"Look at my oriole," Old Hunter said with a proud chuckle. "I took it to the Suzhou opera theaters before they disappeared, so it speaks with a mix of Suzhou and Shanghai accents."

That morning, however, the oriole was stubbornly silent despite its master's repeated urging to speak.

"As the old saying goes, a man had better have one hobby or another. This is even more true for an ancient failure like me. When I lose myself in Suzhou opera, I forget about everything else. But it seems the opera is dying out. So a friend gave me this little bird. It's truly a cute, clever one."

"The fresh morning air at the park is good for your health too."

"You've been to my place. Now, with three generations squeezed altogether, what can I do in a small tofu-sized room? The bird corner in this park gives me an excuse to escape our place early in the morning."

They sat down on a wooden bench under a weeping willow tree, at a distance from the other bird master.

"Tang told me something new," Old Hunter said, coming straight to the point. He pulled out a piece of folded paper. "He overheard a phone call between the squad head Ji and an unknown man. The call came in to Ji's direct line, and Tang and Ji aren't in the same office. But you know those office cubicles—the partition walls are so thin that they're not even close to being soundproof. From fragments he overheard—and those fragments were largely out of context—it was difficult for Tang to grasp what the call was about. But the caller must have been somebody. Ji spoke respectfully, almost subserviently.

And even though Tang only heard fragments of the call, he did catch a few interesting things. The phrase 'the Heavenly World' was repeated several times. Tang also thought that they might have been talking about a possible leak in the bureau. At one point, Ji protested in a louder voice, 'No, that's not possible. I didn't know anything until I stepped into the club.' It was quite a long phone call. I've written down those fragments Tang overheard so you could study them later. Nowadays, my memory sucks."

"I'm surprised that Tang was so cooperative. It's just more proof of your persuasiveness."

"If you listened to Suzhou opera as much as I do," Old Hunter said with a mysterious smile, "you wouldn't have been surprised."

"Well, I've just got a new Suzhou opera CD, but most of the time I've been listening to the cassette from Peiqin. Thank you, Old Hunter. The way you approached Jin at the café was a stroke of inspiration from the Suzhou opera master."

"I'm planning to go back there again, but the agency has been busy lately."

"There's no hurry. By the way, did you see any foreign customers when you were there?"

"Foreign customers? There was a Korean businessman, but he left shortly after I got there. I only heard him say a word or two. Why?"

"I'm just curious. Now, what's Jin like?"

"She's young. Voluptuous. Possibly in her midtwenties. Very fashionable too. She was playing with her cell phone a lot, and she was constantly sending text messages or checking e-mail. She has a genuine Shanghai accent, so she's not some provincial ernai." Old Hunter then added, producing an envelope, "About Jin, I have something for you."

"Something else?"

"At the agency, we have an errand boy. He's not that young, almost eighteen, but he can't find a full-time job. To run errands and other small tasks, Zhang Zhang pays him fifteen yuan an hour whenever he needs a little help. Yesterday happened to be a busy day, so I gave him some work to do. He proved to be quite capable and competent. For one thing, he got hold of a copy of the property certificate. The apartment Jin lives in is registered under the name of Qiang, who turned out to be Sima's son. Given the soaring prices for property, that's not too hard to understand. Within the subdivision, however, the apartment is registered under Jin's name, showing her as the owner, not a renter. Also, her car is registered with the government to Sima, but with the neighborhood committee, that car is also registered as hers."

"Sima probably did it that way for the sake of convenience."

"I don't know why he did it that way, but I know it makes for hard evidence of a relationship between the two. Also, the errand boy managed to get a snapshot of Sima and Jin standing by the window, his hand on her shoulder. It's from a fair distance so it's not very clear, but it's still useable. Our errand boy has promised that he will station himself there every evening, and the whole weekend too, until he gets some higher-quality pictures."

"That is fantastic. I don't know how I can ever thank you enough."

"No need to thank me. You can call me whenever you need me," Old Hunter said. "For a man of my age, I really don't have anything to worry about. And I'm old enough to give you a piece of my mind, Chief Inspector. You believe that you can make a difference, but you should think about qingguan—those honest, incorruptible officials in Suzhou opera, like Judge Bao or Judge Dee. They were popular in the ancient dynasties, and they're still popular today. Why? Because, like you, they're rare, in a society without justice or law. Just last night, I watched a TV show about Judge Bao. Guess how Judge Bao solves a crucial case? The solution emerged when a fitful wind blew someone's hat away. It was just one small thing leading to another, leading eventually to the emperor's real mother, who was hiding in a hut. Ultimately, however, the resolution all depended upon the intervention of a still-conscientious, filial emperor. As for Judge

Bao, even with incredible luck on his side, he got into much trouble. At one point, he was marched out to the execution grounds, only to be spared at the last minute because of the emperor's mother."

"Yes, I've thought about the issue of qingguan. It's sort of an archetype in our collective consciousness. The continued popularity of the archetype speaks to the problems of the system. But I've never heard of the Judge Bao story you just described."

"It's not a commonly told one. In fact, only in Suzhou opera is there such a detailed version of that story," Old Hunter said, standing up abruptly, "But I've got to get to work. I think I'll leave the cage at the market for the day, even though Zhang Zhang wouldn't say anything if I brought it to the office."

Chen rose, watching Old Hunter walk to the gate at Huangpi Road. Chen then turned and headed back to the gate at the People's Square, where he could get to the subway and from there to the railway station.

SIXTEEN

THE NEXT MORNING, CHEN woke up in his hotel room in Suzhou with a dull headache, his neck stiff, and his back sore. He hardly had the strength to get out of bed. For several minutes, he lay there, staring up at the ceiling, his mind blank, before he noticed that the laptop was still on with the Suzhou opera CD inside. He must have fallen asleep while listening to it.

The day before had been an exhausting one—after meeting with Old Hunter at the People's Park early in the morning, there was the hustle and bustle at the subway station, the long line waiting for a ticket at the railway station, then standing for the entire trip in the slow, inexpensive, and overpacked train back to Suzhou. He was pretty much worn out when he got back to the hotel. When he got there, he shut himself up in his room for hours, going over all the information he had. In spite of all his efforts, the multifarious pieces of information remained unconnected. It was exhausting, and, drained, he must have fallen asleep, having just put in the CD.

It was still quite early in the morning. So, ignoring his headache and pains, he decided to pick up where he'd left off last night. He decided to treat the nightclub raid as the central piece of the puzzle and try to fit the other pieces around it.

The Heavenly World was represented by the law firm founded by Kai, the wife of the First Party Secretary of Shanghai, which accounted for its being untouchable. So a raid against the club, even a secret one made against the ex–chief inspector, couldn't happen without Kai being notified.

Was Kai the one working against Chen behind the scenes?

But despite the failure of the raid, it didn't make sense for her to continue putting pressure on Shen. After all, Chen would never step back into that nightclub.

By why did Shen call Kai a bitch when he was talking to White Cloud?

And what about the sudden shift of topic—when Shen went from talking about Kai to bringing up the dead American? Was there some unseen connection? It wasn't simply that the American died in the nightclub or not. Kai didn't have any reason to be concerned about that.

The death of the American was also mentioned at the ernai café. Chen recalled hearing a fragmented sentence on the tape about "the death of a laowai"—a "foreigner." Some of the ernai's men were high-ranking officials, and the ernai might have heard something from them.

He got up, made himself a cup of coffee, and started surfing the Internet again, this time focusing on Kai. But, after a half hour of searching, all he could find was a short bio of her.

Kai was born into the family of red generals. After graduating from Beijing University, she started her own law firm. Her marriage to Lai was believed to be a "red alliance." As a capable attorney, she won a number of major cases, including high-profile international ones. Her practice expanded rapidly, establishing branch offices in several large cities. When Lai was appointed Shanghai Party Secretary, Kai was then referred to as the "First Attorney," her firm ranking as the top in the city, and also as the "First Lady," because of her marriage to Lai. But shortly after he became First Party Secretary, Lai made a surprising announcement: Kai had resigned from her firm to avoid any appearance of conflict of interest due to his official position. After that, she seemed to have faded from public view.

To the best of his knowledge, Chen hadn't been involved in any investigations related to her law firm.

Perhaps all of this was just a red herring. He couldn't afford to waste any more time looking in a direction that might have nothing to do with his crisis.

He broke out into a cold sweat, soaking his shirt. He felt weak. Staring at the cup of coffee he'd made, he decided against drinking it.

Perhaps a good Chinese breakfast could help. He had eaten so little the previous day.

Ten minutes later, he was walking up the stairs to the second floor of Cai's Noodles.

The waitress recognized him, meeting him at the landing of the staircase. "Morning, sir. Are you alone today?"

"Yes, it's just me this morning."

He'd eaten here with Qian just the other day. He didn't see her case as particularly urgent or relevant to his own troubles, though Old Hunter had already started working on it. She had, however, alerted him to the connections between the nightclub and Kai.

"You know how to appreciate noodles," the waitress said. "Is there any particular table you'd like?"

"Could I have the same table by the window?"

Sitting by the window, he checked his cell phone and found that he'd missed a call from Old Hunter last night. Perhaps it was about some new pictures taken by the errand boy, which would be something he could show Qian. He wondered whether she'd been able to ferret out more about the nightclub or had learned anything else that she could share.

"Good choice. The section is quiet this morning." The waitress came back with a menu. "Today's special is organic rice paddy eels. Mr. Cai has several acres of rice paddies where the eels are raised. We guarantee that the rice paddies are pesticide free, and the eels are raised without hormones or antibiotics."

Chen was struck with a feeling of déjà vu. The waitress had recommended almost the same special the other day, but then she couldn't be expected to remember what each customer had ordered.

"Fine," Chen said. "I'll take the rice paddy eels. I'll have them wok-fried with chopped green onion as a separate cross-bridge dish, as well an order of noodles with stewed pork, and a bowl of white soup."

"May I recommend a seasonal topping of sliced pork, bamboo, and pickled cabbage? I think you'll find it has a surprisingly fresh and delicious taste."

"Very well, I'll take your recommendation."

"The chef will start deboning the eels, and once he's done, it'll take a short while to cook them in the traditional way. If you'd like, the noodles can be served first, while you wait. The noodles will be from the first pot of the day."

"Thank you—that's very thoughtful."

As before, two tiny saucers of peanuts and pickles were placed on the table, along with a pot of green tea as well. Sipping at the tea, Chen thought of Qian. He considered calling her, and he pulled out his cell phone. But it was too early to call, so he put it away again.

That impossible romantic. That's what Peiqin had said about him, jokingly.

The noodles were brought out, and the topping of sliced pork, bamboo, and pickled cabbage was as delicious as the waitress had promised.

When he was only halfway through the noodles, the rice paddy eels arrived. "Sizzling oil style," the waitress said, strewing a handful of green onion on top of the fried eels before pouring hot sesame oil over the dish.

"That's the way to serve eel," he said approvingly.

The fried eel surpassed even his most optimistic expectations. He'd become so used to the hormone-injected eel that was found in Shanghai that he must have forgotten how good fresh, traditional eel could taste. He decided to take his time savoring the organic delicacy.

After he finished, Chen felt completely recharged. He paid the tab, leaving a small tip just like the last time. Outside, on Ten Perfections Street, he made a left turn and stepped into the public phone booth at the intersection to make a call.

"Who is it?" A male Beijing-accented voice answered on the first ring. "Qian's not home."

Chen was nonplussed. Qian had told him that she lived alone. But he couldn't rule out her having a visitor—someone on intimate enough terms that he felt he could answer her cell phone.

"I'm just a friend of hers," he said.

"What's your name?"

That was a good question. Even Qian herself didn't know his real name.

"I had noodles with her just the other day. She knows me."

"What's your phone number?"

"Oh, it's nothing important. I just want to say hi," he said. "Who are you?"

"I'm . . . her father. She mentioned you. You met just the other day. She said you like Suzhou noodles."

Something was amiss. Qian's parents had supposedly refused to set foot into her apartment ever since learning about Sima. Of course, they might have reconciled with their daughter, but it was unlikely that she would have told her father about the private investigator she'd engaged to gather evidence against her man back in Shanghai.

"You're from Shanghai, aren't you, Mr. Cao? You can leave your message with me. I'll give it to her as soon as possible. I've got your cell phone number right here."

"Don't worry about it. I'll just call back."

He hung up without waiting for any further response from the other end. Something was terribly wrong. He stepped out of the phone booth and walked away briskly, shaken by a deep sense of foreboding.

He didn't know what to do about this disturbing situation. His mind was completely blank.

He thought he might as well take a short walk, since walking sometimes helped him think. As he walked along Ten Perfections Street, he passed by a local candy shop, which was selling sweet sesame cakes, another favorite from his childhood. Not far away, a rickshaw driver was hawking his services, waving a tourist map in one hand, and a little further down the street, an elderly peddler was displaying colorful paper pinwheels in a holder that looked like a long-handled feather duster.

Chen was in no mood for any of them, nor did his thinking get any clearer as he walked along the busy street. So he gave up and hurried back to his hotel.

Up in his room, he drew himself a bath. Traditionally, a hot bath was how a gourmet would follow up an excellent meal, letting the body relax as the food digested. But Chen had something else in mind. Still at a loss for what to do, he was hoping the hot water would jump-start his brain.

Unsure if he was under close surveillance, he put the CD Qian gave him into a player in the bathroom, to give the impression he was truly indulging himself.

From the speakers, Qian's soft, sweet voice poured out like rippling water.

Myriads of maple leaves / upon myriads of maple leaves / silhouetted against the bridge, / a few sails return late in the dusk. // How do I miss you? // My thoughts run like / the water in the West River, / flowing eastward, never ending, / day and night.

It was a poem written by the Tang courtesan Yu Xuanji. Her social status in the ninth century was pretty close to the present-day ernai. She got involved in a murder case, quite possibly a crime of passion, and was executed. Centuries later, the Dutch mystery writer Robert van Gulik wrote a novel called *Poets and Murder* based on the story. But Chen didn't think van Gulik really appreciated her poetry.

Chen pulled his thoughts back to the present. Who could the man that picked up her cell phone have been? It wasn't her father, not with that strong Beijing accent, and it wasn't Sima, whom Chen would have recognized immediately. Was it possible that Qian had talked about Cao, the private detective, to some other man in her life? It seemed unlikely.

The only other conclusion was that the calls made from or to her cell phone were being tapped.

The man said he had Chen's phone number. His special cell number? He had only given it out to a few: Old Hunter, Peiqin, White Cloud, and Qian.

Panic-stricken, he went over all the calls he'd made and received in the past few days. He had made a point of calling from public phones. Old Hunter was experienced: in spite of the new SIM card, he dialed from public phones. Peiqin had only called him once, and that was to tell him about the ransacking of his mother's room and her subsequent admission to the hospital. Ultimately, it was a phone call that didn't really matter, not to anyone who might be listening in, anyway. White Cloud had, as instructed, called him from a public phone, and the only other time they'd spoken on the phone was when he was at her apartment and she had called him there, at her own home number. That left only Qian who called him on his cell the other day, a call that was quite possibly incriminating.

Even though his replacement SIM card wasn't registered to his name, it was only a matter of time before the "phone police" managed to trace one of his calls to this number. From there, it probably wouldn't be too difficult to trace any incoming calls.

He jumped out of the tub, dried himself in a hurry, dressed and quickly left the hotel.

He would have to change his phone number again and then let his Shanghai contacts know about the new number in person. It was too risky to call them from his old number.

That meant making another trip back to Shanghai.

But before he left, he had to try to find more out about what was going on with Qian.

She said she lived in an area close to the Temple Market. That was about all he knew, but even if she'd given him her address, it wouldn't be a good idea for him to go there and ring her doorbell.

At a newsstand on Ten Perfections Street, he bought several new SIM cards, and then stepped into another public phone booth and dialed her cell phone number.

"Who is it?"

It was the same Beijing-accented voice that had answered her cell phone the last time. Chen hung up.

SEVENTEEN

IT WAS GOING TO be another busy day, Yu thought, when he woke up.

It was still quite early when he heard Peiqin slip out of the room lightfootedly. Her long-standing morning routine was to get to the food market before six a.m., and then back home to prepare the breakfast for the family. Lately, though, she hadn't been getting up that early, what with Qinqin staying at his college dorm during the week, and her going to bed later, after staying up surfing the Internet.

The moment she closed the door, he sat up and reached for the case files. Taking out a pack of cigarettes, he hesitated, but then lit one. He started reading over the files yet again.

About six twenty, Peiqin came back with a basketful of vegetables, fish, and a live chicken.

"Is someone coming for dinner?" he asked, quickly moving the ashtray out of sight.

"No, it's for Chen's mother. She's checking out of hospital today. So I'm cooking something for her."

"That's a good idea. How is she doing? You didn't tell me much about how she's coping."

"There's nothing really wrong with her, but she was badly scared. She's a frail old woman, and the doctor is concerned. He's not sure her heart could stand that kind of shock again."

"That worries me too. Whoever is after Chen will not let him go so easily."

"Then whatever happens next, no one can tell," she said, taking a plastic container out of the basket. "Oh, I almost forget. I also bought soy milk for you, fresh from the market. Drink it. And the earthen oven cake too. Eat it while it's still hot."

He took a bite of the cake. "Another question. You've been spending a lot of time online. Have you found anything special?"

"About your boss?"

"Or anything related to Chen, even remotely related."

"Well, I haven't seen much about the police department, but there seems to be a lot of chatter about Red Prince Lai and his campaign of red revolutionary songs," she said, perching herself at the edge of the bed and breathing into the cup of soy milk in her hand. "You know I'm not interested in politics, but those red songs give me goosebumps. I remember how, during the Cultural Revolution, I trembled, along with my black parents, the moment those red songs started blaring from the street loudspeakers. Are we really going back to those days?"

"I doubt it. I don't think people are interested in going back to those years."

"But Lai is on the rise. He's the head of the red princelings. With his ever-increasing band of followers, it seems that he's on his way to the very top. There are rumors and stories about power struggles in the Forbidden City," she went on, sipping at her soy milk. "For instance, there's an article online about Lai's son, and with it is a picture of him, clearly drunk, standing with the American ambassador's daughter. The caption on the photo is, 'A red prince of the third generation.' The article seems to reveal a lot about his behavior at college, an expensive American Ivy League college, and how he's spending money like water. As for how they can afford to send him to such an expensive university, Lai has told contradictory stories. On one occasion, Lai said his son was able to enroll because he was awarded a scholarship, and on another, he declared that they were able to pay the expensive tuition with his wife's savings, money she earned as a most brilliant lawyer. Even though she publicly resigned, she's rumored to be still in control of the law firm. She was initially nicknamed 'the First Lawyer,' and now that she's resigned from her firm, they call her 'the First Lady.' "

"The First Lady—" Yu cut in. He'd heard that before, but referring to her that way publicly was taboo in China's politics. That title was reserved for the wife of the Party's general secretary, the number one. "But what does all that have to do with Chen?"

"It's about making sure all the prince's men are lined up behind him. That's an absolute necessity in China's politics. Is Chen one of Lai's men? Hardly, and if he's not, how can Lai allow Chen to remain in such a crucial position? He can't. He can't afford anyone who isn't completely loyal. The Party congress scheduled for the end of the year is Lai's big opportunity, and there's not even the slightest chance he'll risk letting anyone spoil that for him."

Peiqin knew what she was talking about. However, it was one thing to remove Chen from his crucial position in the police department, and it was another to go after him relentlessly, determined to publicly destroy him. Events were coming to a crucial juncture, with the Party congress coming up, and such a move against Chen could backfire. Chen had been a popular chief inspector, having conducted a number of high profile anticorruption investigations.

"There's also one post about your new position," she said. "It's in relation to your investigation of the Liang case."

"What about it?"

"Commenters have proposed a lot of different interpretations, speculating about what really happened to Liang. Generally, they believe that Liang was caught off guard but that he had been preparing for his exit, securing a passport or even several of them, a long time ago. So as soon as the Internet started buzzing about him, posting evidence of his corruption, he fled."

"But there's no record of him leaving the country."

"He could have sneaked out under another name, with a false passport, or he could be in hiding somewhere in the country. With all the money that he's hoarded away, it wouldn't be difficult for him to lie low for a while and then, when the time is right, stage a comeback."

"You're right, Peiqin," he said, finishing the cake. "But I think I have to leave early this morning. There are so many pending cases that the squad is investigating."

"You go ahead. After I finish preparing the dishes for Chen's mother, I'll go see her at the hospital, and then I'll leave for the restaurant around noon."

Yu didn't explain what he was going to be working on that day. Yesterday, Party Secretary Li had initiated another talk with him, asking questions about the squad's work, focusing on the progress of the Liang case. Li seemed anxious for Yu to declare it a "cold case." In other words, a case that wasn't yet resolved, but one on which there was no more productive work to be done.

Yu called Xiao Yang, a young officer in the squad, telling him that he had to take care of something and would be in later. After hanging up, he headed to the subway entrance near Huangpi Road.

Liang's company was located on West Nanjing Road. According to the company profile, there wasn't a factory or workshop at that location. In the Shanghai dialect, such a company was sometimes called a briefcase company, meaning all of its assets could be put into a briefcase.

But to his surprise, when he got there, the company had a large, luxuriously decorated office in a tall building next to Henglong Center, another new landmark in Shanghai. The office was partitioned into a large number of cubicles, but there were only five or six people there. The phones, however, were ringing constantly. The office manager, a man named Jun, received Yu with an ill-concealed mixture of indifference and impatience.

"Your people have already been here. What more can I possibly tell you? We're more anxious than anybody to learn what's happened to Liang. His wife, Wei, is worried sick."

"You've heard nothing new?"

"Nothing. But in the meantime, we have to keep the business going, and it's been very difficult. So please find him as soon as possible. He's not shuangguied, is he?"

Shuanggui—"double gui" or "twin designations"—was something beyond the legal system. A corrupt Party official might be detained for inter-Party interrogation at a specific place (the first *gui*), for a specific time (the second *gui*), before going through any legal procedure. It was done to protect the interests of the Party. This way, whatever details the corrupt official might spill wouldn't come out in the media. If a Party official wasn't shuangguied, then it might mean he wasn't in serious trouble.

Yu ignored Jun's question and instead asked, "How long have you worked here, Manager Jun?"

"More than three years."

"So you would be able to answer the questions being raised on the Internet about your company's incredibly lucrative deals from the government?"

"You're asking the wrong person, Comrade Detective Yu. I work under his wife, and I'm only responsible for PR. The boss didn't share any confidential details about the company's business transactions." Jun went on after a pause, "You know we supply parts for the new high-speed trains, don't you? For a country with such a huge population, the importance of the high-speed rail can't be exaggerated. In less than ten years, we've already surpassed the rail systems of America and the more advanced European countries. The safety, as well as the quality, of our products is not just critically important, it's a political priority."

Jun's answer sounded like glib propaganda, an echo from an article in the *People's Daily*.

"But your company only supplies chairs and tables for the new trains."

"Nonetheless, they are integral part of those trains. The designs were studied and restudied, and our products meet all the quality requirements. Everything has to be the best, a point that has been made again and again, and everything we did was legitimate. You can't pay attention to irresponsible hearsay on the Internet," Jun said, raising his voice. "If you have any more questions, you have go through our representatives, the Kaitai law firm. Our bid to supply parts for the high-speed rail project was arranged through them."

Jun handed him a business card.

"Their offices are nearby, in Commerce City. It's just a block away, on Nanjing Road."

Yu took the card, surprised at the hostility in Jun's voice. So far it was still a missing person case, but given all the evidence posted about the company's practices on the Internet, there was no reason for a PR manager to be this uncooperative.

There was also something strange in the way Jun had referred him the law firm. It was as if he thought he was playing a trump card.

Afterward, Yu made his way to Kaitai LLC in the Shanghai Commerce City, one of the top office buildings in the city. To his amazement, the law firm occupied nearly half a floor, and an impressive sign outside the suite indicated that it had branch offices in Beijing and Hong Kong.

A partner in the law firm named Dai received Yu in an office that overlooked West Nanjing Road. Dai was seated at a large mahogany desk, with a laptop next to a desktop computer, and what looked like a tablet as well. On the white wall behind him, there was an impressive array of pictures of Party officials and business tycoons. Some of the people in the pictures were foreigners, including a president of a European country. Yu recognized only a few of them.

Dai turned out to be far more polite than Jun, but also far more guarded.

"The city government people came to us about Liang and his business transactions. We were told not to discuss the sensitive details with anybody else. Besides, Liang is neither charged nor shuangguied. He's simply disappeared. We're not obliged to say anything." Dai added with a smile, "Of course, if you have some general questions, I'll try my best to help."

"I understand. In last several years, Liang landed a number of enormously lucrative deals with the government, but his company didn't have any special expertise or experience, compared to other companies—"

"That's something I can't discuss," Dai said, cutting Yu off. "It was due to the reputation of the company, I suppose. Liang has always delivered on time and met the required specifications."

"Also because of his connections, I would say."

"Yes, his connections," Dai said, leaning back in his chair. "For a successful businessman today, that's not really surprising."

"Liang's company was selected, from all the competing companies, as the designated supplier for the high-speed train, and your law firm prepared all the documents for the bidding process. According to one post on the Internet, however, the company created a special memory drive for which they charged the Railway Ministry more than ten thousand yuan. It was discovered to be nothing more than an ordinary flash drive wrapped in a plastic shell—a flash drive that sells for only twenty yuan in any supermarket."

"That decision was made by the Railway Ministry in Beijing. I'm not a technology professional, so I can't tell you anything about it," Dai said. "We helped them submit their bid, and all the necessary specifications were included and verified. Everything was legitimately done."

"But if everything was legitimate, why did he flee?"

"That's a question for the police, not us. As far as I can see, Liang simply panicked. The storm of accusations on the Internet was terrifying. It was like a lynch mob. His privacy was invaded, his personal life put out on display, and all his company's secrets paraded before the public. Nobody could possibly withstand the pressure."

It was clear that this conversation was going nowhere. Sighing inaudibly, Yu wondered whether Chen could have done any better.

"But there is one thing I can tell you. The company uses a well-known American accounting firm to audit its books. If you're interested, talk to the accounting firm directly."

Dai sat up in his leather swivel chair, his fingers touching a framed picture on the desk. It was a photo of a strikingly attractive woman.

"Our law firm has come a long way," Dai said. "You might have seen pictures of our special advisor Kai in the newspapers. She no longer works in the office, but she founded it single-handedly."

EIGHTEEN

IN THE EARLY AFTERNOON, Chen decided to pay a visit to Suzhou Opera Club.

His hotel room felt oppressive; he couldn't sit there any longer. And ever since his second phone call to Qian, he'd had an ominous feeling.

Qian might not be at the club, but maybe someone there could tell him something about her. At the very least, it could be an interesting visit, something he could talk about with Old Hunter. Chen's knowledge of Suzhou opera had mostly come from his conversations with Old Hunter, but it wouldn't be too difficult for him to toss out a couple of terms and names, pretending to be someone genuinely interested in opera.

The club was in a traditional two-story building, and a small sign on the front door indicated the club was on the second floor. The first floor had been converted into a shoe store, which had a large sign declaring "Suicidal Sale! Bankruptcy!" But the sign looked faded. It could have been posted there for weeks, possibly months.

Visitors to the club had to cut through an extremely narrow corridor leading to a precarious staircase in the back. On the second floor, the door was open, covered only by a bamboo bead curtain flapping slightly in an unexpected breeze. Chen noticed a bell on the doorframe, so, instead of barging in, he pressed the bell.

"Come on in. The door is open."

A woman got up, walked over, and nodded her welcome. She was in her late thirties or early forties, looking haggard and noticeably thin in her oversized dark gray mandarin dress, like yesterday's chrysanthemum.

The club's space was quite large. It looked like it had been converted from the original living room and two wings with the partition walls removed. There were a couple of tables and chairs by the windows, instruments were leaning against the wall, and an oblong opera table stood toward the upper end. That was probably the centerpiece, and singers would perform sitting at the table.

There was also a small bouquet of jasmine flowers on the table.

Four or five kids were gathered in the center of the room, some playing pipa, some plugging sanxian, seemingly oblivious of his intrusion. He wondered whether there was a class going on at the moment.

"I'm staying at the Southern Garden Hotel. It's so close, and I'm interested in Suzhou opera." He decided not to ask about Qian straight off. "Do I have to pay a fee?"

"No, you don't. This is not an opera house, and we don't sell tickets. But if you want to buy a cup of tea, or a buy a CD, you are most welcome."

"A cup of tea first," he said, choosing a fairly expensive one, Hairy Point, for thirty yuan. "I've never been to a Suzhou opera club before."

"It's not like the club in your hotel, Southern Heavenly World, that much I can tell you. And I'm glad you're interested in opera. By the way, my name is Nan."

"No, I'm not interested in that kind of nightclub. And my name is Qiang," Chen said, thinking of Qian again.

"Look around and enjoy yourself," she said, pouring out a cup of tea for him. "If you have any questions, just ask. The kids will start singing soon."

"Thanks."

He seated himself on a mahogany chair by the windows. On the tea table, there was something like a menu, from which a visitor could choose songs or episodes, each with a price listed next to it. It wasn't expensive at all. The mere fact that there was such a club at such a desirable location seemed nothing short of a miracle.

"I have a question for you, Nan. How do you manage to keep this club open?"

"Well, Suzhou opera enjoys a long tradition in this city. I grew up in a family of opera fans, listening to it all the time from my earliest memories on. When my parents passed away, they left these rooms to me. Alone, I didn't need all that space, so I've converted it for the club after the opera theaters were all torn down in recent years. Like me, some other people were sad to see the local opera go into decline like that, so they help in whatever way possible. But it's been really tough to keep the club going."

"I imagine it's not easy, maintaining this oasis in the midst of our materialistic society."

"Usually, the members of the club meet to sing two or three times a week, and nonmembers come to listen and enjoy, buying a cup of tea or a CD as a sort of donation," Nan said wistfully. "Suzhou opera is losing its audience, especially among young people. So we keep the place open for the kids to come by after school, and the instruments are left out so that the children can play them."

"That's something really worth doing," Chen said, nodding. People came here to the club because of their passion for the traditional art, despite all the entertainment available on TV and the Internet. "Not everyone knows how to appreciate a slow pace. Describing

Suzhou opera, a friend always used the well-known example of the one that features a young girl walking downstairs, lost in an internal monologue; it can take as many as eighteen episodes for her to reach the last step."

"Yes, that's from the *Pearl Pagoda.* You can see why times are really hard for Suzhou opera, with its narratives unfolding so slowly in a society that moves so fast," she said with a wan smile. "In the evening, we'll have an informal performance of short pieces. It's free, and anybody may come. Of course, you may want to buy another cup of tea. We won't refuse any donations from people who love Suzhou opera."

A girl, maybe twelve or thirteen, stepped over to the opera table, carrying a pipa taller than herself. After bowing to an invisible audience, she started singing.

To Chen's surprise, it was an eleventh-century ci poem written by Su Shi, titled "Lines Written in Dinghui Temple, Huangzhou":

The waning moon hangs on the sparse tung twigs, / the night deep, silent. / An apparition of a solitary wild goose / glides in the dark. // Startled, it turns back, / its sorrow unknown to others. / Trying each of the chilly boughs, / it chooses not to perch. / Freezing, the maple leaves fall / over the Wu River.

He heaved a sigh. He thought that was one of the songs included on Qian's CD. What was going through her mind while she practiced those lines?

Chen applauded as the girl finished singing. Fifteen years ago, Qian might have been just like her.

He turned to Nan. "What a beautiful piece! I think I've also heard it on one of the club's CDs, sang by someone named Qian. Do you happen to know her?"

"Qian—" Nan said, looking up in surprise. "Why?"

"I met her a short while ago, and she said she sometimes comes to the club."

"You should have come—" Nan murmured, her eyes suddenly filling with tears.

"What do you mean?"

"She died last night."

"What!" The news hit like a personal blow.

"Someone broke into her apartment, killed her, and took all her valuables."

He had suspected something had gone terribly wrong when he had tried to call her from the phone booth and a strange man answered. He was shocked speechless for a minute or two.

A robbery gone wrong? He ruled it out instinctively—it was just too convenient. And the robbery-murder theory certainly didn't explain the man waiting in her apartment, answering her cell phone. But he wasn't in any position to contact the Suzhou police bureau about it.

"You look pale," Nan said. "It's a shock to all of us. Were you close?"

"I didn't know her well, but she helped me," he murmured. "Please tell me more about what happened."

"No one here knows any details yet. Yesterday afternoon, she came here to the club and paid her monthly membership fee, as always. After she left, some visitors came to the club. They bought her CD, and one of them even bought a copy of her poster, which cost two hundred yuan. After they left, I called her. She was pleased, saying that the money the visitors spent would be her donation to the club."

"I don't understand how thieves could have broken into her apartment," Chen said. "Her apartment is close to the Temple Market, near the center of the city."

"I don't know. All I know is that early this morning, while I was still asleep, the cops came to my place. They found me because my number was in her phone's call log as the last person that contacted her yesterday. The cops asked me a bunch of questions before telling me that she'd been murdered."

"That must have been awful for you."

"We're having a memorial performance for her tonight. We're performing all the Tang and Song poems that she set to Suzhou opera tunes. It's our way to remember her. You should come."

Nan then walked over to a pipa leaning against the wall.

"That's hers."

He followed her, reached out to the instrument, and noticed that one of the strings was broken. In ancient China, a broken string was a sinister omen. Touching it, he imagined her playing pipa here, one string, one peg, each reminiscent of the lost years of her youth.

"I'm so sorry I can't come to the performance tonight," he said. He thought it was likely that some plainclothes policeman would also be at the evening performance. "I have an important business meeting tonight. But I would like to buy a CD of hers and order a short piece called 'Zijuan Lamenting at Night' for tonight's memorial performance. I'll pay the fee for the song in accordance to the menu."

Zijuan was a maid to Daiyu, the heroine of *Dream of the Red Chamber*. After Daiyu's death, Zijuan laments the heroine's tragic fate on the night when Baoyu, the hero, marries another girl.

"That is a very thoughtful choice. It's the song I'm planning to sing for her tonight. Don't worry about the fee."

"No, I want to pay for it," he insisted. "I only met her twice, and I know so little about her. Can I also ask a favor of you? Can you start recording tonight's performance as soon as people begin to arrive? I'd like you to record the evening all the way to the end. Not just what the performers sing, but what they say too. Don't bother burning it to a CD. A cassette tape will do. Here is a thousand yuan. Will that be enough?"

"You're generous, sir. It's far more than enough."

"I'll come back and pick up the tape in a day or two."

"Whenever it's convenient. I'm here most of the time, and if I have to step out, I'll leave a note about the tape."

He supposed that was about all Nan could tell him about Qian.

He stood up, holding the CD, which also bore the address and contact information of the club, and said his good-byes.

He almost stumbled walking down the stairs. The narrow corridor led him to an overwhelming question.

Did she die because of him?

He might be jumping to conclusions, but if it had been just a random home invasion robbery, why was there a man at her home answering her phone? At the time Chen called, the man must have known that Qian was dead, but he pretended that he would give her his message.

What's more, the man didn't know Chen's identity, but he did have some knowledge about him, such as the name he'd given her, Cao; that he was from Shanghai; and that he was fond of noodles.

The specificity of his knowledge suggested that the man had been stationed in her apartment to ambush Chen.

That confirmed Chen's earlier suspicion that the phone call she made to him was tapped. It was very likely that that call had led to this tragedy.

While he hadn't said much during that phone conversation, it was only a matter of time before whoever was behind the murder figured out who "Cao" really was.

NINETEEN

AT SIX FIFTY IN the morning, Chen stepped out of the Suzhou-Shanghai train, looked around, almost casually, before he walked into the subway.

At this hour, the subway was already crowded with sleepy-eyed commuters. The subway was a necessity for many, given the perpetual traffic jam in the ever-expanding city. Standing next him, a slip of a girl started dozing off, her head bobbing against his shoulder. He stood still to avoid disturbing her.

He left the station via the number 3 exit, the exit Peiqin had mentioned the other day. It was the one closest to her new restaurant. But it was still too early. He decided to stroll around the neighborhood while he waited. Clustered nearby were a number of convenience stores. A block further east, he glanced down a side street as he walked past, and he came to a stop.

There was a neon sign shining pale, listless in the morning light.

He traced his steps back to the subway, buying a copy of *Wenhui*

Daily on the way. Standing under the subway sign, leaning against a strangely barren tree, and unfolding the newspaper in his hand, he looked like all the others waiting there. Opposite him, a young man planted himself next to a green-painted lamppost, clutching a smartphone.

If this was indeed the exit Peiqin used, he couldn't miss her. The train she usually took arrived at eight fifteen, she'd said, and the subway was fairly reliable. He glanced at his watch again. He was still fifteen minutes early. He might as well stay put jotting down something on his notebook.

It was almost nine fifteen, however, when Peiqin emerged from the station, walking up the stairs, biting into a rice ball that she might have just bought from one of booths down in the subway station.

She was surprised at the sight of him, "Oh—" she said, one hand instinctively going up to her mouth. Her other hand was still clutching the rice ball, a tiny grain of rice stuck to her upper lip. Instead of saying anything more, she looked around, nodded at him, swung around, and walked back down the subway steps.

He followed her in silence, the crowd swirling around them like waves. No one seemed to be paying them any attention.

A couple of minutes later, she led him out through another exit. She led him away from the station for more than two blocks before she stopped, turned around, and spoke to him.

"Morning, Chief," she said. "Sorry, but if we'd stayed near that exit some of my coworkers might have seen us."

"I know. Let's find a place where we can talk."

This time he took the lead. He rounded the corner, circling back to the storefront he'd spotted earlier. It was a neighborhood karaoke club. It looked deserted, even though the neon sign out front was still blinking "Open for Business."

With more fancy and not-so-fancy hotels having opened in the city for customers looking to rent a room at an hourly rate, a KTV private room didn't seem to be a popular choice among the young and the well-to-do anymore. The rooms weren't exactly private, either, since the KTV attendants came in frequently to serve food and drink.

"The morning hours are the cheapest time at a KTV," he said, speaking like a regular customer.

For a karaoke club, the golden period was from seven p.m. to midnight. During that time, a room could cost as much as five or six hundred yuan, not including the fee for the K girls. After midnight, the price went steadily down.

Chen and Peiqin went in, and Peiqin waited while Chen made arrangements at the front counter. They then followed a sleepy waitress to a private room, where she left the song menu on a coffee table in the room.

"Let's pick some songs," he said wryly. "Or people might think we're odd customers—even suspicious."

"Choose whatever you want, it'll just be background music. It's common for people to come here without ever singing or even being particularly interested in karaoke. It's simply a convenient excuse to get some time alone. The attendants never worry about these things."

The first few pages of the menu were full of red songs, and Chen kept flipping pages in frustration. "Just the other day, in the cemetery bus, the driver said he had to play red songs. It was a city government regulation, and it's probably the same here," Chen said.

"As background noise, those red songs might be just as good as any others. You don't have to listen to them," Peiqin said, inputting the number for a song on the remote control. "For some, those songs bring back memories of their lost youth. But I get the chills every time I hear that one." She pointed her finger at a title. " 'The Cultural Revolution Is Great. Is Great. Is Great . . .' The first time I heard that song was during a mass criticism session, where my father was shaking uncontrollably as he was being beaten, struck by the 'revolutionary blows' of Red Guards. It was totally crazy."

"The same thing happened to my father, Peiqin. But it's not politically correct to talk about what happened during those years. For the younger generation, the Cultural Revolution is totally forgotten, almost like a myth. In school textbooks there's no mention whatsoever of the atrocities committed under Mao."

"As a result, red songs are coming back with a vengeance under Party Secretary Lai. It serves his political goals for him to have a chorus of Maoists," Peiqin said, frowning. "Ironically, Lai's own father was denounced as a 'capitalist-roader' at the very beginning of the Cultural Revolution. As a young passionate Red Guard, Lai beat his own father as part of a 'mass criticism,' breaking several of the old man's ribs. Guess what the father said afterward? 'A communist successor should be like this!' "

"Where did you learn all this, Peiqin?"

"On the Internet. Usually, this sort of information about top Party leaders is instantly blocked, frequently in less than two or three minutes, but that piece was up for a couple of days."

It sounds like both the father and the son made enough political enemies that this piece must have been left unblocked on purpose. Chen chose not to say it out loud.

As Peiqin pressed the number for another red song, he tried to change the subject.

"Neither of us likes these songs, so why waste time talking about them?"

"Sorry, I got carried away," she said. "How are things with you?"

Chen began to recount what had happened in the last few days, focusing on Qian's death, while avoiding personal details. He summed everything up by going through what continued to mystify him.

"As a cop, I've ruffled plenty of feathers, and some of them have tried to retaliate. So the attempted raid at the Heavenly World makes sense. But why would they drag an old, helpless woman like my mother into this horrible mess? Why go after a young powerless woman like Qian? I don't think I'm worth all this trouble."

"The burglary might have been a coincidence. An old woman living alone makes for an easy target."

"What about the murder in Suzhou?"

"That, possibly, was a robbery that went wrong."

"But what about the man who was in her apartment afterward?"

"What about him?"

"It couldn't have been her father. I'm positive of that. What's more, anyone who was in her apartment when I called would have already known about her death, yet he kept asking me to leave a message for her. He was trying to set a trap for me."

"You have a point," Peiqin said slowly. "But how could he have known about you? Did he find out from Qian?"

"She wouldn't have discussed what she wanted from a private investigator with anyone. I made a point of calling her from a public pay phone, but she did call my cell phone once. So it's possible that her phone was tapped."

"But why would they do that? They didn't know she'd gone to a private detective. They didn't even know your identity."

"They might have suspected somehow. Or her phone was being tapped for some other reason. For a man in Sima's position, it wouldn't be difficult to arrange. Then perhaps something in her conversation with me triggered her killing."

"The conversation was just about her, wasn't it?"

"No, she had made inquiries for me as well, and she mentioned things that she'd learned about the nightclub."

"Sorry, I didn't know anything about that. Yu and I assumed it was just another of your budding affairs."

"Come on, Peiqin. An affair now? With everything that's going on? But if it was just about her, then after she was dead, why was the man still in her place, waiting by her cell phone, trying to get information about me?"

"No, you're right, that doesn't make sense."

"Perhaps the stakes for them were much higher, for reasons still unknown to me."

"But how can you find out what those stakes are?" She added deliberately, "If they are using whatever dirty means possible, I don't think you have to play by the rules, either. You're no longer a cop—"

There was a knock on the door.

"Free buffet time," an attendant said from outside, her head partially visible through the glass panel in the door.

"Thank you," Peiqin said. "We'll be there in a minute."

"A free buffet. That's not bad," Chen said.

"It's bad for our restaurant. The management here uses it as a gimmick. Some of the overnight customers might stay a couple of hours longer just for the buffet. It's convenient for the customers, and it costs the karaoke club practically nothing."

"You know a lot about this karaoke club, Peiqin."

"Only that the buffet here is terrible. A number of their customers have told us about it. Anyway, we're not here because of the buffet."

"Yes, what you were saying before the knock on the door?"

"We have to hit back, and by whatever means possible, too."

"Well, there's one thing we have to do first," he said, reaching into his pocket. "We have to change the SIM card in our cell phones. I've already changed mine. You need to give one of these new SIM cards to Old Hunter as soon as possible. I've got one for you, and one for Yu too. But don't contact me unless it's absolutely necessary. And if you do, use a public phone."

"I see. So these are just for receiving calls. I'll give the SIM card to Old Hunter today. Don't worry about it." She then said emphatically, "If only we could find out who they are, and why they are so anxious to get you out of the picture."

Chen had been wishing the same thing for a long time, but he chose not to respond to her statement, instead pressing the buttons to play another red song.

"Is there anything new in the case Yu's investigating?"

"He visited Liang's company and the law firm that represents it."

"The law firm?"

"Yes, Kaitai. It's a very powerful firm." She added, "With the construction of the new high-speed train being seen as symbolic of China's economic reform, it is also a highly political case."

Peiqin then briefed Chen about what Yu had discussed with her about the case.

"Yu has quoted an old saying a number of times," she said. "'*To treat a dead horse like a living one*.' I think that's something he picked up from Old Hunter."

"Like father, like son."

It meant Yu didn't think the investigation was going anywhere or had any relevance to Chen's troubles.

"Based on what Yu told me about these latest cases for your squad, I tried to comb through the Internet as much as possible. With the firewall-climbing software Qinqin installed for me, I was able to look at some forbidden 'hostile Web sites.'"

"What did you find?"

"With regard to the dead pig scandal, they don't see it as an isolated incident. To them, it's just a part of the general moral landslide resulting from the uncontrollable corruption rooted in the one-party system."

"The moral landslide. That's a term that was used by the premier, but the day after he said it, the *People's Daily* ran an editorial denying the very idea."

"There's something unusual happening at the top. Several of the overseas Web sites touch on the idea that there's a power struggle in the Party between the left and the right wings," Peiqin said. "But back to the dead pigs. People have been bringing powdered milk in from Hong Kong and elsewhere ever since the scandal about the contaminated powdered milk. Now some are talking about bringing in pork from other countries too. It's a devastating blow to the Shanghai government's image."

Chen thought about his meeting with Sima the other day and nodded.

"Also, a Chinese meat company is trying to buy an American meat company as a kind psychological assurance. 'Only the Communist Party can save and rule China'? Surely you remember that red song. Well the netizens—the people who post and comment frequently on various newsgroups and Internet sites—have posted a parody version of it: 'Only the Americans can save and rule Chinese pork.' It's another slap at the city government. Lai is said to have been livid when he heard the parody.' "

"What black humor!"

"And it's related to another matter too. In the eyes of the Maoists, the netizens are being hard on Shang's son because Shang is a symbol of those red songs. So the Maoists believe that investigation of Shang's son is being carried out for political reasons," she said. "That may be true to some extent. By the way, did you quote the old saying that 'A prince, if found guilty, should be punished like an ordinary citizen' in a recent article?"

"Yes, but that was just an old saying. I wasn't using in reference to anybody in particular."

Once again, he was surprised. In an interview for *Wenhui*, Chen had indeed said something about everybody being equal before the law, along with quoting the old saying Peiqin had noted. The interview wherein he made that statement had been conducted a couple of days before the scandal involving Shang's son broke. But the son was hardly a prince in any real sense, and Shang was just nominally a general. Nevertheless, some people might have been enraged by Chen's remark.

That was a direction Chen hadn't considered before, and it was even more alarming in the light of what White Cloud had said regarding Shang's well-connected wife.

Any one of these cases, when examined under the magnifying glass of Chinese politics, could have been enough to have Chen removed from his position, but none seemed to warrant what had happened to his mother and Qian.

"There is also some discussion in social media about the mysterious death of an American in Shanghai. But that seems to be very vague. My English is not good, and as far as I can make out, it's about how the American didn't eat meat at all, certainly not the bad pork from Huangpu River and yet the authorities concluded that his cause of death was food poisoning."

White Cloud had mentioned that death too, Chen remembered.

"But all these individual events might be neither here nor there. I have no idea which, if any, could be the cause of your trouble."

"What you've learned by searching the Internet really helps, Peiqin. In the meantime, I've been listening to the tapes—your family's conversation, the talk in the ernai café, and the discussion between Old Hunter and Tang. They open up possibilities that I would never have imagined. It may take some time to narrow down the list."

"Yu said these are like a lot of dots that refuse to be connected. And Old Hunter plans to keep going back to the ernai café, but as he puts it: it's like standing by the tree, waiting for a rabbit to run by and knock itself out against the trunk. We can't afford to keep waiting."

"Has Old Hunter exchanged e-mails with Jin?"

"I don't think so. He knows very little about the Internet. He's only just now learning to listen to Suzhou opera online." She went on after a pause, "I just thought of something."

"What?"

"Qian's phone was tapped. Most likely, yours was too. But you can do the same to them. You have some idea of who could be involved, directly or indirectly, don't you?"

"Sima could be one. And Shen, of the Heavenly World, as well. Tapping their lines could help, but I'm not cop anymore. I'm not capable of doing anything like that. I could try to approach some of my connections, but any indiscreet move on my part could get them into trouble."

"What about their e-mails, then?" she said, "I'm no computer expert, but I know some people in that field who are fighting the uphill battle against corruption. I knew someone who is really good at hacking, but he went abroad half a year ago."

Earlier, White Cloud had given him Shen's e-mail address with the idea that Chen could access his e-mails. Peiqin was thinking along the same lines.

"You did an investigation where you got some help from a hacker," she said. "I remember Yu telling me about that."

"That's true, but I've lost touch with him. He changes his phone number every two or three weeks. Given his position, he has to be really careful," Chen said, then added, "Remember the *Wenhui* journalist at the temple? She introduced him to me. I think his name is Melong."

He hadn't contacted Melong for months, in spite of the crucial information he'd provided in one of Chen's anticorruption investigations. But it was different asking for help when it'd been a chief inspector asking for it. Now, professional scruples aside, it wouldn't be advisable to approach the hacker. Melong might be under surveillance, too.

"Of course I remember," Peiqin said. "It meant a lot to us, first your presence with your journalist friend at the temple, and then the pictures that ran in the *Wenhui Daily*. Our relatives talked about it for days." She added abruptly, "Lianping, that's the name of the journalist. What has happened to her?"

"I haven't seen her for a while. She's a happy soon-to-be mother, I think. She gave me the then-current contact information for Melong, but I'm not sure it's fair of me to involve him in this. He could get in trouble simply by talking to me."

"I see," Peiqin said. "Why don't you give me Sima's e-mail address?"

"You—"

There was another knock on the door.

She didn't say any more as a waiter stepped in, holding a menu in his hand. "We can also serve breakfast in the room. Just check the items that you'd like."

Neither of them was in the mood to pick and choose breakfast items, but they did, like typical Shanghainese, pointing at one item after another, discussing them until the waiter withdrew.

"Old Hunter has Jin's e-mail address. Give me Sima's."

"So you are—"

"Don't worry. I'm just an ordinary netizen. No one really pays attention to me. Oh, don't you also have Shen's?"

He hesitated, but he copied them onto a napkin.

"We often keep lists of customers' e-mails," she said with a knowing smile. "It helps our business."

This wasn't for her restaurant, he knew, shaking his head as the waiter came back with a tray.

"It's not too bad," Chen said, after taking a bite of a fried dough stick. He helped himself to a spoonful of the soy soup strewn with green onion and pepper oil.

"But you can never tell if the dough stick here is fried in gutter oil or not," she said. "At least you don't have to worry about that at my place."

TWENTY

PEIQIN WOKE UP, CONSUMED with worry again.

In the dim light peeping through the curtain, she gazed at Yu, who snored lightly at irregular intervals, his forehead knitted.

Last night, Yu hadn't come back until after eleven. It was too late for her to talk things over with him, and she wasn't sure it was something she should discuss with him or not.

She got up, put on her slippers, and walked out into the kitchen. She poured water into a pot of cold leftover rice and turned on the gas.

Waiting for the water to boil, she tried to sort out her tangled thoughts.

Both Yu and Old Hunter had been trying their best to help Chen, each in his own way. *But the water is too far away and the fire too close at hand.* That was another saying from Old Hunter, whose proverbial way was infectious.

She wasn't just worried about Chen, but about Yu too. The camaraderie between the two was no secret in the bureau. Sooner or later,

Party Secretary Li would get rid of Yu too, in spite of his recent promotion to the squad head. Chen's crisis was escalating, and any move on Yu's part could lead to more trouble.

So what could she possibly do?

"What are you thinking, Peiqin?"

Yu walked over to the table in the kitchen area, yawning.

"Nothing," she said, putting chopsticks on the table. "Breakfast is almost ready. It's just cold rice reboiled in water. Sorry about that, Yu. The pickles are in the refrigerator. You can take them out."

"Why are you sorry? I love pickled cucumber and fermented tofu. It's perfect with reboiled rice," he said. "What's your plan for the day?"

"I have to go to the restaurant. Yesterday, after visiting Chen's mother and delivering something to Old Hunter in Pudong, I didn't make it back to the restaurant until three o'clock."

It was an evasive answer, leaving something important out. Luckily, Yu appeared to be absent. He didn't say much while washing down a second bowl of watery rice and then wiping his mouth with back of his hand. She refrained from discussing the vague ideas she had in mind for the day.

After Yu left home shortly after seven, Peiqin called in sick to the restaurant.

"But I'll come in if I feel better this afternoon."

She made herself a pot of strong tea and sat down in front of the computer. But less than fifteen minutes later, she stood up again. The idea she'd tried to put off came back.

What Chen needed wasn't something she could find in an Internet search. The Internet might provide background information, but it failed to cut to the heart of the matter. He needed to know something more about those directly involved.

Had Chen anticipated the move she was likely to make? Had he mentioned Lianping in the karaoke room to suggest it? There was no point in speculating. He hadn't said anything explicit about it. Nor had she.

But the only way that Chen would be able to protect himself would be by turning the tables on the people going after him. And it was the only way to protect Yu, too.

Draining up the bitter tea, she made up her mind.

After checking the subway route to the *Wenhui* office online, she set out.

Near the exit to the lane, a black cat jumped out of nowhere, hissing, its tail trembling like a live whip. It might be an ominous sign. She spit on the ground three times in spite of herself.

An hour and a half later, Peiqin left the Wenhui Office Building and headed for the subway entrance near Shanxi Road. In her hand, she had the new address of Melong the hacker, though Lianping wasn't sure about his latest phone number.

She had but a fleeting impression of Lianping from years ago, thinking of her mainly as a potential girlfriend for the now former chief inspector. But as another proverb said, In this world, eight or nine times out of ten, things don't work out the way one wishes.

Peiqin took the subway to Minghang, then grabbed a special bus, and finally took a taxi to a new subdivision in Nanhui. She was taken aback at the amount shown on the taxi meter. With a wry smile, she paid it and got out. It was a high-end villa complex, where people had their own cars.

The villa matching the address in her hand was a two-story with a red brick façade and a large backyard looking over a creek. Though located far from the center of the city, a standalone house like that would be worth at least three or four million yuan. Melong must have been very successful in his special field, if that was the only business in which he was involved.

A tall man opened the door at her persistent ringing of the doorbell. He was probably in his midthirties, with a receding hairline and deep-set eyes. Alert, he studied her carefully.

"Who are you looking for?"

"Melong. I'm Peiqin, a friend of Chen Cao's."

"A friend of Chen's," he said. He gave a hurried glance around before he moved to let her in. "Oh, come on in. I'm Melong."

She followed him into a spacious high-ceilinged living room. It was simply furnished. To her surprise, she couldn't see a single computer or monitor there. He motioned for her to sit on a black leather sofa.

"How is he?" he asked as soon as she sat down. "I haven't been in contact with him for quite a long while. It isn't advisable for him to be seen with me. I understand."

"He's in big trouble."

"What? Chief Inspector Chen—"

"He's no longer a chief inspector."

He jumped up. "I'll be damned. I've heard nothing about it, it's not anywhere on the Web."

"I spoke with him yesterday and it isn't just that he's lost his position: things are getting worse. He mentioned you and Lianping in passing, but it was my own idea to make an unannounced visit today. By the way, I got your address from Lianping. She would have come with me, but she's pregnant, so I talked her out of it."

"You don't have to explain. If Lianping gave you my address, you must be a very good friend of Chen's. What happened to him? Tell me the whole story."

"The trouble is that Chen doesn't even know what's really gotten him into so much trouble. So what I can tell you may not be that much."

She proceeded to tell Melong what had happened to Chen, speaking as objectively as possible, yet withholding some of the specific details. She wanted to see his reaction before going any further.

He listened attentively, letting her talk without interruption except once—when he heard about someone breaking into Chen's mother's room, he cursed between clenched teeth.

"Now he's dead meat!"

This seemed an odd comment, but Melong must have known that Chen was a devoted son.

After she finished her account, there was short spell of silence. Then Melong said simply, "So what can I do?"

"I've been trying to help. I've been searching the Internet for clues, but what I've found there is limited."

"You're a friend of Chen's. He knows what I do—or I used to. So does Lianping. As well as a number of other people. But only a very few have any idea why I've moved out here."

"Why have you, Melong?"

"It's because of my mother. She's sick. She had a cancer operation not too long ago. That night, while waiting outside the operating room, I thought about a lot of things. I'd made some money by licking blood off the knife edge, and she had worried herself sick about me. What an unfilial son I was! She'd brought me up single-handedly. So I swore to Buddha that I would change and give her nothing to worry about if she recovered."

"How is she?"

"She's in recovery. It was a successful operation, I suppose, but the doctor said that good air quality could be crucial to her continued health. At the same time, the city government offered to buy my Web forum for an incredible price."

"Excuse me, Melong. I visited your Web forum about a week ago. It's still there."

"It's not mine anymore. The government official who arranged to buy it promised to keep the original forum name, and to run it in a way similar to the original. So people might still read those posts there and have no idea that it's now officially controlled. They hinted at the possible consequences if I refused to cooperate. It wasn't the first time they had asked me out for 'a cup of tea.' So I sold the forum, and bought this house with the money. Since then, I've kept myself busy growing vegetables in the back garden."

"Just like General Liu in *Romance of the Three Kingdoms*," Peiqin said, hit with a sense of déjà vu, "so people won't pay attention to you anymore."

"I've also washed my hands of the hacking business. Part of the deal."

"So you don't—" she said, unable to conceal the disappointment in her voice.

"True, I made a pledge to Buddha for my mother's sake," he said with a sudden light in his eyes. "But it's different in the case of Chief Inspector Chen. Without his help, my mother wouldn't have been admitted to the hospital. He got her into East China Hospital, the one for high-ranking cadres. And he also saw that the operation was done by the head of the hospital himself."

"What are you saying?"

"Buddha will forgive me if I do it for my mother's sake. She would want me to help if I told her about Chen's trouble."

"That's a valid point, Melong."

"So it's crucial to find out who's behind all this, and why. Right?"

"Exactly, but Chen's hands are bound."

"Does he have a list of people in mind?"

"Yes, he's has an idea of who some of the people involved in this diabolical scheme are, and perhaps, through them, something more can be found."

"Then give me their names and any information you have on them, particularly their e-mail addresses."

Peiqin pulled out a small notebook and copied the names and e-mail addresses she had onto a page torn from it. "Here they are. I don't know much more than you about these people, but they must be involved in one way or another. Whatever private information you can find out about them, Chen himself should be able to figure out the relevance."

"Okay, I'm going to try to access their e-mail files, and I'll put everything I can find on a flash drive for him. Does he have a laptop with him?"

"I think so, but it's probably best for you to give the drive to me."

"To you?"

"Yes, I work at a restaurant. No one pays any attention to a nobody like me, and even if the authorities are watching somebody like you, it's nothing unusual if you step into an eatery for a bowl of noodles," she said, with a self-deprecating smile. "That's another reason I didn't want Lianping to come out here with me."

"I see. How is she?"

"She's now a Big Buck's wife and a soon-to-be mother," she said. "Anyway, I don't think Chen would want her implicated in any of this. Let me give you my cell number."

"Fine, I'll set up a new phone number for myself, one that's exclusive between you and me. Oh, what's the name of your restaurant?"

"Small Family. It's a new one, on the corner of He'nan and Tianjin Roads. I work there from eight thirty to five thirty every day."

"Oh yes, I remember you now. Your husband is his longtime partner."

"Yes, he is. Detective Yu Guangming."

"Great. I'm sure I'll find my way to your place for a bowl of steaming hot noodles."

TWENTY-ONE

DETECTIVE YU STARTED HIS day on a busy note.

It had begun with a routine phone call about a body discovered at a construction site in Fengxian. While there did happen to be an unsolved missing person case that the squad was working on, that didn't necessarily mean that Yu had to go himself and check out the body. A couple of digital photos would be enough for an initial evaluation. He listened, barely catching all the details about the body: it had been found in nothing but boxers, in an advanced state of decay, with practically nothing to identify it with except for a tattoo on the lower belly, a blue dragon interwoven with someone's name—

At the mention of the tattoo, Yu jumped back as if someone had cracked a knuckle on his forehead. After he took that detail in, Yu decided not to mention it to his young assistant but instead said, "Xiao Yang, let's go and take a look."

The description given to him over the phone reminded him of something he'd learned in a recent interview. It might be a long shot, but it wouldn't hurt to follow up, especially since there were hardly any other steps for him to take in the case at that point.

So he found himself in a police department jeep, sitting beside Xiao Yang, who was excited to going to his first real crime scene. It was appropriate to Yu's new position as head of the squad that he'd been assigned an assistant, but it had been arranged by Party Secretary Li.

Forty-five minutes later, they arrived at the construction site in question. Fengxian, originally mainly farmland, had been recently upgraded to a district and was in the process of being transformed into an urban center. A number of college campuses had been moved to Fengxian from other areas of the city, and there were numerous housing development projects, like everywhere else in Shanghai. The construction site had been a rice paddy field just about a year ago. Yu thought he could still see a narrow stretch of rice paddy not too far away.

"This all happened because of an accident," said the local cop on the scene. He'd come over to greet Yu and Xiao Yang. "The tower crane here collapsed, breaking its heavy arm in a dirt-covered pond. According to the development plan, the pond is to be completely drained, and a parking garage built on that site. When the workers were clearing away the broken crane, they found the body. It had been buried under a layer of dirt, and if it weren't for the accident, it might not have been discovered for months, or even years."

Had the body not been discovered, Yu reflected, soon there would be nothing left for anyone to identify the body with.

Before the local cop finished his report, Yu was fairly sure that this would not turn out to be a natural death or a suicide. At the very least, the deceased could not have buried himself under a layer of dirt.

The degree of the decay indicated that he had been dead for a while. In spite of the strong stench, Yu squatted down next to the body and examined it himself. The tattoo on the lower belly was blurry. The blue dragon was still recognizable, but the two characters intertwined in the figure, possibly someone's name, were barely readable.

"The poor man, he must have been smitten with her," Xiao Yang said, partially covering his nose with his hand. "Some women would have fled at the sight of a tattoo like that."

"Well, if he was rich and high-ranking enough, tattoo or not, some women would have hung on to him—" Yu cut himself short, turning to the local cop. "Was anything else found at the scene?"

"No, nothing else was found. The preliminary examination of the body showed multiple fractures on the skull. Possibly inflicted by a blunt object."

"So the body must have been moved here," Xiao Yang chipped in. "The killer didn't want the body to be discovered anytime soon."

"That seems likely," Yu said. "But let's wait to hear what the autopsy turns up."

Yu started taking pictures, including several close-ups of the tattoo. Xiao Yang looked on, rubbing his hands in excitement.

The forensic team showed up at the scene shortly thereafter. Yu told his assistant to stay with them. They wouldn't have a detailed report ready anytime soon, but the young policeman might learn something from watching the team.

"I'm going to check on something else," Yu added. "I'll take the jeep and be back at the bureau later."

It felt different being in charge of the squad and not merely Chief Inspector Chen's partner. He'd been Chen's second-in-command for so long, that he'd almost taken it for granted. Now he had to make his own calls.

This was a case assigned to the squad, and it was Yu's decision whether or not to take the plunge. If the corpse was indeed Liang, it would stir up another storm on the Internet. A corrupt official exposed on the Internet had been murdered. Interpretations and speculations would inundate the Internet and the city in no time. That would probably put more pressure on the authorities. One result of the extra pressure on Shanghai authorities would be that Chen might be able to take a breath. In the *Art of War*, it was a stratagem called "Come to the rescue of the State of Zhao by surrounding the State of Wei."

Whatever scenario unfolded, Yu saw nothing wrong with investigating further, except that he might have to face a backlash someday, just like Chen.

He set out to visit Wei without calling ahead. Her reaction, if he caught her off guard, could be revealing.

Wei lived in a Western-style condo on a quiet residential lane off Wulumuqi Road. A couple of blocks before the lane, he stopped at a convenience store that offered instant printing and had the pictures printed.

As luck would have it, Wei was at home and alone. She opened the door, surprised to see him. She led him to the living room and waved him over to the leather couch. The room itself was somber, with the curtains drawn over the windows, blocking out the light. Wei looked pale, even haggard, and her eyelids were slightly swollen. Despite the hour, she was still wearing a violet pajama top and pants.

As soon as she sat down in a chair opposite Yu, he got straight to the point by laying the pictures out on the coffee table.

"A body was found this morning, Wei. In Fengxian. Here are the pictures."

She jumped up, snatched the photos, and looked at them closely. She reeled, lurching back a step or two. Her face bleached of color, and she reached out and grabbed the wall. One of her slippers fell off her foot. A vacant look rose in her eyes.

It was Liang. She didn't have to confirm it with words.

Despite her reaction, Yu had a feeling that it hadn't come as a total surprise to her.

"Was he murdered?" she asked, her teeth biting deep into the lower lip.

"His body was moved to a construction site and buried under a thick layer of dirt and construction waste. It took more than one man—along with tools—to do the job. It was probably murder, most likely premeditated."

"Who?"

"As of yet, no clue." He added tentatively, "It's possible they were professionals working for someone high up."

"But why? He had already been lynched on the Internet," she said, slumping back into her chair. She didn't bother trying to retrieve the lost slipper, her bare toes digging into the soft carpet.

"As for motive, my best guess is a coverup of some sort. A dead man can't speak out."

"You think so too?"

It was a rhetorical question, and it didn't require him to respond. It was obviously an ending she'd contemplated, perhaps expected, even before she saw the pictures.

Were there details—a lot of them—that she hadn't told him?

"It's a coverup of something much larger than we know," he said, sort of repeating himself.

There was no immediate response from her.

"Where is his body?" she asked instead. "I want to . . ."

"That can be arranged. I'll call the forensic people, and I'll let you know." He added, "As you've seen in the pictures, the body is badly decayed. If it weren't for the tattoo, I wouldn't have guessed it was Liang."

"The tattoo is still recognizable, right?"

It was another rhetorical question. There was a distinct tremor in her voice. Could it have been a crime of passion? Perhaps there was a secret rival for her affection—someone who had seized the opportunity to get rid of Liang while he was bogged down by the scandal. If it hadn't been for the crane accident, Liang would have simply "disappeared" because of the scandal. If so, she might have known or guessed something.

That would explain the worry she had displayed during the previous interview.

"I'm so sorry about your loss, Wei. The detailed forensic report won't come out until tomorrow," Yu said, standing up. "If you want, I can arrange for you to see the body, but right now I've got to rush back to the bureau. I'll keep you posted."

"Yes, please do," she said, walking him to the door.

"Just one more question," he said, turning over his shoulder. "Has anybody contacted you about Liang?"

"Anybody? No, no one except some business associates who didn't even know he was in trouble."

To his surprise, she took out a business card and jotted something on the back of it. "Please call me on this cell number, Detective Yu."

She was worried for some reason. What that reason might be, Detective Yu hadn't the slightest idea.

On the way back to the bureau, he got a phone call from Peiqin.

"When are you coming home?"

"Probably around six thirty, as usual."

"That's fine. Be back as early as possible. I need to talk to you about something," Peiqin said, hanging up.

From the way she spoke, it was probably something about Chen.

What had he done so far for the ex–chief inspector? Yu thought with a sinking heart.

He pulled off and stopped at the side of road to call a reporter for the *Wenhui Daily* who had contacted him earlier about the Liang case. Yu would reveal the latest news about the body—that it had now been positively identified as Liang—before reporting back to Party Secretary Li. Li might have vetoed releasing the information as not being in the best interests of the Party. This work-around was one of the things he'd learned from Chen.

TWENTY-TWO

CHEN WAS STILL LYING in bed when his cell phone buzzed. The screen displayed a number unknown to him.

It was probably a wrong number, but he pressed the accept button anyway, propping himself up on the pillow.

A female voice, young, buoyant, spoke.

"Would you like to come to the Lion Rock Garden, Chen? It's nearby, and we could enjoy some excellent tea in the garden."

Chen was baffled. On the hotel room phone, he had gotten suspicious calls from "girls" offering a variety of services. But this call had actually come to his cell phone, with the new SIM card, and she knew his name. She spoke as if she were an old acquaintance.

"The Lion Rock Garden?" he repeated. Apparently, she also knew where he was staying.

"I'll be waiting for you there, sitting near the entrance of the teahouse."

Twenty-five minutes later, he stepped into the Lion Rock Garden. It was so named because the grottos there had a number of rocks that resembled lions. In traditional Chinese culture, rocks that resembled other objects were prized and could command unbelievable prices. The last emperor of the Northern Song Dynasty was defeated and captured by the emperor of the Jin Dynasty because the money in the Song state treasury had been squandered on collecting singular-shaped rocks from all over the country. Despite that historical tragedy, the rock fetish lingered. The Suzhou garden, for example, still drew visitors mainly because of those lion-shaped rocks.

It was early in the morning, and there weren't too many visitors in the garden. Chen took two or three turns around the meandering grottos before he saw an ancient-looking teahouse. There appeared to be only one young woman sitting outside, her head bent, her long fingers poking at a smartphone, while an untouched pot of tea sat beside her. She was wearing high heels and a white trench coat made of light material. Chen could see her shoulder-length hair shining in the morning light: it contrasted nicely with one of the teahouse's antique vermillion-painted lattice windows, which framed her silhouette gracefully.

As he approached the table, she looked up and saw him. She stood up, slim and tall, smiling with two dimples.

"So you are Mr. Chen?"

"Yes. And you are—"

"I am Wenting, Melong's girlfriend," she said, gesturing him to sit at the table. "He asked me to come see you this morning. Melong talks about you a lot, and he's shown me several pictures of you on the Internet. It's like I've known you a long time. It's a real honor to finally meet you, Chief Inspector Chen."

"Thank you, Wenting. It's a pleasure to meet you."

So the connection was from Melong to Wenting, and probably from Peiqin to Melong first. Peiqin had taken the matter into her own hands, and she had lost no time doing so. Nor, apparently, had

Melong. Wenting's trip here was certainly not to enjoy a cup of tea in a traditional southern-style garden.

"Melong asked me to deliver this to you in person," she said, pushing a padded envelope across the table, "and, once I'd done so, to hurry back. If there's anything you need, you may call him at this number. He just installed a new SIM card last night."

"I really appreciate your coming all the way from Shanghai for this."

"He owes you a big favor. You don't have to thank me for anything," she said. She smiled with those engaging dimples. "We're getting married at the end of the year."

"Congratulations! Melong's a talented man, and a lucky one too, to have such a pretty girl as his fiancée." After a short pause, he went on, "Was there anything else he wanted you to tell me?"

"He asked me to tell you just one more thing. Everything is in the name of the good doctor."

What could that possibly mean?

He wonder whether it was a reference to Dr. Hou of the East China Hospital, who, at Chen's request, had operated on Melong's mother. Was that Melong's way of saying that he was paying Chen back?

"I have to leave, Chief Inspector. You don't mind my calling you Chief Inspector, do you? That's how Melong refers to you, and I like it." She stood up and reached out her hand. "You can call me, if you need me. You already have my number in your cell."

He rose, watching her depart, her youthful figure finally disappearing behind a gigantic rock that weirdly resembled a pouncing lion.

That had been an unexpected turn of events.

He took the laptop out of his briefcase. There was no point in going back to the hotel room, particularly since it might be under surveillance. He looked around for a power socket.

A young waitress came over, noting his laptop and the cable in his hand.

"We provide free Wi-Fi service with a fifty yuan purchase of tea and snacks. If you prefer, you can also use a table inside. There are several sockets in there."

It was early yet, and no one else seemed to be in or near the teahouse. So he went in, sat himself at a mahogany table, and inserted the flash drive into his laptop.

A screen popped up and, to his confusion, there was a request for a password.

Wenting had said nothing to him about that. Melong was a computer expert, but Chen was not. He was reaching for his phone when he remembered that enigmatic statement of hers—"in the name of the good doctor."

He typed in the doctor's name, and sure enough, the file opened. Three folders appeared on the screen.

Each folder contained e-mails. Those in the first folder were from the e-mail account of Shen, the owner of the Heavenly World; the second, of Sima; and the third, of Jin. Each file contained about two months of e-mails, both sent and received. Sima's folder was thicker than the other two, with an average of thirty to forty e-mails per day, which was understandable for a busy official in his position.

Chen took in a deep breath. It could take him a whole day to read through even just one folder, and most, if not all, of its contents would be irrelevant.

The waitress came back to his table with a tea and snack menu. "What would you like to choose, sir?"

"Anything that meets the minimum of fifty yuan. You choose. I don't have the time to look."

"You're a hard-working customer," she said.

She came back with a pot of tea and a dish of dried tofu cubes, then withdrew light-footedly.

Picking up a tofu cube with a toothpick, he started with Sima's folder. He did a search of keywords, such as "chief inspector," "death of an American," "dead pigs," "Shang's son," "Liang," "red songs,"

"Qian," "high-speed train," and so on. For most of the e-mails, with the names in pinyin and using this or that abbreviation, it was difficult to establish the identities of the senders or receivers. And in the majority of the official e-mails, people tended to be extremely cautious when referring to specific things or people. Still, the keywords appeared here and there.

With regard to "dead pigs," the e-mails revealed nothing new. In several messages, Sima urged the high-end hotels in the city to make certain of the quality of the meat served to international tourists, highlighting it as a political task. There was even a special fund from the city government allocated for that purpose. And in another message to Sima, someone mentioned a secret supply channel of organic food—including high-quality pork—for the top city officials.

"Shang's son" was mentioned mostly as a joke in several e-mails to Jin and to Sima's colleagues. There was also an e-mail on the subject to an editor at *Shanghai Daily*, an English-language newspaper. Sima asked the editor not to say anything about the scandal, as "it concerns the image of our socialist country."

Then Chen keyed in his own name. It actually appeared in a e-mail sent the day he visited Sima. It was difficult to identify who received the e-mail—someone called "Jacoblang"—but the message was clear.

"*Chen came to my office today. Questions about the dead pig case. What is he really after?*"

In response, Jacoblang wrote, "*I appreciate your reporting this to me. Find out as much as you can. If he makes no further move, you may contact him. Don't raise his suspicions, he's experienced. Report to me as soon as you get anything new.*"

Jacoblang, whoever that could possibly be, spoke from a higher, more powerful position.

There was no mail after that. Perhaps Sima didn't think he had anything new or important to report.

Then, all of a sudden, "Chen" appeared in another e-mail, also sent to Jacoblang.

"*Someone named Cao has been in touch with Qian in Suzhou. They're helping each other. Cao claims to be a private investigator, but Qian's actually making inquiries for him through her connections about the Heavenly World—and the people related to it. In a conversation with Cao, she mentioned Kaitai LLC as the legal representative of the club, the 'First Lady,' and some death in Sheshan. All of these are beyond me. As far as I know, Chen Cao is also in Suzhou.*"

The response from Jacoblang was simple. "*What do you suggest?*"

"*The bitch is barking like crazy,*" Sima wrote back. "*It has to be silenced—quick. A long night is full of nightmares.*"

Chen paused, his hands cold with sweat. Sima was devilish, maneuvering, manipulative—he was, as the proverb went, "killing with someone else's knife." Without mentioning Qian's assignment to Cao, Sima had succeeded in moving Jacoblang into action by focusing only on the nightclub.

The day Qian was murdered, a simple message came in from Jacoblang: "*It's done.*"

And the next day, "*Cao called her. Unmistakable Shanghai accent.*"

Chen had no doubt whatsoever about what had happened. Sima's report about Qian's inquiries for Chen sealed her fate in a "home invasion robbery." It was done for a reason unknown to Chen, but known to Sima, and so crucial that Jacoblang deemed it necessary to get rid of her and then to station someone at her apartment to intercept Chen's call.

For the moment, Chen didn't want to read on. He opened Jin's folder instead. It told different stories with two subfolders for her two e-mail addresses. A Sina e-mail account seemed to be for all her social contacts, but there was a Yahoo.co.uk account that was used just for the correspondence between her and Sima.

The subject lines of the messages in the Sina account pretty much indicated the e-mail's contents, such as "Henglong on sale" or "Hotpot Groupon." Those without subject lines were mostly gossip of the sort recorded by Old Hunter in the café. It would take too long to read through all of them, so Chen did another keyword search. Jin touched on some of the those topics, but mostly in the context of her ernai café. For "dead pigs," she lamented about the business she lost because no customer would order pork steaks at the café. "Shang's son" was only referred to in the context of the lurid details of the sexual imagination among the women in the café. "The death of an American" was one of the whispered topics among some of the messages, but Jin didn't seem to know anything specific about it.

In the e-mails between Jin and Sima, Chen performed different searches. As expected, the search for "Qian" yielded quite a lot. Jin knew about the existence of Qian, though from time to time, Jin simply called her "the other woman." In one message, Sima talked about his dissatisfaction with Qian. *"She simply lives in the world of her opera. Otherwise, her body lies there, totally unresponsive, cold, still, like a broken pipa."* Sima was cautious, seldom if ever mentioning his job in his e-mails to Jin. Jin, on the other hand, could be quite demanding. In the last two months, she had had him get her a hair salon gift card for three thousand yuan, a supermarket gift card for fifteen thousand yuan, and three pairs of shoes paid for with a gift card in his own name, among other things. The list was too long for Chen to calculate. The use of "gift cards" was no secret among officials. They readily accepted them from those trying to seek favors. In the meantime, Jin seemed to be pushing him to divorce his wife, or, failing that, to set up some type of long-term financial arrangement for her, in addition to transferring to her the title of her apartment. Sima appeared to be trapped between a rock and a hard place, considering the pressure he was getting from Qian at the same time.

But Sima also seemed to be interested in some of gossip at the café. On one occasion, he asked her what she'd heard concerning the death of an American, and on another, about the disappearance of

Liang, but her responses were vague. Sima also asked her to play red songs in the café from time to time and to tell him how the customers reacted.

Chen then moved on to Shen's folder. Shen proved to be widely connected, certainly not only because of his nightclub, and he was busy dealing in both the white and black ways with a vast number of correspondents. The search for "Chen" didn't yield any results. So Chen changed his tactics and focused on the days before and after the raid. Suspicious e-mails surfaced immediately.

On the night of the raid, Shen got a message from a sender named FL. *"What a disaster! Shame on you for having bragged about the certainty of catching a turtle in an urn."*

Shen wrote back, *"He got a call at the last minute. There is a possible leak at the very top. Nothing to do with us here."*

Shortly afterward, Shen e-mailed again: *"R came back, protesting about the disappearance of C after the raid."*

FL responded, *"Don't worry. I'll take care of him. He knows better than to make trouble if he still wants to do business with the government."*

Chen paused to make a note: "C=Chen?"

One minute later, he added another: "R=Rong? Is he in the dark?"

What White Cloud had told him about that night came back in a flash, filling in the blanks.

Shen also had another strange exchange with the e-mail account named "FL."

Several days before that night at the club, there was a mysterious message from Shen to FL: *"L gone from the surface of the earth."*

The response from FL: *"Good riddance. The boss has to console the black widow of a white tiger."*

Chen stopped again. What did L stand for here? And "the black widow of a white tiger" sounded like a jargon spoken by gangsters. He put another question mark in his notebook.

Another short piece from FL to Shen got Chen's attention. *"Did the American have his favorite in your place?"*

Shen wrote back: *"I've talked to several of them. His lips seemed to be sealed about his business. He knew better."*

There were many Americans in Shanghai, but during the last few days, Chen had heard or read about the death of a mysterious American several times and from various sources.

He lit a cigarette, half closing his eyes, trying in vain for a short break.

There were still so many messages he hadn't read. Many that he'd skimmed were too elusive to reveal their full meaning. Some seemed to be marginally related, but he didn't want to jump to conclusions.

He felt he had reached a point of no return. He might not have been the sole cause of Qian's death, but he was fairly sure she had been murdered because of her contact with him. Finding her killers wouldn't necessarily redeem him, but he owed it to her.

The waitress came over again, carrying a thermos of hot water.

"You have been working nonstop for more than four hours," she said with an enigmatic smile.

"The quiet garden helps me concentrate," he said. But when he looked up, he realized that there were several tourists sitting outside, talking, drinking tea, or cracking watermelon seeds. It was a sunny, glorious day, but he'd been too absorbed in gloomy conspiracies to notice.

It was time for him to leave. He didn't want to appear suspicious, working so long in a garden full of tourists.

He needed to go somewhere else, perhaps that bookstore near the hotel. He needed a quiet place where he could dive back into the depth of these e-mails, however fathomless they were.

TWENTY-THREE

CHEN CAME BACK TO Shanghai the next morning.

But this time, he wasn't coming in quite so surreptitiously, Chen thought, as he walked out of the Shanghai Railway Station. It felt good to be back in the city so familiar to him.

He was exhausted after reading and rereading all those e-mails yesterday. Some of the clues in those messages needed to be investigated more thoroughly. What direction those clues would lead, he had no idea.

Unexpectedly, an empty taxi came to a stop right in front of him, before Chen got into the long taxi line. Chen liked that. It was a stroke of luck and not a bad beginning to the day. Also, for once, the driver turned out not to be very talkative. Chen liked that almost as much.

The traffic was terrible, as always, but he was in no hurry. The car stereo was playing some classical music, not too loudly, and Chen tried to sort out some of his tangled thoughts during the ride.

He had made the trip back to Shanghai today for a conference where he was going to be a keynote speaker. It had been scheduled months ago, and he'd practically forgotten about it. Party Secretary Li had called him last night and said, "The conference sent a notice to the bureau. The organizers must not have gotten your new office address. We know you're busy in Suzhou, but your speech is important to the building of a harmonious society. There are newspaper and TV reporters who will come to cover it."

The event would also function as proof that Chen retained a high-ranking position, thus heading off any speculation about disharmony in the "harmonious society."

Chen, however, thought he'd better attend for his own reasons. The meeting was cosponsored by the Shanghai Writers' Association and the Shanghai Entrepreneurs' Association. He was supposed to deliver a speech about a writer's responsibility to reflect the changes in today's society, focusing on the contribution of entrepreneurs to the unprecedented economic reform. In Mao's time, the proletariat had been portrayed as the sole masters of society, and entrepreneurs as capitalists of the most egregious sort. Now, the role of entrepreneurs was totally reversed. As far as the Writers' Association was concerned, the conference was also arranged to push an undeclared agenda—to solicit financial support from the Entrepreneurs' Association. As a member of the former, Chen considered it his duty to help this effort.

While in Shanghai, Chen also wanted to see his mother, who had returned home from the hospital but remained weak.

Time permitting, he wanted to have another bowl of noodles at Peiqin's place as well.

He felt a net closing in on him, and he knew that any move he made—even a move he didn't make—could pull him deeper into the mire. The consequences of his going to talk to Sima, for instance. He thought he'd had a plausible pretext for the conversation, but then what happened? Immediately, their conversation was reported to someone higher up as evidence that Chen was trying to make trouble. And the consequences of his contact with Qian . . .

It hurt for him even to think about it.

You left, like a cloud drifting away, / across the river. The memory / of our meeting is like a willow catkin / stuck to the wet ground, after the rain.

He'd decided the best thing to do was to attend the lecture as originally scheduled, while taking all possible precautions.

His cell phone buzzed. It was a text message, and it looked to be one of those chain messages that spammers occasionally sent around. Often the message was a joke at the expense of the government. The sender usually used a fake name, so it was difficult to trace. Chen didn't receive too many, since not many people knew his number.

But today's text was strange. It sounded more like a vicious, practical joke in the form of a bit of doggerel:

Prelude

You are sick, dangerously sick / too sick for the higher-up's pick / like her cat tongue's old trick / purring, trying to suck your dick.

Like most doggerel, it didn't make much sense. But he couldn't help reading it again. It wasn't like the usual work composed by a youngster who spent all day and night on the Internet. Then he realized what struck him as strange. As a rule, run-ons don't appear in the syntax of Chinese doggerel. This one was more like a piece written by someone familiar with Western poetry. And then there was the title, which seemed to echo an early poem by Eliot—full of ominous hints and suggestions. It was likely a coincidence—but Chen didn't believe in coincidences.

Then his cell phone rang: another call was coming in. This time, it was his mother. The driver looked over his shoulder and turned the volume down on his radio.

"Where are you, son?"

"I've just gotten back to the city," he said. "How are you, Mother?

After I get out of a morning meeting, I'll come to visit you this afternoon."

"Don't worry about me. I'm fine. I know you're busy."

"I have some new pictures of the renovation of father's grave in Suzhou. I'll bring them to show you."

"Don't go out of your way on this renovation project. Things in this world are fleeting. It's a large sum of money on a policeman's salary. Buddha watches. You act with a clean, clear conscience and you'll be protected."

It was a subtle warning from her. She'd long since given up pushing him to change his career, but she still insisted that he follow the right path. She had no idea that he wasn't a cop any longer, and he doubted he would be protected by Buddha, either.

Ironically, that night at the Heavenly World, he'd been protected by the phone call from his mother, a call related to his filial duty. Karma.

He'd just gotten out the taxi when he received another phone call from Party Secretary Li.

"So you're back in Shanghai. That's great," Li said cordially. "As you haven't yet started work at your new office, I'm sending a bureau car to pick you up."

"There's no need. I can take a taxi."

"It's going to rain today. On a rainy day, it's not easy to hail a taxi. Remember, you're not speaking at the conference for yourself alone. Your speech there will be a credit to our bureau. So, don't worry about it. People here miss their chief inspector. Skinny Wang will arrive before nine thirty."

There was more than an hour before the car was due to arrive.

Back at his apartment, Chen checked in his refrigerator, since he'd left the hotel in Suzhou too early for breakfast. There was only a half a bag of frozen dumplings from a long time ago. He boiled a pot of water and threw in the dumplings. While he was waiting, he began jotting down some points for his talk. He'd given speeches like this before. It wouldn't be too difficult to pull this one together.

Halfway through his outline, however, he got another spam text message on his phone. This one was even more bizarre than the first. It actually consisted of nothing but the last stanza of "Sweeney among the Nightingales" by T. S. Eliot, by no means a frequently quoted poem. Chen recognized it because of its inclusion in the new volume of Chinese translations. In an intertextual twist, the Eliot stanza alludes to the fatal scene of Agamemnon walking across the purple carpet, entirely unsuspicious, the moment when he's murdered by his wife.

But how could that possibly be a practical joke sent as a spam text?

What . . . what if it was the message meant for him alone? From someone familiar with Eliot, sent to him as a warning about some imminent disaster, from something or someone he didn't suspect at all.

He shuddered at the possibility.

Then he was reminded of Rong, whom he had met at the Heavenly World the night he was set up. Rong was familiar with Eliot, and familiar with Chen's knowledge of Eliot. Chen hadn't had the time to check into the background of the banker yet, but judging from the e-mails gathered by Melong, Rong hadn't been involved in the setup at the book launch party. As a literature-loving banker, and possibly a designated donor, Rong might have heard about something that was going to happen at today's conference.

It might be a wild guess, but Chen was starting to think that perhaps it wasn't so important that he attend the conference this morning . . .

He was startled by a metal smell wafting over from the stove's gas burner. The water had boiled away, and the dumplings had burned into a black and reddish mess at the bottom of the pot. He quickly threw the pot into the sink.

Glancing at his watch, he decided to leave.

He tried to think while he was heading out. He turned off his cell phone, lest his thoughts be interrupted by the phone.

As he walked past, several people stood by side of the road, waving frantically at taxis, shouting in vain. Party Secretary Li was probably right about needing to send over a bureau car. Still, it didn't look like it was about to rain anytime soon.

Abruptly, he stopped walking and took out his phone. He checked the weather forecast, and an image of a smiling sun beamed at him. He pondered for a moment, then composed a short text message to Li. In the message, Chen said that there was an accident during the renovation of his father's grave site and that he had to rush back to Suzhou. Then, turning off the phone, Chen headed to the train station.

He wasn't ready to go back to Suzhou. Instead, he planned to continue his research from the train station until evening, when he would go visit his mother. This way, it would be possible for him to claim that he'd actually hurried to Suzhou and then come back to Shanghai.

In *Zhuangzi*, there is a well-known saying: "To hide most effectively is to hide in the busiest section of the city." So here he was, bent over his laptop at a train station café like many others, surrounded by the nonstop flow of commuters. From the train station, if need be, he could easily take the subway to Peiqin's restaurant. She might have something new to share from her firewall-climbing efforts on the Internet. In the meantime, he'd try to sort through more of those e-mails.

Soon the e-mails overwhelmed him again with their conflicting, contradicting currents of possibilities. As he was working on his second cup of coffee, he decided to try a new approach. In the three files of e-mails, was there some intersection, something that all of them touched upon?

There was. To his surprise, it was the death of the American.

The topic came up in various contexts. In the e-mails between the ernai, it seemed it was just a curiosity to gossip about. Though such a death touched upon his work in the Foreign Liaison Office, Sima's e-mails seemed very cautious on the subject. What struck Chen as particularly suspicious was the connection in those e-mails to someone named FL.

Was foul play involved in the American's death?

If so, the death would become an international scandal, which would be far more disastrous to the city government than all of the other cases combined.

Perhaps his having gulped two cups of coffee without any breakfast was making him too intense and paranoid. He was beginning to feel something like coffee sickness.

A waitress came to refill his water glass. "Are you all right, sir? You look so pale."

"I'm fine. I just need to sit by myself for a while."

He turned on his cell phone to check for messages, and immediately the phone started ringing. Chen picked it up.

"Where are you, Chief?" Yu said breathlessly.

"At the Shanghai Railway Station."

"Thank Heaven," Yu said, with an audible sigh of relief.

"What happened?"

"Earlier this morning, Skinny Wang said that he was going to drive for you. He was excited . . ."

"Yes, I was told that a bureau car was being made available and to wait for the pickup," Chen said, "but I had to leave before he arrived. Something urgent came up, so I sent Li a text message."

"Skinny Wang had a car accident."

"A car accident!"

"Just about an hour ago. There was a deafening bang, something like an explosion, apparently, and the car went out of control. There are different accounts about the accident, but it happened on his way back to the bureau. It's so hard to understand. He's such an experienced driver."

"How is he?"

"He's still at the emergency room. His life isn't in danger, but he might end up paralyzed."

"Go to the hospital for me and bring some money with you."

"Don't worry. I'll be there. You take care of yourself," Yu said and ended the call.

Chen was reminded of the "spam" text messages he'd received, particularly the one that quoted "Sweeney among the Nightingales." Now the warning was unmistakable.

Whoever sent that message was someone who had been informed that something devilish was being orchestrated but was too shrewd to send Chen an explicit warning.

For the moment, however, Chen decided not to speculate about who sent the warning. And not to contact Peiqin as he'd originally planned.

He was reminded of a proverb she'd quoted, which she'd gotten from Old Hunter: *Treating a dead horse as if it were still alive.*

He stood up, shaken but ready to move.

TWENTY-FOUR

CHEN STEPPED INTO THE public phone booth at the railway station, pulled out a phone card, and dialed Qi Renli, the associate head of the Songjiang district police bureau. Last year, Qi had worked under Chen on a special case. Afterward, Chen had described Qi's work as "energetic and creative" in a recommendation letter he wrote as part of the Party cadre promotion process.

"Chief Inspector Chen—no, Director Chen."

"Are you alone in the office, Qi?"

"Yes, I'm alone—and I understand. This call is confidential."

"I'm afraid I don't have much time to talk. Last month, the death of an American in Sheshan was reported to your district office?"

"Yes, it was reported to the Sheshan precinct in our district. They got a call from a club and immediately sent two policemen over, but when Internal Security arrived at the scene, they were kicked out."

"But they got there before Internal Security?"

"That's correct. I've met Fei, one of the two cops at the club that day, but he didn't say much about the incident. With Internal Security in the background, few would."

"Do you have their names and phone numbers?"

"Yes, let me find them for you."

Chen could hear Qi typing on a keyboard on the other end.

"Here they are. Fei Yaohua and Jiang Hui." Qi read Chen their cell phone numbers. "And the address of the precinct they work out of is 222 Shexin Road. By the way, Fei may not be there today. I heard that he's helping on a case somewhere else, outside of Shanghai."

"Has anybody else come to the district office asking about the dead American?"

"No, I don't think so. If there were any complications, they would be referred directly to Old Kang, the head of our district office. But I heard that the American died of food poisoning."

"Let me know if you hear anything new," Chen said. "Needless to say, don't breathe a word to anyone else about this phone call."

"Needless to say," Qi said, then added belatedly, "Oh, congratulations on your new position. I've heard that it's just a preparatory step for a higher position in Beijing."

It wasn't the first time that Chen had heard such an interpretation. Whether Qi really meant it or not, Chen saw no need to contradict him.

With the names and address in hand, Chen set out for the Sheshan precinct immediately. But it was a trip he made with a downloaded map in hand, taking three different subway lines and then hailing a taxi. A Shanghai native, Chen had passed though the Sheshan area only once before, and that was years ago. There was a Catholic church there, but that was about all he could recall about the area. The taxi driver hardly knew it any better, making several wrong turns along the way.

Finally, the taxi pulled up to the police precinct. Chen got out and walked around the area for several minutes. New apartments and condos had mushroomed up in Sheshan, just as they had in other parts of the city, but around the corner there were still old, shabby houses built a century earlier. The police station was located in the run-down section.

He walked back to the police station and pushed the door open without even a knock.

Jiang was there alone, bending over a paper bowl of instant noodles. At the sight of Chen striding into the office, he stood impatiently. Then recognition hit home.

"Oh . . ."

"It's a nice day, Jiang," Chen said, lifting a finger to his lips. "Let's get out of here and go have a cup of tea."

Jiang nodded. He was a youngish-looking man in his early thirties. He was wearing a black jacket and khaki pants instead of the police uniform, which wasn't unusual for a beat cop.

"Is there a place nearby we can talk?" Chen said.

"Sure," Jiang said, walking out of the precinct with him.

About a block and a half away, Chen saw a dingy hut with a sign out front reading "Neighborhood Cultural Recreation Center." On the peeling paint of the sign was a hand-drawn mahjong table.

Socialism with Chinese characteristics forebade mahjong, a gambling game, but as "cultural recreation" it was quietly tolerated, even this close to the neighborhood police station.

"It's an open secret," Jiang said with a hint of embarrassment. "When people are engaged over a mahjong table, they don't make trouble. So the city government has always turned a blind eye."

The owner of the mahjong den seemed to know Jiang well, letting them in without a question. Inside, there were three tables, each of them surrounded with energetic, exuberant players of mahjong, which seemed to be the one and only recreation in the center.

"My friend wants to learn how to play the game," Jiang said.

"That's great." The owner led them to a smaller room with a mahjong table set up in the middle of the room.

"If you want to practice for a real game, I'll send in two other players. Just let me know," the owner said before he backed out, closing the door after him.

With the door shut, they had a measure of privacy, even though the noise from the tables in the other room wasn't completely shut out. Mahjong was a unique game, sometimes called the war of a square city, referring to the way that players stood their tiles on end, like walls, along the four sides of a table. Chen knew little about the game, except that there was no way to play a game with only two of them. However, he liked Jiang's choice of location. They could talk there, a side room in a mahjong den, without raising suspicion.

"I want to talk to you about the death of an American in a club here," Chen said, shuffling the bamboo-backed mahjong pieces about, creating a convenient background noise.

"How did you come to hear anything about it, Chief Inspector Chen?"

"Why do you ask?"

"The case was taken from us before we even started looking into it. In fact, we were instructed not to say anything about it."

There was something about the way Jiang spoke, Chen observed. Possibly a hint of hesitancy.

"You've heard about my change of position, haven't you?"

"Yes . . ."

"I'm no longer a chief inspector in the police bureau," Chen said, going on to reshuffle the pieces.

"But you're now the head of another important office."

Working in a local police precinct, Jiang apparently knew little about the politics involved in the city government. His interpretation of events regarding Chen seemed to be similar to Qi's.

"Have you guessed why I was removed as head of the Special Case Squad?"

"No."

"There's an old English proverb: 'When the cat's away, the mice will play.' "

"Now I see, Chief."

"Now you see, Jiang. I was told about this case by an old comrade." Which was a true statement. Who the "old comrade" might be, however, was up to the younger cop to decide. "Suffice it to say that things are complicated and sensitive. So, please, tell me what you know, in detail, about the dead American."

"Fei is the one who can give you all the details, but he's off in Wuxi now, helping the police out there. I can only tell you what I heard from him," Jiang said, holding up a tile and then setting it down with a thud.

"Ours is a new police station for this rapidly developing area. Only two of us work out of this station, and there's a lot of work for each of us. The case of the dead American came to us about ten days ago. Usually, Fei and I would get to the station around eight thirty, but that morning, I had a meeting in the city, so Fei was alone in the office. About nine thirty, I got a text message from him saying, "A dead foreigner was found in the Wugong Club. I'm going there." With so many foreigners living and working in Shanghai, it wasn't surprising that one of them got sick and dropped dead. If it's a case of death from natural causes, the local hospital is in charge, not the police. But since it was a foreigner who died, and in an area club, Fei went over there to take a look. It sounded like a matter of formality, and I believed Fei could take care of it by himself. Shortly after ten thirty, I got another text from Fei. 'As soon as the meeting is finished, hurry back. Come directly to the club.' There was a suggestion of urgency in the message. The meeting wasn't important, so I left before it was over. But there was an accident on the toll road to Sheshan that morning, and I got stuck in the traffic. Around noon, I sent him a text saying I was on the way, and he wrote back, 'Internal Security is coming too.'

"Now, that was weird. The deceased was an American; if the higher authorities were called in, it would be the responsibility of the Foreign Liaison Office. So why was Internal Security coming to the club?

"When I finally got there around two, two Internal Security officers were already there in the room with Fei. Judging by the way they were talking to Fei, they hadn't been there very long.

"There was a body covered by a white sheet lying on the floor. According to Fei, there weren't any obvious signs of a break-in or a struggle in the room.

"One of the Internal Security officers turned to me and said, 'As we've just explained to Fei, we're taking over from here. You two may leave now, but let me repeat what we just told Fei: Not a word to anyone else about any of this.'

"So we left. I was in the room for only ten minutes or so, without even a close look at the dead body. I've got nothing to say even if I wanted to. Which isn't the case with Fei, of course.

"On the way back, Fei didn't say anything for a long time, except to pose a question, 'Why Internal Security?'

"That's my question as well. And that's about all I can tell you about that day."

At the end of Jiang's narration, Chen started shuffling the mahjong pieces, as if that helped him think.

"Did he say anything to Internal Security while you were there?"

"No, not I can recall."

"Now, did you ask him any questions afterward?"

"Nothing specific. Back at the station, I asked him what he'd seen in the club, but he was evasive. He only said that he hadn't contacted Internal Security."

"Let me establish a timeline here," Chen said. "Fei sent you the first message around nine thirty in the morning, and by the time you got to the club, it was two in the afternoon. You said that it sounded to you as if Internal Security got there shortly before you. That means

Fei would have been alone with the dead body in the room for at least four, maybe five hours. What would he have done during that period of time?"

"Normally, he'd take pictures of the scene, and then, if it was a natural death, he'd leave everything else to either the hospital or the mortuary. But if anything was amiss, he might have waited for the forensic team, or called the city bureau. According to Fei, he called the district police bureau and the Foreign Liaison Office. He mentioned that to me the following day . . ."

"Hold on. Fei must have had a reason for making these calls."

"I agree, but Internal Security warned us not to speak about the case, and they might have told him earlier that that meant even me. He had something on his mind, that much I could see. But it's possible that he was just upset with Internal Security for taking over the case like that. We had dealt with cases concerning foreigners before, and there was no need for Internal Security to be dispatched to Sheshan this time."

"Anything else?"

"The next day or the day after, we learned that the American's body had already been cremated. Fei looked very confused, though he didn't say why to me. However, I happened to overhear him talking to somebody about it on the phone."

"Yes. What did he say? If possible, tell me his words verbatim."

"I'll try, but I wasn't paying that much attention at first. What I heard was mostly fragments. I might not be able to give you the exact words, but the basic meaning should be close. One thing he said was something about cremation without autopsy. 'A suspicious death like that should have had an autopsy done.' And another sentence, 'He was a vegetarian. How could he die of food poisoning from bad pork?' "

"So that's what you were told about the American's cause of death?"

"No one told us anything, but Fei made inquiries on his own. By the way, the American's name is Daniel Martin. He was a businessman. At one point, Fei might have tried to contact his wife or something like that, I'm not sure. Fei did tell me that she's Chinese and she has two daughters."

"A different question. What kind of club was it?"

"Wugong is not exactly a fancy club. It was built at the early stage of Sheshan's development as a kind of temporary dorm or motel for the people pouring in. Later, in accordance with new regulations, Sheshan was designated as an area for high-end villas with natural scenery. After that, no more construction of commercial buildings was permitted. Because of its premium location, it's expensive, and modern facilities were installed and then reinstalled into the club."

"So it's somewhere between a club and a hotel for tourists?"

"Well, there are tourists who come here for the National Park and for Sheshan Notre Dame Basilica, but most people chose not to stay in the hotels here. There are lots of fancier hotels in the city, and they're less expensive. It's only a fifteen-minute drive away on the toll road."

"So why did the American choose to stay there?"

"Why? I've no idea. Perhaps the club was convenient. You can stay there for a couple of hours, or the whole night, without it seeming suspicious."

"Did Fei say anything about why he chose the club?"

"Fei could have said something, but I don't remember. Oh, the American had an apartment in the city, so why stay at the club at all? If he was planning a rendezvous, then why not a fancier place at a more convenient location? Unless the rendezvous was with someone who lived nearby, I suppose."

"About Fei, you said he's not in Shanghai now, right?"

"Right. He's in Wuxi, helping the local police with a case."

"What kind of a case?" Chen said. "Fei's just a local cop, isn't he?"

"I don't know the details. The criminal is apparently from this area, and Fei knows a thing or two about him. So Fei left for Wuxi four days ago."

"Have you talked to him since he left?"

"I've called him a couple of times, but his phone was turned off." Jiang added belatedly, "He must be really busy. I really don't know."

With Internal Security lurking in the background, was there something Jiang wasn't saying? In some delicate situations, the less said, the better. He would have done the same, but Chen decided to try and push a little.

"Have you heard of Liang's case?" Chen started, lighting a cigarette.

"No, I've never heard anything about it."

"It came to our squad as a missing person case. At first, nobody could get hold of him: his phone was turned off, and he wasn't returning messages. Then his body was found in Fengxian, buried in a construction site. Detective Yu was told not talk to anybody about it." He added, "Not because Liang's that important, but because the people behind him are."

"So you mean—"

"Did you find anything strange or unusual about his trip to Wuxi?"

"Now that you mention it, there is something strange about it. With only two of us in the office, we touch base with each other a lot. Nowadays it's easy with cell phones and e-mail," Jiang said, trying to pull himself together. "But maybe he's lost his phone, or something like that."

"Tell me something about his contact in Wuxi."

"He did call Gong, a local cop in Wuxi. I happen to know Gong too. If I didn't hear it wrong, Gong promised to pick him up at the station. They've known each other for many years."

"Do you have his contact information?"

"No, but I know he's with the Wuxi Police Bureau. And not just a local cop. That's about all I know," Jiang said.

"Oh, he got a phone call the day before he left for Wuxi. It was possible that it was from someone unknown to him, because he asked for the caller's name a couple of times. It was a long conversation. It sounded like the caller was asking him questions about events in the club the other day. Possibly it was about the surveillance camera there, but I can't be certain. All I heard was some fragmented words out of context. Afterward, Fei looked shaken, but he didn't tell me who called."

"With some political troubles, the less said, the better," Chen said. "Perhaps he didn't want to drag you into it."

"I'm worried."

That was all Jiang could say at that moment.

Chen glanced at his watch, rose, and pushed the wall of mahjong pieces down to the table with a bang, "I have an appointment at noon back in the city. Give me your cell number, and I'll call you if I learn anything about Fei. Of course, don't tell anyone about our conversation in the mahjong room."

TWENTY-FIVE

CHEN DIDN'T HAVE AN appointment in the city at noon, as he'd told Jiang, but he did take a taxi back to the railway station. This time, he had a train to catch.

On the train to Wuxi, he called Huang of the Wuxi Police Department. Not too long ago, Chen had helped with one of Huang's cases in Wuxi. Huang was a young and energetic cop, a fan of Sherlock Holmes, and consequently of Chen. The "legendary chief inspector," however, was a construct of his imagination.

As Chen expected, Huang was more than willing to help.

"No problem, Chief Inspector. I know Gong quite well. I'll have him waiting for you at the restaurant in Turtle Head Park. It'll be my treat. I'll also reserve a hotel room for you under my name."

Huang took it for granted that Chen was on a secret mission. In a way, Chen was. Unlike the others, Huang thought Chen's new position was just a cover for some highly sensitive investigation. Exuberant despite Chen's protests, he remembered well the details of Chen's last trip to Wuxi.

"If there's anything else you want me to do, I'm at your service. I've read that long poem of yours several times. It's so romantic. I know—"

Chen stopped him, knowing what the young cop wanted to say next. It wasn't the time for him to think about his poetry's being romantic.

Around five thirty, Chen walked into the restaurant in the park. The last time he'd been in Wuxi, he'd gone to the park many times, but never to the restaurant, which was a tourist trap.

Huang and a middle-aged man, presumably Gong, were waiting at a table. Gong was a stout man with a reddish complexion and gray-streaked hair. He made quite a contrast to the dapper, energetic Huang.

"After your last trip, I doubt you're interested in the lake specials, so I've chosen some simple dishes. It's a great honor to have you with us, Chief Inspector."

As a local cop, Huang knew only too well about the polluted lake.

"It's getting a little better, or at least the lake looks a little better, but I won't risk eating anything that came out of it," Gong said.

It wasn't the night for a leisurely dinner, but having skipped breakfast, and then lunch, Chen hadn't had eaten anything except an almond biscuit on the train. Chen chopsticked up a piece of Wuxi barbequed rib with a sigh of contentment.

Before they touched the other cold dishes on the table, though, Huang stood up abruptly, saying, "Sorry, I have to make a phone call."

It could be true. But more likely, it was just an excuse to give Chen and Gong the opportunity to talk in private.

"Huang has read too many mysteries," Gong said. He took a gulp of beer, then came directly to the point. "You have some questions for me, Chief Inspector Chen?"

"Yes, about Fei."

"Fei—that's something that puzzles me, too. Fei is an old friend of mine. Many years ago, we were both educated youths in Jiangxi, and since then we've remained in close contact. We both thought this assignment would be an opportunity for us to catch up. I picked him up at the station, then drove him to the hotel. He didn't say much about the job. It could have been highly sensitive, and I understood. We were eating in the hotel cafeteria when he got a phone call. He stepped out to take it, and when he came back, he obviously had something on his mind. About twenty minutes later, a jeep came and took him away. He said that it was for the job, and insisted that I not come out with him because I looked too flushed from the beer. He promised he would call me soon, but he didn't call that night. He didn't call the second day, possibly because he was too busy, so I called him that evening. His phone was turned off. I tried again on the third day, but still no luck. Then I called his hotel, and to my surprise, I was told he'd already checked out. The checkout was done over the phone. Of course, that's possible. As I recall, he only had a backpack with him, when we were in the cafeteria. But if he was leaving, he should have let me know."

"Yes, he should have called you."

"I assumed that, instead of contacting me, he'd hurried back to Shanghai. This afternoon, I called his office, and his partner, Jiang, was no less puzzled. Fei hadn't come back, nor had he contacted him."

"This morning, I talked with Jiang too," Chen said, "and he told me that he's worried. He mentioned that Fei has a daughter in Beijing, but he doesn't have her number."

"I have it at home. She did a summer internship here two years ago. I'll give her a call tonight." Gong added reflectively, "But it's all really strange."

"Anything specific that struck you as strange?"

Gong shook his head in dismay.

"I'm just so worried, Chief—"

He was interrupted by Huang returning to the table, his phone in hand. Huang slumped into his seat, took a large gulp at the beer, and mentioned that he'd made several phone calls. Then he turned to Chen.

"By the way, I've just double-checked, Chief Inspector. Your friend is still here, still alone, still in the same old dorm building. Here's the new number," Huang said, writing down the number on a paper napkin and pushing it across the table.

Chen thought he knew what number Huang was talking about, and he put the napkin in his pants pocket, nodding his appreciation.

"I'll call his daughter," Gong repeated, "and some other people he may have contacted."

"And you have my number, Gong," Chen said. "Call me if you learn anything about Fei. I usually stay up late. I'm taking the train back to Shanghai in the morning."

Chen had decided to come on the spur of the moment, and while he hadn't expected miracles, the trip to Wuxi had been a disappointment.

After dinner, Huang drove him to the hotel.

"Call me if there's anything you want me to do," Huang repeated as he started the car. "I know you can always pull off a masterstroke."

How there could be anything like a masterstroke from him? Chen wondered.

The hotel wasn't fancy, but it was located close to the lake. Nothing about the neighborhood seemed even vaguely familiar. When he got the room key, Chen asked the front desk for a map of the area, though it was too late for him to go out. Then it hit him.

The hotel was close to Shanshan's dorm. Huang had told him at the restaurant that she was still there. That was why Huang had picked this hotel.

Only he was in no mood to visit Shanshan tonight. He'd heard, since his last trip to Wuxi, that she was still single but was applying to study in UK. What was the point seeing her while he was in the midst of all this trouble?

Back in his room, he checked the train schedule for the morning.

There was a fast train leaving for Shanghai at eight thirty. He dialed the front desk and asked them to book a ticket for him.

He felt tired, yet his mind was far from ready to take a break. He didn't want to start working in the hotel room, which struck him as stuffy, so he changed his mind about going out. He left the hotel and walked over to the lake.

The lake looked dark green under the starlight. Here and there, he could still see patches of algae. A lone waterbird flapped off into the darkness.

Perching on a rock by the waterfront, he went over what had happened that day, making notes in his memory. It had been a long day, but he'd succeeded only in exhausting himself, like so many times before, without getting anywhere.

Afterward, he was barely aware that he had started walking again, absentmindedly, along the shore, following an unexpected turn, heading toward the dorm despite his earlier decision. The dorm building appeared little changed, silhouetted against the night. He came to an abrupt stop, thinking he recognized a lit window in the distance, before he walked into a deserted pavilion by the shore.

He also thought he recognized the pavilion with its antiquated vermilion-painted balustrade and white stone-topped bench. It was here that Shanshan had told him an anecdote about when she'd first moved into the dorm. It was quite late, the darksome water lapping against the shore under the moonlight. It would be his last chance to go and visit. No one knew what would befall him tomorrow. Reflexively, he reached for the napkin with the number on it . . .

But he grabbed his vibrating phone instead. It was after ten, he noticed, glancing at the time before pressing the accept button.

"I had to call you this evening." It was Peiqin. "Yu was suspended from the police force for leaking information about Liang to the press without first reporting it to Party Secretary Li. They questioned whether you had conspired with him, controlling him behind the scenes."

So Yu's investigation had rattled them. The hastiness of the move suggested that that Li and the people above him were responding helter-skelter. But was it just about Liang? Chen hadn't thought Yu would last long as the head of the Special Case Squad. Promoting him was nothing but a gesture. However, that Yu had been removed so quickly was a surprise.

Peiqin went on to give a detailed account of the interview Yu had conducted with Wei before his suspension.

"Yu has a feeling that she knows something about Liang's murder," Peiqin concluded. "She is heartbroken, but she chose not to say anything."

"So Liang may have been a scapegoat of some kind. Killed and buried under the waste, lest he speak out against somebody high above him."

"We've also learned that someone in Beijing pointed his finger at the people in Shanghai, recommending you as the one to investigate the recent high-speed train incident. Then the city government arranged for you to be removed from your position in the police bureau. That's unverified, of course. It comes from a so-called 'hostile' Web site." Peiqin then added, "Yu also went to the law firm for Liang's company, a prestigious one for which Kai is a special advisor."

"They felt that to be another strike at them, I believe."

Stories on the Internet may not be reliable, but Yu's move must have been in the right direction. What would be next move for the ex–chief inspector?

Wei might know something. But clearly she also knew it was useless for her to talk, particularly now that Yu was suspended and possibly under surveillance. A push in that direction no longer seemed sensible.

"There's something else," Peiqin continued. "About the American. We found some more info online . . ."

"We?" It was the second time Peiqin had used the plural pronoun this evening. He was worried about Yu, who had enough trouble already.

"Your friend, another filial son, came to the restaurant for our noodles, so we compared notes regarding our wall-climbing efforts. Strangely, the American's death has become a topic of conversation on various Web sites, not just in Chinese but in other languages, too."

Melong, it seemed, had joined forces with Peiqin.

"Here's a short bio of the dead American. His name is Daniel Martin. He came to Shanghai after having been a student at a college in Beijing. That was more than a decade ago. He was clever and industrious and took on all kinds of odd jobs. He was a representative for an American company, consulted on business opportunities in China, dabbled a little in the export-import business, and at one point, even 'played' as a 'special CFO' for a textile company, making occasional appearances to show off the strength of their joint ventures. Anyway, he muddled along like so many other expatriates, with no specific skill or large amount of capital. Then he suddenly seemed to have made a huge fortune. He bought properties in both Beijing and Shanghai, and he married a Chinese ex-model. He set up a consulting office in Shanghai, and with the local housing market on fire, he successfully brought various multinational corporations into the city—he acquired government-owned land for them through his connections. In addition to his consulting office, he apparently had a side business helping the children of Chinese officials study abroad. Before his sudden death in Sheshan, he was said to be a healthy man, rarely drinking or smoking."

"That's quite comprehensive. Thank you, Peiqin."

"But we have no idea whether all this is relevant or will be useful."

Chen already knew the death of Daniel Martin was suspicious. Martin was the very reason Chen was in Wuxi, tracking down the local cop who secured the scene of Martin's death. But the Party might do anything and everything to protect its interests when a potential international scandal was involved. He decided not to tell Peiqin he was currently in Wuxi instead of Suzhou.

After the prolonged phone call, he lit another cigarette. He needed time to digest this latest information, and he had an acute headache even before he started.

It was a little chilly at this hour of the night. He couldn't help looking over at the dorm building once again. In the distance, the solitary window was still lit.

There was no walking back into that favorite poem of his: *"Such stars, but it's not last night, / for whom you stand against the wind and dew?"*

His phone rang again. It was not a night for poetry.

"Are you still up, Chief Inspector?" It was Gong.

"Yes."

"Can I come over to the hotel?"

"Well, actually, I'm at a deserted pavilion two or three blocks east of the hotel."

"That's no problem. You can never tell about a hotel room nowadays. I'm on my way."

About fifteen minutes later, Gong stepped out of his car.

"I couldn't fall asleep, so I took a walk and ended up here," Chen said.

"Nor could I," Gong said. "I called his daughter in Beijing. Fei hasn't contacted her either. That's alarming. She is young, probably busy with her own life, but Fei calls her at least every other day. His wife passed away years ago, so he brought her up single-handedly.

"I went over the details of this trip of his, reviewing it like a movie in my mind. There are things that are not right. He came here to help the Wuxi police with a suspect from Sheshan because he had background information on the suspect. But was that necessary? A phone call or an e-mail would have been enough. In fact, Fei himself seemed to be puzzled.

"Then there was his reticence about it. We're both cops, we know what to talk about and what to be discreet about, but between two old friends, there should be at least a word or two about what we're doing, right? But no, he didn't say anything at all about his assignment here.

"After the phone call he got in the hotel cafeteria, Fei did something else puzzling. He asked me whether I'd told my colleagues about our meeting. He seemed relieved when I told him I hadn't. And then, he insisted that I not walk him out to the car because my face was 'red like a cockscomb.' I don't think that was something that mattered . . ."

"That's a good point," Chen said nodding. "Anything else he said or did after he got the phone call?"

"No, nothing except—he went into the restroom for a minute or two. Then the car arrived, and he looked like he was going to say something, but he gave me a pack of cigarettes instead. Supreme Majestic. 'Just opened on the train,' he said. 'Some of the residents in Sheshan are real Big Bucks.' And then he left in a hurry." Gong paused and looked around nervously before he continued, a catch in his voice. "Unable to sleep this evening, I opened the pack, and I found a mysterious note tucked in there: 'Jiang: If something happens, you may have whatever was left behind, with your nose stuffed or not.' "

"That's strange indeed. Can I have the note, Gong?"

"Of course, you take it. Let me know if you find anything. I'm really worried sick."

TWENTY-SIX

CHEN RETURNED TO THE Sheshan neighborhood police station the next morning. Jiang seemed like he was waiting for Chen. The moment he walked in, Jiang went over and hung an "out of office" sign on the front door and closed it after him.

As Chen took a seat at the other end of the desk, Jiang started talking.

"I'm so glad you're back, Chief. I went to Fei's home yesterday," Jiang said hurriedly. "I was hoping against hope, you know. He's not back yet, but according to the neighborhood committee, there was a break-in at his apartment. Since his only daughter works in Beijing, they believe that someone in the neighborhood must have noticed that no one was home and took the advantage of the situation."

"Even though they know Fei's a cop, someone in the neighborhood broke in? That doesn't add up."

"Exactly. After I came back to the office, I also noticed some suspicious signs here, as if someone had done a secret search of the office. But the lock wasn't damaged, and the windows weren't broken.

Whoever got in must have had a key. Without any hard evidence, it would be a joke to try and report it to the district office," Jiang said. With a bitter smile, he added, "Perhaps I'm imagining things due to all the tension."

"No. It's another inside job."

"But what are they looking for?"

"Something left by Fei."

"You mean something from the scene at the club?"

"Yes, that's a possibility."

"What it could be is beyond me. There was another 'coincidence' yesterday. Internal Security came to the office in the late afternoon, asking a lot of questions about what Fei had said to me after we left the club. But as I've told you, he didn't say anything to me."

"Did they believe you?"

Jiang didn't answer.

"I've told you about Liang, who disappeared so conveniently." Chen went on after a deliberate pause, "Well, I went to Wuxi yesterday. Fei hasn't been seen or heard from after he met with Gong at a hotel. Gong tried to contact him numerous times, without success. He's called you, and last night he called Fei's daughter, who also hasn't heard from her father."

"So you think Fei has disappeared, just like the other man?"

"But that's not the end of it, Jiang. Suppose they're after something they believe was in Fei's possession, something they failed to get from him. That's why he disappeared. And that's the reason for the break-in at his apartment, and the professional search of this office. What will happen if this item in question is still out there?"

"What will happen then?" Jiang asked. He added, "I've heard a lot about your brilliant investigations, Chief Inspector."

"With only Fei and you at the death scene in the club that day, it's not difficult to imagine what will happen next."

Again, Jiang appeared to be momentarily tongue-tied.

"I was only in the room for ten minutes or so," Jiang finally managed to say, "and Internal Security was there the whole time."

"But what about afterward? The only way out for you," Chen said slowly, "is to make them give up looking for whatever it is."

"But how can that be possible? I don't have any idea what it is."

"If it turns up somewhere else, they'll be still worried, but they won't be focused on you."

"I'm confused, Chief Inspector."

"Here is a note to you from Fei, written before he was taken away in Wuxi."

Jiang stared at the scrap of paper for several minutes. The note was unambiguously ominous.

" 'Jiang: If something happens, you may have whatever was left behind, with your nose stuffed or not.' What does this mean?"

"According to Gong, that note was slipped into a pack of cigarettes Fei gave him just before he drove away in the car. If anyone can get to the meaning of the note, it's you."

"If something happens—"

"His disappearance probably counts as 'something,' "

"It is something—but even if we figure out what Fei 'left behind,' " Jiang said deliberately, "I'm afraid these people still might not let us go."

"Whatever it is, it's related to his examination of the American's death scene, right? Now, you have no idea what 'it' is, but somebody else does."

Jiang pulled out a pack of cigarettes. "Let me think."

"What's he referring to with 'your nose stuffed or not?' " Chen murmured.

"Wait a minute—" Jiang jumped up and rushed into the back room. He came back with a glass jar in his hand.

"What's that?"

"Fei's parents came from Ningbo. I don't think he's ever been to Ningbo himself, but he's crazy about Ningbo food. Particularly the stinky fermented tofu. He keeps a whole jar of it in our mini refrigerator. We got along well together in this small office, except for our constant squabbles over this jar. We both bring our lunches with us and eat them here. Once he takes out the stinky tofu, however, I have to flee the building. Except for rainy days, when I simply have to stay inside and stuff my nose with my fingers."

"If that's the case, you can step outside and smoke a cigarette. I'll take a look at the jar in here."

If there was really something in the jar, as long as Chen didn't tell Jiang and he didn't see it, then Jiang wouldn't be responsible for the consequences.

The moment Jiang sidled out, Chen picked up the jar. It was quite large, with seemingly nothing but fermented tofu inside. There were at least thirty small pieces immersed in the amber-colored liquid, some of them with a grayish fuzzy surface.

He wrenched open the lid with a pop, and an overwhelming smell surged out. Jiang wasn't to blame for the reaction he'd described. For people from Ningbo, however, stinky foods were considered delicacies, and fermented tofu was probably the most popular of them.

Chen stuffed his nose with a paper napkin before inserting a ballpoint pen into the jar. Sure enough, it touched something other than fermented tofu at the bottom. With two fingers, he reached gingerly into the jar and pulled out a tiny package wrapped in layers of plastic sheets.

Except for some bits of tofu that had broken off in the extraction process, the jar soon recovered its tranquility. No one would notice any difference, he thought, screwing the lid back on and wiping his fingers with the paper napkin. He put the package in his briefcase.

Then he opened the front door to find Jiang smoking outside.

"That smell is really horrible, Jiang."

"I told you," Jiang said, stepping back into an office still beleaguered by the smell. "You haven't found anything, have you?"

It was a question with the expected answer implied.

"No. Nothing."

"I put my lunchbox into and take it out of the refrigerator every day. If there were something there, I would have seen it."

"Exactly," Chen said. Jiang must have rehearsed his words while he was outside smoking.

"But some people just want to catch the wind and shadow," Jiang said, looking worried again.

"Don't worry too much," Chen said, handing him a SIM card. "That's for you. I'll call you on this number exclusively. But don't try to call me. I'm constantly changing my number."

"But what if they continue . . ."

"Things may change soon, possibly in a couple of days. I'll keep you posted," Chen said, "but I think I have to leave now."

Forty-five minutes later, Chen arrived at a teahouse called Tang Flavor on Hingham Road, close to the subway exit there. He had been to this teahouse before. There were nice private rooms equipped with Wi-Fi.

A waitress came over to him with a menu in her hand.

"I have an appointment with a friend," he said readily, "but I'm a bit early. I want to sit by myself while I wait. What's the minimum charge for a two-person private room?"

"Two hundred for three hours."

"That's fine," he said, counting out the money. "For the moment, just a cup of tea. Nothing else. And no interruptions whatsoever."

"You can also have our Shanghai snacks for free."

"Don't worry about it. Just tea for now. Again, no interruptions."

After the waitress put the tea on the table and withdrew, closing the door after her, he took out his laptop and the plastic-wrapped object from the jar.

He lit a cigarette first, frowning.

TWENTY-SEVEN

IN THE LATE AFTERNOON, Chen stood up to leave the private room at the Tang Flavor teahouse.

How long he'd shut himself up in that room, bent over his laptop, the cup of tea barely touched, he had no idea.

The world is crazier than a crime novel.

What Fei kept in the stinking fermented tofu jar was a flash drive with the contents of the club's surveillance camera from the day Daniel Martin died. The video showed the people going in and out of that particular room—including Kai, the First Lady of Shanghai. She entered the room in the company of the American, intimately, hand in hand, and then, shortly after the estimated time of the American's death, left with a middle-aged Chinese man.

A lot of things clicked, connected, once Chen added the video to the e-mails, but at the same time, a lot more still didn't add up.

Kai had been involved in the death of the American. But why would she get involved in such a thing at the very moment that Lai was advancing to the top of the Party power structure? The American might have somehow become an insufferable threat, but even if he did, she didn't have to do something like that.

For the first time, Chen could start to piece together the cause of his troubles. He'd known for some time that the stakes of some case or cases were too high for certain people, as he'd told Jiang earlier. That accounted for the desperate urgency with which they'd been trying to get him out of their way. But he hadn't known which cases.

He hadn't even heard about the death of the American until after he'd been promoted out of the police department and the Special Case Squad. Now Detective Yu had been suspended while in the middle of a seemingly unrelated investigation.

Emerging from the teahouse, he turned, absentmindedly, toward the subway entrance near Hengshan Road. He'd become gradually familiar with the cobweb of subway lines after losing the use of a bureau car along with his position as chief inspector. In the city, there were more than ten lines woven together, and there were five or six more in partial operation or under construction. Ever-present traffic jams made the subway system the more reliable alternative. For Chen, there was another advantage he'd never known about before: it wouldn't be easy for someone to follow him through the labyrinth of subway lines. He made a point of standing near the train door and abruptly shoving his way out at the stop, without give any advance signs of his intentions.

That afternoon, he pushed out of the train in just such a manner and climbed up the steps to West Huaihai Road, an area that used to be part of the French concession back in the old days. It remained just as fashionable and wealthy now, a symbol of status in the current materialistic age.

Finding himself at an intersection close to White Cloud's hair salon, he toyed with idea of going in for a haircut. He took out his cell phone. There were no new messages from her in the last two days. She might have tried to make additional inquiries for him, but it would have been difficult for even a cop to have found out any more.

Then he realized he hadn't even given her his new cell number. She might have tried to call but without success.

He thought, too, that they might be able to check some of the details they hadn't been able to cover in their hurried phone call that night at her apartment. He decided to give her a call first. It would be too dramatic for him to make another unannounced visit to her salon.

"Oh, it's you," she said, picking up on the first ring. "I was thinking about calling you, too."

So she hadn't tried to call him yet. That's good, he thought.

"Things aren't good, Chen," she went on without waiting for him to say anything. "To put it in a nutshell, it would be advisable for you to take a short vacation, preferably abroad, as Mr. Gu suggested."

Had she discussed this with Mr. Gu?

"It might not be that easy."

"Don't you know some people in the consulate on Wulumuqi Road?"

"Yes, but . . ." he said, without finishing his sentence.

She was referring to the American consulate. He knew a cultural consul there, though he wondered whether he'd ever told her about that. But it wasn't the matter of getting a visa from the consulate: his name would already have been put on some sort of alert list at customs.

It was clear, however, that she'd learned more about his troubles and that they were far more serious than she'd initially supposed.

"You have done a lot here, Chen. It's time for you to start over somewhere else and do something for yourself. You're still dreaming of an academic career, aren't you?"

"I've thought about it," he said, not really knowing how to respond. "But what about things here? Take you, for example: you've worked hard all these years, and now with the salon and the apartment—"

"*I've thought about it*," she said, picking at his words irritably.

"I don't like it, not at all—the salon, the apartment, and everything else that might go onto that list. Whatever you have here today can be totally wiped out tomorrow."

"So—"

"With your command of English, I would have made it out long ago."

He was alarmed. There was something urgent in her vague words, but she didn't elaborate. Still, there was an unambiguous difference between tonight's call and her phone call the night he stood at her Bingjiang apartment windows, overlooking the sleepless river. This time, she was still so concerned about him, and her suggestion was a realistic one. But this time, she chose not to involve herself more than necessary.

It was understandable. What could he possibly give her? Nothing except trouble, particularly in the midst of his own troubles.

There was no point in going to her hair salon. He finished up the phone call like a suddenly hollow man, murmuring polite yet meaningless words. He reminded himself that she had helped him so generously.

The evening was beginning to spread out against the sky. He walked on along Huaihai Road, passing the consulate she had just mentioned, as if in some mysterious correspondence. Then he turned onto a shady side road lined with trees. Ahead of him, he saw a new Sichuan restaurant, with several Westerners talking outside under the flashing neon sign. Heavenly Sichuan. He remembered hearing a lot about this place. On an inexplicable impulse, he stepped inside.

The restaurant, while still designed in the old Sichuan style, was pretty much Westernized in terms of its service. The proprietor must have taken into consideration the consulates located nearby, not only the American consulate but several other Western ones as well. Chen chose a corner table. At a table in the other corner, a waitress was deftly cutting and placing a portion of a squirrel-shaped fish on a dainty plate in front of each diner, all Westerners. It was quite different from the Chinese way of everyone dipping their chopsticks into the same big platter.

At the recommendation of a bespectacled waiter, Chen ordered sliced spicy pork draped like clothing on a tiny bamboo pole, pock-faced granny's spicy tofu, and a steamed live bass with ginger and scallion.

"Are you waiting for someone?"

"Maybe. She might come, but I'm not sure."

"These will be enough for now, I think. When she comes, you can order more," the waiter said considerately. "Anything to drink?"

Chen was thinking of hot tea when the waiter opened up the menu to the wine page.

"How about the Bordeaux? It's very appropriate and fashionable to have red wine with the Sichuan dishes."

"Well, whatever you recommend, but I'd like a pot of green tea too."

He wasn't surprised to see that the two Westerners across the aisle—both men—were dining with three young Chinese women. Each of them was holding a glass of red wine, laughing, and using chopsticks as if they had done so all their life.

He found himself the only solitary diner there. Few, Shanghainese or not, would go to a stylish restaurant alone. The waiter came back to the table, carrying a medium-sized live bass jumping in a hand net for his inspection. He nodded absently.

At the next table, the diners were from Russia, which gave him an idea. Just a couple of days ago, he had planned to visit Overseas Chinese Lu in Pudong but had ended up staying at White Cloud's apartment. This evening, he'd finally go to Overseas Chinese Lu's place. But first, he had to think about what he was going to do, tomorrow, with the footage from the club's surveillance camera.

The spicy tofu was brought to the table. It was quite tasty, but after just a spoonful, he lost himself in a tangle of ideas, one after the next, in a futile attempt to find a way out. He worked through the possible scenarios so many times that thinking only exhausted him.

The next dish that came out was the thin-sliced pork. It was beautifully prepared and looked almost like a table decoration.

Before Chen could take a bite, he thought of something Peiqin had said about Kai's son studying at an Ivy League college and Daniel Martin's business of making arrangements for the children of high officials who were going abroad. Was there a connection? But it was probably such small change for those officials . . .

"The live fish," the waiter said, serving a large, colorful platter with the steamed fish covered with green onion, red pepper, and golden ginger.

Was Chen just like the Watch Boss, anxious to have a last fling before the end?

The dead fish eyes seemed to be staring back at him.

Outside, it started raining. It could be difficult to get a taxi on a rainy night. Most of the customers here had come in their own cars, so they weren't worried. Not so for Chen, but then again, he wasn't anxious to leave for Pudong.

He was beginning to have second thoughts about his plan for the night. Given the present circumstances, there was no telling if visiting them would cause trouble for the Lus. Besides, Chen couldn't afford to spend the night in sentimental conversation about the old days. Overseas Chinese Lu had grown impossibly nostalgic of late. In the meantime, Chen didn't have much time left—the net was closing around him.

Then his cell phone buzzed.

"Where are you?" Wenting asked, her voice energetic and exuberant against a background of muffled noise.

"In a Sichuan restaurant—Heavenly Sichuan—near the American consulate."

"Oh, I know it. It's close to Wulumuqi Road, right? I'm in the subway on the way to the train station. I'm glad I called you to check, so now I just have to take a taxi over to the restaurant. This way I don't have to make a trip to Suzhou to talk to you. I'll see you at Heavenly Sichuan in half an hour."

Twenty minutes later, Wenting scampered into the restaurant, heading straight over to the table as if she were late for a date.

"Sorry I'm late."

"Don't worry about it."

She reached across the table to peck him lightly on the forehead, her hand taking his tenderly. She put something in his hand.

"Oh, you look terrible," she said with a note of affectionate concern.

That might be true. He'd slept little, what with Gong's phone call that stretched late into the night, and then the train back to Shanghai so early in the morning.

"The latest update," she whispered in his ear, her finger touching his unshaven face like a lover.

The waiter hurried over, carrying a bottle of red wine in his hand.

"No, I have to leave soon," Wenting said. "I've got some urgent business."

Nodding, the waiter withdrew in quick steps.

"He's waiting for me," she said to Chen, standing up. "He insists I shouldn't take up too much of your time."

After Wenting left, Chen turned on his laptop and inserted the new flash memory drive she had delivered from Melong. It had the same three folders as before, updated to include recent e-mails. There weren't too many e-mails in the past two days. He skipped over those between Sima and Jin.

But some of the e-mails in Shen's folder caught his attention. The date stamp on these e-mails was today. Melong must have captured them this afternoon.

In one message from FL earlier this morning: *"The widow may have started talking."*

Shen's response was curt: *"Talking about the guy buried and dug up again? I'll have her place bugged tomorrow."*

"Do whatever necessary," FL wrote back. *"Better something done once and for all."*

FL wrote again five minutes later, as if in afterthought. *"Just like in the club."*

There were no further e-mails from Shen.

Was the widow in the e-mail Liang's widow? If so, she could be the next target. But Liang was dead and buried with all his secrets—why were they being so ruthless toward her? Whatever the answer, once again it pointed to some high, unknown stake that had put them on an unbearable edge.

It also meant that surveillance cameras or secret agents would be installed outside her house. Fortunately, Yu had been suspended, unable to visit Liang's widow again, no matter what breakthrough might come from her. It was good that Yu wouldn't be caught on the new surveillance.

Was FL the First Lady? If so, then the Chinese man caught on the camera beside her must be none other than Shen. Judging by the latest e-mail, Shen knew something about what had happened at the club. Whatever the real identity of FL, it seemed they were becoming really desperate.

But the cell phone buzzed again and broke his train of thought. To his surprise, it was Huang from Wuxi.

"I have to report the latest development, Chief."

He hadn't really instructed Huang to do anything, but Huang had taken the matter into his own hands.

"What's that?"

"I've checked the missing person files. A body was found not too far from the Grand Buddha temple. Nobody has reported a missing person or tried to claim the body. It originally looked like it was a tourist who fell sick suddenly and died. But the body matches the description of Fei that I got from Gong. I'll need some more data to be a hundred percent sure. I'm on the way to check out the body,

Chief. I'll send you a list of its traits, and once we identify the corpse definitively, I'll let you know—before anyone else."

"Thanks, Huang. You might want to send pictures of the body to my phone too. His colleagues can help us to identify it."

One victim after another in quick succession. Liang had been killed, and Qian, and Fei, and Skinny Wang, who lay paralyzed in the hospital.

It was just a matter of time before they silenced Wei, too.

Wei had chosen not to talk, but what if she was made aware of the impending danger to her? Detective Yu hadn't been able to change her mind, but Chen thought he might be able to do something different, particularly with all the new information that he had to share. He helped himself to another spoonful of cold tofu, which tasted slightly greasy.

The waiter came by to add hot water to the teapot. How long had he been sitting here? Customers around him were beginning to leave. It was eight thirty. Once again, it seemed too late for him to go out to Lu's apartment in Pudong. A Shanghai melody was coming out of a speaker somewhere. It wasn't a red song; rather, it was a black, decadent song banned during the Cultural Revolution.

After our parting tonight, / when can you come again? / Drink the cup, / help yourself to a delicacy. / How many times can you get really drunk? / Enjoy! Seize the moment . . .

He noticed the waiter hurrying past, carrying a large box to the entrance, where a young man in a restaurant uniform took it and rode off on an electric bike.

"Your restaurant also does delivery?" he asked the waiter when he came back to his table.

"Yes, we do. Because of our location, some of the deliveries are for the consulates nearby. Some of them place orders quite late in the evening, too. Our delivery men wear the restaurant uniform and ride electric bikes with our logo painted on the side so the guards there recognize them."

"That's a good idea. People in those offices might work late, and it's convenient for them to order delivery. But hold on . . ." Chen said. He counted out five hundred yuan. "That's for dinner, and the rest is a tip for you. Also, can you lend me a uniform and a bike?"

"Why do you need that?" The waiter looked confounded.

"You don't have to know. The bike and uniform will be returned to you tomorrow."

"Don't do anything stupid. The guards at the consulates check every delivery and call for confirmation before letting anyone in."

"Come on. What do you think I am?" Chen showed him his police bureau business card as well as his ID card. "It's highly confidential. Don't say a word to anyone."

"So you are . . ." The waiter stopped and broke into a smile. "Of course, anything you want, Chief Inspector Chen. You should have told me earlier. Of course, not a word to anyone."

Fifteen minutes later, Chen walked out dressed in a restaurant uniform, carrying an insulated box, and picked up an electric bike.

TWENTY-EIGHT

IT TOOK CHEN ONLY five or six minutes to ride over to the lane off Wulumuqi Road where Wei lived. He circled the area before he got off the bike and locked it to a poplar tree near the lane. Then he trotted over to a European-style condo, one hand carrying the box like a delivery man, the other pulling out his cell phone.

"You gave me this new number just the other day, Wei," he said the moment she picked up. "I'm at your door."

"What?"

Wei opened her door with surprise on her peculiarly pale, fatigue-laden face. She was wearing a black embroidered silk robe and black silk slippers. She was in mourning, as Yu had described. Her sadness was not something temporarily put on for a cop or a delivery man.

"Delivery from the Heavenly Sichuan," he said, and then added in a hushed voice before she uttered another word, "Detective Yu gave me this number."

"Come on in," she said, managing to respond, "I love the spicy tofu from your place."

Chen stepped inside, and she quickly closed the door after him. It might be suspicious for a delivery man to step into her condo without leaving again almost immediately, but it was a quiet residential neighborhood with apparently no one around to notice.

Chen set the box down on the corner table. "The box is from the restaurant, but I'm the partner of Detective Yu. Or, rather, the ex-partner, and an ex–chief inspector of the Shanghai Police Bureau. My name is Chen Cao. At this moment, I'm also the head of the Shanghai Legal Reform Committee."

He handed her his new business card. It was only the second time he'd ever used that card. The first time had been back in the office of the cemetery where his father was buried. Perhaps this was another bad omen—to a widow.

On the wall behind Wei, there was a long silk scroll painting of a white tiger crouching on a lone singularly shaped rock. The painting bore the signature of Zhang Shanzi, a celebrated modern painter. The artist's winged aspiration had created a tiger vividly ferocious, its eyes burning bright in the forest of the night. The painting was probably worth a fortune.

She looked confounded, but she waved him over to the leather sofa, which was covered in scattered books, magazines, newspapers, a white blouse, jeans, and other random items.

"I remember seeing your picture in the newspaper," she said. She changed her mind and pulled out a chair for him, then seated herself on the sofa. "But why are you here, dressed in a restaurant uniform?"

"No one pays attention to a delivery man."

"Liang talked to me about you as well, Chief Inspector Chen. I'm sorry that the room is such a mess . . ."

"It's not a night for formality, Wei. I'm here to talk about what happened to Liang, and about you. I've worked on quite a number of complicated cases, as you know, but this is the most difficult and dangerous one. And quite possibly, my last one, too. Now, to answer your question, why do I have to approach you like this? It's a long story. Let me start by telling you what has happened to me in the last few days. A lot of things that seemed unrelated, at least initially, are actually connected. I'm just beginning to see from what direction they were coming."

He hadn't prepared what he was going to say. He was just going to present a comprehensive picture, with all the necessary details, of the diabolical intrigues that threatened to ruin both their lives. He hoped to make her see the impending danger and then persuade her to cooperate with his plan, even though he had no idea how that would play out. He also hoped that talking about it might help him sort out the tangled ideas that were still crowding his mind.

It was like a win-or-lose move in a *go* game. So much remained as yet unknown, he felt as if he were jumping into an abyss. But he didn't have much left to lose anyway, and soon, there would be nothing left.

"Please go on, Chief Inspector Chen."

There was half a bottle of whiskey on the coffee table, along with a single glass. Was she drinking alone? She got up and fetched another glass from the cabinet, poured out a finger, and offered it to him. There was a faint touch of alcohol on her breath as she leaned over to hand him the glass.

"This evening, I'm not talking to you as a police officer, which I'm not, though I still can't help feeling like one," he started. "You might have heard that I was moved to a new position outside of the police bureau. As a cop, I've ruffled high feathers, so I wasn't totally surprised. But after that, things happened in such quick succession that I was overwhelmed. To begin with, I nearly fell prey to a setup in the Heavenly World last week."

"The Heavenly World?" she interrupted.

"Yes, it was touch-and-go. If not for an unexpected phone call from my mother, I might have ended being another Pan Ming that night."

She didn't appear to be mystified by the name Pan Ming. It had been a notorious setup.

"Detective Yu thought that all of this—my sudden removal from the police department, the attempt to discredit me in a setup—must have something to do with one of the cases recently assigned to the squad. In other words, it was to prevent me from looking into one of those cases. So that's exactly what we did. Detective Yu and I checked into each and every one of those cases, including those involving Shang's son, the dead pigs on the river, and your missing husband. To our surprise and confusion, though, everything turned out to be unbelievably bizarre. I've translated some mysteries, as you may have heard, and from time to time, I find fault with the implausibility of the plots. That's just fiction, you may well say. But things in China can be far stranger than fiction.

"I don't have time to dwell on some of the cases Yu and I have explored and reexplored in the past few days, so I'll stick to the pertinent details.

"Now, shortly after I was removed from the police bureau and made a director, I went to Suzhou on some personal business. There I met a young woman named Qian, who mistook me for a PI. She offered me the job of catching her cheating man back in Shanghai, and I took on her case in exchange for her help making inquiries about the nightclub. Before any progress was made on my part, however, Qian was killed in a home invasion robbery. As it turned out, her phone was tapped and her calls recorded, including the inquiries she made on my behalf."

He produced the CD, with her profile still smiling wistfully on the cover.

"She was also a very attractive woman, like you," he said with difficulty. "I hold myself responsible for her death."

Wei made no response, studying the cover of the CD intently.

"Meanwhile, Detective Yu, who took my place as the head of the Special Case Squad, was working on the Liang missing person case. He investigated various scenarios to find out what had happened to Liang. When officials who are the subject of a corruption investigation disappear, the most likely scenario is that they've gone into hiding with the hope of staging a comeback later. With so many scandals in today's China, any given transgression might easily blow over. But when Liang's body turned up in Nanhui, that changed things. Both Detective Yu and you ruled out the possibility of suicide. Then what had happened?

"Somebody must have been anxious to quickly and permanently get him out of the way. With Liang in the limelight, his death had to be orchestrated as a disappearance, so that the real cause of his death wouldn't come to light for months, or years, if ever. It might have played out that way but for a crane accident at a faraway construction site.

"Now, Qian's death and Liang's might appear unrelated, but there was one thing the victims had in common. Both were threats to a person or persons in power. The murderers wanted them out of the way to make sure they couldn't speak out against them.

"Speak about what? About something in which the stakes were too high for the murderers to risk failure. Were there several important secrets to protect, or just one? I didn't have any clue initially.

"I came back to Shanghai two days ago to deliver a long-promised lecture. The car that the police bureau sent over to take me to the conference was practically destroyed in an explosion. I happened to have already left to take care of something else before the car arrived, but the driver, my former colleague Skinny Wang, was paralyzed in the incident.

"In the meantime, in the midst of my bumping about like a headless fly, I also heard about the death of an American in Sheshan. Intriguingly, I heard about it more than once, and from various sources. That death wasn't even a case for our squad. Nor for the bureau. But the topic came up repeatedly."

She nodded contemplatively, picking up her glass but putting it down again without touching a drop.

"Have you heard of it?"

"Yes, different versions."

"People talked about his connections to the top."

This time, she didn't respond.

"Now, that death may have had nothing to do with me, with Qian, with Liang, or with the other cases we've been looking into," Chen went on. "But then there was another missing person, a local policeman from Sheshan named Fei. At this moment, Fei's still listed as missing, but I got a call from Wuxi just about an hour ago. A body was found there, matching Fei's description. He was the first one in the room where the American died. Later, he was joined there by Internal Security and another local cop. Fei and his colleague were told to turn the investigation over to Internal Security. The American was cremated the next day without an autopsy being performed. The cause of his death was announced as food poisoning. The dead man, however, was known to be a vegetarian who wouldn't have touched pork, according to the gossip in social media.

"Back in the room, Fei had sensed this American's death was something more than merely gossip material. He moved fast, and he got the recordings from the club's surveillance camera before Internal Security arrived. He didn't report this to the higher authorities immediately, for the people implicated by the footage were untouchable. Before he could do anything, however, he found himself under suspicion and questioned about his actions at the crime scene. It could only mean more trouble, he knew, if he turned over the footage from the surveillance camera. He'd seen too much, and had become too much of the threat to those involved in the murderous conspiracy resulting in the American's death. Fei was suddenly sent to Wuxi, where he went missing . . ."

"Yes, horrible things are happening, Chief Inspector Chen," Wei said, "but I'm having a hard time following you. What's the connection among all of these and, in particular, with my husband's death?"

"You're right. It's difficult to see the connections. That's why I didn't think of coming to you earlier. That's also why I'm telling you the story in this way. It's a long chain of related and interrelated links. Almost too long. All these diabolical actions weren't just about Liang, about me, or about any other victim. It's a particularly high-stakes political move at this crucial moment that is the hidden common denominator among all of them."

"At this crucial moment?"

"The National Congress of the Communist Party of China is scheduled for the end of the year, when the members of the most powerful Politburo Standing Committee will be replaced by new people. Shanghai Party Secretary Lai is on the rapid rise and has a good chance to grab one of the top positions. But he has political rivals within the Forbidden City. So he can't afford to have anything go wrong at this moment. As luck would have it, things went wrong."

"You mean Liang's . . . trouble?"

"That's part of it. Under normal circumstances, Liang might have gotten shuangguied and punished for the high-speed train contracts, and then the newspaper would have declared it another victory attributable to the Party's great determination to fight corruption. But what if Liang spilled his guts out about the other people involved in the scandal? You know what law firm Liang hired as the company's legal representative, don't you?"

She kept her head hanging low, muttering an inaudible word, her chin involuntarily quivering. Beside her, the bronze pendulum in a mahogany antique clock went on swinging, measuring the seconds in perpetual tranquility.

"Coincidentally or not, Liang's company and the Heavenly World were both represented by the Kaitai law firm," he resumed after a pause. "But perhaps most significantly here, the dead American, Daniel Martin, was also connected to the law firm. For some reason still beyond me, he posed such a threat that he had to be removed—or at least, so it seemed to Lai, or the people close to him.

"Now, there's one thing I've learned during all my years as a cop.

Murderers are capable of seeing something that makes sense only to their twisted and paranoid imagination. So what would paranoid people in power do? For one thing, anything or anyone that might be in their way would have to go. That's why I was removed from my position. But that wasn't enough: they were worried that I would still try to find out what was going on. For that reason, they put together an elaborate setup at the nightclub, one that would result in my complete disgrace. Then there was the explosion of the police bureau car. I'll accept the consequences of my choices as a cop, but I can't bear to see an innocent victim caught in the crossfire."

"An innocent victim? You mean . . ." She didn't finish her sentence.

"After the revelation of Liang's death, you could have reacted in any number of ways." He added after a deliberate pause, "Detective Yu told me you nearly collapsed when you recognized the tattoo on his body."

"He told you that?"

"These kinds of details are important to a cop. But how might his killers interpret your reaction? In their minds, Liang might have confided in you, and you might try to do something with that knowledge. So what would people like that do? Such people live by Cao Cao's statement, 'I would let down all the people, rather than have any of them let me down.' Furthermore, they see themselves as representing the Party, so they feel that whatever they do is politically justified. As the red song goes, 'Only the Communist Party can save and rule China.'

"So I'm here now trying to help you—and to be honest, trying to help myself too."

"Are you saying that you can't even help yourself, Chief Inspector Chen?"

"No, I can't. We have to find a way out, and we will. Not just for ourselves. You have to think of Liang, and I have to consider all of the victims," he said in earnest. "Now, let me show you something. Yesterday in Wuxi, I came across the video that Fei took from the club's surveillance camera. This is the reason for Fei's disappearance. Kai was caught on tape entering the room with the American, and leaving around the estimated time of his death."

He produced the flash drive, and continued on without immediately putting it in his laptop. She stared at him without saying anything.

"In the meantime, I also came across these e-mails, some of which I just got a couple of hours ago. I have reason to believe they directly concern you," he said. He turned on his laptop and opened the e-mail messages Melong had obtained for him. "You should take a look for yourself."

"Now?"

But she moved over, kneeled beside him, started reading.

Not long after, she leapt to her feet shakily, shuddering. Chen reached out a hand to support her.

"I've come to the conclusion," he went on, "that you most likely will be the next target. Tomorrow or the day after tomorrow, a surveillance camera will be installed here, as indicated in the e-mails. Twenty-four hours. But there are worse scenarios than surveillance that I'm worried about."

"But why should I be worried? An ill-fated woman like me, it's all destined," she said, with a hysterical note in her suddenly husky voice. "The black widow of a white tiger."

It was Chen's turn to be astounded. That phrase again.

"And blue dragon and white tiger indeed!" she went on. "He believes that he is a dragon, meant to eventually take the throne."

In Chinese slang, "white tiger" was sometimes an obscene expression used to describe a woman without pubic hair. There was also a superstitious belief that such a woman brings bad luck to her man. Chen wasn't sure what was meant by "blue dragon." In ancient China, an emperor was believed to be a dragon incarnate. But whatever the correct interpretation was, a "blue dragon" was believed to be able to mate with a "white tiger" without worrying about any bad luck.

But she used the present tense in her last sentence. So she couldn't be referring to Liang. And that last part—"eventually take the throne . . ." It began to hazily dawn on him.

"Thank you for telling me all this," she said, making a visible effort to pull herself together. "Now, please tell me what I should do."

That was an unexpected turn. She leaned forward, grasping the chair arm with one hand, the other adjusting her silk robe embroidered with a soaring dragon.

"Tell me what you know about what was going on with Liang," he said.

TWENTY-NINE

A SHROUD OF SILENCE fell over the living room.

The moonlight streamed through the flapping curtains and landed on her face, which was bleached of color, yet infinitely touching.

"I appreciate your telling me about this, Chief Inspector Chen," Wei said, finally. She picked up the Suzhou opera CD with the profile of Qian on the cover. "Your story is so unbelievable that no one would have tried to make up something like that. I believe every word of it. There was actually a catch in your voice when you declared yourself responsible for her death.

"You're worried about me, I understand. An ill-fated woman like me, though, is beyond worrying about. I'm going to tell you all I know, but do you know why?"

"Why?"

"Because I want to do something for Liang, just as you are trying to do for the other victims. Years ago, I also tried to do my best for him, but it all went terribly wrong. Did you read Kai's e-mail joking about the 'the black widow of a white tiger'? That really clinched it.

Lai must have told her everything in bed, in an ecstasy of cloud rolling into rain."

"Lai?"

"He must have been told about her murderous plan. After all, they're the archetypal couple of a red prince and a red princess. What he's said to me means nothing."

There was something incomprehensibly confusing yet alarming in her words. Chen had a difficult time following the beginning of her revelation. Picking up his glass, he waited for her to go on.

"There has been a lot of gossip about me and Liang. What I'm telling you, though, is the truth. Like your story, mine has to be told from the beginning. As you said, only when all of the background is revealed can things come to light."

"That's right, Wei. I'm all ears."

"You're a writer, and someday you may write about us. If so, I hope you do Liang justice, at least in the part about our marriage. Believe it or not, Lai once told me you're a good poet, but you're just too bookish to be a politician. I remember that because my grandfather was a very bookish man. I grew up with him in a Jiangsu village, and he taught me how to read and write."

"I wish I could write like in my college days," he said, "but please go on."

"After high school graduation, I failed to pass the college entrance exam. In the Jiangsu countryside, girls usually marry young. I was just seventeen when I married someone in the same village in a sort of arranged marriage. He was really good for nothing—gambling, drinking, hanging out with his wine-and-meat buddies during the day and beating me up at night. Soon lurid stories started to spread about me being a white tiger. Imagine him joking with other rascals, sharing the most intimate detail about my body, and blaming his bad luck at the mahjong table on me. White tiger! You know what it means, don't you?"

He nodded.

"Then he died in a tractor accident. He was barely twenty at the time. His family all blamed me—a white tiger—for bringing the worst luck on him. I could no longer stay in the village, where people constantly pointed their fingers at me. So I came to Shanghai on my own.

"As a provincial girl without any skills or connections in a new city, I ended up working as a foot-washing girl. You know how things are like in a job like that. I spent my days bent over a stool, holding men's feet in my lap, wiping the cracked skin on a worn-out towel, and pouring out dreams with the dirty foot-washing water. Day after day after day. . . . My life was a long black tunnel with no light at the end! After a couple of years, Liang came to the salon one evening. He came the next day, then quite regularly, and always to me exclusively. At first I took him for just another Big Buck customer who took a fancy to my service. With his company, and his official position, Liang could have easily targeted someone younger and prettier, not a pathetic widow from the countryside. One of the well-to-do clients had made an ernai out of one of the other girls at the salon, and most of us would have jumped at such an opportunity. Instead of treating me like trash, Liang showered affection on me, and to my astonishment, he then proposed. I told him about my disastrous marriage, along with being a white tiger, but he was determined. He said he didn't care about the superstitions, and a week later, he came back to the salon, dragged me into a private room, and showed me the tattoo on his lower belly. It was a blue dragon interwoven with my name, and he declared, 'Now I'm a blue dragon. We don't have to worry.' That's another superstitious belief, as you may know. It's said that only a man who is a blue dragon can sleep with a white tiger without being harmed."

Chen had no idea what kind of man qualified as a blue dragon or whether or not, according to Chinese mythology, such a tattoo could make one a blue dragon.

"I was more than touched. For someone like me, what more could

I possibly ask? I moved in with him that night, and I swore to be a good wife. After our wedding, Liang signed over a large number of his company shares to me. He loved to bring me around, to all his dinners and social parties, so I thought I should try to help him. If anything, I'd learned how to talk to men. Needless to say, his business associates knew nothing about my past, and they congratulated him on his choice of a wife. Coincidence or not, his business then picked up dramatically. According to him, it was because of the combined luck of the blue dragon and the white tiger. After that, he put me in charge of public relations for his company, though I didn't have to go to the office every day.

"The job required me to meet with more of his business associates and connections, some of whom turned out to be really powerful. You know what networking means in today's business world, don't you? It means drinking, partying, karaoke, and whatnot. Liang trusted me, and I was anxious to be really helpful to him, not simply washing his feet in the bedroom. Some of the people at those parties were high-ranking officials, and that included Lai, who had just been appointed the Shanghai Party secretary. I knew how important these associations could be to Liang's business. Believe it or not, it's much easier for a young woman to cultivate connections. Some of them proved to be so useful that Liang declared the expansion of his business was all to my credit. I knew better as I got deeper into his company's PR work. Still, I drew a line for myself. Associates of Liang's, the ones for whom three-accompanying girls are easily available, knew not to push too far with me. They all knew that I was out of bounds, and they knew they might have business to do with Liang in the future. Lai was the exception. One evening, after three cups in a private club room, Lai put his hand on my shoulder, caressing, though only for a short moment. I thought he might have simply had a drop too much to drink.

"There's an old saying: 'No boat can enjoy smooth sailing all year round.' Liang's company got into trouble during the nationwide economic crises. Liang quickly transferred more of his properties to my name, but he was heading for an irrecoverable disaster, unless he could get a huge order from the city government. So I thought of Lai, and contacted him. Lai invited me to his office. That evening he was alone there, looking beat, with documents piled high on the large desk, but he offered to help. Out of gratitude, I told him I had learned how to do massage. And I did a good job that night, I think. It's not difficult to imagine what happened next. But you have to understand—I had to help Liang, no matter the cost."

"It's understandable," Chen said. "As in the Confucian classic, 'He treats me as the most special one in the whole country, and I have to pay back to him accordingly.' "

"Thank you for saying that, Chief Inspector Chen. But to be honest, I was also flattered by the attention from a powerful man like Lai. It didn't take too long, between this and that, for Lai to tell me that, despite all the glories in the political world, he wasn't happy at home. Kai was an ambitious, greedy, and vain woman from another high-ranking official family. Because of his position in the city government, he had to make her resign from her law firm, a decision she deeply resented. And her suspicion that he was being unfaithful had further derailed the marriage. Kai was said to have started having affairs of her own, and at home she cared only about their son, Xixi, who was now studying abroad. At one point, Lai said to me that they were staying married only out of political convenience. But I knew he would never leave Kai, whether the story about his family life was true or not. And that was fine with me. I would never leave Liang, and Lai knew that too.

"Oh, there's another coincidence about the superstitious idea of a white tiger. Lai also declared himself to be a blue dragon, for he actually believes that I could bring him luck—"

"Hold on. What made Lai a blue dragon?"

"He's ambitious, always has his eye on the top. When he was still a little child, he told me, his father had a well-known fortune-teller examine him. The fortune-teller predicted that Lai would have a chance at the throne . . ."

"And in the fortune-teller's jargon, an emperor is a dragon," Chen said, shaking his head. It was hard to believe that a Politburo member would have chosen to believe in fortune-tellers.

"Damn the dragon." She reached up and crumbled the golden dragon embroidery on the front of her robe. "He chose this robe for me and for that very reason. And the dragon-embroidered slippers too," she said, kicking them off in disgust.

"Except for that first time, I never asked anything of Lai again," she went on. "That's perhaps why he told me that he felt so stress-free with me. In the meantime, Liang continued to get large orders from the city government, but not just because of me. Liang's company paid a large sum to engage the Kai's law firm as its legal representative. As for the thing between me and Lai, Liang may have somehow guessed, but he never said a word about it. If anything, he seemed to be more secretive about his business. But he trusted me as before. He managed to obtain a green card for me and transferred a substantial amount to a foreign bank account under my name. When I asked him why, he said that one could never tell what would happen next in China. About six months ago, there was a sum wired from my account to someone in the States. It was his money and Liang could use it however he liked. Still, he explained to me that this sum was going to Lai's son Xixi in the name of a scholarship foundation. Going from a prestigious private high school to a prestigious private university, the cost for Xixi's schooling and expenses was more than a hundred thousand US dollars a year. I checked the transaction later and the money was indeed wired to this scholarship foundation.

"Things went on like that until the scandal about the high-speed train equipment broke on the Internet. Liang was worried sick. He got the order through his connection with Kai. He'd mentioned to me that more than half of the profit went into that so-called scholarship account. One or two days before Liang's disappearance, I called Lai, who promised that it would work out all right for Liang. If Lai really wanted to help, he could have. But instead, Liang disappeared. I didn't know what had happened. If he'd left on his own, Liang would have discussed it with me first. And he couldn't he have slipped out of the country on his own. While he'd obtained a green card for me, he didn't get one for himself, saying that as a Party official, he would get into trouble if he did that. After I heard nothing from him for several days, I suspected serious trouble. So I contacted Lai again, and like before, he promised me nothing would happen to Liang.

"The last two times that I begged Lai, I knew something wasn't right, so I recorded our conversation. Not for myself, but for Liang.

"Then Detective Yu came to me with the pictures of Liang's corpse. I think you know the rest only too well. I'm not saying that Liang conducted his business properly, but he wasn't alone in today's society. It was just his luck. And my luck too. When all is said and done, I did Liang terribly wrong. He cared for me so much, but what have I done for him? If I hadn't slept with Lai, Liang might have lost his company, but not his life."

"You don't have to say that, Wei."

"It's a too crucial moment for the Lais. Liang was murdered because they couldn't afford to have anything go wrong—especially not something high-profile like the high-speed train equipment orders, which had been orchestrated by Kai."

"I think you're right."

"How pathetically naive I was, believing Lai cared for me just a little. He must have shared all the sordid secrets with Kai, telling cruel bedroom jokes about a hairless, brainless white tiger." After making a visible effort to control herself, she went on, "If you have any questions, Chief Inspector Chen, go ahead and ask me anything that may help your work."

"Yes, I do have some questions," he said slowly.

Her story was absurd, even unimaginable, but he believed it. For the same reason she believed him earlier. *"It would have been difficult to make up something like that."* Still, it was sadly shocking that Lai, a powerful member of the Party Politburo Committee, could have stooped so low, and for that matter, that his wife Kai had as well.

Much of what Wei described sounded impossible, absurd. But this was the story in an age of absurdities, and for all the light her story threw on a lot of things, others still puzzled him. It would take some time to sort them out. At the moment, he felt Wei was both relatable and reliable. He didn't want to judge.

"Liang paid a substantial sum to Kai's law firm," he started, "so that's how he came to know the things going on at the top?"

"I don't know, but Liang became quite close with Kai."

"What about the money transferred to that special account—do you still have a copy of that?"

"Yes, I've kept a copy."

"So Lai knew how the so-called scholarship was being funded?"

"He didn't talk to me about it. Like other high-ranking Party officials, he knows how shady these business transactions can be, but he let Kai and others take care of that."

"Now, a different question," he said, jumping to a different subject. "About the death of the American, did you hear anything about it from Lai?"

"Lai mentioned him one evening. He looked very upset, so I offered to massage him. He almost felt asleep in the middle of it, and he muttered drowsily that the American had been so annoying, actually threatening Xixi."

"Why?"

"He didn't say much about it on the massage table, but from some of his remarks on other occasions, I gathered it was probably something like this. The American helped to take care of Xixi in the States, and in return, he'd been working, with Kai's help, on a large real estate project in the center of the city. If the land deal was approved by the city government, the project could have made him a huge profit. But someone high up in Beijing was watching the project with alarm, so Lai scrapped the deal at the last minute. The American must have lost some of his initial investment, so he tried to get compensation by threatening Xixi.

"Possibly connected to that, Liang mentioned one evening that Kai needed additional money for her son because she'd fallen out with an American business partner. I'm not sure if it was the same American. She needed money quick, so Liang had no choice but to touch that account of mine again."

"Liang got more deals from the city government after that?"

"Yes, he did. He promised to put everything back into my account as soon as possible. I didn't doubt or blame him. After all, he didn't have to quietly set up the account for me in the first place," she said. "Again, he said I shouldn't worry about these things, about which, sometimes, the less said, the better . . ."

"Can I smoke?" Chen said abruptly, struck with a sense of déjà vu. It was if he himself had said something like that.

"Sure," she said, her hand reaching into the clutter on the sofa, as if in an effort to find something, but without success. "You must be disappointed with what I've told you. As I've said, I'm beyond being worried about."

"No, your account really helps. Now I see why they are so desperate and so cold-blooded."

Many more questions came up in an ever-accelerating swirl of thoughts, but for the moment, the most pressing one was what he was going to do. He'd made the decision to visit Wei on the spur of the moment. To his surprise, the visit yielded far more than he'd expected. Whatever plans he devised for himself, how was he going to keep his promise to help her? The next day, Shen and his thugs would be here. At that point, an ex-cop wouldn't be able to turn the tables. Not even with this new information he'd gotten from her, he calculated and concluded, would he have a chance to do anything—not for her, and not for all the others.

Looking up, he saw the silk scroll painting of a lone white tiger on the wall. Was that also something bought for her by Liang? The tiger crouched in ferocity, framed in fearful symmetry. He shifted his glance and leaned slightly forward, gazing down, holding his head in both hands. In the soft lamplight, she sat still like a forsaken wax image, her face ghastly pale, the worn-out red polish peeling on toes looking like petals in rainwater. She must have been so distressed and distracted the last few days. *The west wind sighing and vexing / the green ripples, / it is unbearable to see / the beauty ravished by the grief of time.* Some lines by Li Jing came out of nowhere. The ex–chief inspector, annoyed with the impossible poet within himself, started tapping on his laptop sitting on the coffee table.

"In the light of what you have just told me, the files and information I've got on my laptop would have made convincing evidence—under normal circumstances," he said. "But as it is, the minute all of this was turned over to the higher authorities in Beijing, the official in charge would make a phone call to Lai in Shanghai.

"Quite simply, Lai is too high for the system to allow him to fall. It would deliver a irrecoverable, catastrophic blow to the legitimacy of the regime. With the Party's interest placed above everything else, they would have to cover it up. Consequently, more innocent people would disappear, including you and me. That's the way the Party machine works.

"As I mentioned, I made a recent trip to my father's grave in Suzhou, where I realized how I'd let him down by working within the system. I had hoped to make a difference despite many setbacks, but it was of no avail. It's time to redeem myself by venturing outside the system, and doing something that was unimaginable before. That pledge to my father has informed me ever since that morning at his graveside—has been with me every step in the investigation, or rather the investigations, which appeared to be unrelated until I started looking into the death of the American. That turned out to be the last straw for the conspirators.

"Now, this afternoon, I happened to get a phone call from a friend, who suggested that I go abroad as soon as possible, and with the help of a visa official in the American consulate. It was a practical suggestion, but even if I didn't have to worry about the blacklist at customs, I don't think I'll do it."

"What do you mean, Chief Inspector Chen?"

"With the death of the American, the evidence on the video clip, and with the e-mails, plus what you have in your hands—the phone records and bank transaction receipts—if you take it all with you to the American consulate, as a holder of a green card in real danger, the consulate will have to protect you. Then it could turn into an international scandal, something too huge for the Party authorities to cover up. After all, there are ways the ensuing scandal could be interpreted as being in the Party's interest."

"Yes, that's a possibility," she said with an incredulous note in her voice. "But what about you, Chief Inspector Chen? With all the evidence, you could do this for yourself."

"A couple of weeks ago, I would never have dreamed of having such a discussion with you," he said with a rueful smile. "In my college years, I dreamed of being a poet, not a Party member cop. But when you have given so much to the work, for so many years, it becomes a part of you, even though that part isn't pleasant. There are obligations to being a cop, there's no point in denying that. I can't write that off in one stroke. It's inconceivable to me, as a Shanghai police officer, to go and seek protection in an American consulate.

"That's not the case with you, Wei. When all is said and done, you shouldn't be the next victim."

She looked at him, her large eyes brimming over with disbelief.

"Do you have a copy machine here at home?" he asked.

"Yes."

"Make copies of the bank transactions, and of the phone records showing the calls to Lai. Give them all to me. They'll be kept in a secure place," he said. "In the meantime, you'll have the evidence I'm holding, the video clip and the e-mails."

"I'm still lost. What will happen to you?"

"You don't have to argue with me anymore, Wei. We are fighting against impossible odds. There's no time left for us to discuss—"

Suddenly, he heard something like a bell ringing out in the lane, moving ever closer, as an old woman's voice, tremulous in the depth of the night, spoke.

"Close your windows and doors. Be careful with fires. Be on the alert against the sabotage of the class enemy."

It was like something he'd heard many years ago, possibly during the Cultural Revolution, or even earlier.

"The neighbor security committee used to do that at midnight back in the seventies. Liang told me about those years of class struggle under Mao," she said, as if relieved by the unexpected change of topic. "It's all coming back now, like something fashionably nostalgic."

It was a surreal touch. Was it part of Lai's campaign of singing red songs? The slogan-chanting at midnight through the lane sounded like a parody of the past.

"So it's a new day," he said, rising. "We have to hurry."

EPILOGUE

IT WAS THE MORNING of the fourth day after Chen returned to Suzhou.

He'd been busy with the renovations, staying there most of the time, supervising, running errands, making suggestions, though he had no idea if all that really helped. But he was racing against time to see that it was completed, before anything happened to him. He kept telling himself that this was perhaps the only achievable redemption for him.

He felt much calmer—"the boat burnt, the wok smashed," as the *Art of War* described.

When he left Wei's place early in the morning, he thought he'd done all he could.

Perhaps it was more than he should have. He didn't know.

But he didn't want to think about it anymore. There was no point in doing so anyway. There were too many possible outcomes, like wild weeds overgrowing the cemetery hills.

He'd turned off his phone, and his computer too. Already there had been too much collateral damage; he didn't want to do anything that might implicate or incriminate anyone else. He himself was beyond worrying about, to use Wei's own words, but he still had to worry about others.

Helpless the water flows, and petals drift. He wondered how things had been going with her, but he knew better than to make any calls or inquiries. He didn't want to be distracted by any more new information, glimmering like the will-o'-the-wisp in the dark.

So that morning he was sitting out in the hotel garden, at the stone table, sipping tea like a leisurely tourist, before going out to the cemetery to oversee the completion of the renovation project. He carried with him the book written by his late father, which he was going to place in the casket that afternoon.

The waitress brought him the *People's Daily*, a hot water bottle, and an engaging smile, as usual.

Raising his teacup, he cast a glance at the headlines on the front page.

LAIKAI IN CUSTODY AS SUSPECTS IN THE DANIEL MARTIN MURDER CASE

What in the world did that mean?

It was unprecedented. In China, after 1949, a married woman kept her maiden name. So it was as an unmistakable message to have the two surnames of Lai and Kai juxtaposed in the official newspaper. It was too eye-catching to miss. Even with no real news about Lai in the *People's Daily*, the fate of the ambitious red prince appeared to be sealed.

The editorial in the Party's newspaper mentioned in one short sentence, among other things, the cooperation of the American consulate in Shanghai in the investigation.

Wei had managed to do something for Liang in the end.

Chen scrambled to turn on both his phone and his laptop.

There were no voice messages from Wei. That was no surprise. She knew better. As for the messages left by others, he would check those later.

There was an e-mail, however, from Comrade Zhao sent last night from Beijing, marked urgent.

> I've been in the hospital with no access to a computer until this evening. Sorry for having not written back earlier. You have been doing a great job at the Shanghai Police Bureau. So I've made a suggestion to the Party Central Committee: While you start your new job at the Legal Reform Committee, you should keep the old job at the police bureau.
>
> I'm old, sick, so there's nothing I can really do. I'm still reading Wang Yangming. He put it so well, "It's easy to kill the enemy in the mountains, but it's difficult to kill the one in the heart."

What could that mean? Chen had no idea how to respond, but he knew he wasn't in a hurry.

He spread out the newspaper and began to read in earnest.

"Another corruption and conspiracy story," he said to the waitress, who was bringing over a dish of white-sugar-covered scarlet yang mei berries, his favorite sweet in the ancient city of Suzhou.

"Just like so many stories in today's China," she said, shaking her head like a rattle drum. "Are you writing another poem this morning?"

"No, I was thinking of a poem by Du Mu from the Tang dynasty. *'At the bottom of the river still lies / the broken anchor, which I wash and wipe / for traces of the bygone dynasties. / If the eastern wind had not turned, miraculously, / in favor of General Zhou Yu / the two beauties would have been locked up / in the Bronze Sparrow Tower, deep in the spring.'* "

"I think I read that poem in school," she said with a slight frown, "but what does it mean?"

"There's a real historical event behind the poem. In the Three Kingdoms period at the beginning of the third century, a war broke out between the Wu State and the Wei State. Cao Cao, the prime minister of the Wei State, was allegedly motivated by his wanton lust after two celebrated beauties in the Wu State, so he led a powerful fleet down the river. Cao Cao even composed a fu poem about it, bragging about the construction of the Bronze Sparrow Tower to house the two beauties there. Now, one of the two in question happened to be young General Zhou's wife, so the enraged general was determined to fight him against incredible odds. Luckily, in a crucial battle near the Scarlet Cliff, the wind changed in Zhou's favor, and with it he burned out Cao Cao's fleet."

"But why these lines this morning?"

"It's a poem about the contingency of history. I was reading about the LaiKai case just now. You know what it's about, don't you? The editorial acclaims it as another triumph in the government's unwavering battle against corruption, no matter how high-ranking the officials involved. Hence all the credit goes to the great, glorious Party," he said, pointing at the newspaper article. "But what about the contingencies . . ."

"Like the eastern wind, right? Lai was such a powerful figure only yesterday, with a mighty fleet of the red song–singing leftists following him all the way. You're truly a man of learning, sir," she said with admiration. "So, you're a university professor?"

"I would love to teach that poem to a class," he said, "if there were enough students interested."

He wondered whether that poem was included in Qian's CD, as a new wave of sadness washed over him.

He took the CD out. An insect started chirping somewhere in the garden. It was as if he were taking it from her slender hand in Cai's Noodles only this morning.